TH
OF THE
GENERALS

Books by Hans Hellmut Kirst

What Became of Gunner Asch
The Officer Factory
The Return of Gunner Asch
Forward, Gunner Asch
The Revolt of Gunner Asch
The Night of the Generals
Soldiers' Revolt
Brothers in Arms

THE NIGHT OF THE GENERALS

Hans Hellmut Kirst

Translated from the German by J. Maxwell Brownjohn

Pantheon Books, New York

 Published in the United States by Pantheon Books, a division of Random House, Inc., New York.
Originally published in Germany by Verlag Kurt Desch GmbH., Munich. English version first published in Great Britain by William Collins Sons & Co. Ltd., London, and in the United States by Harper & Row, Publishers, Inc., New York.

Library of Congress Catalog Card Number: 63-20304

ISBN: 0-394-72752-5

Manufactured in the United States of America

First Pantheon Paperback Edition

The Night of the Generals

PART ONE

Even death has its funny side

WARSAW, 1942

1

The body lay in the middle of the room between the table and the bed. Anyone looking at it from the door would have mistaken it for a bulging sack. It lay huddled up, face buried in the carpet.

"Nice carpet, that," said the man who stood surveying the scene, legs planted firmly apart. "Pity about the blood, though. It's completely messed up."

He looked like a healthy, contented boy. His cheeks were plump and ruddy and his eyes friendly and appealing, as though on the look-out for congenial playmates.

"Death occurred barely two hours ago," said another man, who was leaning against the door-post. "We notified you immediately in accordance with standing instructions."

The cheerful, boyish-looking man, whose name was Engel, nodded. Kneeling down, he grasped the corpse by the hair, pulled the head back and inspected the face. It stared back at him with waxen rigidity, mouth agape and eyes wide with horror. Something of the dead woman's wild, dark beauty remained in spite of her contorted expression.

"She must have been spectacular in bed," mused Engel.

His companion, who was still leaning against the door-frame, motionless as a graven image, gave no sign of having heard his remark. His eyes were like extinct craters, grey, inaccessible and hard as volcanic rock. He looked gnarled and desiccated, like an old gnome.

"Did you hear, Liesowski?" Engel asked the gnomelike man. "For a corpse, I think she looks pretty good—or don't you agree?"

"Naturally I agree," replied Liesowski.

"Even when you agree with me you manage to be irritating," said Engel. He rose to his feet with a grunt. Having made an excellent dinner on the pick of the left-overs from the generals' table, washed down with schnapps, he ha been planning an agreeably strenuous night with a woma agent in military intelligence. Instead, his after-dinner entertainment had turned out to be a dead body. "What's th matter, don't you like her?"

Detective-Inspector Roman Liesowski of the Warsaw police shook his head a trifle indulgently. "I've never been abl to see much charm in a corpse, Herr Engel."

"Not even in your capacity as a Polish patriot?"

"I've been a policeman for almost as long as I can remember and I've come across a lot of dead bodies in my time, but my sole reaction is always: who did it? I've spen a lifetime hunting down murderers without developing th slightest sense of patriotism."

"That," said Engel cheerfully, "is probably the reason why you're still alive and kicking, Liesowski. We Germans giv you a chance to do your duty, and in return you're allowe to breathe our air, eh?"

Engel laughed gaily and slapped the breast of his leathe raincoat, which gleamed dully in the subdued light. "Well my friend, why did you send for me? Not just to show m a beautiful corpse, surely?"

"The woman's name was Maria Kupiecki."

"Well? She's only one corpse among many. They're a thick as fleas on a dog's back in this city. The world's full o them, so why disturb my well-earned night's rest?"

"Maria Kupiecki—also known as 'Countess' Kupiecki—wa one of the people whom we have to provide with polic protection on request. Her name figures in your official list so she must have been working for German intelligence."

"Ah, now I get it!" Engel beamed happily like a schoolbo who has been given a new football. "That explains why was struck by your smug attitude the moment I came in. know exactly what you're thinking: one traitor less! An murder's all right with you, but a patriotic murder's twice a welcome."

"Take a closer look at the body," recommended Liesowski unruffled. "This piece of butchery had nothing to do with patriotism."

"Why not? Don't you think any of your keen and determined fellow-countrymen would go to such lengths?"

"This isn't what one would call a normal murder. The ma

didn't just finish her off. He made a revolting mess of the body."

Engel slowly withdrew his gaze from the Inspector and transferred it to the inert bundle, once a human being, which lay on the floor in front of him.

"Get this straight, Liesowski," Engel said softly, as if anxious to avoid being overheard. "If you try and concoct any unpleasant surprises for us you'll end up a corpse yourself."

Roman Liesowski raised both hands as though in surrender, but it was a half-hearted and not particularly convincing gesture. His expression was morose. "We seem to be at cross purposes. I'm talking about a bestial murder, nothing more. I've drawn no political conclusions whatsoever."

For a brief instant Engel seemed disconcerted and his smile lost some of its ebullience, but he quickly regained his air of exuberant geniality.

"All right then, you can proceed with your inquiries under my supervision, but I shall have to notify my superior. Until Major Grau arrives I can only hope you don't come up with anything stupid. I don't want to have to find a replacement for you if I can avoid it."

"I shall be glad to do all I can," Liesowski replied drily, "but judging by the look of things I can't promise that you'll be overjoyed at the results of my investigation. Perhaps it would be better—better for you, I mean—if you took over the case yourself."

But Engel had resumed his inspection of the body. "Why did the bitch have to die?" he asked with the sudden petulance of a child whose balloon has burst. "She looks as though she'd have given one a good time. It's always the same, though. Women like her bring nothing but trouble in the end."

The air in the room was close and muggy. It was a compound of stale perfume, the foetid sweetness of blood-soaked clothing and the acrid smell of Engel's Brazilian cigar.

Major Grau, head of counter-espionage for the Warsaw area, arrived an hour later. His overcoat, which was draped negligently round his shoulders, made an elegant rustling sound, audible evidence that he selected only the finest materials for his wardrobe.

"There's no need to apologize," he announced, "not in

advance, at least. I'm at your disposal day and night if necessary. Was it necessary in this case?"

Before Engel could reply the Major demonstrated his observance of formalities by extending his hand to the Polish policeman—not forgetting to remove his pigskin glove first—and uttering a few cordial words of greeting. Liesowski sketched a small bow.

"First, let us deliberate," said Major Grau, his features illumined by a look of gentle, scarcely perceptible irony. "Be good enough to send your men outside, Inspector. I think it would be appropriate if we opened the proceedings in private. Allow me to commandeer your chair, my dear Engel. It looks extremely comfortable—but then the whole room gives a cosy impression. I know it already, by the way. This isn't my first visit, though from the look of things it will probably be my last."

Major Grau chatted away like a guest at an afternoon tea party. He selected a cigarette from his gold case, but not before offering one to Roman Liesowski, who tucked it away in his breast pocket.

"I'm listening," said Major Grau, when the Inspector's assistants had left the room as instructed. His air was that of a business man awaiting a proposition.

Liesowski recounted the known facts with due objectivity: at 11:05 p.m. screams had been heard, but produced no immediate reaction from anyone in the house; shortly afterwards someone telephoned the police and a policeman called to investigate; towards midnight the homicide squad turned up, identified the body without difficulty and informed the German authorities; Sergeant Engel arrived, postponed further investigation and notified Major Grau.

"What a frightful smell there is in this house!"

"It's the smell of war, Major." Roman Liesowski's tone was explanatory, like that of a sewer-worker speaking from professional experience. "Poor food, insufficient soap, windows hermetically sealed because of the black-out, clothes caked with months of sweat—and now blood as well. It's the characteristic aroma of our time, at least in this part of the world."

Major Grau smiled faintly in apparent agreement, then raised one pigskin glove. "For the moment I'm solely interested in facts, Inspector. You've told me your findings

Now I should like to know what conclusions you've drawn."

The Major seemed reluctant to lavish undue attention on the body, which still lay in its original position on the carpet. His gaze rested on a portrait hanging between the two windows. It depicted a Polish noblewoman of Chopin's day, mysteriously dark and graceful but endowed with a pale, almost transparent skin and provocatively scarlet lips, a blend of delicate sensitivity and passionate abandon.

"There's not much doubt about the motive," declared Engel, who lost little of his boyish enthusiasm even in the presence of his superiors. "It looks as though one of her more energetic boy-friends was at work here. She's as full of holes as a dummy after bayonet-practice. Maybe she drove him to it."

"She was remarkably uninhibited," remarked Grau. He turned to Liesowski with a look of bland inquiry. "I knew this lady. Indeed, who didn't?"

"I didn't," said Engel gloomily.

"Our associates are a mixed bunch, Engel. You ought to devote a little more attention to them," recommended Grau with extreme amiability. "Have you had the room searched, Inspector?"

"There were no documents of any kind," answered Liesowski, "nothing in any way suspicious, no sign of papers having been removed and not the slightest indication of any so-called patriotic motive. It's murder, that's all, probably the ugliest I've ever come across—and I've seen plenty."

"Very good," said Major Grau. "Maria Kupiecki was a valuable collaborator of ours, but the reason for her death probably lay in her personal mode of life."

"You may well be right, Major."

"Are you in any doubt?" Grau put the question in a gentle voice. He smiled expectantly, almost as though he hoped for an affirmative answer.

Of all the Germans with whom Liesowski was compelled to work, Major Grau of Abwehr was the oddest. He fell into none of the predominant categories. He was neither cold-bloodedly brutal nor cynically condescending, neither officious nor prosaically bureaucratic. Roman Liesowski had every reason to think himself a good judge of human nature, but Grau remained an enigma and he found this disconcerting.

"Shall I repeat my question, Herr Liesowski? I should be glad to know if you feel any doubts about my line of reasoning?"

Liesowski's gnomelike figure seemed to shrivel up even more and his eyes dimmed like two guttering candles on the verge of extinction. "Does that mean," he asked with suspicious diffidence, "that you intend to take the case under your jurisdiction? For my part, I'm quite happy to regard the matter as closed."

"The man's incorrigible!" Engel grimaced at Major Grau and fished another cigar out of his breast pocket. "We're dealing with an out-and-out patriot, Major. He may not realize it himself, but that's what he is. I'm pretty sure he's planning to drop us in the dirt. I don't know exactly how yet, but that's his game—I felt it the moment I got here. Something smells fishy round here, but what?"

"Your cigar, among other things, Engel. It's worse than any corpse."

Engel's laugh was unabashed. He took the remark in good part, especially as his chief gave an impression of cheerful expectancy. Whatever his reasons, Major Grau seemed to be enjoying the situation.

"Engel is not only a valued colleague but a professional funny-man." Grau smiled encouragingly at Liesowski. "I hope you'll bear with him."

"Then the case is closed as far as I'm concerned," said the Inspector with alacrity. "I'll put all the available details at your disposal, if you wish, also the witness my men have unearthed."

"Witness? What witness? That's news to me." Engel shook his head. "This isn't the first time an informer has been killed, you know. It could always be a simple case of robbery with violence, of course, but it's far more likely to be revenge for reasons of misguided patriotism—and I admit that patriotism means different things to different people. All right then, wipe these people out and keep mum about it—that's the usual rule, Liesowski, so why don't you stick to it?"

"I don't quite follow you," said the diminutive policeman.

"My dear Liesowski," said Grau in his best drawing-room manner, "allow me to try and clarify the situation. Two things seem firmly established: first, the murdered woman worked for us, and, secondly, she was no better than she should be.

The question is, was she murdered because she was a whore or because she worked for us? In the former instance the case becomes a criminal matter and one which does not concern my department; in the latter, it becomes something aimed more or less directly at us. And now you produce a witness like a rabbit out of a hat. Engel finds this suspicious, but I must confess that my only reaction is one of curiosity. If your intention was to intrigue me I must ask you to explain your motives."

"My men have merely found a witness. I have no idea what his evidence consists of. All I know is that he was only too ready to make a statement at first, but when he heard that the German authorities were being called in he flatly refused to say another word." Liesowski looked inquiringly at Major Grau. "Shall I have him brought in?"

"Please do," said Grau.

Engel stood the witness against the wall with his arms above his head and felt him all over like a butcher examining a cow before slaughter. "All clear," he announced. "Now we can pick his brains."

The Pole ventured a faint smile, encouraged by the unwavering cheerfulness of Engel's expression. Whatever Engel said sounded cheerful.

"Kindly put your questions, Herr Liesowski," said Major Grau. "Engel will assist you if necessary."

Liesowski nodded. He glanced at the Major's hands, which lay folded in his lap as though in prayer. Engel sucked audibly at his cigar.

"Was it you who informed the police?" began the Inspector.

"Yes," said the Pole, cautiously.

"Did you discover the body?"

"Yes." The man's eyes betrayed alarm.

"Monotonous, isn't he?" remarked Engel.

"We have time," said Major Grau amiably, "plenty of time. We're prepared to be patient, too, provided it's worth our while—and there's no reason why it shouldn't be."

Further questions elicited the following facts: while the witness, whose name was Henryk Wionczek, was sitting in the communal lavatory on the second floor, he heard screams coming from the floor above. He had the distinct impression that they originated in the region of Maria Kupiecki's room. It didn't surprise him—she was an odd type, after all. Well, while he was sitting in the communal lavatory . . .

"It's right by the stairs," Engel explained. "If you squat on the pan you can see through the keyhole quite comfortably. The keyhole's big, too. Isn't that so, Liesowski?"

"Quite so."

Major Grau sat up slowly, the silky cloth of his uniform jacket growing taut as he inhaled deeply. With a touch of impatience, he said: "Well, now ask him what he saw through the keyhole."

Liesowski did so. Wionczek flinched almost imperceptibly, opened his mouth and promptly closed it again. Raising his head, he stared fixedly at the network of cracks that ran across the ceiling.

"Nothing," he gulped, "absolutely nothing. Nothing special, anyway, and the light on the landing was bad. I really didn't see anything. May I go now?"

Liesowski closed his eyes momentarily. Major Grau's gaze narrowed as though it had suddenly fallen on a painting of particular interest. Engel laughed delightedly, like a boy who has just seen a deck-chair collapse under a fat old lady.

"It looks as though I'll have to go to work on this lad," he said. "He obviously thinks we're a bunch of idiots—and I don't like that."

"I feel the need for a short breather." Major Grau got up, carefully smoothing a few imaginary creases from his immaculate tunic. "Meanwhile, Engel will continue the conversation with our witness. Make him an offer, Engel, and don't be stingy. Herr Liesowski, may I ask you to accompany me?"

Grau stepped out into the corridor followed by the Inspector. It was a long, narrow passage with a high ceiling and pale green, peeling walls. Several Polish detectives stood there in the semi-darkness like stone sentinels. There were no civilians in sight.

Grau glanced at Liesowski's worried face and gave a fleeting smile. "Don't worry, Inspector. You mustn't forget that there are certain differences between us and the S.D. or the Gestapo—differences which we set store by. Engel's methods are a picnic by comparison, I can assure you."

He went into the communal lavatory on the floor below,

sat down on the seat and peered through the keyhole. The whole corridor was visible. He could even hear, with comparative ease, snatches of apparently amiable conversation drifting down from the room once inhabited by the murdered woman. Engel was administering one of his guaranteed cures for a defective memory. He was haggling like a horse-trader, offering foodstuffs in exchange for a full and immediate statement.

"Let's go back," Major Grau suggested, glancing at his watch. Little more than five minutes had elapsed, but past experience told him that this was long enough for Engel's efforts to yield preliminary results.

They found Engel standing in the centre of the room. In front of him, not far from Maria Kupiecki's body, stood the witness, wearing a more co-operative expression.

"I've had a few words with our lavatory-man." Engel clapped his hands. "Now then birdie, start singing! What did you see?"

Wionczek shuffled self-consciously. Detective-Inspector Liesowski leant against the wall as though seeking support. Major Grau sat stiffly erect in his chair.

"Well, I sat there listening to the screams. At first I thought, Maria's tight again. She was always drinking and making a racket, you know. But then it struck me that she sounded really frightened. Then everything went quiet."

"Go on," prompted Engel. "You looked through the keyhole."

"Yes, because I heard steps coming downstairs from the floor above."

"What exactly did you see?"

Wionczek hesitated. "I must have been mistaken."

"Why not?" said Engel cheerfully. "You're only human, after all. Anyone can make a mistake. The main thing is, tell us what you saw—mistakenly, of course."

"There's no need to be afraid," Liesowski said gently.

"I caught sight of a man," Wionczek blurted out. "He was wearing uniform—the sort of uniform the Germans wear, grey or greenish—the light in the corridor was too dim for me to see clearly."

"You don't say!" exclaimed Engel. "A German soldier? He'll be telling us it was a German officer next."

"Kindly don't interrupt him," said Major Grau. "And don't make any leading remarks. Let him speak for himself."

"It could well have been a German officer," said Wionczek. Words suddenly gushed from him like water from a spring. "At least, that's what I thought at the time. Of course, I could be wrong. I was in a bit of a state—not feeling too good—that's why I was sitting there in the first place. Anyway, I caught sight of something else, something red, like a red stripe running down the man's trouser-leg—a wide red band. And there was something that looked like gold up by his collar."

"Great balls of fire!" exclaimed Engel. "Can you beat it? He goes the whole hog and describes a German general. I've half a mind to withdraw my generous offer and . . ."

Major Grau cut him short. "You can forget that idea, Engel," he said curtly. "Let the witness repeat his statement."

"The man must be wrong." Liesowski looked shocked. "These alleged patches of red could have been bloodstains."

"It's possible," said Major Grau ruminatively, "but you can't deny that his description fits a German general to a tee."

Engel gazed round somewhat dismayed, vainly looking for someone to share his consternation. "But that's utterly absurd!"

"I agree," said Liesowski with some emphasis.

Major Grau sprang to his feet. His lean and expressive features betrayed an odd glimmer of satisfaction. "What's to prevent us from taking this witness's statement seriously?" he inquired. "Personally, I'm inclined to believe in the man's sincerity. He may be mistaken, but why should he be lying? His evidence is unusual, but that only makes it more interesting. We shall draw our own conclusions and act on them—exhaustively and without compunction, as our sense of duty demands. Am I right, Engel?"

"As always, sir. After all, nothing's impossible in our line of country."

"I still find it difficult to take this witness's statement at its face value," said Liesowski.

Grau led the Inspector aside and laid a hand on his shoulder. "I think we should proceed as follows. You, my dear Liesowski, will record every detail of this inquiry. Do so without fear or favour. Bear in mind that the truth is all that matters, however unpleasant it turns out to be. Also bear in mind that I am prepared for any eventuality. Act as though justice were the one factor involved. No exceptions are to be made, even if a general's head has to roll."

INTERIM REPORT

PRELIMINARY DOCUMENTARY RECORDS

Excerpts from conversations dealing with events in Warsaw, 1942. These conversations took place eighteen years later and were recorded on tape.

Track 1
Place: Cologne
Speaker: Engel, Gottfried, ex-sergeant, now employed by a firm of carriers in Cologne. What follows is an abstract of Engel's statement, omitting the interviewer's questions:

"Did I know a man called Roman Liesowski? Yes, that's right. We used to call him 'tortoise' or 'gnome'. We took Liesowski over from our predecessors for the simple reason, I seem to remember, that he was one of the few senior members of the Warsaw police force who spoke fluent German. That's all I know about him.

"I can't remember much about Maria Kupiecki's body. I ask you, there were so many bodies lying around! It was just another lousy murder—in a crummy lodging-house somewhere off the main street, as I recall. It was three flights up and well after midnight. I was out on my feet.

"This Kupiecki woman was a tart of the first order. It's quite possible she worked for us—not as a tart, of course. She was more of a post-box for secret agents. Anyway, someone bumped her off. There wasn't the slightest indication of any political motive.

"I don't know how the case turned out. Major Grau took over all the particulars, so it wasn't my affair any longer."

So much, thus far, for Gottfried Engel. A further meeting was arranged with his consent, of which more later.

Track 2, also recorded eighteen years after the events in question.
Place: Warsaw
Speaker: Roman Liesowski, still a detective-inspector in the Warsaw police. Now living at No. 2a, Block 1c, one of the massive new apartment houses in the city centre. The following are extracts from Liesowski's statement, with intervening questions omitted as before:

"It was just about midnight when I arrived at the scene of the crime and began my inquiries. The name Maria Kupiecki rang a bell, so I told them to run a check on her at Headquarters. It turned out that Kupiecki was on our list of German agents, as I'd half suspected. Accordingly, I informed the competent German authority.

"The body was appallingly mutilated. Three of the knife-thrusts—possibly inflicted with a large clasp-knife—would have been sufficient to cause death on their own. Two of them had pierced the woman's breasts at the nipple and the third had penetrated her navel. There were dozens of other wounds, all apparently inflicted with the same insensate fury and all with the same end in view: the disfigurement of every feminine sexual characteristic. Would you like me to give you any more details? No? I'm glad. It wasn't a pleasant business.

"Conclusion: murder committed during an outburst of obsessive passion. There was nothing to indicate that Kupiecki had been done to death by a member of the Resistance—and even if it had been so I shouldn't have hesitated to bring him to book for an instant. The man was obviously as dangerous as a wild animal.

"I didn't hesitate to call in Major Grau, either. There wasn't anything particularly daring about this course of action. It was more calculation on my part—instinct, you might call it. Grau was a lone wolf, you see. Everything about him was unusual.

"Grau reacted promptly, just as I had expected. He took the witness's statement seriously and seemed determined to act on it. What was more, he actually seemed pleased to have got his hands on the material I gave him and took over the case himself.

"Needless to say, I did a little ferreting around on my own account. There were seven German generals in Warsaw at the time of the crime. A lot, you think? Well, there were several thousand generals in the Wehrmacht—upwards of four thousand. Many of them were busy in Russia at the time. A large number of others were engaged as organizers and administrators in the Balkans and Scandinavia and on the so-called Home Front. Several hundred more were waiting behind the Atlantic Wall—and Warsaw had seven: one in the suburb of Praha, three, normally in transit, at the Hotel Metropol and another three in the Liechnowski Palace.

"The Praha general spent the evening and most of the night with his troops—women signals auxiliaries, to be precise. Of the three generals living at the Hotel Metropol one was asleep in his room, the second was night-clubbing at the Mazurka with his A.D.C. and the third was playing host at a stag party in the hotel bar. In short, these four had an alibi.

"It was impossible for me to check on the three gentlemen in the Liechnowski Palace. It was a sort of fortress, hermetically sealed and kept under strict surveillance from the wine-cellar to the chamber-maids' attic. Eighty or more people lived in the Palace—staff officers, aides-de-camp, clerks, signallers, women service personnel, batmen and visitors of various kinds—and the three generals, namely:

i General von Seydlitz-Gabler, General Officer Commanding a Corps;

ii Lieutenant-General Tanz, commanding the Nibelungen (Special Operations) Division;

iii Major-General Klaus Kahlenberge, Chief of Staff to the Corps Commander.

"Is that selection good enough for you?"

2

General von Seydlitz-Gabler had the distressing sensation that he had been buried alive in an avalanche of cotton wool. His head buzzed as though it were a built-in concrete mixer and the skin of his scalp seemed taut to breaking point. It was agony even to open his eyes.

When he did open them, the first thing he saw was a bottle. It stood there fatly on his bedside table, and it was empty. It had once held a red burgundy by the name of Château Confran, a wine which had shrouded his memory of the night before as effectively as a blanket of fog. Perhaps it was just as well.

The General heaved his corpulent body on to its side and groaned deeply. The light streaming through the tall windows of the Liechnowski Palace hurt his eyes and his head throbbed steadily to the rhythm of his heart-beat. Suddenly he clamped his eyes shut in something akin to terror. Silhouetted against the centre window, where his desk stood, was the seated figure of a woman—his wife, to be exact. He breathed stertorously through his gaping mouth and feigned sleep.

"Well, have you slept it off?" asked Wilhelmine von Seydlitz-Gabler.

"I'm utterly exhausted."

"You had far too much last night," said Wilhelmine in a tone of melancholy reproof. "Why are you drinking so much lately?"

The General tried to sit up, but the throbbing inside his head rose in a crescendo and he swayed like a ship in a storm. Groping for support he knocked over the bottle, which fell to the floor with a dull thud. "Sheer pleasure, my dear," he said faintly, his bleary eyes pleading forgiveness, "sheer pleasure at having you with me again."

Wilhelmine von Seydlitz-Gabler had the patrician good looks of a thoroughbred horse, not exactly beautiful but undoubtedly striking. Glancing across at her husband sitting hunched up in the enormous bed, she saw a jumbled heap of yellowish-white bedclothes and blue-and-red striped pyjamas surmounted by a fleshy face like that of an aging operatic tenor, majestic but flabby, strong in profile but flaccid as a lump of dough when viewed from the front.

"Nonsense, Herbert. Tell me why you're drinking so much."

"Why?" The General sank back impotently on to his pillows. "I'm completely overworked, that's why."

Wilhelmine got up from the desk with reluctance, evidently fascinated by the piles of papers that lay strewn across it.

The General eyed his wife's approaching figure with dismay and endeavoured to burrow down into the bed.

Wilhelmine was arrayed in a thick hard-wearing woollen night-gown, but her husband had a momentary illusion that he could see right through it to the protuberant bones, blotchy skin and scanty flesh beneath. An acrid smell assailed his nostrils, simultaneously erotic and repellent, like the odour of distant decay. It was his misfortune to see more acutely than other men, he reflected, to probe more deeply and think more logically. He looked on himself as a blend of general and philosopher.

Von Seydlitz-Gabler became oppressively aware of his wife bending over him. Her foam-rubber flesh touched his and her breath soughed across his face like a tropic wind. On the walls around him, on the heavy silk tapestry of vernal green interspersed with a pattern which might have been water-lilies, on the vivid white ceiling whose moulding resembled the work of some eccentric pâtissier, on the unnaturally plump and rosy figure of the effeminate baroque angel in the corner.

"I'm getting old," he said with an effort, averting his face.

Wilhelmine von Seydlitz-Gabler straightened up, her thoroughbred features betraying pain of some unspecified kind.

Von Seydlitz-Gabler raised his imposing head from the pillow, the head of a heroic tenor seasoned by a thousand public performances. "These are trying times," he announced dramatically. "All the powers of concentration at our command must be directed toward a single goal: the future of our nation!"

Frau Wilhelmine von Seydlitz-Gabler breathed deeply. "Believe me, Herbert," she said, bosom heaving, "I have always been conscious of my responsibility toward you and your career. You must have confidence in me."

She kissed him, very lightly, on the lofty dome of his noble brow, and then released him. He closed his eyes in momentary relief. When he opened them again his wife was once more seated at the desk, as she had been when he first awoke.

It was not an unfamiliar sight. Wilhelmine made it her business to take an interest in everything to do with his work. She had played an active part in every stage of his career, and even in war-time she hurried to his side whenever circumstances permitted, as they did from time to time. General von Seydlitz-Gabler, it should be explained, was a specialist in pacification. Having mastered the art of appearing strict and paternal simultaneously, he made an acceptable conqueror. Thus it was no accident that his headquarters were located in Warsaw, and it was this fact which made it possible for his wife to visit him.

"How do you interpret these suggestions from Supreme Headquarters?" she asked, holding up a document resembling a diagram.

The General's limp skin looked grey as a worn-out dishcloth, but he summoned up a brisk nod of approval. "You've put your finger on the essential point, my love. It contains nothing but suggestions."

"And you can interpret them as you think fit?"

"Of course, but my interpretation must be dictated by the conditions prevailing here." The General hoisted himself up in bed slightly, as though trying to enhance the dignity of his appearance, but conditions were hardly in his favour. He sank back again.

"Surely, Herbert," she inquired gently, "isn't it always advisable to be decisive in a position like yours?"

"By all means," he replied, fidgeting with the buttons on his pyjama jacket, "but the decision involved here is one of far-reaching importance. Under certain circumstances I might be compelled to burn parts of this city to the ground."

"And what would your conscience say to that?"

"Decisions of this nature must be very carefully weighed." Growing restless, the General rolled out of bed, his pyjamas billowing loosely except in the nether regions, where they moulded themselves tightly to his haunches. He disappeared into the bathroom, leaving the door open. "The consequences could be simply catastrophic."

"Why do you imagine Supreme Headquarters has allotted you General Tanz's division?"

"Purely a safety measure. Just because I'm allotted a division of that sort, it doesn't necessarily mean that it will be used."

A fierce jet of water shot into the basin as von Seydlitz-Gabler spun the taps in an endeavour to drown his wife's observations, however valuable, but his efforts were in vain. Wilhelmine had followed him in and stood leaning against the door-frame smiling pensively.

"Damn it all!" exclaimed von Seydlitz-Gabler in an access of sudden but muted energy. "I really can't understand your everlasting preoccupation with this chap Tanz. There's a great deal to be said for him, I've no doubt, but he hasn't got a Regular Army background—never went through the mill as we did. I find it a little irritating, the way you always sing his praises."

Wilhelmine smiled. "I have my reasons, and they should be good enough for both of us. After all, Ulrike is just as much your daughter as mine and Tanz is more than a successful general—he's a bachelor as well. Besides, there's a sort of tradition at stake. When Father was your C.O. he told Mother that I was going to marry the best man in the regiment—and that happened to be you."

Major-General Klaus Kahlenberge, Chief of Staff to General von Seydlitz-Gabler, tilted his chair back from the desk, digging the heels of his boots into the floor as he did so. The chair tottered alarmingly, but Kahlenberge had an admirable sense of balance.

"Do me a favour, Otto," General Kahlenberge told the pancake of a man who stood facing him. "Don't ask me any trick questions at this ungodly hour of the morning. What's a human life worth?—I could say, a pinch of cow-shit. I might equally say, a very great deal. No, the real answer is, it all depends. Every human being has his market value. It fluctuates according to supply and demand, that's all."

"I know Lance-Corporal Hartmann pretty well, sir," said the rotund man in corporal's uniform.

"So what?" Kahlenberge gave a long, dry-as-dust laugh. His hairless skull glistened as though it had been basted with oil. It always shone like this, hence the nickname "Moon-face," a sobriquet which his subordinates used whenever they were absolutely sure he was not within earshot. His eyes, greenish and phosphorescent like those of a lynx, twinkled with amusement. The rest of his face was smooth, round and inflated, as though modelled in plasticine.

"You say you know Lance-Corporal Hartmann. Where from, may I ask? Did you play in the same sand-pit as children or were you drafted into the same shower when you joined up?"

Otto the Fat, corporal clerk and plaything of General Kahlenberge, grinned broadly. The General had put his finger on the spot as usual. Kahlenberge possessed what amounted to a sixth sense. You couldn't pull the wool over his eyes, which was why he was never boring to work for.

"My dear Otto," Kahlenberge continued, rocking to and fro precariously, but with evident pleasure, on the hind legs of his chair, "you're a clown, and as such indispensable to me for purposes of light entertainment. If I can ever do you a favour you only have to ask me. Why not, after all? War gives us a chance to play God. All right, let's play."

"The question of justice comes into it too, sir."

Kahlenberge burst into another peal of laughter. It was a mirthless sound like the distant croaking of a vulture.

"The concept of justice varies according to who defines it, Otto. Besides, Hartmann must either be a blithering idiot or an idealistic dreamer—which usually comes to much the same thing. If he had an ounce of common sense he wouldn't be where he is today. The only thing he can be, as long as he's here with us, is what he's already listed as in official records: dead. A dead man doesn't get into trouble and doesn't make any for other people. All the same, it's quite a challenge, raising someone from the tomb."

Sensing that his request was as good as granted, Otto allowed his spherical features to radiate gratitude. He gazed up at the General Staff maps on the wall with the expression of a true believer glimpsing heaven. Hartmann's fate was really a matter of indifference to him, but he liked to maintain a pleasant working atmosphere and thought it advisable to give the General a chance to demonstrate his generosity from time to time. General Kahlenberge found it enjoyable.

"Very good, sir," said the fat corporal, "I'll classify the Hartmann case as top priority."

"Do that thing, Otto," Kahlenberge replied tersely, slapping his riding-boot with the flat of a ruler. "I always welcome it when my men try to serve the cause of justice, so-called. Humanitarianism gives one an appetite for work. Besides, a senior officer likes to feel that he's surrounded by willing numbskulls."

Otto received the last observation with the composure of a man for whom such pronouncements were a daily occurrence —which they were, at least in General Kahlenberge's entourage. Kahlenberge uttered aloud, and with relish, things which others hardly dared to think, and Otto provided him with a loyal audience.

"I can hear the Almighty coming," said Kahlenberge.

"Half an hour earlier than usual, sir."

"I might have guessed it. He develops a tremendous capacity for work whenever his wife honours him with her presence."

At that point von Seydlitz-Gabler entered the room and conversation ceased. Otto froze to attention like a bowl of jelly that has suddenly and miraculously set. Even Kahlenberge interrupted his perilous balancing-act and stood up, doing his best to assume an expression of alert deference.

The G.O.C. raised one hand in greeting. It was a friendly gesture which included the corporal clerk as well as the Chief of Staff, but it also served as a signal to Otto to make himself scarce. The first and most important conversation of the day was always conducted in private.

"I devoted last night to a thorough study of the suggestions contained in the Supreme Commander's directive."

General von Seydlitz-Gabler enunciated these words in an almost oracular tone. With his slightly rotund frame encased in an excellently tailored uniform, he now resembled a photograph in one of the more flashy illustrated magazines—the sort normally adorned with a caption reading: "One of our military chiefs."

"My intensive study of the directive has convinced me that we are being given a special opportunity, Kahlenberge, an opportunity whose successful exploitation almost certainly depends upon the skill and effectiveness with which we put General Tanz's division to work."

Kahlenberge's greenish eyes glowed briefly. "Tanz's division," he said, selecting his words with some care, "has apparently been very successful—in its own way—at carrying out assignments of the utmost difficulty. One word of command from you and Tanz will raze Warsaw to the ground. But what would be the point? An unbroken sea of rubble is a pretty enervating sight and dead men don't offer any resistance—they just stink, as any fool knows. A corpse can't shoot back but it can't be useful to you either. In my submission, sir, the most radical solution isn't necessarily the best one."

The G.O.C. nodded sagely. Whatever he did, as long as he was in full regalia, looked impressive. There was something grandiose and heroic about his gaze, something prophetic, too. The only question was, what did the future hold in store? Kahlenberge was prepared to venture a guess.

"Given half a chance," he went on, "Warsaw could become a living hell. There may well be a Jewish uprising in the ghetto and the Resistance movement will certainly make its presence increasingly felt elsewhere in the city. If so, we shall be partly to blame for tolerating the filthy slaughterhouse tactics that are being employed in this country. If we don't do something soon we shall go down in history as collaborators in mass-murder."

"I didn't hear that last remark," said the G.O.C. with dignity. "My dear Kahlenberge, you're continually letting yourself be drawn into making bold and, if I may say so, dangerous assertions. You can't say I haven't warned you."

"All right, sir, as far as Warsaw's concerned we've been more leisurely—so far, anyway. But we're not going to be allowed to sit around in Warsaw for ever. That's why I recommend playing a waiting game. Sending in Tanz's division prematurely would be the worst thing possible. It would be tantamount to the radical solution I mentioned. Tanz has almost certainly been granted special powers by

Supreme Headquarters. His favourite hobby is arson, and the one thing we can't afford to do is give him a chance to indulge in it."

General von Seydlitz-Gabler's jaw muscles tightened. "As you may be aware, Kahlenberge, I was reared on the classics, but as a student and admirer of ancient Greece I know that one cannot escape the responsibilities thrust on one by Providence. They may be an immense burden, but one has no right to evade them."

"But what if history takes even half a step in the direction of normality, as it occasionally has done in the past? Do you want to be branded as the man responsible for the destruction of Warsaw?"

Von Seydlitz-Gabler glanced at the staff map of Warsaw lying on Kahlenberge's desk. Thick red arrows transfixed the stubby, narrow shape of the ghetto and those quarters of the city which had recently given trouble.

"Have you been working on something, Kahlenberge?" asked the G.O.C. hopefully.

"These are General Tanz's plans, sir. They were submitted to us for scrutiny. As you can see, the General wastes no time in getting down to business."

"Not bad," said von Seydlitz-Gabler admiringly. It was the experienced professional speaking. Nothing could cloud his evident pleasure in matters of pure strategy. "General Tanz is undoubtedly a man of action. I'm sure it will pay to establish friendly relations with him—in the most tactful way, of course. What would you think of inviting him to lunch?"

"A lunch party for General Tanz," mused Kahlenberge. "What about including some ladies?"

The G.O.C. agreed with alacrity. "Not at all a bad idea, Kahlenberge. I know my wife would be happy to attend, and my daughter too, no doubt."

"To put a little more life into the party we could also invite Major Grau of Abwehr," Kahlenberge suggested casually. "Grau's an adept at entertaining the fair sex. He's always got a fund of interesting little anecdotes. At the moment he has a murder story on his books—one which promises to have sensational repercussions. He mentioned it to me on the 'phone a few minutes ago."

"He's welcome to come as far as I'm concerned," said

von Seydlitz-Gabler with a characteristic air of *noblesse oblige*.

"I'll lay it on, sir," Kahlenberge said crisply. His eyes narrowed to slits. "People like Major Grau can be extraordinarily amusing—as long as they don't amuse themselves at your expense. It's hard to tell sometimes."

Lieutenant-General Wilhelm Tanz, commander of the Nibelungen Division, stood erect in his open Mercedes staff car. His left hand rested on the windscreen frame. In his right, with elegant nonchalance, he held a sub-machine-gun. He surveyed the stretch of road ahead with eyes as clear as a mountain stream, and when he spoke it was with sovereign calm.

"We'll set up the first road-block here."

Tanz looked like a painting by someone who had tried to capture the essence of heroism. With his lithe athletic figure, slender boyish hips, gladiatorial width of shoulder and finely chiselled features, he gave the impression of being a successful cross between a mountaineer and a seaman. He towered above everyone around him.

The General's driver, Stoss by name and—for the moment at least—sergeant by rank, stared rigidly ahead. It was his duty to watch the road even when the staff car was stationary. His gloved hands rested on the steering-wheel—another of Tanz's whims. As the General's personal driver, Stoss had to be ready to drive off at a moment's notice.

Major Sandauer, the Divisional G.S.O.1, considered it superfluous to ask any questions and silently pencilled in the General's road-block on his map. He looked colourless and schoolmasterish, rather like Himmler only more intelligent. His eyes had a penetrating quality.

"We'll take a leaf out of the fisherman's book," Tanz continued. "First we'll mark out a wide perimeter and then we'll start combing the outlying streets. That should set the fish in motion. Naturally, they'll try to make off in the opposite direction, but we'll have road-blocks there to cut them off. By the time we've closed the net we'll have the rebels exactly where we want them—with their backs to the ghetto wall."

"What about the civilian population, sir?" asked Major Sandauer.

"One can hardly talk of a normal civilian population in this place." General Tanz described a chopping movement with the hand that held the sub-machine-gun. "We'll put them through the sieve. Anyone who looks in the least bit suspicious will be held for questioning."

Major Sandauer noted down three points for discussion with Corps: means of transport, additional support and the maintenance of security. The last item covered temporary prison camps and ancillary arrangements such as latrines, a hospital, food distribution and interrogation facilities.

"At a conservative estimate," said Major Sandauer, "the sections of the city which we propose to search contain eighty thousand inhabitants."

"Take the necessary steps," replied the Divisional Commander.

Leaving the G.S.O.1 to his paper work, General Tanz thoughtfully scanned the street up which he intended to launch his first drive. It was lined with grimy old three- and four-storeyed houses with massive windows and doors, most of which had hardwood frames—probably Polish oak from the forests round Cracow and Lublin. They were like little fortresses but they wouldn't present any great problem if they were overrun quickly enough.

"Drive on," said the General.

The G.S.O.1 hastily scrambled back into the staff car. He always sat behind and on the right when accompanying his General. The seat beside him was occupied by the Divisional Commander's current "No. 2 orderly"—commonly known as his combat orderly, to distinguish him from the No. 1 orderly or batman who ministered to his needs in quarters. The combat orderly's job was to produce, at a moment's notice, anything the General might require while conducting an engagement, to whit: one Thermos flask of coffee; one packet of salami sandwiches; one flask of high-proof liquor reserved for special emergencies, so it was said, because the General never drank in action; three packets of iron rations; a hard pillow and a supply of pistol and sub-machine-gun ammunition. The combat orderly's name was unimportant. He seldom lasted in the job more than a week.

"Hold it at thirty," said the General.

A hum emanated from the Mercedes' bonnet, but Sergeant

Stoss carefully avoided gunning the engine. With clockwork regularity, the wheels began to turn.

Lieutenant-General Wilhelm Tanz, commander of the élite Nibelungen (Special Operations) Division, drove at a measured pace down Potocki Avenue. Once the go-ahead was given, he reflected, this was where he would instal his first road-block. Sergeant Stoss stared dourly ahead, the current combat orderly fingered his various items of equipment nervously and Major Sandauer busied himself with his notes, but the General seemed intent on impressing the surroundings on his mind. Whatever he saw became transformed in his mind's eye into a map.

"Flame-throwers," he remarked as the houses glided by. "Make sure our requirements are fully met, Sandauer."

"To be on the safe side, sir, I'll indent for three times as much as we need," replied the G.S.O.1, and made notes accordingly.

Tanz nodded. Being an expert staff officer, Sandauer relieved him of all the time-wasting donkey work. Tanz knew that he could rely on him, realizing that the Tanzes of this world could fight on regardless as long as there was a Sandauer to take care of logistics.

General Tanz registered every detail of what he saw, house by house and door by door. Though the buildings were large, their entrances were narrow and comparatively few and far between. Three or four men per house would do to begin with. First seal off, then search—that would be the procedure, with machine-gun sections covering the street, tanks blocking the main thoroughfares and all available scout cars maintaining an uninterrupted patrol of the intervening spaces. Then there were the flame-throwers . . . Once the ground floors were cleared the survivors would crowd upstairs like rats into a trap and could be mopped up at leisure. The roofs, however, presented a special problem.

"We ought to have a few helicopters," the General told his G.S.O.1. "Low-flying fighter support too, if possible. We must seal them off above and below simultaneously. Any man who slips through the net during this type of operation represents a potential danger later on."

"I'll indent for everything possible," Sandauer replied mechanically. His schoolmaster's face wore the anxious look of a man about to undergo a rigorous examination. He could indulge in such facial contortions because the General never looked at him closely, being far too preoccupied with himself and the enemy of the moment.

"Stop!"

Stoss braked judiciously and the Mercedes rolled to a halt as gently as if it had been driven into a snow-drift. A group of children who had been playing in the gutter froze into immobility and stared at the General wide-eyed.

The Divisional Commander raised his hand, then leapt lithely from the car like a victorious tennis-player vaulting the net. He strode over to the children and looked down at the hungry eyes and prematurely old, fearful faces.

"What are you scared of, youngsters?"

Major Sandauer translated the question into Polish, but the children did not venture to move.

"I think they're hungry," said Major Sandauer after a brief inspection.

Tanz turned to his combat orderly. "What have we got in the way of food?"

"Only two sandwiches, sir—Hungarian salami, meant for the General's lunch."

"The General," put in Sandauer, "is invited to lunch with the G.O.C. today."

"Even if I weren't," declared Tanz, "nothing would prevent me from foregoing my normal ration if circumstances rendered it necessary. Show me the sandwiches."

The combat orderly opened a brief-case with tremulous fingers and brought out a packet wrapped in a paper napkin. Inside were the prescribed two sandwiches. He held them out for Tanz's inspection.

Tanz's eyes wandered to the orderly's hands. As they did so, they took on the glint of freshly fallen snow in arctic regions. The hands holding the sandwiches were rough, chapped, uncared-for and dirty into the bargain.

"Filthy pig," said the General.

With one abrupt and powerful sweep of his left hand he sent the packet of sandwiches flying. They disintegrated into their various components and fell to the cobbles, salami, butter and bread standing out vividly against the dusty surface—russet red, creamy yellow and fluffy white bordered with pale brown. The children gazed at them with eyes in which greed and fear struggled for pride of place.

"Filthy pig," repeated the General. "Even Polish children don't deserve to be offered muck like that."

Major Sandauer nodded to the ragged onlookers, who promptly fell to their knees and scrabbled for what lay on the ground, tugging at it like birds with a worm. Having crammed the bread and sausage into their mouths, they sucked the butter off the cobbles, ignored by the members of General Tanz's entourage.

"Make a note: bread," the General told Sandauer. "Bread and other foodstuffs as well—sweets too, if available. These children appear to be hungry. Even starvation can prove a welcome ally in time of need."

"Duly noted, sir."

"As for this specimen," General Tanz continued, curtly indicating his current No. 2 orderly, "return him to general duties at once. I don't wish to see his grubby face again. Last week he had the effrontery to hand me an unwashed glass. He scratched my belt and tried to grease the inside of my gas-mask. He persistently swaps my sheets round so that the foot end turns up at the head and vice versa—and now, to cap it all, he dares to enter my sight looking as though he'd just exhumed his grandmother with his bare hands."

"Returned to unit, sir," Sandauer said hastily.

"Absolute cleanliness," pursued the Divisional Commander, "that's what I demand from the people round me. Do I make myself clear?"

"Yes, sir!" Tanz's erstwhile combat orderly looked almost relieved, possibly at having forfeited the dubious privilege of serving in the General's immediate vicinity.

"Drive on," said the Divisional Commander briskly. "I propose to inspect another four streets this morning and we must be finished by lunchtime. Sandauer, transmit the following message to the G.O.C.: operational plans under way, arriving G.H.Q. at appointed time. Has anyone else got any food? Throw it to the children. It can't do any harm to gain their confidence."

INTERIM REPORT

EXTRACTS FROM VARIOUS LETTERS

Letter 1, written eighteen years after the events described here.
Sender: Professor Dr Kahlert. Resident at Münster, Westphalia, between 1945 and 1946. Active in the field of popular education and contributor to several periodicals. Moved to Berlin in 1947, where he has since been closely associated with nationalist groups. The following are excerpts from Kahlert's written depositions, reduced to bare essentials:

"I was attached to General von Seydlitz-Gabler's staff, first as a lieutenant and later as a captain. One of my duties, which I still recall with pride today, was to keep the Corps' war diary.

"The General trusted me implicitly, a sentiment which was fully reciprocated. I regarded him as a born commander-in-chief, and history has confirmed that he was one of the Fatherland's greatest strategists.

"Apart from that, however, General von Seydlitz-Gabler was what might be termed a philosopher. His utterances, which I was privileged to record in writing, were couched in global terms. This has become clear only in latter years. As he told me during the Polish campaign, for instance: 'To be the dung of humanity is a tragic thing but a useful one.' Again, when we were alone once, during the conquest of France, the General said: 'The impulse towards what is good and right is comparable with the pangs of childbirth: we must overcome it if it is not to destroy us.'

"I can provide you with further striking examples of his insight, and shall be glad to do so in my humble capacity as an historian. I shall never forget something he said during the Russian campaign, one evening when we were sharing a bottle of Mâcon together. I recorded it verbatim. 'We have a weary road to tread,' he said, 'and it may well be that only posterity will fully understand us. What seems a daring pipe-dream today will go down in history as a piece of modest realism.'

"You make repeated inquiries about his wife. I can assure you that, whatever the occasion, she showed herself worthy of him. I was privileged to see them together at many crucial moments, and I can only say that I have never met a finer embodiment of the phrase 'Whither thou goest I will go'. Their relationship was one of mutual dependence. I shall always remember the time she turned to him one evening after a Chopin recital and said: 'Real human values, Herbert—how could we recognize them if they weren't within us?'

"As to the child of this fortunate marriage, I fear that I cannot give you very much information. The young lady's name was Ulrike, and I regret to say that she was living proof of the age-old theory that prominent men rarely produce offspring worthy of them. There was something ill-starred about her. She had a father who left his mark on history, but how many children are capable of recognizing parental greatness?"

Letter 2, also written nearly eighteen years after the events described here. –
Sender: Otto, occasionally known as Otto the Fat.
The following passages are also in extract form:

"General Kahlenberge was quite something, you can take it from me. I was with him for years and he never gave me a dull moment. He had X-ray eyes and ears like wireless aerials. I often used to think—that fellow could hear a sparrow fart at ten paces!

"Kahlenberge had a sort of sixth sense for everything that went on round him. He could always tell when the G.O.C. was on the war-path or when he was going to be easy meat. He was the sort of chap who could give you tomorrow's weather forecast or next week's casualty figures in advance. He was so sharp it took my breath away sometimes.

"He was probably the only brass-hat who never tried to shoot us a line. If someone started talking about dying like a hero he'd say it was all a question of keeping a tight arsehole, and when he saw a slogan like 'The Fatherland Calls!' he'd say 'They're after our money again.' He also liked to talk about 'the Greater German sewer-rat' (meaning our revered Führer and Supreme Commander)—and when he said 'shit' you could smell it!

"Kahlenberge could twist anyone round his little finger. He was a ball of fire. The G.O.C. may have had big ideas, but where would he have been without Kahlenberge? He really ran the show, and I helped him do it."

Letter 3, also written eighteen years later.
Sender: ex-Colonel Sandauer, currently a senior provincial government official. Owns a private residence in the Swabian Alps near Geislingen-Steige. Sandauer's written remarks are reproduced here unabridged:

Geislingen-Steige, November 9, 1960

"Dear Sir,

I must apologize for the fact that pressure of work has prevented me from replying to your letter until now. Although I am only too willing to answer your questions, I fear that my answers will prove of very little value because my knowledge of the more intimate details is extremely limited.

"You are correct in saying that I served under Lieutenant-General Tanz in the Nibelungen (Special Operations) Division. I was his G.S.O.1 for nearly two years, from 1942 until 1944, successively holding the ranks of major and later lieutenant-colonel. My duties were not of the easiest, but I did my best to perform them conscientiously and efficiently.

"No form of personal contact existed between myself and the General, a fact which would surprise no one who had any knowledge of that unusual man. He was unapproachable in the truest sense of the word. He had no private life and was completely wrapped up in his work.

"At the time, General Tanz struck me as an ideal soldier, but I should like to emphasize that I can only judge by what I saw during the two years I served under him. Moreover, my observations must necessarily be subjective and incomplete. General Tanz would not tolerate weakness or contradiction. He gave his orders and we carried them out. Suggestions were offered only when he asked for them, and any sort of discussion was unthinkable.

"You make a point of asking about the General's human qualities and mention the incident in Potocki Avenue, when he gave the Polish children his rations. I can only say—he was like that. He enjoyed eating in field kitchens surrounded by his men. On more than one occasion I saw him give a dying man a last drink from his canteen, and he once offered an old woman a lift from one village to the next in his car. He always treated women with exemplary courtesy. Although he never drank spirits or smoked himself, he made a practice of sharing out his cigarette ration among the troops or members of the civil population. You can read further details of a similar nature in army newspapers, of which I should be glad to send you any particular copy on request.

"I should be genuinely grateful if you would make every effort not to abuse my confidence. Misunderstandings of a painful and even dangerous nature can arise only too easily these days. It is true that we have not yet been as successful as we could wish in overcoming our past, but it is surely incumbent on us all to do so as speedily and effectively as possible.

"Trusting that you will understand my position,

Yours very truly,

Sandauer"

3

The intimate little luncheon party to be given by the Corps Commander, General von Seydlitz-Gabler, was evidently a function of some importance, for Frau Wilhelmine had taken all the preparations under her personal supervision. The orderlies were having a dismal morning of it, and they were not the only ones. A.D.C., staff supervisor, head cook, orderly officers and female personnel were all going through hell.

"I wonder if I might ask you?" was the mode of address normally adopted by Frau Wilhelmine on such occasions. The *Generalin* did not exactly give orders or issue directives. She had no right to. She merely requested, but when she made a request it had all the force of an order of the day issued by the G.O.C. himself.

"Dear Fräulein Neumaier, I wonder if I might ask you to arrange for a fresh tablecloth and matching napkins?"

Melanie Neumaier, the General's personal assistant and long-time chief secretary, was Frau Wilhelmine's favourite victim. Melanie cherished a profound and transparent devotion for "her" General and probably dreamed about him at night, but she hardly represented much of a danger. Her potential attractions were to a great extent nullified by an ample nose. What was more, her inordinate shyness with men had won her the nickname of "the Iron Maiden."

"Dear Fräulein Neumaier, I wonder if I might also ask you to look around for some glasses that harmonize with each other? It would be so nice if we could have four matching sets. We need hock, claret and champagne glasses, as well as tumblers. Would you mind doing that for me?"

No one could have withstood Frau Wilhelmine's frosty courtesy. Besides, past experience indicated that the General's mood was largely dependent on that of his wife, and the

General's well-being was very close to his subordinate's hearts.

"I wonder if I might ask you to polish these glasses?"

This time the victims were Lehmann, the General's batman, and two orderlies detailed for the occasion. They polished away, possibly consoling themselves with the thought that when the war ended—if it ever did—they would emerge as trained hotel staff.

Frau Wilhelmine von Seydlitz-Gabler seemed to be everywhere at once: in the kitchens, where a capon was sizzling fragrantly; with General Kahlenberge, who as Chief of Staff was theoretically responsible for organizing the lunch; with Melanie Neumaier, who wrote out table-cards, arranged flowers and made telephone calls; and with the staff superintendent, who was persuaded to part with special stores of various kinds after a short struggle.

"I wonder if I might ask you to find some ice-buckets for the wine—silver ones, if possible?"

The *Generalin* was not one to shy at fences, most of which she took at the first attempt. She had wasted no time in combing the multitudinous rooms of the Liechnowski Palace for articles of value and gathering them around her, well aware that the effect of a painting is often determined by its frame.

By the time she had finished, the suite occupied by her husband and herself resembled an inhabited museum. It was filled with damasks from Lyons, marble from Carrara, paintings from Paris, furniture from Rome and, scattered among these, fine examples of Polish craftsmanship, notably a massive and elaborately decorated table from a Cracow workshop of the late eighteenth century.

Wilhelmine von Seydlitz-Gabler's majestic features grew stern as her daughter Ulrike entered the room.

Ulrike was a slim, bony girl with an air of extreme reserve. If her father's prayers had been granted she would have been a boy, but Ulrike resolutely emphasized her femininity. Her hair-style, for instance, was downright provocative—a long smooth creation which enclosed her head like a silken curtain.

Ulrike was a source of some worry to her parents. She was largely devoid of the sovereign self-confidence which might have been expected in a general's daughter, nor was she particularly choosey about her friends. So, Ulrike had to be watched, and that was why, when she took up war-work, she was always "posted" somewhere within her parents' reach. At the moment she was working at garrison headquarters.

"Ah, there you are, my dear," said Frau Wilhelmine. "You must be wondering why I sent for you."

Ulrike von Seydlitz-Gabler was young. Her eyes were blue and untroubled as a Mediterranean sky in summer. "I suppose I've put my foot in it again," she said sweetly. "What have I done wrong now?"

"My dearest child," said Wilhelmine, all mother and general's wife, "I worry about you more than you give me credit for. I worry about your future, too." She indicated one of the tall chairs that stood round the table. "After all, you're a woman now."

"Maybe," said Ulrike, almost sadly. "Sometimes I think so too. It's the war, probably."

"You're not an innocent girl any longer, Ulrike. We needn't pretend to each other."

"Why should we? Nobody's to blame. It's not your fault or Father's either. I'm doing war-work here because you insisted on it, but when you do war-work you meet a lot of soldiers—and they're not all as old and respectable as a Corps Commander."

"Don't misunderstand me, Ulrike. I've no intention of reading you a moral lecture. On the contrary, we all have to learn from our mistakes. I'd like to know whether you're happy, that's all."

"Is it essential to be happy with things the way they are?"

Frau Wilhelmine brushed the question aside. "I'm no stranger to this sort of situation, my dear. When I was your age I gave myself to a lieutenant—one summer night in the park. I need hardly add that he was an exceptional man, but who was I to tie myself to a young, impetuous lieutenant? Later I met a captain, a much more balanced, mature and stable man. He became your father."

Ulrike crossed her legs. It was a defiant gesture, but her mother refused to be distracted. When Frau Wilhelmine could see the winning-post ahead she pressed on regardless like the thoroughbred she was.

"We women," she pursued, quite unperturbed, "have our occasional moments of weakness, but when the hour of decision comes we choose a man of solid worth, the man who seems worthiest of our love."

"And who do you suppose that might be in my case?"

"A general at the very least, Ulrike. That's why I asked you here today. I think it's high time you settled down. I'm thinking of General Tanz, of course."

"Tanz! You want me to marry a war memorial?"

"What could be finer than to become the wife of a unique man like that?"

Frau Wilhelmine spoke with immense conviction. She had a hundred arguments at her finger-tips, each one more cogent than the next, but she was not given a chance to produce them because at that moment the generals entered the room.

There were five at table. The G.O.C. presided over the gathering with Lieutenant-General Tanz on his right and, since they were an odd number, his wife on his left. Ulrike was seated between Tanz and Kahlenberge.

Frau Wilhelmine led the conversation, keeping an eagle eye on the mess waiters meanwhile. "Major Grau of Abwehr will be joining us for coffee," she announced. Her tone hinted that this was a piece of skilful planning—first the generals and their womenfolk, then the lower ranks—but the real reason was rather more prosaic: the capon would not stretch to more than five.

"I'm no slave to the pleasures of the table," declared General von Seydlitz-Gabler, plying his knife and fork with gusto, "but I appreciate my food."

"It's all a question of refinement," said Frau Wilhelmine, always quick to corroborate her husband's pronouncements whatever the subject under discussion. "Don't you agree, Ulrike?"

"As far as I'm concerned," said Ulrike carelessly, "the main thing is to have enough. I'm always hungry. The kitchens at garrison headquarters don't produce food like this."

"We also live frugally here," said von Seydlitz-Gabler in a tone of mild but unmistakable reproof, "but we enjoy offering hospitality. This is a special occasion. We often have nothing but bread and butter with artificial honey for breakfast."

"A man can conquer the whole world," interjected Major-

General Kahlenberge, busying himself with a chicken-leg, "without ever being able to satisfy all his acquisitive urges."

Remarks of this sort obviously irritated Frau Wilhelmine von Seydlitz-Gabler, who liked to steer conversation along less abstract lines. Pushing back her plate, which was not entirely empty, she said: "Whatever our normal standard of living, we must always be prepared to do without things when occasion demands, as it does in times like these. Don't you agree, General Tanz?"

"I do indeed," he replied tersely.

These were the first words that General Tanz had uttered since his arrival. He had endured the preliminaries in silence and had wordlessly offered Ulrike von Seydlitz-Gabler his arm when they went in to lunch. He had not seemed particularly interested in his table-companions' conversation and devoted all his attention to the business of eating. He drank water instead of wine, but no one was surprised at that. The General was known to be a man of iron self-discipline.

Frau Wilhelmine regarded him with a frank blend of tenderness and admiration. "Ah yes, we all have to make sacrifices, don't we?"

"And what sacrifices do you make, General?" asked Ulrike casually.

"I am a soldier," said General Tanz, who evidently considered this a sufficient answer.

"My dear child," said von Seydlitz-Gabler, gently reproving, "it's about time you realized that you were born into a world of self-denial. I'm a soldier too, and so were my ancestors before me."

"I happen to be a woman," said Ulrike.

"I'm aware of that." The G.O.C. smiled like a perfect host watching one of his guests smashing a priceless heirloom. "But the female members of our family have always married soldiers."

"And never regretted it!" put in Frau Wilhelmine.

"Some soldiers lie and rot on the battlefield, so I'm told," Ulrike said defiantly. "They aren't all lucky enough to rot in comfortable staff jobs."

"You're mistaken, Fräulein," said General Tanz in measured tones. "For instance, the members of my staff are given every opportunity to train the healthy body on which the healthy mind depends. In my command, even staff officers take part in early morning sports, cross-country runs and field training. Nobody rots with me."

"Nor with us," remarked Kahlenberge. "We practise club-swinging with bottles and dig trenches with knives and forks. Our conferences are marathon efforts. Anyone who wants to survive with us has to be an all-round athlete."

Frau Wilhelmine von Seydlitz-Gabler endeavoured to inject a more friendly note into the proceedings. "General Tanz," she said, "to my mind, you're a model man in every respect save one: you're not married. May I ask why not?"

"No opportunity," replied the General. "Greatly regret it."

"Perhaps you've had plenty of opportunities and just let them slip?"

"Maybe," said General Tanz, with the look of a man surveying a battlefield. "We cannot choose the age we live in, but it's our duty to shape it. That leaves us precious little time for what is commonly known as private life. We live in a period which makes great demands on us."

"One of them being the extermination of the Jews, I suppose?" asked Ulrike aggressively.

"Child, child!" Frau Wilhelmine raised her right hand in protest. "What a subject—and lunch not over yet!"

"Life is a struggle," said General Tanz, dissecting his cheese. "Anyone who proposes to build a world order must be capable of destroying anything that threatens it."

"Human beings are capable of the most incredible things," commented Kahlenberge bitterly.

"I merely try to do my duty," said General Tanz.

"Only your duty, nothing more?" Kahlenberge leant back in his chair as though evading an unseen blow. "To do nothing but one's duty can be a demoralizing process."

Frau Wilhelmine said firmly: "General Tanz is a man!"

"We're all men," declared the G.O.C. He raised his champagne glass as though it was a field-marshal's baton. "We are fighting a war that was forced on us, but we wage it unflinchingly."

Coffee, brewed in the Turkish fashion, was served in the Blue Room. The carpet that covered the floor was a mixture of deep blue and subdued marine tones, heavy midnight blue hangings swathed the walls, and the pale crocus blue of the moulded ceiling shimmered like a clear sky in early spring.

Into this extravagant symphony in blue stepped Major Grau. His lean, slightly saturnine face wore an ingratiating smile. "I have what I hope will be an entertaining item of news for you," he said when introductions were complete. "That is, if you're interested. It concerns a highly unusual corpse—a female corpse, to be precise."

"I think," Wilhelmine von Seydlitz-Gabler said stiffly to her daughter, "that it would be better if we left the men alone."

Ulrike followed her mother out of the room. An uneasy silence reigned for a moment after the door had shut.

"Our good ladies," declared the G.O.C., "have a marked sense of tact where official matters are concerned."

Kahlenberge glanced keenly at Grau. "Is this official?"

"It's not beyond the bounds of possibility," said Grau.

"Are you still talking about a woman's corpse?"

"Why not? Does anyone mind?"

General von Seydlitz-Gabler threw back his head and laughed. It was a melodious sound, the product of years of practice, and he was well aware of its effect. "What is all this about a corpse, my dear chap? Surely you can find a more entertaining subject. Perhaps you'd do better to concentrate on the Hartmann case."

"The Hartmann case doesn't concern me, sir," said Major Grau. "Officially, it's the S.D.'s pigeon. Besides, the whole business seems to be little more than a comedy of errors. The man was declared dead. Let the matter take its course, I say."

"Are those patent leather shoes you're wearing?" asked General Tanz abruptly.

Major Grau raised his decorative head. "Are they forbidden?"

"I find them ludicrous," said General Tanz.

"I don't belong to your division."

"Unfortunately."

Kahlenberge shook his glistening skull as if trying to dislodge a fly. "What are we talking about, anyway, that poor devil Hartmann—or are we back on the subject of dead females?"

"Are you wearing perfume, by any chance?" General Tanz asked with a face like granite.

Major Grau retained his expression of unruffled serenity. "I occasionally use a strong after-shave lotion."

General von Seydlitz-Gabler kneaded his fingers until the joints cracked, but his rubicund features lost none of their disarming benevolence. He emitted a series of conciliatory sounds.

The G.O.C. was a man who liked harmony to reign in his immediate circle. In an endeavour to change the subject he recalled an amusing incident from the days when he was a young officer in the first world war. It concerned some British prisoners and a bet which he, then adjutant of his regiment, had made with his commanding officer. Under the terms of the wager he, von Seydlitz-Gabler, had to induce his prisoners to sing the German national anthem within the space of three days. They ended by singing not only the Deutschland-Lied but also *Ich bin ein Preusse, kennt ihr meine Farben?* (he assured them on his word of honour) in four parts!

This truly hilarious anecdote was greeted with general laughter, although it was a standard item in the General's repertoire and everyone in the room knew it of old. Even Grau seemed amused. There was an improvement in the atmosphere, further enhanced by the appearance of a mess waiter with a bottle of Napoleon Brandy, guaranteed thirty years old. Even Tanz accepted a glass.

Major Grau exploited the appreciative silence that followed by interjecting: "I do hope you'll permit me to return to the corpse I mentioned earlier. I'm sure you'll agree it's a unique case."

Kahlenberge shook his head indulgently. "You must be joking, my dear Grau. We live in an age in which bodies lie around in the streets like cobble-stones. What's so unique about this one."

"Ah, General, there are corpses and corpses. This one was literally perforated like a block of postage stamps—by hand, too."

The G.O.C. raised a well-manicured hand. "How ghastly," he murmured.

Tanz said coolly: "We all have to die some time."

"And even death has its funny side." Kahlenberge refilled his glass to the brim with cognac. "Even gentle Juliet and sweet Desdemona finished up as cold as wet flannels on a winter's night."

Major Grau regarded General Kahlenberge with bright, inquisitive eyes. "You sound preoccupied with death, sir."

"I occasionally do some reading," replied Kahlenberge sardonically, "Shakespeare included."

Grau smiled faintly. "This is a case which appears to fall outside the usual run of murders."

"Let's abandon the subject," suggested General von Seydlitz-Gabler. "In my opinion, the dead only die once and should be buried as quickly as possible."

"But every death has a cause."

"And every victim has a murderer," Kahlenberge put in. "The dead already number millions in this absurd age of ours, Grau. What about their murderers—perhaps millions of murderers?"

Von Seydlitz-Gabler shook his head disapprovingly. General Tanz gazed into the distance with apparent indifference.

"The dead woman worked for us," said Grau. "She was useful to us. The question is, should I let someone murder one of our agents and get away with it?"

"Splendid!" cried Kahlenberge, reaching for his glass of brandy. "How comforting to know that even in this day and age there are people who don't bite the dust unavenged."

"In this particular case," Grau continued, "something quite extraordinary and entirely untoward has come to light. I can assure you that our findings are accurate and based on inquiries conducted by men of professional integrity. In brief, these experts have unearthed a credible witness who informs us that the murderer may be . . . Gentlemen, I am reluctantly compelled to inform you that the only possible suspect is a general. A German general."

Von Seydlitz-Gabler again raised a protesting hand, his fleshy face pale as ashes. Kahlenberge ventured a laugh, but it was more like the yelp of a dog in pain. Tanz seemed turned to stone. One of the brandy glasses fell over and its contents spread across the table-cloth like blood.

The G.O.C. was the first to speak. "A joke in poor taste," he said with an effort.

Kahlenberge mustered up a half-hearted smile. "All things are possible."

"An outrage," declared General Tanz in glacial tones. "An outrage such as only a cretin could devise."

Major Grau looked the generals over like a row of dustbins, savouring his triumph. A moment like this seldom came twice in a lifetime.

"A most entertaining story, Major," said von Seydlitz-Gabler. "We appreciate your telling us, but we mustn't detain you any longer."

Major Grau rose gracefully to his feet, bowed and left the room, confident that he had left behind a time-bomb of mammoth dimensions.

Back in the Blue Room, the three generals eyed each other in silence for a moment.

Kahlenberge screwed up his eyes and peered through an imaginary pall of smoke.

Von Seydlitz-Gabler muttered: "It can't be true!"

And Tanz snapped: "That's the end of Grau as far as I'm concerned."

"God Almighty!" Major-General Kahlenberge said mildly. "Who do you think you are—a knight in shining bloody armour? I've never heard such concentrated tripe all my life."

"I can only tell you what I know, sir." Lance-Corporal Hartmann sounded eager to please. "And I really don't know any more than I've told you already."

Rainer Hartmann was a fresh-complexioned young man whose head sat a trifle crooked on his shoulders. This was not a congenital defect but the result of a neck wound received some weeks earlier. For a long time he had been unable to do more than croak—a circumstance which had saved his life—but the danger of his position had increased with every step he took on the road to recovery.

"Must you shoot off your mouth, Hartmann?" asked General Kahlenberge. "Or are you absolutely hell-bent on self-destruction? There are people like that, I know. But what's the point of it?"

Hartmann blinked as though the sun was shining straight into his eyes, but he preserved the immobility of a statue in a city park. His youthful face was handsome but lacking in animation, his brown, gently waving hair fell appealingly on to a high forehead and his body looked well-proportioned even in its graceless sack of a uniform.

Hartmann's trouble was that he had survived what he regarded as an epic ordeal with flying colours and could not understand why no one seemed ready to take an equally uncomplicated view of the matter.

"He doesn't get the drift, sir," asserted Otto the Fat, who was standing in the background. "He's a good-hearted lad, that's why he behaves like a clot sometimes."

"A valid enough excuse, Otto, but I'm afraid your views aren't going to do Corporal Hartmann much good." General Kahlenberge tapped the document lying before him on the desk with distaste. "This piece of bumf is as good as a death warrant. It's all very well for you to believe in Corporal Hartmann's innocence, but there's no getting away from the fact that he's got to prove it."

Otto hung his pink and porcine head in apparent dejection, but knowing his General he felt that all was not lost. Hartmann opened his mouth as an aid to breathing, rather like a fish caught in a swirling torrent of muddy water.

"If I'm forced to pass on what I have here unaltered, Hartmann will be handed over to the S.D. Once they get their claws on him it'll mean curtains." Kahlenberge's left shoulder twitched a little. Almost inaudibly, he went on: "And I don't want that. Why should I do their dirty work?"

Hartmann's head drooped. It was a weary but graceful gesture. "I really don't know what they could accuse me of. I'm not aware of having committed any crime."

"As though it mattered two hoots what you think, man!" Kahlenberge leant back in his chair. "All I know about you, Hartmann, is that you seem to have had a lot of bad luck. For some peculiar reason you're still alive. That's neither to your credit nor the reverse. You're obviously a wide-eyed innocent, but what's to be done with a curiosity like you?" He smiled grimly. "Well, you're lucky in one respect. We don't propose to hand you over—not because of your big blue eyes but because it doesn't suit our book. Do you follow me? No, of course you don't. Never mind, it's just your good luck. Remember one thing, though. There can't be many people as dumb as you still in the land of the living."

Kahlenberge once more bent over the transcript of Lance-Corporal Rainer Hartmann's statement. He saw no reason to concentrate on details but merely absorbed what seemed important. The gist of the story was as follows:

". . . I was assigned to a unit which had the job of transporting supplies to the forward troops. We were a party of six under a sergeant whose name I don't know. The convoy consisted of three medium-sized trucks—four-tonners. When we reached a place whose name I don't remember we were suddenly fired on by Soviet troops. All the vehicles went up in flames and all the members of my unit were killed except me. I crawled off somewhere half-conscious and eventually fainted. . . .

". . . Finally—I don't know how long afterwards—I came to in a barn which was being used as an emergency hospital. I was surrounded by Russian soldiers. My uniform had gone and I was bandaged to the neck and wrapped in blankets. I couldn't speak, so the Russians treated me as though I was one of theirs. . . .

". . . Some days or weeks later the hospital fell into the hands of our troops. I wasn't able to keep track of time. I had a high temperature and was always drifting off into unconsciousness, but I know I regained my voice almost as soon as our chaps arrived. I was released and managed to find my way back to my unit."

Kahlenberge slowly shook his gleaming pate. "What unadulterated idiocy," he said. He spoke like a man who was shouldering a burden which no one else cared to take on. The fact that he did so willingly was beside the point.

"It's the truth, sir, every word of it," protested Lance-Corporal Hartmann.

"No doubt," said Kahlenberge wearily. "The truth as seen by one Lance-Corporal Hartmann, but not the whole truth as we are compelled to see it. All this happened on December 5th, 1941. On December 10th it was announced that one of our units, to wit yours, comprising six men and a sergeant, had fallen into Russian hands. According to official reports you were brutally murdered—eyes gouged out, balls cut off, bellies slit open, etcetera, etcetera. None of you escaped. The Propaganda Ministry gave the case the full treatment and played it for all it was worth."

"It's true," Otto interposed. "Thanks to some first-class public relations work by various propaganda units and the S.D., the so-called neutral press flocked to the scene of the crime in droves. You should have seen the ink flow! They really went to town when they saw the bodies. There was nothing but mincemeat left."

"As the details suggest," Kahlenberge went on, "the Propaganda Ministry got weeks of material out of this piece of butchery. They even published a 'Red Book' on the subject, full of the most blood-curdling details. What's more, our historian Captain Kahlert has collected a whole filing cabinet of data on the case."

Otto the Fat nodded. "There's no doubt about it, Hartmann. Officially, you're dead."

Kahlenberge excavated his right ear with his index finger. "And now you've turned up again. You're alive, and that's your personal bad luck. Unfortunately for you, you're living proof that our Propaganda Ministry published a pack of lies."

"How can I help it?" Hartmann asked helplessly. "I only did what anyone would have done. I don't see how anyone can blame me for that."

"What a dangerous attitude to take, Hartmann." Kahlenberge eased himself back into his chair and raised his chin as though surrendering himself to the attentions of an invisible barber. "Are you seriously asking me how you can help being still alive? How can a man help being born a Jew or a Pole or a Prussian? Why does a human being happen to be on the receiving end of a bomb? Why do some people die in bed while others end their lives in a ditch or on the field of honour? The only valid question at this moment is: how can we decently save your neck?"

Lance-Corporal Rainer Hartmann looked bewildered. Otto the Fat regarded this demonstration of resentful incomprehension with growing disillusionment. "Heavens alive, man," he exclaimed. "Can't you get it through your thick head? You're in the shit up to your neck."

Kahlenberge massaged his hairless skull until it shone like a billiard ball. "Listen, my lad," he said kindly. "You've escaped death by the skin of your teeth and it's obviously proved too much for you. The very fact that you're still alive is enough to hang you. You're alive contrary to official instructions and in defiance of widely published reports. People will be wondering how you managed to survive. Don't you get it? According to official information you're dead—mutilated past recognition. A couple of dozen newspapers say so. But since you still exist, Hartmann, that makes you perfect material for every conceivable kind of enemy counter-propaganda. Don't you see that?"

"I shall be happy to follow any advice I'm given, sir," said Hartmann, trying unsuccessfully to brush a leaf of hair off his forehead. "But I'm still not clear what's expected of me."

"In the view of the S.D.," said Kahlenberge, "there can be only one explanation for your survival. These people are convinced that only a man who had sold himself to the Russians could have survived. Therefore, you betrayed your companions and let them be slaughtered. Your fellow-soldiers' appalling death was the price you paid to save your own miserable neck. Q.E.D."

"But that's not so!" exclaimed Hartmann, visibly shattered. "Really not, I swear it!"

"For the present, Hartmann, I'm only interested in useful facts, nothing more. That being so, you'll have to make some fundamental changes in this statement of yours. Otto will help you—he knows the ropes. If you're to convince them, your only possible line is that you purposely misled the Russians. Purposely, do you hear! No twaddle about fainting-fits or temporary loss of memory and voices or other doubtful jokes of that sort. Make a note of that, Otto. People only believe what they want to believe. Hartmann fought for his life methodically. He outwitted the Russians and waged a dangerous and determined battle for continued existence. He was a hero, not a victim. There's no other way of explaining things. Are we agreed?"

"All clear, sir," declared Otto vigorously. "Isn't that right, Hartmann?"

"Why not?" Hartmann's voice was resigned. "I want to live, after all."

"That's the ticket!" Kahlenberge pushed the papers back decisively and dealt them a playful slap with his hand. There was something final about the gesture. "We all want to live—as long as we can, that is. Ours is a heroic age."

The room was cold and smooth as a metal box. The predominant colour was a chalky white against which the wall-maps stood out like blemishes. Even the few pieces of furniture dotted round the room failed to alleviate its depressing monotony.

The harsh light illuminated a bottle and two tumblers, and, just beyond the immediate radius of the lamp's glare, the faces of Sergeant Engel and Major Grau. Engel was slumped wearily in his chair, while Grau smilingly studied the light through his glass.

Engel grinned discreetly. "You wouldn't put anything past those generals, would you, Major?"

There was a rustle of silk as Major Grau leant forward slightly, but his expression betrayed no identifiable emotion. His elegance had an irritating quality. No one who saw him would have believed that he was associated with one of the dirtier aspects of war.

"Impatience is not one of my vices, as you know, Engel," Grau said blandly, "but I should be interested to hear if you've managed to verify any details."

"Of course, sir, as far as I was able. From all that has come out so far it really seems on the cards that a general was responsible."

"And why shouldn't it have been a general?" asked Grau with a disarming smile. "After all, someone must have done it."

Engel played a scale on his knuckles. "All the same, Major, it's a case of brutal murder."

"Experience tells us that murder is far from being a prerogative of the insane—or even of the lower classes, so why shouldn't a general join the club for once?" Major Grau smiled pensively. "To the gaping mob, a Prussian or a German general is much the same as a national monument, but compared with some of the specimens I've met any village schoolmaster's a genius and any tramp's a gentleman."

"Oh yes," said Engel, "that's all very true. I've caught a general with a male tart before now on a raid. But surely, sir, the real question is—who's going to believe us?"

Grau's voice took on the deliberate tones of a don delivering an important lecture. "Don't you see, Engel? We can beat these lads at their own game: history. We can wrap their past round their necks until it chokes them. We can take it for granted that these inflated idiots who enjoy sounding off about honour and tradition whenever it serves their purpose are really poor whipped curs. We can also take it for granted that they've always run off with their tails between their legs whenever they've been treated accordingly. We can tell ourselves that they were better at their job in the days of the Great Elector. Frederick the Great made marionettes out of them. In 1848 they let themselves be cut to pieces in Berlin by a handful of comparatively harmless revolutionaries. Under William the Second they became tailor's dummies. During the Weimar Republic their sole remaining wish was to survive. And when Adolf Hitler arrived on the scene they crawled to him on their bellies and licked his hand."

Engel picked up his glass and silently held it to the light.

Major Grau passed a hand across his eyes as though dazzled, then continued in the same urbane tone. "Of course, generalizations are always absurd. Not all generals are epic figures or political time-servers. I've no doubt there are some worthy men among them."

"Some bastards too—eh, Major?" said Engel. "And one of them's the man we're after—eh?"

"That's about the size of it," said Grau.

INTERIM REPORT

FURTHER DOCUMENTS

Extracts from diaries and letters, also an excerpt from a situation report and the results of further inquiries.

Extracts from a diary kept by Frau Wilhelmine von Seydlitz-Gabler. This journal, entitled "My Personal War Diary" and comprising several volumes, was made available only after protracted negotiations with the authoress's relatives, in whom sole rights are vested.

Warsaw 1942

"How grim this city would seem if Herbert were not here. His pure and kindly nature sheds a sort of universal radiance. Clarity of thought is his distinguishing characteristic. I need hardly say that I am proud of him, but it is pride coupled with humility.

"How popular he is with his staff! I really believe they would go through fire for him. And how wonderful that their regard for him extends to myself. Do I deserve it? When I asked my husband he said yes—another proof of his greatness.

"Arranged a small luncheon party today. Everything went swimmingly, as far as it ever can in this city. Quite a festive table, of which Herbert the undisputed centre of attention. On his right: General Tanz, one of the Reich's finest soldiers and many times decorated. Touching, the well-bred gallantry with which he paid court to Ulrike, our daughter! Ulrike was deeply impressed but tried not to show it. Young people are like that, but our experience of life will guard her against making any silly mistakes.

"At a convenient moment I said to General Tanz, in confidence: 'I'm so glad that it's you who are to work with my husband at this important juncture.' And I added, spontaneously: 'My husband thinks the world of you!' Whereupon Tanz: 'The feeling is mutual!' What more is there to say?

"Herbert is literally wearing himself out. He works all day and even during the night. A few days ago he didn't get to bed until dawn. How touchingly anxious he was not to wake me! I couldn't bring myself to disillusion him. Later, when I tidied his clothes, which he had thrown down untidily in a state of utter exhaustion, I was horrified to see traces of blood on them. He must have been visiting the front, but he didn't make the slightest fuss about it. How typical of him!"

Situation report by Lieutenant-General Tanz, commanding Nibelungen Division.
Written in Warsaw in 1942 and prepared in quintuplicate: one copy for the Corps Commander, one for Supreme Headquarters, Wehrmacht, one for the Reichsführer S.S. and two further copies for filing. One copy of this reposes in the "Collection of Historic Documents" in Warsaw. What follows is the fourth paragraph of the report, which originally comprised seven type-written sheets:

"As things stand now, there is obviously no longer room for so-called subtlety and flexibility, i.e., caution. Our efforts should much rather be directed toward a radical solution. The population of Warsaw is dangerous. Nothing further can be achieved by kindness and consideration. An uprising could occur at any moment. The fact that German soldiers have been shot down from ambush is established beyond doubt. Casualties are not yet heavy—in the past week only seven men lost as against three hundred and sixty-four deaths inflicted in the course of immediate reprisals—but this figure could increase overnight. I therefore find myself compelled to urge unremitting severity."

Deposition by ex-Corporal Otto recorded on tape in summer 1960. All that are reproduced here are extracts which appear to have a bearing on the events in Warsaw and their sequel.

"I'm a sensitive sort of chap—always have been. I enjoy

talking, but I can't understand why everyone harps on the Hartmann business. Hartmann was a nut-case, I tell you for a fact.

"There was something odd about Hartmann. If I'd thought about it properly at the time I could have told how everything was going to turn out. Some people snuff it as easily as others catch cold. Hartmann was like that. He always used to say: 'How can I help it? I ask you—how can a donkey help having long ears?' It wouldn't have mattered what Hartmann did, believe me, the final result would have been the same.

"Gentle as a lamb, he was. The women used to go gooey-eyed when they looked at him. He was a good-natured lad, too. You could have a game of cards with him and he'd never go off the deep end when he lost. He lost most of the time, I might add."

Deposition by ex-Sergeant Engel, also recorded eighteen years later. Like all statements made by Herr Engel (and sundry other individuals) it was subject to the express qualification: "as far as I can remember."

"Don't ask me what sort of person Major Grau was. I don't know. I worked with him for nearly two years but I never got to the bottom of him. To look at the man you'd think he was mild as milk, but he could be stubborn as a mule when he wanted to be. He was no respecter of persons. I once heard him tell Gauleiter Koch, the Reich Commissioner: 'I'm not interested in what you represent here, only in what you do!'

"He knew his job, there's no doubt about that. He had ideas, too. I once saw a letter on his desk from Admiral Canaris. It began 'My dear Gottfried.' Gave me quite a turn, I can tell you. I never even knew that Major Grau's Christian name was Gottfried.

"Life was full of surprises when he was around. There were days when I didn't know whether to treat him like a friend or an enemy. Once, he even said to me—referring to a general—'You can't tame a mad dog!' "

4

Major-General Kahlenberge, Chief of Staff to the Corps Commander, liked to pretend that he enjoyed choral singing. As a matter of fact, he didn't, but as he once said to a friend: "Men who sing can't think, and men who can't think make congenial subordinates—so let them sing. It makes a senior officer's job that much less complicated."

Kahlenberge often sat and listened to the G.H.Q. choir going through its paces. This choir—a male voice ensemble, needless to say—was drawn from every branch of the Corps Commander's staff. The sergeant cook was a member, as was the chief of the map-making section; clerks sang beside technicians, the leading tenor was a signaller and the mightiest bass belonged to a medical orderly. The choir-master's duties were performed by a dentist who enjoyed a great reputation as a festival conductor in his home town. He conducted with verve and endurance but wasted no time on musical subtleties.

"*Westerwald!*" General Kahlenberge called encouragingly.

The choir, which had just been allowed a short break for throat-clearing and nose-blowing, set to again with a will. Kahlenberge leant back comfortably in his chair and stretched his legs. The other ranks' mess hall in the cellar of the Liechnowski Palace, which provided the venue for this prodigal outpouring of emotion, seemed to quake.

Without warning, the singers' fervour suddenly redoubled in intensity. Kahlenberge was at a loss to explain this phenomenon until he swivelled round in his seat and beheld the G.O.C. He rose to his feet with decorum and came to attention. The choir continued to sing lustily of the wind that blew so cold in the Westerwald.

The G.O.C. took his Chief of Staff by the arm and led him

out into the cellar passage. When von Seydlitz-Gabler treated one of his subordinates with this degree of intimacy his motives were bound to be interesting. Kahlenberge's eyes began to gleam like those of a cat scenting a plump mouse.

"A splendid choir," declared von Seydlitz-Gabler.

Kahlenberge nodded. "Practice makes perfect."

The G.O.C. cleared his throat. "We Germans have an inexhaustible repertoire of choral music. I'm particularly fond of *Lützows wilde, verwegene Jagd.*"

"We'll practise it," Kahlenberge assured him. His curiosity mounted.

"Choral singing is an embodiment of the purest German traditions. It's not surprising that all our most characteristic virtues can be found in it—profound romanticism, for instance, and boundless love of nature, especially the German forests. Unquestioning loyalty, too."

Kahlenberge smiled. Digressions of this sort meant that something quite extraordinary was in the offing, but the G.O.C. was finding it patently difficult to steer the conversation round to it. "Let's go into the inner courtyard," said von Seydlitz-Gabler eventually.

The inner courtyard boasted a fountain, a stretch of lawn and some comparatively unobjectionable early baroque cloisters. Here the G.O.C. liked to pace up and down in peace and seclusion, lost in thought processes which he deemed creative, and here, once he and Kahlenberge were safely within its precincts, he turned on his Chief of Staff with the air of a man about to impart a revelation. "Imagine it, Kahlenberge! That man Grau is sitting in my outer office!"

"Not for the first time, sir, surely?" inquired Kahlenberge drily.

"No, no, but he's sent a message asking permission to put some questions to me—in an official capacity! What do you think of that?"

Kahlenberge could not find the right words at first—he was so surprised and delighted. With relish, he mentally reconstructed the sequence of events. Grau had turned up in the outer office and announced that he proposed to ask the G.O.C. some official questions—and the G.O.C. had promptly raced out of the back door and gone to find his Chief of Staff. "What a remarkable thing," he commented ambiguously.

"Something must be done—and quickly!"

"But why, sir?" Kahlenberge's tone was innocent.

"Now see here, my dear chap!" The G.O.C. drew himself up imperiously as though inspecting a whole division on the eve of battle. "This is an alarming state of affairs. We must map out a course of action at once. We can't just lie down and let the Abwehr ride rough-shod over us."

"Has Grau given any hint as to what questions he intends asking?"

"Oh, that's clear as daylight. The man's obviously trying to provoke me. Yesterday I thought he was just having his little joke, and since it was a joke in doubtful taste I treated it as such. In my innocence, I thought he would come to his senses if he were given a chance to do so—but what happens? He has the effrontery to waltz in here and try to ask me questions—me!"

"And you really think it has something to do with the story he told us yesterday? May I ask what makes you so sure?"

"My instinct tells me—instinct coupled with experience. Believe you me, Kahlenberge, this man Grau wouldn't shrink from following up the most preposterous red herrings. He's the sort who'd send his own mother to the gallows if it helped him to wrap up a case. We must put a stop to his game at all costs."

Kahlenberge's luminous cat's eyes narrowed. "Grau is not without influence," he said slowly. "It would be unwise to ignore the fact."

"I don't want any unnecessary complications," replied von Seydlitz-Gabler, "but I refuse point blank to overestimate this fellow's importance. He must be put in his place."

"Nothing could be easier," Kahlenberge said, watching von Seydlitz-Gabler's face keenly. "You've only got to answer his questions and he'll be forced to see how pointless it was to put them in the first place."

The G.O.C. folded his handkerchief into a pad and mopped his brow. His forehead was a high one and it took some time to pat it dry. "You're right as usual, my dear Kahlenberge—at least in principle. Under normal circumstances what you suggest would certainly be the simplest solution. Unfortunately, circumstances are anything but normal in this instance."

Kahlenberge paused near one of the cloister pillars. "Does

that mean, sir," he asked gleefully, "that you wouldn't be in a position to answer Grau's questions fully?"

"You might put it that way," von Seydlitz-Gabler conceded with an effort. "Not, of course, that I feel in the least bit guilty about anything. However, I'll frankly admit to you in confidence that such an interrogation might prove embarrassing to me."

"That," said Kahlenberge, barely able to conceal his delight, "changes everything, of course."

"On the evening when the appalling incident Grau told us about took place I was, shall we say, in transit. I assure you that I have nothing whatsoever to hide, but it was—so to speak—a masculine excursion. You follow me?"

Kahlenberge nodded. He had every sympathy with masculine excursions.

"If you mean," he said, "that Grau should be choked off because he's being a nuisance, I'd agree. He urgently needs a change of air, somewhere as far away from Warsaw as possible."

Now it was von Seydlitz-Gabler's turn to prick up his ears. He could read between the lines. If Kahlenberge was so ready to commit himself on the subject it meant that he had reasons of his own, possibly of an equally intimate nature.

"Let's assume," the G.O.C. said, not without curiosity, "that I simply passed Grau on—to you, for instance, my dear Kahlenberge. Let's assume that I told Grau: put your questions to Kahlenberge first and then come and see me. How would that strike you?"

"Most unfavourably." Kahlenberge's reaction was unambiguous. "I have a private life too, and I'm just as anxious to avoid sharing it with strangers. With all due respect, we're in much the same boat."

"There you are!" von Seydlitz-Gabler exclaimed jubilantly. "We're both in the same boat, Kahlenberge, but we're an experienced team. What do you think we ought to do under the circumstances?"

"What everyone does when there's no other alternative—declare war," replied Kahlenberge with quiet irony. "If Grau refuses to be choked off we'll just send him to General Tanz. I can't think of anyone better equipped to deal with him. Tanz has an uncomplicated way of handling people—he just ups his horns and tosses everyone who crosses his path."

"Agreed," said von Seydlitz-Gabler with relief. Then, cautious as ever, he added: "You really think Tanz is the right man for the job?"

"The only man," said Kahlenberge.

General Tanz seemed to be magically attracted by one particular street intersection in the western half of central Warsaw. There was nothing noticeably different about it. It was just an intersection like a hundred others, a drab expanse of cobbles, trees, groups of houses—alternately grey and green—and dirty window-panes like dull, sightless eyes.

On the ordnance survey map in General Tanz's hands, however, this intersection bore the legend "P1", pencilled in bold, vigorous characters as red as fire. P1 stood for Point One—the place chosen as the jumping-off point for General Tanz's proposed mopping-up operation.

"So the G.O.C. hasn't rejected our plan," Tanz said thoughtfully.

Major Sandauer stood a pace or two behind his General in an attitude of alert and respectful attention. "We haven't received official confirmation yet," he replied cautiously.

"No rejection is the equivalent of approval," asserted General Tanz.

Sandauer did not dispute the point. Disagreement had an explosive effect on General Tanz.

"Coffee," said Tanz.

The Divisional Commander's current combat orderly, new at his job and destined never to grow old in it, sprang out of the staff car. Bustling round to the back he opened the boot, removed a Thermos flask, a china cup and the saucer belonging to it, wiped the two latter articles with a linen cloth, poured out some coffee and extended the result of his labours to the General with a slightly tremulous hand.

"Too cold," said Tanz after a brief appraising glance.

The combat orderly froze in his tracks, realizing that he had committed some inexcusable blunder. Either the coffee had not been hot enough when he poured it into the Thermos, or the flask itself was defective, or he had paid insufficient attention to the external temperature. Whatever the reason, he was to blame. His hands started to shake so violently that the coffee slopped over the rim of the cup and flooded the saucer. However, he had ceased to be the centre of attention.

General Tanz was contemplating, almost lovingly, the houses on the far side of the intersection. Major Sandauer was watching the General. Sergeant Stoss, sitting at the wheel of the Mercedes, appeared to see nothing but the street ahead of him. Behind the Mercedes stood two armoured scout cars, both equipped with wireless, and the Divisional Commander's permanent dispatch-rider detachment, four soldiers encased in gleaming black leather and mounted on powerful B.M.W.s. For all of them, nothing existed save what lay ahead, least of all the trembling orderly, who slunk back to his place.

"We'll carry out a tactical exercise," said Tanz.

"Without the G.O.C.'s approval?" Major Sandauer, G. S.O.1 of the Nibelungen Division, asked the question in an undertone. His words were intended for the ears of the Divisional Commander alone.

"An operation of this type," said Tanz undeterred, "requires the most meticulous planning. I consider it vitally necessary that we first try out on a small scale what we shall have to carry out later on a large scale. Only then will we be able to operate with any guarantee of success. Alert the division, Sandauer. Code word: Waldfrieden."

Sandauer nodded, but permitted himself a small aside. "Is Corps to be notified?"

"Later. The operation will be little more than a test exercise, but I regard the experience to be gained from it as absolutely indispensable. We'll try out on four or five streets what we may have to do later with forty or fifty—without arousing any unnecessary attention. Afterwards we'll see."

"Is the whole division to be alerted?"

"Down to the last man. When I do a thing I do it properly or not at all."

"You must keep up appearances," declared Frau Wilhelmine von Seydlitz-Gabler. "People expect it of you. You owe it to your position."

"Of course." The G.O.C. was convinced that he had possessed a marked talent for keeping up appearances ever since his infancy. His father, also a general and land-owner, had instilled it into him at an early age, and one of his earliest recollections was of shaking family retainers' hands at harvest festivals and on Christmas Eve. He still remembered the moist and fleshy hand of the housekeeper, the dry leathery fingers of the first coachman and the soft, velvety little paw of the chamber-maid who used to sigh at him provocatively in the upstairs corridors.

"You're absolutely right, my dear," he said, mustering a smile. "As always."

"An evening of convivial good taste," she declared, as though issuing an edict.

General von Seydlitz-Gabler groaned almost inaudibly. His feet hurt. The new shoes which his wife had put out for him that morning had a certain solid elegance, but they were too tight. Wilhelmine's solicitude was something of a trial at times.

"We ought to make the occasion a cultural event," announced Wilhelmine. "I'm thinking of a reception for a few specially invited guests, with music."

"Excellent," said the G.O.C. deferentially.

"Not a big concert—no orchestra, not even a string quartet—just a pianist."

"We'll dig one up."

"He must play some Chopin, of course."

"Of course."

"We are in Warsaw, after all."

"True, my dear. Don't worry, we'll arrange it—some time in the next few days."

"This evening," Wilhelmine said blandly.

The General nodded in reluctant but unequivocal agreement. "I'll get Kahlenberge to lay it on."

"He is already doing so." Wilhelmine subjected her husband, who sat slumped exhaustedly in his arm-chair, to a look of searching tenderness. "Take those new shoes off if they're pinching you, Herbert. Be comfortable while you have the chance."

Major-General Kahlenberge was organizing things. As always, he made it his first concern to organize the organizers. Otto the Fat was detailed to make the reception rooms look festive. Captain Kraussnick, an acknowledged specialist in the field of entertainment, was made officially responsible for the guests' comfort, and Melanie Neumaier, the Corps Commander's "Iron Maiden," was entrusted with the compilation of the guest list.

Having got his plans safely under way, the chief planner found himself sitting around with time on his hands. He decided to send for Lance-Corporal Hartmann.

Hartmann duly appeared, but stood in the doorway eyeing Kahlenberge mistrustfully. Kahlenberge's initial reaction was a long paroxysm of almost soundless laughter. Then his face grew abruptly serious.

"Well," he asked, "have you got things straightened out? Do you see why one wrong answer would be enough to send that handsome head of yours rolling? You must learn to be practical, Hartmann. Right, tell me this: have you ever had the smallest contact with the Russians, that's to say, the Communists?"

"Never!" protested Hartmann vehemently. "How could I have?"

"Wrong first time!" Kahlenberge shook his head. "Ringing assurances always sound fundamentally suspicious. If you want people to believe something, say it simply—unless of course you're addressing a political rally. It's always a mistake to bellow one's convictions in private, so don't yell 'never'—just say 'no.' And remember: look them in the eye like a good German and hold yourself like a proper soldier, confidently but with respect. That's what counts."

"Yes sir," said Hartmann promptly.

"Think carefully before you answer these questions—you're bound to be asked them. Have you ever been in contact with Communists? Did your father belong to the Party? What about your brother, your uncle, your brother-in-law? Has your sister or fiancée ever had an affair with one?"

"No," Hartmann answered simply. The General's admonitions were beginning to sink in.

"That's right. Stick to the word 'no' wherever possible," Kahlenberge recommended. "Never say 'I don't know' or give a qualified answer. It sounds suspicious."

Hartmann began to smile for the first time, sensing the goodwill Kahlenberge felt for him. "I think I'm beginning to get the hang of it, sir."

"To help strengthen your position a little, I propose to take you on to my staff. You'll work in my department until further notice—Otto will break you in. But just remember—

make one mistake and you'll never get a chance to make another. What's more, you'll be endangering me as well. Is that clear?"

Hartmann understood. He nodded, breathed a sigh of relief and withdrew, rightly concluding that the interview was at an end.

General Kahlenberge did not watch Hartmann's departing figure. Instead, he picked up the 'phone and asked for Major Sandauer. Kahlenberge and Sandauer entertained a mutual regard for each other's tactical skill, which meant in effect that they intrigued against one another only when circumstances rendered it unavoidable.

Without special preamble, Kahlenberge asked whether General Tanz would be prepared to answer some questions which a certain Major Grau of local Intelligence proposed to ask him. The questions involved might well be of an embarrassing nature, to say the least. Indeed, said Kahlenberge, defamatory or insulting might be a more appropriate description.

"General Tanz," said Sandauer, wholly unimpressed, "is not in the habit of dodging an issue. However, may I draw your attention to the fact that the General is a man of very strong views and that he never hesitates to express them forcibly?"

"I'm aware of that—in fact I'm counting on it."

"With respect, General, may I ask what you're driving at?"

"Certainly," answered Kahlenberge with equal frankness. "I should esteem it if a certain gentleman could be reminded of the golden rule which states that subordinates may normally ask questions only when expressly requested to do so."

"That," said Sandauer, "is a view which General Tanz unquestionably shares. I shall hardly need to remind him of the fact."

"In that case I shall send our inquisitive friend to see you at a particularly suitable time. What has your General got in mind for this afternoon, my dear Sandauer?"

"A sort of dress rehearsal, sir," replied Sandauer. "That is to say," he added prudently, "he plans to try out a new technique on a very limited scale and for a very limited period."

Kahlenberge concealed his disapprobation and astonishment at Tanz's high-handed decision. As Chief of Staff, he would normally have intervened at this stage, but he was not a man to make two mistakes in succession. One ill-considered question was enough for the moment, so he contented himself with asking: "Is what you have just told me an official report or merely for my personal information?"

Sandauer was not slow to take Kahlenberge's point. "I thought we'd just been having an informal little chat, sir."

"Exactly what I thought too."

"But to return to your suggestion, I think the most unfavourable time and the most inconvenient place to ask General Tanz questions would be at fifteen hundred hours this afternoon, on the south side of Promenade Square."

Having concluded his business with Major Sandauer, Kahlenberge made another telephone call, this time to Major Grau of the Abwehr. He informed Grau that the G.O.C. was unfortunately prevented by social obligations from placing himself at Grau's disposal and would therefore have to forgo that pleasure for the time being. He, Kahlenberge, was also unable to spare the time, and for similar reasons, but Grau would be quite at liberty to see General Tanz at fifteen hundred hours on the south side of Promenade Square.

Major Grau extended his thanks for this information. Kahlenberge was irritated to detect a trace of a smile in Grau's voice, but he had no time to dwell on such things because the evening's arrangements once more claimed his full attention.

Wilhelmine von Seydlitz-Gabler was scrutinizing the preparations for her soirée, in particular the activities of Melanie Neumaier.

"You're doing an invaluable job as usual," Frau Wilhelmine told her. "My husband and I appreciate it so much. I know the General's extremely fond of you. No, don't blush, my dear girl, I'm sure you're fond of him too."

"I admire the General immensely," breathed Melanie. "He's a great man."

"But a very human one." Frau Wilhelmine conducted this exchange as though she were discussing clothes, the weather or National Socialism, running her eagle eye over the list of invitations meanwhile. Not a name escaped her, and she discovered three or four important omissions which Melanie Neumaier dutifully added to her list. Frau Wilhelmine nodded approvingly.

"My husband, dear Fräulein Neumaier, has led an arduous life in the service of his country. He isn't the strongest of men, you know, and it has taken its toll of his health. Unfortunately, I can't always be with him. This posting in Warsaw is a fortunate exception to the normal rule. If he ever falls ill, can I rely on you to look after him?"

"I should be honoured, madam!" said Melanie fervently, welling over with gratitude. She felt like the recipient of a sacred trust. "You can rely on me. I'll do everything within my power."

Frau Wilhelmine was entirely satisfied with this reaction. She thought she knew her husband far too well to be uneasy about the passionate devotion of a doubtless highly inhibited girl. In fact she had no scruples about amusing herself—in a well-bred way, of course—at Melanie's expense.

In high good humour, Frau Wilhelmine decided to seek out the second of Kahlenberge's organizers, Captain Kraussnick, the recreation officer. Kraussnick hailed from the restaurant business (dancing and entertainment section) and was destined to return to it after the war.

Kraussnick was quite equal to introducing a little culture into his programmes of entertainment when so desired. On this occasion he had paid a visit to the Warsaw Conservatoire, lined up the entire establishment, staff included, and issued the simple order: "Pianists stand fast! The remainder, dismiss!" He was left with a round dozen individuals of either sex, none of whom disclaimed a special ability to play Chopin, especially as it had been announced that the fee was to be a parcel of "fodder." Looking them over with the eye of a connoisseur—though not of music—Kraussnick had settled for a firm-fleshed, lusty-looking brunette named Wanda.

Wanda now stood before him with Lance-Corporal Hartmann at her side. Hartmann had been assigned to Kraussnick by General Kahlenberge, who had hinted in confidence that the young man was something of an art historian and had pretensions to culture. Accordingly, Kraussnick had detailed Hartmann to discuss Wanda's recital programme with her.

At this moment Frau Wilhelmine entered the room. Kraussnick hurried over to her, came to attention and delivered a semi-military report. He bent over her graciously extended hand and kissed it with near reverence. Then he drew the attention of the *"verehrte gnädige Frau"* to sundry details of organization, pointing to the numerous baskets full of bottles, the battery of glasses, the piano, Wanda, and Hartmann.

Frau Wilhelmine assumed an air of unwonted interest and approval. She even nodded benevolently, though with a touch of condescension, at Wanda. Then, looking down from the invisible platform on which she always stood, she directed an inquiring gaze at Hartmann.

"Are you new here?"

Hartmann did not reply "Yes ma'am." He merely bowed, but with a grace and deference which made an immediate impact on Frau Wilhelmine. The young man not only made a pleasant impression. He obviously had manners too.

"You mustn't let me detain you, my dear Captain Kraussnick. Please finish what you were discussing."

"Certainly ma'am!" The recreation officer obediently turned to Wanda and Hartmann. "Well, ladies and gentlemen," he said briskly, "what are we going to give them afterwards? Frau von Seydlitz-Gabler wants Chopin and her wish is our command—but which pieces by Chopin?"

"The Polonaises," suggested Wanda.

"Sounds a good idea," said Kraussnick approvingly. "Polonaise—that's a sort of dance, isn't it? Plenty of go. No one'll doze off, and that's an important consideration."

Frau Wilhelmine looked at Hartmann. "What do you think? Do you agree with the suggestion?"

"Chopin's Polonaises are superb," Hartmann observed politely, "but not perhaps what might be termed appropriate under present circumstances. The Polonaises are patriotic compositions. In fact Robert Schumann once described them as cannon garlanded with flowers."

"Out of the question!" exclaimed Kraussnick. "If we're going to have cannon they'd better not be Polish ones. And garlanded with flowers, too! That's all we need!"

"You're a very alert young man," Frau Wilhelmine told Hartmann, "and obviously not without talent. I leave it entirely to you to find a suitable programme for this evening's recital. When you've done so, come and report to me. Would you be so kind? I'm only expressing a wish, of course, but I know you'll do me this little favour." She smiled benignly. "Good, then I look forward to seeing you later."

"Promenade Square, south side!" Major Grau called to his driver.

As he spoke the sun broke through the clouds, dazzling him a little. He leant back in his seat and blinked at the road ahead. "Are you armed?" he asked.

"Of course, sir."

"We're on our way to see General Tanz," said Grau affably.

The car swept through the almost empty streets of Warsaw, its engine humming like a swarm of bees. Glancing skywards, Grau saw that the sun had disappeared behind the clouds again. They looked like a thin pall of smoke, and for some reason he was vividly reminded of the fact that he had gained his first real success as a policeman in the old days by solving a case of arson.

"They've sealed off the approaches to the square," announced the driver.

Major Grau emerged from his reverie with a start. He now saw what had been apparent to his driver for some time. Fighting units were deployed everywhere, dressed in mottled grey-brown-green denims and equipped with small arms. An oppressive silence enveloped them. Hardly anyone spoke, and no one spoke loudly. They stood there like a herd of cattle waiting for someone to open a gate.

"Men from Tanz's division," said the driver.

"Some exercise, probably," said Major Grau. "When they're not in action they're training and when they're not training they're asleep. Take no notice, the regulations don't apply to us."

Grau's expression did not change. It was as though he merely registered what was going on round him but was not particularly interested or impressed by it.

"Halt!" cried a clear, incisive voice. "No vehicles beyond this point."

A tanned, hard-bitten face appeared at the car window, half obscured by a jutting steel helmet. Dour determination was written in the pale blue eyes that stared into Grau's and in the grim slit of a mouth beneath. Any obstacle erected by Tanz had to be dislodged by force.

Grau attached no importance to complications of this sort. He calmly got out of the car and completed the hundred odd yards that separated him from the south side of the square on foot. There he caught sight of General Tanz, a powerful figure despite his rapier-like build, standing aloof from the men who surrounded him.

Looking round for Sandauer, Grau found him leaning against an armoured scout car some distance to the General's rear. He was not examining the map in his hand but appeared to be lost in a sort of expectant day-dream.

The same applied to the General himself, except that he looked incomparably more impressive. Sandauer stared at nothing: the General gazed into infinity. A war correspondent attached to the division was improving the shining hour by taking a few photographs while the General stood there motionless. A better contemporary subject for the camera could hardly have been imagined.

"Phase One," said the General.

The General's A.D.C. transmitted this order to Sandauer, who straightened up and said: "Away we go." These words, uttered in much the tone of a housewife buying a pound of sugar, were addressed to the wireless operator who sat waiting in the scout car.

"I have an appointment with the General," said Grau, "but I don't want to disturb him."

"It's impossible to disturb the General if he doesn't intend to be disturbed." Sandauer preserved his schoolmasterly demeanour whatever the circumstances. "But you're quite at liberty to approach him. He's expecting you."

Grau went over to the General and made his presence known. Tanz seemed to be wrapped in a shroud of silence, so much so that Grau could almost detect a faint odour of decay.

The General continued to stare fixedly ahead, and it was impossible to tell whether he had heard Grau or not. Eventually he said: "Another few minutes, Grau. It's almost time."

The minutes ticked by and nothing in particular happened—nothing, that is to say, which seemed to account for Tanz's attitude of tense expectancy. The fronts of the houses looked flattened, like a dingy stage-set, the tightly shut windows like clouded spectacle lenses, the trees like the skeletal remains of huge cadavers.

Small groups of men moved almost noiselessly along the walls and then froze like statues. A grinding roar came suddenly from a neighbouring street as tanks crawled into position.

Tanz's face had become a bronze mask, his cheek muscles prominent as whipcord. His slender but powerful hands caressed his sub-machine-gun like those of a lover fondling the neck of his beloved.

The first shot rang out, followed immediately afterwards by the explosive crump of a bundle of hand-grenades. Within what seemed like a split second, the scene changed. The brooding stillness gave way to a roaring, boiling torrent of sound, and pin-points of flame began to flicker like lights darting across the console of an electronic brain. Thin wisps of smoke wreathed their way into the sky as though the city's inhabitants were puffing at a myriad cigars.

Tanz's features relaxed into an austere smile, a strange rictus which seemed to grow more pronounced as bullets began to patter round him like hail-stones. A sudden shaking sound came from somewhere near by, then the dull thump of a body hitting the ground. Shortly afterwards a second soldier slumped to the pavement. General Tanz did not move.

"All according to plan," said Sandauer a moment later.

The General gave an almost imperceptible nod, then turned his head as if unwilling to deprive his faithful G.S.O.1 of an appreciative smile.

"Good," Tanz said contentedly. "And now Major Grau can put his questions."

"He seems to have abandoned the idea for the time being," said Sandauer.

Tanz looked contemptuous. "What do you mean? Has the fellow wet his pants or something?"

"I don't think so, sir." Sandauer forced himself to meet the General's searching gaze with equanimity. "He merely took his leave."

"Without saying anything?"

"He said something, sir, but I didn't catch it." Sandauer lied with a good conscience. He couldn't possibly tell the General what he had heard or the world would have fallen about his ears and buried him. Major Grau's quite audible comment had been: "Not even a subnormal human being could be expected to watch an idiotic display like this of his own free will."

Though intended as a brilliant social occasion, the G.O.C.'s proposed reception—complete with Chopin recital—threatened to become a fiasco of the first order.

The G.O.C. himself was detained by the necessity for making what were described as "momentous decisions", which automatically meant that his Chief of Staff, General Kahlenberge, was also delayed. General Tanz was still at large somewhere in the city. When the windows were open, the martial din made by his embattled division drifted in. Consequently, the windows were kept shut.

The order to close the windows issued from Frau Wilhelmine, who continued to supervise arrangements and played the part of sole host, performing the former function with vigour and the latter with dignity.

Once the first few uncomfortable minutes had been overcome the atmosphere took on a comparatively festive note, thanks mainly to the efforts of that seasoned entertainer Captain Kraussnick. His method was admirably simple. Instead of greeting the guests with a glass of port or vermouth, as had been planned, he enterprisingly took a short cut and plied them with hard liquor—chartreuse for the ladies, cognac and kirsch for the gentlemen—in wine glasses. It was hardly surprising if the room was quickly pervaded by a glow of intimacy.

One of the momentous decisions which were occupying the G.O.C. concerned Major Grau, who stood in his outer office displaying a mixture of pig-headed obduracy and bland affability. He wanted to have his say.

Kahlenberge said: "Why not?", left Grau in the outer office and went in to see his chief.

The G.O.C. was still preparing for the reception. His words of welcome were to be sonorous yet profound, courteous yet admonitory—in short, edifying. He had already mapped out the more important passages and was now engaged in polishing the finer details. Any distraction at this juncture was unwelcome.

"We're not going to be able to avoid seeing our friend Grau, I'm afraid," Kahlenberge told him. "As a matter of interest, he's in a most peculiar state at the moment—still behaving like a gentleman but apparently determined to stage a sort of bullfight here with himself in the role of matador. It would be advisable to disabuse him of the idea immediately."

"Didn't Tanz manage to send the man packing?"

"No." Kahlenberge sounded relieved rather than disappointed, almost as though he derived a perverse pleasure from being confronted with the problem of Grau once more. "Grau obviously realized that Tanz meant to give him a rough time. We couldn't foresee that. Anyway, he beat a hasty retreat—in our direction, unfortunately."

"Deuced embarrassing," commented the G.O.C. "What do you think we ought to do now?"

"What one usually does in such situations, sir: keep talking."

"Couldn't we put him off—say, until tomorrow?"

"I shouldn't advise it."

As normally happened when he was confronted by a grave decision, von Seydlitz-Gabler experienced a moment or two of faintness and his stomach threatened to rebel. Then, as if he were controlling an unruly horse, he gathered himself for the next hurdle.

"All right, send him in."

Major Grau entered the room like a man who intended to take possession of it, lock, stock and barrel. His usually immaculate clothing looked slightly crumpled but his smile was as bland as ever.

"I was under the impression," he began, "that I was going to be able to pursue my official inquiries this afternoon. This had been agreed to, and General Kahlenberge personally made the necessary arrangements with your consent and approval. As it was, I found myself involved in a—hm, military engagement."

"Most regrettable," said the G.O.C. resonantly, "really—most regrettable."

"Regrettable, yes—but true." Grau still managed to preserve a smile. "And all the more regrettable in that it was a matter of which my department should have received advance notification."

"Major Grau," said the G.O.C., puffing like a weight-lifter in training, "I thank you for your interest and your gratifying willingness to co-operate. I fully appreciate it and shall draw the appropriate conclusions. When occasion arises I shall take the matter up again."

Major Grau seemed to be amused. "I could insist on immediate clarification. I could even take the view that postponement is tantamount to concealment."

"Is that meant to be a threat?"

"Perhaps only a warning," replied Grau undeterred. "I have some questions to ask and I shall ask them."

"Later please," said von Seydlitz-Gabler with comparative vigour. "And kindly remember that military operations always take precedence over other matters."

"Even when the solution of a murder case is being systematically impeded?"

"Even then, I'm afraid," put in Kahlenberge with an inscrutable smile. "Military law takes precedence over criminal law. You won't find that written down anywhere, but it's a generally accepted fact—and for obvious reasons."

General von Seydlitz-Gabler cleared his throat. "And now I must ask you to leave me alone with my Chief of Staff."

There was something deliberately irritating about Grau's smile as he withdrew, making his exit like an actor who was due on stage again in a minute or two. His parting salute bore no resemblance to the regulation movement and the G.O.C. did not deign to return it.

"Well," said von Seydlitz-Gabler, "that settles his hash. His latest performance went a bit too far. High time for that change of air you mentioned, eh, Kahlenberge? It shouldn't be difficult to arrange.—No, what I'm much more worried about at the moment is the news that there has been fighting in the city. What do you know about it?"

"Nothing much, sir—only that General Tanz laid on an exercise for this afternoon."

"Without consulting us?"

"He only planned to hold an exercise," Kahlenberge said cautiously. "Major Sandauer, Tanz's G.S.O.1, informed me accordingly. I don't know what it developed into."

"Kindly request clarification," ordered the G.O.C.

The process of clarification lasted nearly an hour. Kahlenberge conducted a prolonged telephone conversation with Sandauer over a newly laid direct line leading to Promenade Square.

Von Seydlitz-Gabler did not remain idle either. He also did some telephoning, in this instance to Supreme Headquarters, where he had an old Staff College friend who was in the closest touch with Admiral Canaris. It was a highly satisfactory conversation and one which demonstrated the value, if demonstration were needed, of the "old boy net."

Meanwhile, Frau Wilhelmine continued to receive her guests as they streamed into the festively decorated salon. She noticed that Lance-Corporal Hartmann had stationed himself respectfully within reach. His efforts to put together a representative programme had been crowned with success. There was to be Chopin, but only some waltzes and a few undemanding preludes. If any encores were needed, the gap could be plugged with an étude or two.

"You're a very efficient young man," Frau Wilhelmine told Hartmann appreciatively in an interval between guests—she had just extended her bony hand to the Reich Commissioner—"I feel I can rely on you."

Hartmann blushed. He always blushed when he was uncomfortable, and he was uncomfortable most of the time. The new world into which he had been launched presented more surprises than he had bargained for. Within a bewilderingly short space of time he had been shuttled back and forth, willy-nilly, between life and death, Russians and Nazis, Chopin and Frau Wilhelmine.

"I'll look after him," said Ulrike, eyeing Hartmann with pleasure. "I'll make sure we don't lose him."

"I hope," Frau Wilhelmine said severely, "you haven't forgotten why you're here."

Ulrike grimaced. "There's not much hope of that."

"Good," said Frau Wilhelmine. "Then behave accordingly." She turned to Hartmann with a gracious smile. "I'll call you when I need you. Hold yourself in readiness."

"Certainly, ma'am," said Hartmann, glancing cautiously at Ulrike.

Meanwhile, the two generals had been doing what they could to sort out their problems, and that, in the third year of the war, was a good deal. Satisfied that his private network was still functioning admirably, von Seydlitz-Gabler felt that the world had resumed its ordered course.

"The following facts have emerged from my conversations with Major Sandauer and General Tanz," Kahlenberge reported. "Units of the Nibelungen Division were engaged in an exercise this afternoon. Object: to explore methods of dealing with scattered hostile groups in a built-up area."

"How did fighting break out?"

"Quite simple," Kahlenberge went on. "General Tanz's troops had just started their exercise when, according to Major Sandauer, they were suddenly fired on by members of the Polish Resistance. In consequence, the units engaged returned their fire."

"Entirely understandable," declared the G.O.C. without hesitation. "It amounted to a case of self-defence, which takes the matter out of our hands."

"Certainly, providing someone like Major Grau doesn't try to put forward his own version of the story. It could, for instance, be painted as a piece of deliberate provocation which we tolerated almost without a murmur."

"We needn't worry on that account, my dear Kahlenberge." The G.O.C. beamed contentedly across the desk. "I did a little telephoning myself just now. As you're aware"—here he winked confidentially—"I cherish the highest regard for Major Grau. His achievements on behalf of local counter-intelligence are beyond dispute. I have therefore impressed upon the appropriate authorities that Major Grau has an unrivalled claim to be transferred to a wider and more important sphere of duty."

"And?" Kahlenberge inquired eagerly. "Have you really managed to get him kicked upstairs?"

"Major Grau is to be promoted lieutenant-colonel and will receive an immediate posting to the Abwehr in Paris. He is to be congratulated—and so are we."

INTERIM REPORT

DOCUMENTS CONCLUDING THE FIRST PART OF THIS BOOK

Recorded remarks of ex-Sergeant Lehmann, long-time batman of General von Seydlitz-Gabler.
Place: Berlin.
Date: 17th February, 1962.
Lehmann on General von Seydlitz-Gabler, with special reference to his private life. Reproduced in heavily abridged form:

"The General was one of the best, you can't get away from that. A proper gentleman in any situation.

"Here's a typical example. Just after the fall of France we were quartered in a villa somewhere. I came in late—saw a light still on in the General's study—thought: he's working himself to death. Then thought: maybe he needs something—a sandwich or a glass of soda water or a bottle of burgundy. Knocked and went in. Saw the General sitting there brooding in an arm-chair, medals and all. Then saw a woman stripped to the buff and doing a sort of dance in front of him. Nice bit of stuff. Said: 'Excuse me, sir,' and the General said: 'I'm afraid you're in the way for the moment, my dear Lehmann.'

"Do I remember Melanie Neumaier? I should say so. She was potty about the General. Not that she showed it of course, but I could read her like a book. She used to get hot pants whenever she'd been near him for any length of time. Once she led me on—*me!* We had a roll on the General's bed—he was in conference at the time. She puffed like an engine going up a gradient and babbled: 'Herbert, oh Herbert!' My name's Alfons—Herbert was the General's Christian name.

"Frau Wilhelmine was a right one. She just about did

for us, the way she kept us all on the hop. Sometimes I was almost as worn out as the General—and I didn't have to sleep with her. But she was a real lady, I will say that. No one ever got a sniff there, not even the people she encouraged—not even Rainer Hartmann, I'd stake my oath. He just acted as a sort of lap-dog for a while—wagged his tail nicely too, but that's as far as it went.

"Her ladyship always spoke to me in the third person. Something like this: 'I'm sure our faithful Lehmann will take care that . . .' or: 'Seeing that our Lehmann is so reliable, I hope that he will . . .' and so on. —Our Lehmann! It wasn't long before everyone on the staff was calling me that. Even a girl who was keeping the General happy called me 'our Lehmann.' She had a point, too. The General wasn't getting any younger, you see. Too much red wine and worrying about his work didn't help—so, to cut a long story short, I helped him out occasionally.

"Things got a bit complicated sometimes. Once when I was waiting next door for the girl I heard her start screaming fit to bust and rushed in. The first thing I saw was what I expected to see—follow me? Then I saw that the girl was purple in the face—bloody near strangled, she was. The General must have had a sort of heart attack, because he was hanging on to her with his hands round her neck. Pathetic, isn't it? That's what comes of knocking yourself out for your country. And what thanks do you get, that's what I'd like to know."

Extract from a leading article published in the magazine Sword and Spirit *in November 1942. Its author was Captain Kahlert, the war historian attached to General von Seydlitz-Gabler's staff. This article appeared under the title:* "Resistance and the Consequences:"

"We are waging this war in order to create a better world. It is an historic mission of which no one who is conscious of his responsibility toward Greater Germany and a New Order in Europe can or may deprive us.

"But, as always occurs when light wrestles with darkness, the most sinister forces are unleashed. Sub-humans are incapable of observing the clearly defined rules of fair play. Their favourite weapons are cunning and deceit. We must not only be prepared for this but take positive measures to meet it, and this plainly entails the extermination of all criminal elements.

"Such is the situation that has been forced on us in several places, notably Warsaw. While we regret it profoundly, we should not hesitate for one moment to draw the necessary conclusions. For what are the real facts of the matter? Poland persistently provoked the German Reich and imposed a war on her by force of arms. We had no alternative but to meet this challenge, and we did so victoriously. We occupied the country and began to govern it according to the historic rights of the victor and the eternal laws of humanity."

Statement by a man named Valentin Gebhardt. Gebhardt is not mentioned by name in the present book. The only reference to him is the short sentence which describes how a man standing beside General Tanz on the edge of Promenade Square in Warsaw was hit by a bullet and collapsed. Gebhardt, then a sergeant, was severely wounded. He belonged to the dispatch-rider section of between two and four men which had to accompany General Tanz everywhere in action:

"The General never turned a hair, even under the heaviest fire. He never wore a steel helmet either. Some of the lads used to say he had an arrangement with the Devil and others said he just couldn't care less. One of them even reckoned he wanted to die. But that was all bullshit. General Tanz had more guts than the rest of them put together.

"In the days when I knew him he was always in the thick of it with that sub-machine-gun of his, loosing off one magazine after the other. His belt was always stuffed with grenades and he had several pistols. One he always wore himself, the second he kept in the glove compartment of his car and the third had to be brought along in reserve by his orderly.

"Tanz was a crack shot. We used to say that if one of the enemy saw the whites of Tanz's eyes it would be his last sight on earth. No quarter—that was his rule, and he stuck to it even when things started to go to pot.

"I was still with him then. That was during the first winter in Russia, just short of Leningrad. Tanz was going at the enemy hell for leather, as usual. Even the special shock troops couldn't keep up with him, and my number two had to be replaced five times in seven days. It was a tough number, I can tell you. Then we suddenly found ourselves cut off. It took us two days and nights to fight our way out—partly with arms and ammunition taken from the Ivans. Nearly half the division bought it in the process. There were some companies which could hardly muster a platoon.

"I went out like a light when I stopped one that time in Warsaw, but when I came to there was a bottle of brandy by my bed. 'With the General's best wishes,' the Sister told me. That was Tanz all over! And I was one of his best D.R.s."

Further conversations with Gottfried Engel, formerly assigned to Major Grau as a sergeant in counter-intelligence. Extracts from tape-recordings made eighteeen years after the events described:

"I can only repeat that I was in a subordinate position. I was not authorized to dictate policy and never did so. I was what they call an executive agent.

"As for the three generals you mention, I'd sum them up as follows:

"1. General von Seydlitz-Gabler, Corps Commander. One of the old school, with all its virtues and vices. He'd really have been more at home in the last century. His wife was the power behind the throne, and there must have been times when he hated her guts. She pushed him too hard, and no man can stand that indefinitely.

"2. Lieutenant-General Tanz, Commander of the élite Nibelungen Division. A career-general of the first order with no inhibitions whatsoever. Rose from the ranks of the Freikorps and had just what it takes to go places. There were only two alternatives for him: a cross on his chest or another over his grave. He had an almost legendary reputation, and anyone who didn't help to foster it became his personal enemy. Presumably that applied to Major Grau and me.

"3. Major-General Kahlenberge, Chief of Staff of the Corps Commander. Middle-class origins. Hard to sum up. Kept himself and his opinions very much to himself. No one ever really managed to get to the bottom of him. Tough to deal with and a shrewd negotiator. Extremely competent in almost everything he did and considerate towards his subordinates. Had a rather odd sense of humour at times. He was the real brains of the outfit. He certainly acted as von Seydlitz-Gabler's throttle and brake, and for all I know he may have steered him as well.

"The rest is common knowledge. We were sent to Paris, and a murderer—who might or might not have been a general—was reprieved for the time being.

"Fate plays funny tricks, though. Almost two years later, in July 1944, we all met up again in Paris."

PART TWO

Human lives for sale

PARIS, 1944

1

Lucienne sang, beseeching her audience to speak to her of love. She had closed her eyes as if dreaming, but it might have been because she was dazzled by the harsh glare of the spotlight. It might also have been because she preferred to shut out her surroundings, for many of the men who were watching her wore uniform, and it was not the uniform of her own country or its allies.

"Isn't she terrific!" whispered Captain Kraussnick.

He bent forward confidentially as he spoke, not unlike a black marketeer commending the quality of some merchandise to a prospective customer. Kraussnick regarded Lucienne as his personal discovery, and a special table was permanently reserved for him next to the stage.

"Are you getting a percentage out of this?" asked General Kahlenberge.

General von Seydlitz-Gabler, who sat beside him, murmured: "The creature's got a voice like silk!"—which reminded him that his wife had recently expressed a desire to buy some dress lengths.

Lucienne went on singing. She was not a performer like the great Sasha. Lucienne had to live and her establishment needed the business. The great Sasha liked to scintillate, to demonstrate his regal superiority. He regarded himself as an essential component of French history, but Lucienne was a Parisienne, no more and no less. It was almost a matter of indifference to her who listened to her as long as she was loved as an institution devoted to the *chanson*.

People who heard Lucienne seemed to be bathed in the glow of her reputation. She sang in a pool of rosy light, and the fleshy faces bordering it radiated pleasure and satisfaction. The sameness of their uniform was not so far removed from the uniformity of dinner jacket or tails. Even generals could let themselves be seen in uniform here because a visit to Lucienne counted as a sort of cultural outing.

There was a scattering of night-club femininity—identical ivory faces partitioned by the black and scarlet streaks of eyebrow and lip, the former thin and the latter thick, but both applied with panache. Here and there was a naked-seeming expanse surmounted by a pair of blue eyes—female members of the occupying forces clad in blue or field grey. Women in uniform; but women for all that.

The song which begged the listener to speak of love—and nothing else—had several verses. Lucienne sang them all in the same abstracted way, as if immersed in a sea of emotion and melody. Her audience hardly dared breathe.

The last notes died away and the lights went up to a burst of applause. There was a universal raising of glasses to lips—at least six bottles' worth inside five seconds, the manager calculated swiftly. Lucienne's nightly appearance was the establishment's most lucrative asset.

"Well, did I exaggerate?" asked Captain Kraussnick.

"I found her most stimulating," conceded General von Seydlitz-Gabler. The General had been highly decorated since Warsaw but was still in command of a Corps. Kahlenberge, his indispensable assistant, was still Chief of Staff but had been invested with the Knight's Cross and was now a lieutenant-general.

"Has the General any special request to make?" Kraussnick inquired.

"Not at the moment," said von Seydlitz-Gabler.

"But you can sound out the ground, my dear chap," added Kahlenberge with an eye to the future.

The entertainments specialist rose promptly to his feet, not forgetting, before he went off to make inquiries, to see that a new bottle of Veuve Clicquot Rosé 1933—the third, and what a year!—was placed within reach, chilled to a temperature of between twelve and fourteen degrees. Although Kraussnick was a connoisseur it was not an easy job to maintain his reputation, let alone enhance it. In his experience generals preferred young flesh, but that was just where the market was shortest.

"One can forget one's troubles in a place like this," General von Seydlitz-Gabler said pensively. "We ought to make the most of it."

Kahlenberge drained his glass with relish. He found himself doing everything with relish these days. It was as though he were being challenged to choose between life and death. As long as no one forced him to die he chose life, but anything might happen, especially in a world in which soldiers were compelled to behave like bandits.

Kahlenberge smiled opaquely and leant forward. "One way or another, we're going to have to make up our minds what sort of country we want. All the signs are there if you know where to look for them."

The G.O.C. stared at the ceiling, screwing up his eyes at the brightness of the overhead lighting. He saw a vista of snowy white and glistening gold interspersed with a red as rich and warm as life-blood. The cross-beam above his head was adorned with squatting *putti*, firm-fleshed and compact as Würzburg baroque, except that these *putti* were pink as marzipan and rouged like miniature whores.

"I refuse to resort to underhand measures," he said. "Candour has always been my watchword."

Kahlenberge nodded cheerfully. "Which is precisely why you ought to find it easy to define your position when people ask you what sort of Germany you want."

"I'm a man of moderation," said the General, with all the caution of an experienced angler. "I refuse to accept things unthinkingly just because someone tries to ram them down my throat. What's more, I've always been conscious of my duty to Germany, which is one reason why I'm a general."

"And that," said Kahlenberge gently, "is why you must automatically be against everything which claims to represent Germany today."

Von Seydlitz-Gabler blinked at the lights again. "I have tried to serve my country faithfully for as long as I can remember."

"No one expects anything else of you."

The G.O.C. slowly shook his imposing head, deaf to the still muted laughter that rippled round his table like water from a fountain playing at half strength. The joys of Parisian night-life had not yet reached their zenith. Von Seydlitz-Gabler sighed a little and drank a good deal, temporarily overcome by the feeling that there were hard times ahead.

Kahlenberge regarded the G.O.C. through narrowed eyes, savouring his agony of mind with unrestrained enjoyment. He had recently seized upon every opportunity to make disquieting allusions to an inevitable catastrophe which lay in the immediate future.

"Either tonight or tomorrow I shall be meeting a group of officers. I am convinced that their intentions are above reproach."

"For heaven's sake be careful, my dear chap!"

"Something positive must be done as soon as possible. What can I tell them about your own attitude?"

The G.O.C. was perspiring heavily like a man in a Turkish bath and his ruddy features had taken on the sheen of wet varnish. "My sympathies," he said, "are always with what is right and good."

"Can you tell me what that means in practical terms?"

Kahlenberge's question remained unanswered for the time being because a shadow had fallen across the table. It belonged not to Kraussnick but to Grau of the Abwehr—now Lieutenant-Colonel Grau. He bowed sedately. Far from diminishing, his innate self-assurance seemed to have increased with the years.

Kahlenberge looked annoyed. "Well, what are you doing here? I thought you spent your whole time chasing spies and traitors?"

"Why not here?" Grau inquired blandly.

General von Seydlitz-Gabler had straightened up in his chair. He looked forbidding. "Must you ruin our meagre ration of enjoyment?"

"As a matter of fact, General, I came to bring you some news which I thought might prove of interest. General Tanz is on his way to Paris."

"Has he got another of his divisions cut to ribbons, then?" asked Kahlenberge bitterly.

"More or less," Grau gave a smile of concurrence. "General Tanz's division is to be quartered in the Versailles-Fontainebleau area for regrouping."

"And you get a kick out of the idea?"

"It always gives me pleasure to look back on our instructive times together in Warsaw."

On that note Lieutenant-Colonel Grau withdrew, strutting through the room—so it seemed to von Seydlitz-Gabler at least—like a peacock. He gave the impression of being on home ground wherever he went. Even the band, which had just struck up a *musette* waltz, seemed to match the rhythm of his stride.

The G.O.C. blinked at his Chief of Staff. "Surely he wouldn't dare to bring up that Warsaw business all over again?"

"We only got as far as the first act." Kahlenberge folded his hands Buddha-fashion. "The next act may prove superfluous if more important events intervene. I've no idea where the senior members of the Abwehr stand—whether our friends have won them over or whether Grau figures on their black list."

"Let's hope he does," said the G.O.C.

"Be that as it may, do you sympathize with what these men are trying to do?"

The G.O.C.'s face darkened as though he were straining hard to hear some inner voice. "Perhaps. All the same, I don't feel happy about it."

Shortly afterwards Captain Kraussnick reappeared, bringing word of "various charming creatures," well-developed and "anxious to please."

The General shot Kahlenberge a reproachful sidelong glance. "I just don't feel like it," he grumbled with the air of a disgruntled Jupiter. "I'm not in the mood any more."

The Mocambo Bar was packed. Inside, the temperature had risen to tropical heights. A saxophone howled its way up the scale, performed a few velvety somersaults and then plunged back, gurgling and choking, into the muddy depths of its lower register. Lance-Corporal Rainer Hartmann took his uniform jacket off.

"Why not your shirt too while you're about it?" asked the girl beside him.

"Maybe later on," said Hartmann, meaning it as a little joke, nothing more. He pulled the girl to her feet and prepared to push cheerfully through the packed dancers, but they stood aside for him.

Hartmann was saddened. He wanted to belong, to be just one of the pleasure-seeking crowd. The people around him were like himself—young, greedy for life, filled with a yearning for the scent and warmth of other bodies—but they avoided him. It was probably because he was wearing uniform, for almost all the other habitués of the Mocambo Bar were Frenchmen in civilian clothes.

"Something worrying you?" asked the girl he was dancing with.

Hartmann's reaction was almost violent. "I'm happy," he assured her. "I like it here. I come here often. I virtually discovered this place. Do you like it?"

"My name's Ulrike." The girl in his arms relaxed against him. "You're welcome to call me Ulrike."

"But do you like it here?" Hartmann asked hopefully.

"I like it because I'm here with you." Ulrike's lips were so close to his ear that he could almost feel them. "I've always wanted to be in a place like this—with you."

Hartmann recoiled instinctively. Ulrike was the G.O.C.'s daughter and his friend Otto was under instructions to look after her, but Otto was hitting the bottle at the bar. His broad hindquarters and amorphous back were visible across the dance floor.

The next time Ulrike von Seydlitz-Gabler pressed her body gently against his, Hartmann did not recoil. It must have something to do with the atmosphere, he reflected. Just the attraction of the unfamiliar—a meaningless game, that was all, but yet another proof of how wonderful Paris was.

Everything Hartmann saw and heard pleased him: the sparse lighting with its soft gradations of red, the solid brick walls and the hypnotic beat of the drums, like the pulsing wing-beats of a flock of birds on the rise. He also liked the people who frequented this modest place of entertainment.

"Where can I wash my hands?" asked Ulrike when the music stopped.

Hartmann showed her. He was no stranger to the amenities of the Mocambo Bar—kitchen, bottle store, office and solitary toilet—all of them the size of a pocket handkerchief. He wandered over to the bar. Otto, his friend, companion and guide was there, and so was Raymonde. Raymonde meant Paris to Hartmann, even if it was the Paris of suburbs and back-yards, short-time hotels and Métro entrances.

Raymonde rinsed some glasses and smiled at him.

"You're going great guns with Mademoiselle von Seydlitz-

Gabler," said Otto admiringly, his suety, pig-like face beaming. "But don't go burning your fingers."

Without waiting for Hartmann to ask, Raymonde put a *crème de menthe frappée* in front of him. Jealousy was alien to her, probably because she felt confident of her own special qualities. She didn't regard Ulrike von Seydlitz-Gabler as competition, and lack of space did not prevent her from waggling her hips provocatively at Hartmann in the diminutive cubby-hole behind the bar counter.

"Why not hand Raymonde over to me for the night?" Otto suggested casually. "I'm sure Ulrike would make it up to you."

"Are you speaking from experience?"

"Heaven forbid!" Otto sounded shocked. "I'm not tired of living. I leave that sort of caper to you."

Rainer Hartmann felt a firm but gentle hand on his shoulder. It belonged to Ulrike. "Shall we dance again?" she asked..

He felt himself swept away by the music. The band was playing a blues—the Basin Street Blues—with a mixture of passion and attenuated melancholy. The extra-strong *crème de menthe,* his seventh of the evening, hung about him like a heavy velvet curtain. His uniform jacket was draped limply over a chair somewhere.

"I feel wonderful," said Ulrike, hugging him. "I may even be happy too—I'm not quite sure."

"One can be happy here," Hartmann assured her. He was hopelessly enraptured, a condition which always afflicted him when he was being lapped by waves of private yearning. Out of spontaneous gratitude more than anything else, he pressed Ulrike von Seydlitz-Gabler to him. Glancing across at Raymonde he saw that she was still smiling at him. His happiness was complete.

Except for one thing. He wanted all the French people in the room to smile at him—not only Raymonde. He loved them, surely they could feel that, but there always seemed to be a vacuum round the Germans dancing there—round him too, even though he had taken off his uniform jacket. It began to get on his nerves.

"Why are they so prejudiced against us?" Rainer Hartmann asked sadly. He surveyed the solid wall of faces round him and had a violent impulse to smash through their cold indifference. "Something ought to be done about it."

"We'll just have to be patient and hope for better times," Ulrike told him.

"It's not good enough just to hope for better times. Why shouldn't we try and do something about it?"

Ulrike smiled at him. "Don't they say that when two people are happy it's catching? Or isn't that enough for you, Rainer?"

"What about humanity as a whole?" Hartmann's voice rose to a shout. The combined effects of seven *crèmes de menthe,* the viscous heat and pulsating music had done their work only too well.

He left Ulrike standing, pushed his way through the jungle of dancing figures and climbed on to the platform, gently dislodging the saxophonist. He raised both arms as though in supplication. The music stopped, and a hundred upturned faces swam before his gaze like extinguished lanterns.

Hartmann stood on the stage in a rather obscure cellar bar in a street just off the Champs-Elysées. At that moment, the Eastern and Western fronts were threatening to collapse, men were dying by thousands in places no one had ever heard of, war material thundered against war material and the world seemed to be parcelled up into mass graves.

But Hartmann stood there, a figure clad in clumsy ammunition boots, crumpled wood-fibre trousers and a greyish-yellow shirt dark with sweat at the shoulders, the whole surmounted by an excited, perspiring face.

"Friends!" cried Rainer Hartmann passionately. He spoke French with difficulty. His "*mes amis*" sounded hoarse, but it seemed to have an arresting effect. At least no one shouted him down.

"When I say 'friends'," Hartmann continued in his wooden schoolboy French, "I mean it. I'm sorry, I speak your language badly, but I mean what I say."

"That's something, anyway!" a Frenchman called out encouragingly.

A number of people laughed, women mainly, but their laughter sounded almost affectionate. Raymonde, his beloved Raymonde, who was still behind the bar, clapped. Quite a few of the others joined in the applause—whether in fun or not it was hard to tell.

"I am a German!" Hartmann cried with enthusiasm. "You are French! But we're all human beings! I can't help this war—I didn't start it and neither did you. But we're all part of it, so we have something in common. We belong together. We want to live. Let's live as best we can!"

"Bravo!" shouted a number of Frenchmen.

The few Germans in the room stared at each other, more in amazement than anything else. One who sat near the exit seemed to be writing something down. Presumably he was taking notes. Ulrike von Seydlitz-Gabler stood rooted to the spot. Raymonde was still smiling, but Otto sat frozen to his bar stool like a hunk of ice.

"Are you completely off your rocker?" he asked Hartmann when things had returned to normal. "You could be shot for what you did just now—don't you realize that? You belong in a nursery school, not a war. You know, sometimes I have a horrible feeling you're dead but you won't lie down."

Just over half an hour later a military police patrol, duly alerted, marched in and arrested Hartmann.

Police Headquarters in the Quai des Orfèvres worked a twenty-four hour day. The more violent the age, the more violent the crimes committed in it. As Monsieur Henri Prévert—commonly known as "*Henri le doux*"—used to say in private: "We'll soon be living in policeman's paradise. It won't matter what you do—you'll automatically be committing some crime or other."

Henri Prévert was a pear-shaped man whose hindquarters appeared to dominate the rest of his body. His face looked as though it had been hurriedly kneaded together out of baker's dough and his eyes were reminiscent of old, worn out buttons. Behind this façade, however, lurked an accurate and highly sensitive instrument, for Prévert had what was probably the best brain currently available to the Paris police force.

The telephone on his desk buzzed briefly three times. This signified the presence of a visitor—to be precise, the sort of visitor who could walk in unannounced. Under prevailing circumstances this could only be a member of the German counter-espionage service. Prévert guessed that it would be Engel, the bloodhound who spent most of his time making life difficult for him, but he was wrong. The door opened to reveal Lieutenant-Colonel Grau himself.

Prévert's doughy features betrayed no reaction whatsoever. They never did—indeed, they seemed incapable of registering any expression other than indifference.

"This is an honour, Colonel Grau!" Prévert's voice sounded as if it had been filtered through absinthe, but his manner was cordial and welcoming.

Grau sat down with the easy grace of a cavalryman mounting a charger. He raised his chin inquiringly. "Have you got a bad conscience, Monsieur Prévert?"

"No, why should I have? After all, you've come to see me, Colonel. If I had blotted my copy-book you'd have sent for me."

Prévert had what was probably one of the most difficult jobs in occupied France. As chief of a newly formed department within the Sûreté Nationale, it was his duty to maintain the requisite contacts between the forces of occupation and the French police authorities. No one envied him his task, and his colleagues were convinced that his head sat lighter on his shoulders than any other in France.

Grau got down to business without any preamble. Empty courtesies and diplomatic shadow-boxing were superfluous with a man like Prévert. He said: "I want to make a deal with you."

Prévert nodded readily. He knew that it was not a question of silk, cognac or antiques. When people bargained with him it was for human lives. "I shall do my best not to swindle you," he said.

"Monsieur Prévert," said Grau, "what I have to offer is something which will presumably interest you as a Frenchman: the lives of a few French patriots. I might be able to hand over half a dozen of your heroes, providing they're still in our custody and I can exert pressure in the proper quarters."

"And what is your particular interest, Colonel?"

"Not small fry, Monsieur Prévert, I can tell you that. I'm interested in bigger fish—really big ones, perhaps."

Prévert inclined his head and shoulders in a gesture of complete understanding. He was not particularly surprised by Grau's suggestion because Engel had already made hints in that direction. Grau was evidently after big game.

"A tall order, Colonel, but not entirely out of the question.

Some of the necessary material may already be to hand. I'm thinking mainly of the work done by our special agents in the security section which I set up to represent your interests."

This "security section" was Prévert's own personal brainchild. Its official task was to give the Germans free rein and effective backing, its true function to record incidents, conversations and behaviour—in short, to register everything from petty misdemeanours to serious crimes. One extremely efficient team of operatives had been installed in the brothel in the Rue St. Honoré, which was frequented by senior officers. They employed listening devices of the highest technical precision—all, be it noted, for the benefit and protection of the Germans, who dreaded to think what might happen if a German officer fell into a pimp's clutches.

"It's not easy," Prévert went on. "There's always some reshuffling going on. For instance, a flourishing establishment specializing in perversions has sprung up in the Avenue Montaigne. Another new house just round the corner in the Rue François employs minors only. We've got all these establishments under surveillance, of course. There are German officers among the regular patrons of the Rue François and I could give you a sizeable number of names which appear on the books of homosexual houses—those of three members of your department among them."

Grau brushed this aside much as he would have a fly. "I'm not particularly interested in that sort of thing," he said contemptuously. "Almost everyone has a little lapse now and then, depending on how drunk he is, and there are homosexuals everywhere. I'm interested in bigger perversions. Naturally you could give me lists of names, Monsieur Prévert. But I want more than that—considerably more."

Prévert raised his bull-dog nose as though snuffing the air. If he could actively help to decimate the Germans—whatever Grau's intentions were—why shouldn't he, especially as he would be preserving a few of his compatriots from certain death. He meditated for a moment and then shrugged his shoulders.

"What, for instance," he finally asked in his husky absinthe-laden voice, "would one of your generals be worth?"

"Three Frenchmen," Grau replied promptly. "Three taken from any list you care to give me, except that it must contain at least ten names. I reserve the right to choose. I'm not omnipotent, you understand. I have to take great care not to tread on the toes of the S.D. or the Gestapo.— But I don't need to explain that to you. Paris will soon see the last of those unpleasant organizations, anyway. Our business takes priority. Can you tell me which general may be involved in your offer?"

Prévert hesitated. Grau was not the sort of man to haggle with. He was tricky to handle, but he always put his cards on the table.

"Are you familiar with a general named Kahlenberge?"

"It's a deal!" said Grau. "What can you offer me in this connection?"

"Give me a day or two to assemble my material. There are still a few gaps."

"I shall be back tomorrow, Monsieur Prévert."

INTERIM REPORT

FURTHER PARTICULARS

Notes supplied by a journalist who is an expert on the events that took place in Paris in July 1944 and has written several important articles on the subject:

"There is scarcely anything to add to what is already known about the group which formed itself round General von Stülpnagel, commander-in-chief of the German forces in France. The conduct of most of the officers who were directly involved in the conspiracy against Hitler merits our unqualified respect, and the conduct of Lieutenant-Colonel Cäsar von Hofacker, in particular, was distinguished by historic greatness.

"Apart from this clearly defined group at the top there existed numerous others composed of sympathetic but passive accomplices, and others of men who had become party to the conspiracy by accident. Then, again, there were officers who guessed a great deal but knew nothing for certain. These individuals circled the main groups like satellites, cautiously trying to make contact but failing.

"Still other men, regimental officers as well as staff officers and generals, formed their own independent groups and tried to build up their own networks. They conspired with and sometimes—unwittingly—against each other. Each felt that things could not go on as they were, but all lacked centralized direction—though it must be admitted that this was scarcely possible under the circumstances.

"As a result, attempts at conspiracy sometimes took curious forms. One important rule was to put nothing in writing and avoid suspicious turns of phrase on the telephone because the enemy might be listening in. In this instance, the enemy was the S.D. and the Gestapo, although many also regarded the Abwehr as such. The only comparatively safe method of communication was direct contact between two individuals or very limited groups of individuals.

"It was essential to avoid attracting attention. Conversation between two officers in the same department presented no special difficulty, but when the officers in question had no official connection with one another the problem became exceedingly awkward.

"Neutral and inconspicuous places were favoured as venues for this type of conversation. Among them was the Métro, especially Lines 1 and 7 between Palais Royal and Hôtel-de-Ville. It was not unusual for contact to be made in cafés, and von Falkenhausen of the Commander-in-Chief's staff developed a craze for taking bicycle rides dressed in civilian clothes, complete with typically French basque beret.

"Consider the general situation. The Eastern Front was steadily contracting, the Allies had landed in Sicily, and the Normandy front, which had held hitherto, was now showing signs of collapse. Still based in Paris were numerous headquarters staffs and various units belonging to all three services—e.g. an army, a navy and an air force headquarters, each with its own garrison troops—the Commander-in-Chief, France, the senior S.S. and police chief, France, the headquarters of the S.D., France, the staff of the Quarter-Master-General, Western Command, and so on.

"Furthermore, stationed in and around Paris were numerous units of varying size, some held in reserve, some ordered there for regrouping and transfer and some intended as garrison and 'pacification' units.

"Outwardly, however, Paris hardly seemed to have changed at all. It was still, to quote an expert, regarded as an El Dorado by many Germans."

Statement by ex-Sergeant Johannes Kopisch, formerly a member of the Provost Corps and as such permanently engaged in disciplinary duties within the garrison area of Greater Paris:

"Why do I still remember that evening so well? Because the whole business seemed so goddam stupid. You come up against a lot of funny things in the Provost Corps, but what happened that night was just plain idiotic.

"I can't tell you the precise date and time, but it was after midnight and damned sticky—it was like a Turkish bath the whole of that July—up till the 21st, that is. I can still remember the exact date. Why? Because that's when it began to rain. My notebook fell into a puddle and I was bloody near transferred to the front on account of it. My captain was a pernickety sod. I could tell you a thing or two about him!

"All right, I'm coming to it. It must have been a few days before the 21st. We were out on patrol as usual, me and a pal in a truck. Up and down the Champs-Elysées all the time, from the arch to the square and back again.

"Well, while we were driving up the Champs—or were we driving down? I can't remember—someone stops us and says: 'There's a chap giving a defeatist speech in the Mocambo Bar.' I said: 'Breathe!' but he wasn't tight or we'd have sent him off with a flea in his ear. As a matter of fact, he was an N.C.O.—a real spit-and-polish type. There wasn't anything for it but to go and take a gander at the Mocambo Bar.

"We collared the lad who was supposed to have spoken out of turn and I winked and said: 'Well?'—encouragingly, if you understand me. And what does the fellow say, the stupid bastard? Just says: 'Yes.' Admits the lot. Never thinks of shooting the only possible line—you know: I was drunk, I was misunderstood, I meant the exact opposite—and all the rest of the old bullshit.

"I couldn't believe my ears! This chap Hartmann was actually proud of his night's work—even asked what all the fuss was about. I ask you, how dumb can you get?—Stirring up the French and calling the war a load of crap in front of a few dozen witnesses! Mind you, he may have had a point, when you think about it today, but you just don't do things like that.

"Well, I had to take this Hartmann along, and a few witnesses as well. One of them said she was a general's daughter. I had a good laugh at that until I found out her old man really was a general. Anyway, I reported the matter. What else could I do? It was my duty.

"What sort of impression did Hartmann make on me? Well, as I said, he was a poor stupid bastard. Nice chap all the same—a bit soft, but nice, there's no denying that. He sort of tickled me. I got the feeling he wasn't quite right upstairs. Why? I don't know. It was just a feeling."

Deposition by ex-Lieutenant-Colonel Sandauer, formerly G.S.O.1 in General Tanz's division. This deposition was accompanied by an assurance that it could be used as an affidavit at any time. It was supplied in writing, seventeen years after the events referred to.
Exact date: 18th September 1961:

"I should like to stress that there can be no talk of 'squandered lives' in connection with the Nibelungen Division of which General Tanz was the commanding officer, neither during operations in Poland and Russia nor during similar engagements in France. The transfer of our division to the Greater Paris area in July 1944 was not in any way a reflection on its commander.

"The true facts are as follows:

i The losses sustained by General Tanz's division remained within what may be described as normal limits at every stage.

ii Even if our casualties sometimes appeared unusually high by layman's standards, this was attributable solely to the fact that, as an elite division, we were always in the forefront of the fighting.

iii The division's chain of command remained intact at all times, and was never for a moment endangered or interrupted. The only possible exception to this was the situation which developed outside Leningrad in December 1941. On that occasion General Tanz was cut off while personally leading an assault, and our command post was subjected to concentrated artillery fire. Due to a combination of these two unfortunate circumstances the division temporarily ceased to be operational.

iv The widespread rumour that General Tanz received orders, allegedly from the Führer himself, to refrain from direct and personal participation in military operations does not accord with the full facts.

"As a private individual, I should like to add the following rider:

"General Tanz was essentially a fighting man, but after the

Leningrad incident he was always at pains to keep the division under strict control at all times. Since the only normal method of doing this was from Divisional Headquarters, the General was compelled to avoid personal involvement in the field."

2

General von Seydlitz-Gabler's nights had recently been growing more and more unendurable. He lay there like a lead soldier slowly melting in a furnace, the blood creeping reluctantly through his ageing body. He was thoroughly miserable.

One of the main reasons for his insomnia was an increasing propensity to brood about his country and its leaders. How many times in German history, he wondered, had a general found it necessary to dwell so persistently on the subject?

The General tossed to and fro on his bed, gasping like a stranded fish. He even found it impossible to dream clearly any more. In his younger days he had been able to picture whole battlefields, coronation ceremonies and parades in his dreams—all with such overwhelming clarity that he could identify the battle honours on a flag or the colour of a plume on a helmet. Now he found himself submerged in a confused blur of murky colours to the accompaniment of massed brass bands blaring out *Parlez-moi d'amour.*

"Time to get up, sir," said Sergeant Lehmann.

The General struggled painfully to the surface. He levered himself on to his elbows with a groan and swung his bandy legs to the floor. Then he groped for the glass in his batman's outstretched hand. It was tinned orange juice, a morning treat which von Seydlitz-Gabler got only because Lehmann drank it regularly himself.

While he stood there drinking, a short and rather pathetic figure in a night-shirt, he cocked an eye at his watch. For the first time that day his face assumed a human expression.

"Good God, Lehmann, were you trodden on by a rooster

this morning, or something?" he asked testily. "It's only seven o'clock!"

"The General is breakfasting with her ladyship at the hotel today." Lehmann spoke as though he were reading the weather forecast. "Her ladyship telephoned yesterday evening and expressed the wish that you should join her, and since the General did not return to quarters until late . . ."

"All right, all right." Von Seydlitz-Gabler cut him short and hastily began his morning toilette.

"I've already had the car brought round, sir," said Lehmann, when the General's normal veneer of majestic elegance had been restored. The batman looked him over critically and seemed satisfied with the result.

Leaving his headquarters at the Auberge Moulin Noir on the eastern edge of the Bois de Vincennes, von Seydlitz-Gabler drove to the Place Vendôme in the centre of the city and stopped outside the Hotel Excelsior, which was his wife's temporary abode. At least, he hoped it was temporary. Fortunately, circumstances in Paris made it impossible to duplicate the domestic arrangements which had existed in Warsaw.

"I see you so little these days," said Frau Wilhelmine, after she had greeted him in her hotel room.

"Duty, my love, duty. There are critical times ahead."

The General gazed into his wife's blue eyes with unflinching gallantry, then past her at the twin beds, one of which had been intended for him. The virgin counterpane stared at him accusingly. To his relief he noticed that they were not alone in the room. His daughter Ulrike stood by the window, firm-fleshed and graceful as a young racehorse. Even her corn-coloured mane of hair reminded him of a horse.

"We're all going to have breakfast together," announced Frau Wilhelmine.

It was a long time since they had eaten *en famille*. They exchanged a few amicable remarks and chatted about home and Paris. Ulrike, who was temporarily stationed in Fontainebleau, complained that it was dull compared with Paris and said she would rather live in the city.

"Paris is not for you," Frau Wilhelmine said resolutely, glancing at her husband. "Paris does no one any good. For all that, I may let you come up for a day or two soon. General Tanz is on his way here, I gather, so we shall have to entertain him a little."

"In that case give me Fontainebleau!"

Ulrike's spontaneous outburst evoked a stern reprimand from her mother, who was duly backed up by the General. Frau Wilhelmine launched into a lengthy monologue in which she summarized all she had to say on the subject. Numbed by the ruthless logic of her mother's arguments, Ulrike maintained a sullen silence. Her father, on the other hand, repeatedly assured his masterful spouse how greatly he appreciated her advice.

"I shall discuss the necessary arrangements with Kahlenberge immediately after breakfast."

"So your bosom pal Hartmann is in it up to his neck again."

General Kahlenberge was addressing Otto, who had left a report from the garrison authorities on his desk without prior comment, knowing that Kahlenberge would learn the more embarrassing details of the Mocambo Bar affair soon enough.

"Hartmann's idiotic behaviour is becoming dangerous. Preaching his kindergarten idealism in public is going too far. Don't misunderstand me, Otto. I've nothing against his personal opinions and I don't demand gratitude or any other kind of emotional twaddle from my men—all I expect is a grain or two of common sense. There are some things people can't do if they want to go on working for me. I've no use for emotional blockheads."

"But, sir, what's he done that's so terrible?" Otto asked ingenuously.

"He's been making speeches, so-called defeatist speeches. In the presence of Frenchmen, what's more."

"Oh, they didn't understand half of it. Hartmann speaks French like a first-term beginner."

"Otto," said General Kahlenberge, suspicion dawning in his eyes, "were you there, too?"

"Pure coincidence, sir. I was sitting at the bar having a drink when Hartmann suddenly sounded off."

"Why didn't you shut him up?"

"He was well away by that time, sir. Also, I didn't quite

get what he was blathering about to begin with. It was all about international understanding, I think."

"And this was in a brothel?"

"Not a brothel, sir, I swear it—just an ordinary bar."

"Fair enough," said Kahlenberge good-humouredly. "I'll keep you out of the firing-line if they start making any inquiries. But I shan't lift a finger to help Hartmann—not yet, anyway. Let him cool his heels for a day or two. Maybe it'll teach him how dangerous it can be, fooling around like that. Later on I'll dig him out of the shit again. God knows why! He'll probably have another paroxysm of brotherly love before long. Well, is that all?"

"There's one point, sir." Otto switched abruptly to the role of spiritual adviser, a part which he played execrably—much to Kahlenberge's amusement. "It might be worth remembering that if Hartmann is questioned and has to mention names it won't be only my name he mentions. There's someone else involved."

General Kahlenberge tilted his jaw and studied Otto silently for a moment. His thoughts appeared to be travelling along the right lines. "Otto! You're not suggesting that Fräulein von Seydlitz-Gabler is mixed up in this, too?"

"Yes, sir." Otto's voice was tinged with admiration for Kahlenberge's sixth sense where matters of delicacy were concerned. "I was detailed to pick up the young lady from the opera yesterday and drive her to her hotel. We made a little detour on the way."

Kahlenberge seized a ruler and smacked his palm with it loudly, fixing Otto with a quizzical stare. At length he said: "I trust you aren't planning to spend your leisure time hobnobbing with generals' daughters."

"You needn't worry about that, sir," Otto protested vigorously. "I'm not a fool. Quite apart from that, the girl's not my type. I like something you can get hold of."

Although Kahlenberge was overloaded with work, anything to do with the von Seydlitz-Gabler family interested him intensely. He pressed Otto for details.

Otto hesitated for a few moments to whet Kahlenberge's appetite. Then he came out with it, eyes alight with glee. Ulrike von Seydlitz-Gabler had quite a thing about Hartmann, he said. Her voice went all husky whenever she spoke to him or talked about him. The whole business had started in Warsaw under cover of a common interest in music, notably Chopin. It had all been very romantic—little walks hand in hand, exchanges of letters, etc., etc. "Touching, sir, isn't it?" Otto concluded.

General Kahlenberge replaced the ruler on his desk. Crow's-feet of merriment appeared at the corners of his eyes.

"Call garrison headquarters for me, Otto. Hartmann is to be transferred here immediately. I'll take care of any details later."

Otto withdrew happily and Kahlenberge, surrounded by members of his staff, at once plunged into the mass of paper work that littered his desk. He issued instructions with the crisp precision of a computer punching cards. After an hour, his assistants were drenched in sweat while he still looked as pink and contented as a freshly bathed baby. This buzz of activity continued until General von Seydlitz-Gabler appeared.

The G.O.C.'s arrival signalled the beginning of the so-called overall planning phase. Immediate objectives were defined more clearly and long-range objectives examined more closely. Human beings were converted into the columns of figures so dear to the hearts of logistics experts. Finally, conversation turned to more specialized problems.

"Yesterday evening," Kahlenberge said confidentially, "I had a talk with a group of reliable officers. There were two generals among them. Shall I quote names?"

"Please don't!" Von Seydlitz-Gabler discreetly raised a well-manicured hand.

"Anyway, they're unanimously agreed that something must be done if we're to avoid total disaster, and in their view the situation warrants extreme measures. They're counting on you, sir."

Von Seydlitz-Gabler demanded fuller information on various points, his intellectual's brow furrowed in thought. He gave several portentous nods.

"Please keep me *au courant*, my dear fellow," he said finally. "I'm not fundamentally opposed to your aims, but I refuse to sanction them unthinkingly. Above all, I emphatically warn you against any ill-considered use of force. I need hardly impress on you that this conversation never took place—but I think I can say with a good conscience that if my country need me I shall not ignore the call of duty."

Kahlenberge accepted this noncommittal assurance at its face value. He hadn't expected anything more, but he made a point of praising the Corps Commander's unequalled foresight and sense of responsibility.

"Now for the next point," said von Seydlitz-Gabler. "Tanz is on his way here with orders to report to me. He's been temporarily placed under my command, and it's our job to see that his severely depleted division is brought up to strength as soon as possible."

The next half hour was spent in routine discussion. Both men realized that Tanz's division would soak up more than just their reserves. Since Tanz enjoyed the favour of the Supreme Commander, only the best would be good enough for him.

"There are going to be a lot of problems," said Kahlenberge. "Tanz is not a man to be trifled with."

"He and his men have fought heroically. A pause for recreation would do him a world of good."

"An excellent idea, sir!" Kahlenberge at once saw possibilities opening up. They might be able to divert Tanz—isolate him, even. However long the respite lasted, it would be worth it.

"General Tanz," said von Seydlitz-Gabler in his most paternal tones, "is universally respected, by my family in particular. I'm sure my wife will be only too happy to entertain our worthy colleague to the best of her ability, and I've no doubt my daughter will help her."

"Splendid!" said Kahlenberge.

"We can't entertain him the whole time, of course. That would be overdoing it. What I suggest is that we arrange a few pleasant, peaceful days for General Tanz. Let him devote himself to the Muses, as it were. He shouldn't find that too irksome in this city. What do you think?"

"I think I know just the man to handle General Tanz's concentrated programme of entertainment," said Kahlenberge. "A lad named Hartmann—you may remember him."

General Tanz's arrival was scheduled—or ordered, whichever way one cared to regard it—for four o'clock. At three fifty-five, Generals von Seydlitz-Gabler and Kahlenberge posted themselves at a window in the Moulin Noir, confident that they would not have to wait a moment in vain. General Tanz was as punctual as Radio Berlin, the State Railways, or death itself.

At three fifty-seven precisely a motor-cyclist hove into view—General Tanz's outrider—immediately followed by a Mercedes staff car. It was the same model as that used by Tanz in Warsaw but the fourth in the series. The other three had vanished into the limbo of war.

In the front seats, motionless as statues, sat General Tanz and the durable Sergeant Stoss, whose gloved hands grasped the steering wheel in text-book fashion. In the back sat Lieutenant-Colonel Sandauer, tried and tested G.S.O.1 of the Nibelungen Division, and beside him the General's combat orderly—the latest in the unending succession.

Completing this small but impressive cortège was the General's second outrider, an equally solemn and motionless figure—more puppet than man, but a puppet forged in steel. To Kahlenberge, there was an icy aura of naked power about General Tanz which seemed to freeze the very air around him. Mars himself had arrived.

"He certainly knows how to set the stage," grunted Kahlenberge.

"He leaves nothing to chance. A man of iron self-discipline, General Tanz." There was a trace of rueful admiration in von Seydlitz-Gabler's voice. "If one didn't know what a Prussian general was, one would only have to look at him."

"Poor Prussia!" Kahlenberge murmured to himself.

There followed an exchange of official courtesies. It unfolded with the fluency of a solemn and carefully planned ceremonial. Tanz stood there motionless for a second or two, his eyes seeking von Seydlitz-Gabler's. Two paces behind him stood Lieutenant-Colonel Sandauer, his faithful shadow. Then Tanz raised his hand, encased in grey doeskin, to his peaked cap in salute. He reported his arrival in firm and ringing tones.

The G.O.C. responded, endeavouring to match Tanz's firmness and clarity. "I am delighted to have you under my command once more. You and your division have seen heavy fighting and acquitted yourselves admirably. I congratulate you."

"Thank you, sir." Tanz's reply was as crisp and economical as the bow that accompanied it.

With the official part of the proceedings over, von Seydlitz-Gabler's face relaxed into a smile of manifest relief. "And now, my dear Tanz, allow me to extend to you a hearty welcome."

They all exchanged handshakes, strictly observing the rules of protocol: von Seydlitz-Gabler and Tanz, Tanz and Kahlenberge, von Seydlitz-Gabler and Sandauer, Kahlenberge and Sandauer.

"Well, gentlemen, let's make ourselves comfortable," said the G.O.C. as they went inside. "Would anyone care for some refreshments?"

"The regrouping of my division," Tanz said, ignoring the suggestion, "must be tackled without delay."

"Of course," said von Seydlitz-Gabler with a touch of asperity, "but let's sit down first."

Tanz duly sat, taking his signal from von Seydlitz-Gabler, and the other two followed suit. Even when seated, Tanz looked as though he were standing up—straight as a ramrod and controlled in every sinew. Sandauer, who vainly tried to copy him, looked like a sack of potatoes by comparison. His schoolmaster's face wore a worried frown.

Von Seydlitz-Gabler cast a brief glance at his Chief of Staff, who was sitting slightly behind and to the left of General Tanz. Kahlenberge gave a bland smile. "The regrouping of your division," he said, "will not be an overnight job."

"I know," said Tanz, "but that doesn't affect my instructions, which explicitly state: 'soonest'."

"Soonest could mean two or three weeks."

"In my estimation, seven to ten days at the most."

General Tanz was a man for whom each day, including the night that went with it, was a working day. There were no rest days in war-time—not, at least, in any war in which he was engaged.

"Thoroughness," declared Kahlenberge, "takes time."

"But it doesn't preclude speed."

Tanz had demonstrated his imperturbability. Von Seydlitz-Gabler disliked demonstrations of any sort, but he did his best to smile sympathetically.

"Our list of requirements, Sandauer," ordered Tanz.

Sandauer removed a wad of papers from his briefcase and handed them to Tanz, who handed them to von Seydlitz-Gabler, who in turn passed them to Kahlenberge, who propped them on his knees. There was an expectant hush.

"Ten days," said General Tanz insistently, "perhaps only a week."

At a nod from the G.O.C. Kahlenberge once more stepped into the breach, and the conversation soon developed into an intricate series of negotiations. Kahlenberge started by speaking of difficulties, then hinted that some of them might possibly be overcome. From there he went on to introduce his next delaying tactic. Corps, he stressed, was in something of a cleft stick because it continually had to meet the requirements of reserve formations as well as front-line units.

As expected, Tanz remained obdurate. He even hinted that he might be compelled, if circumstances warranted it, to contact Supreme Headquarters direct. Von Seydlitz-Gabler hastened to reassure him.

"Don't worry, my dear chap, we're used to overcoming difficulties. We work fast, but we don't rush into things blindly. By the way, did I tell you that my wife sends her warmest regards?"

"Thank you. May I take the liberty of reciprocating them?"

"My daughter Ulrike also asked after you."

A remote smile flitted across General Tanz's face. He clenched his hands. "Please convey my warmest regards to the young lady."

"By all means." Von Seydlitz-Gabler contemplated Tanz with the air of a fond father—no mean feat in the circumstances. "I hope we shall have a chance of entertaining you to a modest meal in the next few days."

"I hope so, too," said Tanz with mechanical courtesy, "but I doubt if I shall be able to spare the time."

Here Kahlenberge intervened again, arguing that even if it proved possible to bring the division up to strength within ten days—and he would make every effort to do so—the first three, four or even five days would necessarily be occupied with routine work. "And that's something I and your G.S.O.1 can handle on our own. Don't you agree, Sandauer?"

"Certainly," said Sandauer with alacrity. A few days of preparatory work with Kahlenberge would mean a few days without Tanz. The thought seemed to appeal to him.

"That's splendid!" cried General von Seydlitz-Gabler enthusiastically. "A few days off will do you good, my dear chap."

"Out of the question!" Tanz repudiated the suggestion with the disdain of a bullfighter who has been asked to herd cows. "I must be there from the start."

Von Seydlitz-Gabler flung himself energetically into the role of father-figure. He was anxious, he declared, and his anxiety sprang from a sense of responsibility. Tanz was a model of self-denial and had given of his best. He never thought of himself and the idea of leave never occurred to him, but even the best motor needed an overhaul sometimes—and human beings even more so.

"You must relax occasionally, my dear fellow."

"I can't afford to."

Von Seydlitz-Gabler, a past master in the art of persuasion, refused to give up. He painted the advantages in glowing colours, but Tanz seemed to be colour-blind. He appealed, implored—even begged, but Tanz remained adamant. Finally, enlightenment dawned.

"You leave me no alternative but to compel you to enjoy yourself. I consider it essential that you should relax for a few days, and I shall be happy to shoulder the consequences of my decision. I order you to take some leave. Is that clear? I order you to!"

"Yes, sir," Tanz replied promptly.

Von Seydlitz-Gabler was patently delighted with his success. Diplomacy had been quite superfluous when he was dealing with a soldier. How could he have forgotten that a world ruled by discipline is the most convenient of all worlds?

"We'll put General Tanz up at the Hotel Excelsior," he said with new-found authority.

"I'll make the necessary arrangements," Kahlenberge replied. "I imagine the General would like to see as much as he can in the shortest possible time. In that case, I suggest civilian clothes, a private car and a guide with a comprehensive knowledge of local conditions. I happen to have just the man, a lance-corporal on my staff named Hartmann. He has ambitions in the field of cultural history and a wide range of other interests as well. I'm sure you couldn't do better, General Tanz."

"Splendid," said von Seydlitz-Gabler.

INTERIM REPORT

FURTHER DOCUMENTS FROM THE PERIOD IN WHICH THE EVENTS UNDER REVIEW TOOK PLACE

Extracts from notes (not an official activity report) made by an agent known to the Sûreté under the designation A17A. These notes were in the possession of a Herr B., formerly a sergeant in German counter-espionage, who has since published several informative works on his activities in Paris:

"Notes made by A17A in the course of inquiries into a murder in the Rue de Londres. Third of seven conversations. Person interviewed: Ulrike von Seydlitz-Gabler. Subject of conversation specified by M. Prévert.

"I opened by saying that I was there on behalf of the Sûreté. I realized that there was no legal basis for my interrogating a member of the Wehrmacht. This was not an official interview, therefore, but the Sûreté would be grateful for co-operation.

"I also emphasized that my questions would be of a purely routine nature and were designed solely to fill in gaps. Their subject-matter was not directly related to any criminal offence at present under investigation. Five agents had been assigned to the case, and each of them had between seven and ten interviews to conduct.

"Fräulein von Seydlitz-Gabler eventually declared herself willing to co-operate with the Sûreté as requested. My first question: How long have you known a man named Rainer Hartmann?

"Ulrike von Seydlitz-Gabler: 'I met Herr Hartmann in Warsaw. That was in 1942, almost two years ago, at a reception during which a Chopin recital took place. We only exchanged a few words that evening, but a few days later we bumped into each other at garrison headquarters. We talked for some time and then went for a walk, after which we arranged to meet again the following Sunday. Herr Hartmann always treated me as though my father were present and his behaviour was never anything but correct. To be frank, I had a hard time breaking down his reserve, although that didn't happen in Warsaw. It happened much later on, here in Paris. However, I really don't see what business that is of yours.'"

Extracts from instructions regarding Lieutenant-General Tanz, Officer Commanding the Nibelungen Division, drafted and issued by the G.S.O.1's office:

"To the clerk on duty,

The surface of the Divisional Commander's field desk is to be thoroughly wiped with a woollen cloth every morning before the commencement of duty. Additional polishing with wax is to be carried out every Monday morning and immediately after every change of position. Any scratches or dents are to be dealt with at once. Ink-spots must be treated with ink eradicator without delay. This is kept in the G.S.O.1's office.

"The Divisional Commander's desk must at all times be equipped with the following: ink, black and red; two penholders each with pen; a set of ball-point pens; three pencils, medium hard; two chinagraph pencils; one red pencil, thick; one green pencil, thin. All pencils to be sharpened, but none to within less than two-thirds of its original length. A double quantity of the above-mentioned writing-materials is to be kept in reserve. The reserve compartment is in the left-hand drawer. No india-rubbers!"

To the Divisional Commander's No. 2 orderly:
(The General had two personal orderlies. The No. 1 orderly was responsible for indoor duties and the No. 2 for outdoor. The following is an extract from their instructions, which covered a total of eight type-written sheets.)

Re: Iron Rations:

"Since neither the commencement nor duration of any operation can be foreseen, care must be taken to ensure that a complete basic ration, or iron ration, is available at all times. This consists of the following items: one half-pound tin of dripping (rendered down and free of meat content); one half-pound tin of corned beef; one half-pound tin of game sausage; two packets of rusks, one white, one brown; a salt-cellar two-thirds full of dry, best-quality salt.

"Further equipment must include the following basic items: steel eating irons (not silver) comprising knife, fork, spoon and teaspoon; two Thermos flasks with corresponding pouches, blue for cold drinks, red for hot drinks; two large napkins for use as tablecloths; six small napkins, white, linen; two cups; at least fifty folded sheets of toilet paper, strong and coarse-grained, white or grey (no bright colours)."

Statement by ex-Sergeant Otto with special reference to the relationship between Ulrike von Seydlitz-Gabler and Lance-Corporal Hartmann:

"Looking back on it now, I reckon those two led me up the garden path. I should have guessed, I suppose, but they were so bloody careful about it. They had every reason to be. If her ladyship had caught on there'd have been hell to pay.

"Kahlenberge must have got wind of their little game because he was always going on at me to tell him all I knew about it. I didn't know much, so I invented a few things to keep Kahlenberge happy. What's the point of having an imagination if you don't use it?

"I'd lay odds on one thing, though. Running a general's daughter like that must be a bit of all right. Handled the right way it could be a sort of insurance policy. Handled the wrong way—well, it'd be the exact opposite. Hartmann never had much luck. It didn't matter where he trod, he always ended up with his foot in a turd.

"All the same, he still had Raymonde!"

3

Paris was beginning to get on General von Seydlitz-Gabler's nerves. He felt increasingly old and enervated, surrounded by temptations and never at liberty to succumb to them.

The General often sought refuge in red wine, pretending that he wanted to bury himself in his work. On this particular evening he sent for a bottle of Mâcon and Melanie Neumaier, and had two glasses and a pile of papers brought to his study.

He eyed Melanie solicitously, a little like a breeder examining his favourite rabbit.

"It's very late. I don't want to overwork you."

"Oh, don't worry about that," she exclaimed. "You know I'm always at your service."

Melanie was an incomparable assistant, von Seydlitz-Gabler reflected, punctual as a clock and reliable as sunrise—ready for anything. This evening he felt inclined to test the extent of her readiness. He felt sure that it was unlimited, and the thought was immensely flattering.

To begin with, they concentrated exclusively on the files in front of them. None presented any particular problem, but each needed working on.

At intervals they refreshed themselves with Mâcon. The first bottle went quickly. Sergeant Lehmann, his face expressionless as a sheep's, brought a second. His gloomy eyes were entirely devoid of interest. Years of experience had taught him that Melanie Neumaier was no more to the General than a piece of office furniture. It didn't occur to him that the situation mightn't last for ever. He left a third bottle ready and went to bed.

The night, however, had hardly begun. Von Seydlitz-Gabler raised his glass to Melanie with a wide, world-encompassing gesture. He drank with evident enjoyment and Melanie did the same.

"Perhaps you'd rather call it a day," he said. "I'm sure there's someone waiting for you."

"Let him wait!" cried Melanie archly.

"I find that very flattering, my dear Melanie." Von Seydlitz-Gabler's voice had grown suddenly husky. The time was ripe and the fruit long since over-ripe. His bedroom was immediately next door to the study. He felt tempted.

"Come and sit next to me, my dear. We'll be able to work more comfortably."

Melanie Neumaier pulled her chair round the desk and placed it next to his.

Casually, as if to prop himself up, the General laid his hand on Melanie's left thigh. She cautiously shifted her leg to give him a better purchase and, though she needed no fortifying, took another swig of red wine.

Melanie had waited literally years for this moment, but she knew that she must not abandon her self-control prematurely now that the end was in sight.

"Angry with me?" asked von Seydlitz-Gabler softly.

"I'm happy!" There was an artificial catch in Melanie's voice as she answered.

The General hesitated, still not fully resolved to jump the last hurdle. His satisfaction at the knowledge that he could do so temporarily outweighed his desire for the act itself. He blinked at the files lying in the pool of light cast by the desk-lamp. The muted glow which pervaded the rest of the room, ranging from warm flesh-pink to dark and dramatic red, lent it a vaguely theatrical air. Oppressed by this, the General closed his eyes and abandoned himself to pure sensation.

However, borne in on his sense with far more immediacy than the warmth and softness under his groping hand was something else. He became aware of a loud and persistent booming sound. Someone was knocking at the door.

Melanie leapt to her feet and smoothed down her skirt with trembling hands, face beetroot red and eyes dilated like those of a frightened deer. Von Seydlitz-Gabler recovered himself with miraculous speed. He had just turned back into a general when Kahlenberge entered.

"I was sure I wouldn't be disturbing you. I caught that

lazy dog Lehmann slinking off to his kennel for the night and he told me that you and Fräulein Neumaier were still working, so I thought I'd pop my head in. I've got something rather important to discuss."

"Of course you're not disturbing us."

"Really not?" asked Kahlenberge, thinking that Melanie looked slightly dishevelled but dismissing the notion as absurd. "Would you mind leaving us for a few minutes, Fräulein? That is, if the General doesn't mind."

Von Seydlitz-Gabler sanctioned this customary display of independence on the part of his Chief of Staff with a silent nod. Melanie departed crestfallen, feeling as though a door had been slammed in her face. She had never found Kahlenberge particularly congenial. Now she hated him.

"You said you had something important to discuss?"

"Yes. I've just been told—in the strictest confidence, of course—that our network has been considerably extended and strengthened. Field-Marshal von Kluge is reported to be definitely sympathetic, General von Stülpnagel is actively involved, and General Fromm has been initiated and is only waiting for the word."

"Good, good. But couldn't all this have waited until tomorrow?"

"Plans have been brought forward. According to latest indications from the Bendlerstrasse the balloon may go up on the 20th—only three days hence—so now is the time to muster our resources. There ought to be immediate consultation with the groups already involved—C.-in-C. France, for example. Time is running short, sir. May I go ahead with arrangements on those lines?"

"We must, of course, be prepared for every possible eventuality," said von Seydlitz-Gabler. "I repeat—every eventuality. We owe it to the army and our country."

"I agree. But my colleagues and I foresee a special problem arising in our area. I refer to General Tanz. It's true that we've managed to isolate him temporarily, but he's quite likely to create further difficulties."

"You know my motto," said the G.O.C. in measured tones. "Look before you leap. All in good time. Thorough preparation is half the battle. I strongly advise you not to make any premature moves. However shrewd one is, there's always the risk that ambition will take a hand, so be careful. As far as

General Tanz is concerned, he's safely out of the way for two or three days at least, and that's surely good enough for the time being. Incidentally, I hope your arrangements in that respect leave nothing to be desired."

Lance-Corporal Rainer Hartmann felt sure that there were a few pleasant days ahead. Everything pointed in that direction. He had been excused normal duties and issued with a good and unobtrusive suit of civilian clothes. He had also been entrusted with a gleaming eight-cylinder Bentley—a 1939 model requisitioned during the French campaign—a wallet stuffed with French money, a sheaf of petrol coupons and numerous permits of various kinds.

His special assignment, as transmitted by Kahlenberge, was to accompany General Tanz on an excursion through Paris lasting several days. Kahlenberge had concluded his instructions with the words: "Carry the job out properly, Hartmann, or you'll be carried out yourself—feet first."

Undeterred, Hartmann viewed the days ahead with a thrill of anticipation. Few military assignments could have presented such an enjoyable prospect.

"Don't worry, sir."

"Now go and report to Lieutenant-Colonel Sandauer."

Hartmann did so. He stowed his civilian clothes away in the suitcase which he had also been supplied with and drove off to Romainville, where the headquarters of the Nibelungen Division were temporarily located. There he asked for the G.S.O.1 and was duly directed to Sandauer's office by a crowd of soldiers who gawped at the Bentley with befitting admiration. He might have been an ambassador presenting his credentials.

Sandauer inspected Hartmann's pass, examined his civilian clothing, scrutinized the Bentley and checked the papers that went with it, exchanging scarcely a word with Hartmann in the process.

"Show me your hands," Sandauer said.

Hartmann did so, feeling as though he were playing charades. Sandauer reminded him of a pompous uncle.

"Now get the Bentley ready for inspection," ordered Sandauer. "Sergeant Stoss, the General's driver, will supervise you. You'll receive further instructions in due course."

As Hartmann emerged from the office a bullock of a man

lumbered over to him. It was Sergeant Stoss. He eyed the massive silver-grey Bentley with a blend of mistrust and envy and said: "The car's to be cleaned from top to bottom. Get cracking."

Hartmann got cracking. It was three o'clock in the afternoon when he started. At five o'clock he hadn't even finished the body-work. Stoss spoke little, and then only to criticize. He circled the Bentley like an alert sheep-dog, barking out complaints in a hoarse voice. By six o'clock he was not wholly dissatisfied with the body-work, and at seven he pronounced the interior to be "just adequate."

"Now the engine," he said.

Hartmann was glistening with sweat. He ground his teeth, muttered some inaudible imprecations at Sergeant Stoss and all the other sergeants in the world, and set to work again. Stoss seemed to relish his fury. He made him clean the sparking-plugs, polish the engine-block until it shone and rub the contacts down with emery-cloth.

At nine o'clock Sergeant Stoss declared himself satisfied. He nodded with evident reluctance, barked "That'll do!" and departed grumbling.

Shortly afterwards Lieutenant-Colonel Sandauer appeared. His pale blue eyes examined Hartmann's exhausted figure critically. "Change your overalls," he said, "clean yourself up—especially your hands—and then report to me. I want to introduce you to the General."

A quarter of an hour later Hartmann reported to Sandauer as ordered. The latter rose, opened an inner door and motioned to Hartmann to follow.

It was not the first time Hartmann had seen General Tanz. He had had an opportunity of observing him from a respectful distance in Warsaw, but now they were face to face. He saw a lean, angular countenance whose every detail was as clean-cut and precise as if it had been designed on a drawing-board.

"Lance-Corporal Hartmann," announced Sandauer in a flat, almost indifferent voice. "Christian name, Rainer. Height, five foot nine. Weight, eleven stone four. Has been in the army since the outbreak of war. Infantry. Driving licence since nineteen thirty-nine. Matriculation. Intends to study art history. Born in Berlin, age-group nineteen-twenty-two. Father, railway official medium rank, now dead. Mother resident near Berlin. No brothers or sisters. No criminal record. Unmarried."

The General did not stir. His eyes were narrowed to the point of invisibility, but his Knight's Cross with its various bars twinkled brightly. He gave an almost imperceptible nod.

"Come closer, Hartmann," bade Sandauer.

Hartmann complied. The General's immobile face seemed suddenly to grow in size. His thin, knifelike mouth moved, and Hartmann heard a voice, chill and clear as the reaches of outer space, say: "Show me your hands."

Hartmann obediently extended his hands towards the seated figure. After a short pause he turned them over so that his palms were uppermost. His fingers did not tremble.

"Carry on, Sandauer," said the General.

This concluded the interview. Back in his office, the G.S.O.1 indulged in a smile. He lowered himself into his chair and removed his glasses.

"You didn't make a bad impression." Sandauer sounded as though Hartmann had passed a stiff examination against odds. "The General has accepted you, and that's as good as a medal. However, it's early days yet. Everything will depend on whether you really do your stuff. You'd better sit down. There are still a few matters I want to discuss."

Sandauer began to ply Hartmann with questions. They struck him as superfluous, if not absolutely pointless, but he did his best to answer them fully. The G.S.O.1 wanted to know where he had spent his childhood, what schools he had attended, what subjects he had specialized in, what his special interests were, where he had normally spent his school holidays and what his favourite reading-matter was.

Hartmann was tempted to ask what it was all about, but Sandauer's patient inquisitorial technique allowed of no digressions. He fired his questions with the regularity of a man reading from a carefully devised questionnaire.

"Don't bother to work out whether there's any point in my questions or not," Sandauer said with a smile. "You're not qualified to judge, Hartmann—not yet, anyway. You'll just have to take it from me that there is. Right, let's get on with it."

Hartmann found the next group of questions even more peculiar than the preceding one. Sandauer wanted to know if he had ever had an unusual illness, if any of his family had had an unusual illness, if he had any medical knowledge, if any close or distant relation of his was a doctor, if he had any friends who were interested in illnesses and discussed them with him.

"No," answered Hartmann resignedly.

"Don't be surprised by my curiosity, Hartmann." Sandauer wiped his glasses with meticulous care. "Anyone who is to be introduced into General Tanz's immediate vicinity has to be put through a fine-tooth comb."

"Yes, sir."

Sandauer leaned back and heaved a deep sigh, closing his lustreless eyes. "You will begin your duties with General Tanz tomorrow, July 18th, at eight o'clock in the morning. At that hour you will be waiting outside the Hotel Excelsior in the Place Vendôme with the Bentley. The General's room number is thirty-three. At eight o'clock, mark you, not a second before or after. Detailed instructions have already been worked out and will be handed to you at the end of this interview. Sergeant Kopatzki, who is the General's No. 1 orderly for the time being, will be able to give you a number of tips. Pay the utmost attention to all he tells you. By tomorrow morning you will have worked out an exact itinerary for submission to the General. It must take in all the main places of interest in Paris. Concentrate on works of art. But steer clear of tombs—even Napoleon's! Remember, the watchword is relaxation."

"Yes, sir."

Sandauer replaced his glasses. "Among the particulars I shall give you will be a telephone number at which I can be reached at any time. If anything out of the ordinary happens—anything which exceeds your competence, Hartmann—ring me at once. It only remains for me to wish you good luck. You'll need it."

Rainer Hartmann felt an overwhelming desire for a double cognac, but that was not the only reason why he made for the Mocambo Bar late that night. Raymonde would be there, Raymonde with her gentle smile, tolerant good humour and straightforward willingness to please. To Hartmann, she was like a life-line in a sea of troubles, and he could happily have spent the rest of his life with her.

He forced a path through the closely entwined couples.

One or two French people nodded to him, and his spirits rose slightly at this mark of distinction.

Hartmann pushed his way up to the bar and grasped Raymonde's cheerfully extended hand. He didn't say "Good evening" or "How are you?"—just held her hand tightly for as long as she would let him. It was not a situation which could last indefinitely because Raymonde was on duty and he wanted his double cognac.

"I'm out on my feet, Raymonde. I don't know why, but I feel as if I'd swallowed the cat."

"Cheer up, it won't last." Raymonde flashed him an encouraging smile. "There are a couple of people over there just dying to take your mind off things." She pointed to the far corner of the cellar.

Otto, who sat there beaming like an amiable dumpling, raised his hand and beckoned Hartmann over. Then he jerked his thumb sideways at the girl sitting next to him. It was Ulrike von Seydlitz-Gabler. Otto's gesture was rich in unspoken hints of primitive pleasures to come.

Hartmann muttered something which Raymonde failed to catch but was certainly not expressive of delighted surprise. She told him not to keep his friends waiting and remonstrated with him when he protested that the two at the corner table were acquaintances, not friends.

"She's a nice girl, and really attractive. Most men would be happy to have her as a girl-friend."

"But I've got you."

"Not tonight you haven't," she said with a grin. "I'm a bit off-colour."

As ever, Raymonde was entirely undismayed by the presence of competition, being convinced that any man who knew her and went elsewhere would only find confirmation of her own superior charms.

Reluctantly, Hartmann strolled across to the table where Otto and Ulrike were sitting. Otto shouted a few words of welcome above the noise of the band, waving his arms like flails. Ulrike said simply: "I'm glad you came."

Before Hartmann had a chance to reply a mountainous figure loomed over the table. It was Sergeant Stoss, but a new Sergeant Stoss, apparently inflamed by vast quantities of alcohol.

"Hartmann!" he yelled, flinging his arms wide. "So you're

still alive, old cock! You won't be for long, take it from me. You're as good as dead—done for—finished—kaput! Just a heap of manure—good for daisies and dandelions and nothing else!"

Hartmann tried vainly to extricate himself from the Sergeant's clutches, but there was no stopping him. Stoss had tanked up with alcohol for the first time in years because tomorrow morning he would be able to sleep off the effects like a hibernating bear. After an eternity of abstinence, he was enthralled by the prospect of two or three days' concentrated drinking. And he owed it all to Hartmann—that poor, clueless, good-natured imbecile Hartmann!

"Write him off, girlie!" hiccupped Sergeant Stoss, bowing unsteadily in Ulrike's direction. "Believe me, he's done for only he doesn't know it yet. Come on, give us a dance. Cheer up, sweetie-pie, Hartmann's had it but old Stoss is here. Let's go!"

Hartmann got up and stood between him and Ulrike. "I'd better warn you, Sergeant," he said in an undertone. "This young lady is General von Seydlitz-Gabler's daughter."

"Marvellous!" Sergeant Stoss roared ecstatically, swaying like a flag-pole in a high wind. "That's the best story I've heard for a long time. As a man who appreciates a joke—and I'm one—I can only say: if she's the Corps Commander's daughter I'm Goering's brother!" He slapped his thigh with a noise like thunder.

"I'm off duty now," Hartmann said warningly.

"Shit!" said Stoss. "Don't talk to me about your private life. You haven't got one any more."

"You're drunk," said Hartmann.

"Of course I am!" yelled Sergeant Stoss, clinging to the back of a chair. "Of course I am, but I'm a sergeant too, and I don't like to see lance-corporals being annoyed by drunken sergeants. So get lost, Lance-Corporal. That's an order!"

"You can't do that!" cried Ulrike, outraged.

"Keep out of this, sweetie-pie," Sergeant Stoss told her contemptuously. "This is man's business. It's above your head."

Hartmann stationed himself protectively in front of Ulrike. "Sergeant, you've absolutely no right . . ."

"Shut up! Go off and get some kip—right now. That's a

direct order. You've got a heavy day in front of you, take it from me, and if you aren't out of here in five minutes I'll call the M.P.s and have you locked up. Got me?"

"I'm going," said Hartmann, his face dark with shame and fury. He knew he couldn't risk another brush with the military police. "I'm going, but you haven't heard the last of this."

"I hope not," Stoss growled. "If you're still in a condition to discuss it this time tomorrow I'll be the first to congratulate you."

"What about me?" Ulrike asked.

"You can stay as far as I'm concerned," said Stoss condescendingly.

Hartmann strove to save his face. He turned to Ulrike. "Otto will take you home. Try to understand my position. I must go—there's no alternative. We'll have to say good-bye for now."

"Will I see you tomorrow?"

"Perhaps, I don't know. I hope so."

"So do I."

"Your five minutes is just about up," barked Sergeant Stoss. "Either you make yourself scarce or I go and 'phone the M.P.s. I'm sure you wouldn't want me to do that, or your girl-friend either."

"I don't put up with boorish behaviour from anyone," Ulrike said pugnaciously.

"No?" Stoss grinned at her. He liked a girl with spirit. "I tell you what. Go and complain to your daddy—you know, the general. I'd be interested to see what happens."

INTERIM REPORT

FURTHER DOCUMENTS

Expert opinion of Herr B., the former sergeant in German counter-espionage who has a special knowledge of events which occurred in the Paris area during July 1944:

"Frenchmen were generally kept under surveillance by Frenchmen, as much for linguistic reasons as anything else. However, since Germans also came into contact with Frenchmen, it frequently happened that members of the occupying forces were watched at the same time. As a result, many confidential discussions were recorded by the French authorities, and it is highly probable that these included conversations relating to the officers' conspiracy.

"I met Monsieur Prévert, who has been repeatedly mentioned in this connection, on only one occasion. Prévert was a strange man. He did not seem particularly impressive at first sight, but as soon as he opened his mouth one knew without doubt that he had extraordinary ability.

"In a profession such as his, it is far from uncommon to trade in human lives. The rules of demand and supply operate there as elsewhere, and Prévert would naturally have been an expert at conducting such negotiations.

"Initiates into the conspiracy were not certain which way General Kahlenberge's sympathies lay. Apparently, he never established contact with the main group of conspirators, and it seems far more likely that he acted off his own bat and formed his own little circle. He is not, therefore, a clear-cut case.

"Thus the crucial question here is not: what were General Kahlenberge and his possible backers worth?—but: what was a man like Kahlenberge worth to a man like Prévert? To Prévert, French patriots were naturally more important than a German general. Only this explains what actually happened.

"The role played at that time by Lieutenant-Colonel Grau has never been fully explained. He had the reputation of being an unusually accomplished expert on espionage and sabotage. Some classed him as one of the Canaris circle and others as a member of another opposition group, but he may have been a lone wolf. On the other hand, certain circles regarded him as a potential danger, probably because no one ever managed to sum him up."

Statement by Jacques Dumaine. Though not mentioned by name anywhere in the present book, Dumaine was the proprietor of the Mocambo Bar in Paris in 1944. He is now (1961) the proprietor of a restaurant (credited with one star by Michelin) at Les Sables, north of La Rôchelle. The notes reproduced here cover only a few sentences taken from a three-hour interview:

"The Mocambo Bar was always jammed full—mostly with young people. All they wanted to do was live it up—forget, get drunk, make love. It didn't matter what language they spoke or whether they wore uniform or not.

". . . I remember Hartmann well. He always looked as if he was hungry but didn't quite know what for. He spoke appalling French. It still makes my ears hurt to think of it. But what spirit!

"Perhaps my weakness for the lad had something to do with Raymonde. I wonder if he ever realized how lucky he was to have her. . . .

". . . Yes, he gave a speech at my place. I could have hugged him, but I never got the chance. I was busy serving customers, and a little while later the Boches came tramping in looking like a lot of tortoises in those helmets of theirs. . . .

"The next day Hartmann was back again. He was like one of those toys—you know, you stand them on their heads or give them a shove and they bob up smiling.

"What ever became of him?"

Further comments on Lieutenant-Colonel Grau by ex-Sergeant Engel:

"I spent a lot of time with him, in private as well as on duty. He talked to me a great deal, but I never made out what his real ideas were. Sometimes, when he made a risky remark I didn't know whether he meant it or whether it was just a sort of joke.

"There were times when he had to keep five balls in the air at once. It was part of the job. People were always sticking their oar in—the S.D. and the Gestapo, for instance. Grau had his hands full, shaking those lads off, and every so often there was a rumpus. For example, the S.D. swore that Grau had knocked two of their men off.

"But a lot of the army boys in the Paris area also got hot under the collar when Grau appeared on the scene. He enjoyed hauling senior officers out of their beds late at night and arresting them—in the politest possible way, of course."

4

It was the morning of July 18th 1944, and Paris lay there radiant in the splendour of high summer like an attractively dishabille woman of mature years and warm-blooded beauty who was preparing to rise and begin another in a long succession of pleasurable days.

Or so, at least, Rainer Hartmann felt, though others might have described the morning in more prosaic terms, e.g.: sky cloudless, temperature average for the time of year and traffic normal, or rather, normal for war-time conditions. Anyway, it was Paris as it had always been and would always be—endless façades of petrified grandeur in every conceivable shade of grey, grey-black and black, sweltering in brilliant sunlight.

It was precisely eight o'clock, and Hartmann was standing beside the Bentley in front of the main entrance of the Hotel Excelsior. His forebodings of the previous night had vanished, leaving him pleasantly excited at the prospect of what he was sure would be an unusual experience. The thought of General Tanz's rugged, adamantine inaccessibility did not perturb him unduly. Even Tanz, he told himself optimistically, would succumb to the unique enchantment of the city sooner or later.

A sergeant emerged from the hotel and hurried up to him. He looked pale as death and was carrying a briefcase —though "transporting" might have been a better description. He handled it as gingerly as if it contained a live bomb which might explode at the slightest jolt.

"Are you Hartmann?" the sergeant inquired. "My name's Kopatzki, but you're welcome to call me Paul. I'm General Tanz's No. 1 orderly—for the time being, that is. I may have lost the job already. I forgot to take his laces out before cleaning his shoes this morning. If he notices it I'm done for."

"I'm sorry," said Hartmann.

"You needn't be." Sergeant Kopatzki showed the whites of his eyes like a cowed but cunning mongrel. "I ought to have done it ages ago. He'll throw me out on my neck and get me fourteen days' spud-bashing, but it'll be a rest-cure after all I've been through."

Hartmann was at a loss for an answer, but one thing seemed certain: Kopatzki, Paul, was hardly a bundle of joy. "Is the briefcase for me?"

"You bet your sweet life it's not! This briefcase belongs to the General. It's got his holiday rations inside, if you like to call them that."

Kopatzki held out the briefcase to Hartmann. Its dark pig-skin surface gleamed like a mirror.

"Hand-polished!" Kopatzki said bitterly. "It only takes a quarter of an hour a day to bring the shine up, but the General's got three of the sods."

Hartmann made to take the briefcase, but Kopatzki stepped back hastily, his face betraying alarm. "Don't put your sweaty paws all over it! Haven't you got any gloves?"

"What do you mean, gloves? I'm not a flunkey."

Paul Kopatzki laughed hoarsely but without malice. "Please yourself, it's all the same to me. You can dig your own grave as soon as you like, but you're not going to do it at my expense. I'm responsible for this briefcase until you and the General drive off."

So saying, Kopatzki stowed the case away with his own gloved hands. He put it in the back of the Bentley, first satisfying himself that the floor was spotlessly clean. "I never mind helping a pal," he said. "Sometimes there's no choice."

Hartmann was informed that the briefcase contained "refreshments," to whit: a bottle of cognac, a bottle of gin and a Thermos flask of strong black coffee, seventy beans per cup, temperature forty degrees centigrade. "One degree over or under and the General will throw it at your head or the nearest wall."

"Does the General drink?"

Hartmann's face clearly showed that he entertained the strongest doubts about the sergeant's statement. Kopatzki seemed to deplore this.

"Drink? He soaks it up—not that you'd notice. He can put away buckets of the stuff without tripping over his words. Holds himself like a ramrod, too. I reckon he swallows a couple of iron bars every morning before breakfast. He smokes like a chimney as well—when no one's looking."

"So he suffers from nerves too," Hartmann mused, searching for an explanation. "You've got to remember he's been through a lot."

"So have we, but no one spares a thought for the likes of us."

"I'm sure his bark's worse than his bite."

Kopatzki snorted contemptuously at Hartmann's comfortable generalization. "I guarantee you'll change your tune before you've been with him two minutes," he prophesied. "Here's one piece of advice, anyway: polish everything polishable or he'll have your guts for garters."

Remembering Lieutenant-Colonel Sandauer's orders, Kopatzki proceeded to enlarge on this theme. There were a number of commandments, among them:

Don't speak unless requested to do so.

Carry out all orders without a word, even when they seem pointless or asinine.

Take advantage of every halt—whether the General is inspecting something, eating or relieving himself—to clear up any mess that has accumulated in the interval.

Always deal with the ash-trays first, then the floor and finally the seats.

If without gloves, always use a duster when touching polished surfaces and objects. Paper will do in an emergency.

Answer the General's questions loud and clear, even if he puts them quietly, as he normally does. He never asks twice.

Watch the colour of his notebooks.

"For heaven's sake!" exclaimed Hartmann, dumbfounded. "You must be joking. What do you mean—watch the colour of his notebooks?"

"He's got two," Kopatzki informed him patiently. "You needn't worry about the black one. He just jots down his ideas in it. But watch out for the red one! He uses it for recording all the omissions, mistakes, oversights, slips and misdemeanours of his personal staff. One entry means fatigues, two entries mean jankers, and so on down to special duties and transfer for disciplinary reasons—and that's as good as an indirect death sentence."

"You're pulling my leg."

"You'll find out soon enough."

"But this is ridiculous." Hartmann's voice rang with a self-confidence he didn't entirely feel. "You can't scare me. I spent a week with General Schörner in Russia. That was something, I can tell you. He's the biggest fire-eater I'm ever likely to come across."

"Schörner a fire-eater?" scoffed Sergeant Kopatzki. "He's a dear old lady compared with Tanz."

"But Tanz is only human. The fact that we're standing around gabbing proves it. I was ordered to be here at eight o'clock on the dot and it's gone half past already. It's a human failing, being late like this."

Kopatzki sadly shook his jowly, doggy head. "You poor fool! Sandauer ordered you to be here by eight, but only to give us a chance to put you straight on a couple of things. The General won't be here till nine—and he'll be here on the dot, you take it from me. He's having breakfast now."

Hartmann took a step back as though in self-defence. As he did so his sweaty palm touched one of the wings, leaving a damp mark. Almost automatically he pulled out his handkerchief and started to polish the paintwork. Kopatzki grinned sympathetically.

At that moment Lieutenant-Colonel Sandauer appeared. Like Kopatzki he was grey with fatigue, but his eyes looked alert and observant behind their thick lenses.

"Haven't you got any gloves?" he asked.

"No, sir, I didn't realize that . . ."

"Kopatzki, dig up some gloves. Better try the hall porter. He'll help you out."

While Kopatzki trotted off into the foyer, Sandauer began to circle Hartmann and the Bentley on a tour of inspection. Minutes passed. The already hot sun shone brightly down on this unusual military spectacle in the heart of Paris, but the few passers-by seemed to avert their gaze. What was happening belonged to a world which had nothing to do with them.

"Not bad, Hartmann," Sandauer said finally. "You seem to be the adaptable sort. Have you got everything buttoned up? The General will expect you to submit some concrete suggestions. He'll only visit the most important places, but he'll insist on doing them thoroughly."

"Yes, sir."

"And as I said—no tombs or similar items of interest. We see enough graves as it is. That rules out the Invalides and the Arc de Triomphe and the Panthéon. Grandeur and beauty are what the General needs for relaxation, understand?"

Hartmann absorbed sundry further instructions from Sandauer and then donned the pair of gloves which Kopatzki had managed to extract from the hotel porter. Shortly afterwards a clock began to chime the hour.

"Nine o'clock," said Sandauer. "Here's the General."

As he spoke the General appeared, clad in a pale grey suit which he wore as though it, too, was a uniform. He glanced briefly up at the sun, then down at Hartmann, his eyes focusing on him with a fighter pilot's knack of instant orientation. Finally, he advanced on the Bentley with measured tread.

Hartmann opened the rear door. The General paused for some seconds, scrutinizing the cleanliness of the car's interior. His three satellites—Sandauer, Kopatzki and Hartmann—watched him with bated breath.

All was well. General Tanz climbed in without a word and settled himself in his seat, though his ramrod back scarcely seemed to touch the cushions. He gazed straight ahead through the windscreen at the massive triumphal column in the Place Vendôme. Perhaps its dark metallic sheen appealed to him.

"First a tour of the city," said the General in a quiet, not dissatisfied voice.

However, before Hartmann had even started the engine he spoke again, this time to Sandauer but without turning his head. "Sergeant Kopatzki is relieved of his duties. He has smeared shoe-cream all over my laces. Fourteen days' cookhouse fatigues."

"Yes, sir," said Lieutenant-Colonel Sandauer with palpable indifference.

"Drive on," said the General.

General Kahlenberge was prepared to make any sacrifice provided it gave him a chance to work on his commanding officer systematically. He even accepted an invitation to lunch from Frau Wilhelmine. His overriding aim at the present time was to strengthen the conspiratorial network and ultimately to make contact with one of the main groups.

Although the crucial moment seemed to be approaching with lightning speed, von Seydlitz-Gabler had still not shown his colours. Not that von Seydlitz-Gabler was particularly important in himself. His name coupled with his rank and position were useful assets, but everything else would be handled—as usual—by able and efficient members of the General Staff. However, the G.O.C. was as slippery as an eel.

"There have been a series of discussions," Kahlenberge reported. "Various plans have been worked out in the fullest detail."

"Excellent. Just what one would expect from staff officers." General von Seydlitz-Gabler tacked elegantly like a yacht beating into the wind. He did not question the nature of the discussions nor express any wish to be acquainted with the plans. He seemed to tolerate the situation, if not actively approve of it, but he avoided committing himself.

"I'm told that Field-Marshal Rommel has finally joined us."

"A first-rate soldier," declared von Seydlitz-Gabler, "though his generalship is open to criticism. Nevertheless, I must admit that some of his operations in Africa showed a certain finesse."

It was becoming increasingly difficult, even for the Chief of Staff, to speak to the G.O.C. in private. Either Melanie Neumaier was present or Sergeant Lehmann was skulking around in the background, and on the trip to the Hotel Excelsior the driver sat in front like a steel-helmeted listening post.

Once they reached the hotel itself, Wilhelmine never let her husband out of her sight, even though she appeared to listen to what Kahlenberge was saying. Kahlenberge took care not to mention anything that might have the slightest bearing on the conspiracy in her presence. She was a woman and, as such, a security risk.

Then came one of the rare opportunities to speak, and Kahlenberge seized it with both hands. Between dessert, which had been served in the hotel dining-room, and coffee, which was to be taken in her ladyship's suite, the two generals ound themselves alone in the corridor for a few minutes.

While they were strolling up and down in post-prandial armony, Kahlenberge said, with sudden and deliberate deiance in his tone: "We'll probably have to get rid of him, ou know."

Von Seydlitz-Gabler betrayed no emotion whatsoever. Alhough he must have known that "him" referred to Hitler, e controlled himself admirably. "Let's go and have some offee," he suggested. "It will do us good."

Ulrike had been invited to coffee, though not to the meal hat preceded it. Frau Wilhelmine had thought it better to pend the meal concentrating on the two generals and heir official business. She took an interest in everything that vent on in the Corps, but for the lighter conversation that vas to follow she had selected a very special subject—General Tanz.

"Is he being properly looked after?" she wanted to know.

This question, like all important questions, was directly ddressed to Kahlenberge.

"Everything has been laid on with the utmost care," he ssured her. "We've detailed a reliable man to look after im. General Tanz will be adequately occupied, and that's he main thing."

Frau Wilhelmine gently corrected him. "Surely the main hing is that General Tanz should have a few pleasant and elaxing days. No one deserves them more than he."

"And no one needs them more," Kahlenberge agreed.

"They say he's a secret boozer," said Ulrike.

"Who told you that?" asked Frau Wilhelmine sharply.

"Someone told me."

"Who is 'someone'?"

"Just someone."

"What 'someone' says, Ulrike, is not worth listening to." Frau Wilhelmine regarded her challengingly. "A person of haracter abhors malicious gossip." Her gorgon gaze transerred itself to Kahlenberge. "Isn't that so?"

Kahlenberge hastily assented, adding some comments of is own, e.g.: No general ever boozes—the most he does is drink—everyone has a drink now and then—an inevitable ymptom of war—abnormal strain, exertion, fatigue, hardship, etc., etc.

"And why shouldn't one, now and then?" demanded Frau

Wilhelmine. "Always providing one has a strong head, which you haven't, Herbert, unfortunately. How do you fare in that respect, General Kahlenberge?"

Conversation proceeded along these lines for a while, with Frau Wilhelmine in full command of the situation and exploiting every opportunity to wind yet another laurel wreath about General Tanz's noble brow. Her reasons were obvious.

"I propose to invite General Tanz to dinner tonight. How does that appeal to you, Ulrike?"

"It doesn't," said her manifestly ill-bred daughter.

Fortunately, Frau Wilhelmine chose to disregard her reaction, and von Seydlitz-Gabler contented himself with a few remarks on the inevitability of social obligations. Kahlenberge, however, scented a special reason underlying Ulrike's pig-headed refusal to co-operate and wondered if it could be turned to account.

"May I ask what you have against General Tanz?" he inquired politely.

"His men are a lot of coarse, impudent louts. I find it rather indicative, don't you?"

Kahlenberge decided to explore the matter further. "Are you speaking in general terms, Fräulein, or do you have a special case in mind?"

"Do you know a sergeant called Stoss?"

"What is all this?" asked Frau Wilhelmine, determined to nip this line of conversation in the bud. "General Kahlenberge has better things to do than worry about sergeants."

"Unless I'm mistaken," said Kahlenberge, "General Tanz's favourite driver is a Sergeant Stoss."

"They make a nice pair," snapped Ulrike.

There were sound reasons for her belligerent contribution to this coffee-time conversation. She was desperately trying to get herself excluded from the threatened dinner party so that she would be able to make the Mocambo Bar in time to see Hartmann.

However, Ulrike was up against a shrewd opponent. When Frau Wilhelmine saw smoke she also wanted to see the fire that caused it.

"Ulrike," she said severely, "how do you come to be acquainted with such people? How, where and when could you have met them? I insist on an answer to my question."

Frau Wilhelmine met with a point-blank refusal. Von Seydlitz-Gabler appealed to the mutual trust which should exist between a daughter and her parents. Meanwhile, Kahlenberge sipped his coffee with enjoyment, eyeing Ulrike over the rim of his cup.

Ulrike persisted in her refusal because she had no choice. To give anything more away might provoke unpleasant repercussions. If her mother found out that she had been spending time with other ranks in disreputable dives her days in Paris would be numbered. One false move and she would pine away the rest of the war in some god-forsaken spot in East Prussia or Pomerania or Saxony. She regretted having opened her mouth in the first place.

"Anyway, at least we've got a name to go on," said Frau Wilhelmine. "I wonder if I might ask you to make some enquiries, General Kahlenberge."

"Always at your service," Kahlenberge assured her without a moment's hesitation. "Even when the General and I are confronted by grave decisions we can always find time to carry out your wishes. You can rely on me implicitly."

Lance-Corporal Hartmann was chauffeuring Tanz round Paris. Object of the exercise: a general sightseeing tour. Maximum speed: thirty miles an hour or twenty miles an hour when passing buildings, monuments and places of interest, on which a brief commentary was required.

Hartmann's hands, swathed in the white gloves belonging to the porter of the Excelsior, instinctively grasped the Bentley's wheel at ten-to-two. His head was tilted backwards slightly so as to catch any orders the General might issue.

For a full hour the General remained silent. Although Hartmann dared not glance round, he could make out a few stray sounds above the opulent whisper of the Bentley's engine.

The noises made by the General were as follows: the muffled plop of a bottle being uncorked, the clink of glass against glass, the gurgle of liquid and the sharp hiss of matches being struck. There were no accompanying sounds. The General appeared to remain immobile throughout these operations.

Having chosen the Ile de la Cité as his jumping-off

point, Hartmann began to describe ever-increasing circles round it, taking in the best-known sights in central Paris *en route*. He named them and gave a brief description of each, totally unaware of whether or not his passenger was listening.

Rounding a corner, Hartmann stole a glance in the driving mirror. Tanz had not budged since he got in, but his right hand held a cigarette and his left a tumbler brimming with brownish liquid, evidently cognac. Hartmann was half appalled, half fascinated to see his wood-carving of a face twitch several times in succession as though convulsed by a violent electric shock. Deep, sharply defined creases appeared between his ear and the corner of his mouth, but only the left side of his face was affected. His forehead remained smooth and glossy as the brow of a Greek god.

"Stop," said the General.

Hartmann cautiously applied the brakes, pulled the Bentley over to the kerb and eased it to a halt. He waited. They were almost exactly in the middle of the Pont Alexandre, and the silver-grey ribbon of the Seine flowed sluggishly beneath them.

"Now a more detailed inspection of the main places of interest," said General Tanz. "Your suggestions, Hartmann."

Hartmann was ready for this moment. He recited his schedule without pausing for thought.

"This morning, Notre Dame. Then lunch at the Quasimodo. After lunch, the paintings in the Louvre."

"No old daubs, Hartmann."

"After lunch, the Impressionist paintings in the Jeu de Paume," Hartmann amended. "Then a trip to Versailles to see the Château, steps and gardens."

"Agreed," said the General.

They continued across the Pont Alexandre, turned right along the Seine, drove past the Tuileries and the Louvre, crossed the Île de la Cité again and finally pulled up in the square outside Notre Dame. Hartmann jumped out, ran round the car and jerked open the near-side rear door. Tanz got out.

"The main dates," he said.

Hartmann reeled off what he knew about Notre Dame. Built between 1163 and 1330—designed by a brilliant but unknown architect—ground area 60,000 square feet—interior length 425 feet—in front of a pillar in the transept a fourteenth century Madonna known as Notre-Dame de Paris—in the cathedral sacristy relics including wood from the Cross and part of the Crown of Thorns.

"Good," said the General. "Wait here."

Tanz strode off into the cathedral, his pale grey suit as immaculate as if it had just come off the hanger. There was something statuesque about the unbending rigidity of his body.

Hartmann leant against the Bentley, sweating slightly. Tanz had scarcely indulged in a single remark or gesture which might indicate how he was faring. He was as unapproachable as ever.

On examining the back of the car, Hartmann saw that the place where Tanz had been sitting was marked by a litter of cigarette butts and ash. Remembering Sergeant Kopatzki's injunctions on the subject of cleanliness, he searched the boot for a small dust-pan and brush—rather like the implements his mother used for sweeping up cake-crumbs at home—and systematically began to clean the back of the car. Then he polished the tumbler which had held cognac with one of a large set of linen cloths. Finally, he took a duster and polished the seat, grab-handles and side windows.

Having completed his chores, Hartmann stepped inside the cathedral. He soon caught sight of Tanz standing in front of the *Travaux des Mois,* scenes from daily life in the thirteenth century. He was evidently examining them with care, but whether or not with interest it was impossible to tell.

Hartmann found it moving to see a twentieth-century warrior standing entranced before an immortal work of art, trying to forget the horrors that dominated his own daily life. He felt a thrill of elation at the thought that he was privileged to be the man's guide, but his elation vanished when it suddenly occurred to him that he had forgotten to clean the ash-tray in the back of the car, and he hurried off to remedy his oversight.

An hour and twenty minutes later General Tanz emerged. He strode up to Hartmann and the Bentley as though he were seeing both for the first time, then halted. After a pause of five seconds he began to circle the car. He made only one tour, but his eyes missed nothing. "The ash-tray," he said.

Hartmann unclipped it and displayed its gleaming interior. General Tanz nodded. Then he spurned up a corner of the floor-mat with his toe, exposing the carpet beneath. It, too, was clean.

"Your hands," said Tanz.

Hartmann peeled off the porter's gloves and held his hands out. They passed muster.

"Break for lunch," said Tanz, adding: "I may inspect the engine afterwards."

Hartmann drove the bare two hundred yards to the Restaurant Quasimodo, whose speciality was *canard à l'orange* served with champagne. While Tanz was lunching there, Hartmann polished the engine block and consumed a cold chicken sandwich washed down with mineral water. He used up two rags and a wad of cotton waste during his lunch break.

Shortly after two o'clock Tanz reappeared. He seemed to have dined well and wined still better. There was even a suspicion of a smile hovering about his lips.

"Open the bonnet," he said.

Hartmann did so. The General bent forward slightly, withdrew a snowy white handkerchief from the left-hand breast pocket of his pearl-grey suit and rubbed it against a section of casing in the region of the distributor head. It failed to retain its dazzling whiteness.

"I dislike soiling my handkerchiefs with filth which any subordinates have failed to remove," stated General Tanz. "This is your first warning. I advise you not to merit a second. What is next on our programme?"

"The Impressionists, General."

"Right." Tanz ensconced himself in the back of the Bentley with manifest satisfaction. "Kindly note the following: I do not wish to be addressed as 'General' in the presence of a third party during our excursion. While it lasts we are off duty. Remember that at all times."

Hartmann drove to the Place de la Concorde and drew up immediately outside the strangely named pavilion, separated from the Louvre proper by the Jardin des Tuileries, which is the home of the Impressionists. The Jeu de Paume,

Hartmann announced with barely disguised enthusiasm, housed nearly all the major contributions made by France to the world of painting during the past hundred years, including works by Monet, Manet and Cézanne, van Gogh, Renoir and Gauguin, Degas, Toulouse-Lautrec and Rousseau.

Tanz stood before each painting in turn and called upon Hartmann to interpret it. Hartmann did his best to comply, carefully moderating his genuine enthusiasm for the subject. He spoke in subdued tones of van Gogh's explosive strength, Renoir's luminous colours, Cézanne's ability to capture natural forces on canvas. Tanz listened attentively. He even repeated one or two pieces of information in an undertone, presumably because he felt them to be important, e.g. "Degas, Edgar, *Woman combing her Hair,* pastel, 80 x 57 cm., circa 1880-5, signed."

The General inspected picture after picture as though each one posed some arithmetical problem which he had to solve. He seemed to allocate his time with care, never spending more than a specific number of seconds before each picture and never favouring one at the expense of another. He might have been inspecting a ceremonial parade. Hartmann followed at his heels, poring over his catalogue and murmuring names, numbers and dates.

Tanz's measured progress continued until he came to van Gogh's *Self-portrait,* 1889, oils, 65 x 54 cm., sometimes known as "Vincent in the Flames." The description in the catalogue read: ". . . Taut to breaking-point, it testifies to van Gogh's struggle to master his inward turmoil. . . . An expression of supreme equilibrium on the brink of the abyss."

Hartmann limited himself to the bare title and reference number, thinking that there would be no time for more. Mechanically, he started to move on to the next picture, but General Tanz lingered in front of "Vincent in the Flames" longer than usual. He stared at the picture, or rather, he stared straight ahead and consequently—since it hung at eye level—at the picture.

Hartmann approached with due caution. Suddenly, he saw the General's right arm begin to twitch convulsively. His hand, twisted into a claw, groped its way upwards and clutched his forehead in a vicelike grip. His body, usually as erect as a ferro-concrete tower, tottered and threatened to collapse.

Hartmann rushed forward and grasped the General's left arm. Simultaneously, he felt the muscular flesh beneath his fingers grow taut as steel cable. Tanz's arm jerked one way and then the other, throwing him off balance. Hartmann staggered back, his childlike eyes filled with astonished incomprehension.

Tanz turned to face him, looking as craggy and inaccessible as he had ever done. "How dare you lay hands on me?" he asked softly, his eyes as cold as a snake's.

"Excuse me, General, I thought . . ."

"Never do that again."

Tanz spun on his heel and made for the next picture. Hartmann followed him. His mind was a whirl, but he managed to find his place in the catalogue again.

Tanz strode on ahead as though his moment of weakness had never been, passing from picture to picture with clockwork regularity. He broke his rhythm only once, and that was when he came to Renoir's *Bathers*, that colossal, intoxicating symphony in rosy flesh-tones. This he passed by with scarcely a glance, the back of his neck even stiffer than usual.

Finally, the General chose a sheaf of post-cards from the counter in the entrance hall. He was extraordinarily methodical about it, displaying not the slightest preference for any one painter but apparently bent on achieving as comprehensive a selection as possible. Telling Hartmann to pay for the cards, he tucked them carefully into an envelope.

Their next port of call was Versailles. Tanz stalked through the palace with an unheeding and almost contemptuous air, evidently repelled by the extravagant splendour which met his eye at every turn. The gardens, on the other hand, he surveyed with a certain admiration, presumably because their decorative symmetry recalled the excellent staff work which must have gone into their design. As for the great steps, he traversed them once in either direction with slow, possessive strides.

At seven o'clock the first day's sightseeing tour ended and Hartmann drove the Bentley back to the Hotel Excelsior. He jumped out and opened the door.

"A satisfactory day," said Tanz—which was probably high praise. "Call Colonel Sandauer in half an hour for further instructions. Meanwhile, see to the car."

He disappeared into the hotel and Hartmann drove round

the corner to a garage which catered for Wehrmacht personnel. While cleaning the Bentley he came upon the General's briefcase. He opened it and looked inside.

Two cigarette packets, each of which had contained twenty-four cigarettes, were empty. So was the cognac bottle.

They met in one of the private rooms on the first floor. The restaurant on the Quai des Grands Augustins was celebrated, and not only for its high prices. Its *poulet docteur* was second to none and the same could be said of its *crêpes Mona.*

"Who's going to foot the bill?" asked Lieutenant-Colonel Grau.

"You're in Paris," Prévert replied in his absinthe voice. "Consider yourself my guest, at least on this occasion."

They began their meal with lobster accompanied by a Chablis. Prévert had the honour—he used the word without irony—to know the head chef; and this exercised an effect not only on the bill but on the food itself. Prévert and his guests were assured of the best that kitchen and cellar could produce.

Although Grau and Prévert were meeting on neutral territory, their encounter had been preceded by an amusing episode. Once time and place had been agreed, each had sent a plain-clothes man along in advance to search the room for concealed microphones. The two agents bumped into each other, raised their eyebrows and decided that if both sides feared the same thing neither had any grounds for apprehension.

"Don't you trust me?" Grau asked amiably.

"I'm just careful, like you." Prévert dissected his lobster with artistry. "And in times like these one can't be careful enough. To be frank, Colonel, I can't afford to have any conversations overheard even by my own men."

"Nor can I," said Grau.

He looked at the large mirror, bordered by fragile old damask curtains, which almost entirely covered the far end of the room. It was one of those mirrors which bore a jumble of numbers and initials scratched into the glass, presumably left there over the course of the years by girls who had used their diamond rings to engrave a record of their gay nights out. In the old days the *salons particuliers* of the establishment had always been reserved for lovers, but the matters now under discussion demanded equal privacy.

"Well, can you deliver?" inquired Grau.

Prévert nodded, seemingly at his Chablis. "Two generals, a colonel and a whole host of lesser fry."

"Is Kahlenberge included?"

Prévert nodded again, his expression morose. He was pained that an exquisite dinner should be abused by the introduction of subjects more suitable to the coffee stage, but Grau persisted.

"His crime?"

"What you would call high treason."

"Only that? I'm disappointed. Haven't you found anything out of the usual run—a nice little murder, for instance?"

"Well," said Prévert, not certain what Grau was driving at, "perhaps high treason with murder in mind—or at least complicity in murder. Would that suit you better?"

Grau wrinkled his brow, picked up his glass and drained it almost hurriedly. "Have you got the requisite details with you?"

Prévert nodded once more like a salesman granting a favoured client's special request. Then he rang for the next course. The head chef had recommended *canard Colette* served with a Château-Laffitte 1908, and to the friends of his kitchen such recommendations carried the force of law. Prévert sniffed his burgundy with an expression of bliss.

But Grau was not to be put off. As soon as the waiter had retired he again turned to the subject of documentary evidence.

"As I told you, I have it with me." Prévert forked up a morsel of duck and conveyed it reverently to his mouth. "What about my list?"

"It's acceptable. I've already made the necessary arrangements." He rang for the waiter, an aged indivual with the dignified mien of an elder statesman, and asked him to send up a Herr Engel, who was dining downstairs in the main restaurant.

Engel appeared almost at once, radiating his customary good-humour. There was something infectious about his beaming smile.

"Deliver the first three names on the list to the appointed place at the pre-arranged time," Grau told him.

"It shall be done." Engel grinned and vanished through the curtains, his cheeks puffed out as though he were whistling an imaginary tune.

Prévert tore his gaze away from the succulent skin of his duck, pale brown like the leaves of a tulip-tree after the first frost of autumn, and regarded Grau with a worried frown. "I only hope there's no misunderstanding. My information is reliable and I'll turn it over to you immediately, but what if you can't use it—if you don't want to use it?"

Grau, too, laid down his knife and fork. "Why do you think that's likely?"

"Because you aren't a Nazi." Prévert made this statement in the same matter-of-fact tone which he would have used if he had been commenting on the quality of the cuisine. "On the other hand, you seem determined to get rid of a number of senior officers. Why?"

"Let him serve the next course," said Grau.

There was another lull in the conversation. The lights sparkled festively in the old mirror, the decrepit waiter took on the appearance of a priest performing some mystic rite, and the dark hangings which had heard so many whispered endearments and so much gay laughter in the past enclosed the two man-hunters in a little world of cosy contentment.

Prévert drew a bundle of papers from his breast pocket. "What I have to offer you is this: a conspiracy by generals and other senior officers against Hitler. It seems fairly certain that they mean to eliminate him."

Grau reached for the notes and leafed through them impatiently. His eyes skimmed across the sheets one by one, taking in the gist of their contents. A dark flush of excitement rose to his cheeks.

"A deal's a deal," he said finally. "I'll hand over three of your chaps and you can do what you like with them. The same goes for me. I'll do what I like with my three—if I do anything at all."

"Now let's have some champagne," suggested Prévert. "I had a bottle of Mumm Rosé '33 put on ice. I hope you don't object?"

The champagne was served and the two men drank to each other, draining their glasses at a gulp.

"You know," said Grau, "we're as different as chalk from

cheese, but I have the feeling that fundamentally we have a good deal in common."

"That's quite understandable," said Prévert, refilling their glasses. "There's a sort of brotherhood which isn't dependent on the accident of blood relationship and has nothing in common with the herd instinct." He raised his glass. "I drink to the brotherhood of reasonable men."

"My people," Grau declared, when the third glass of Mumm Rosé was circulating inside him like gentle rains irrigating a parched landscape, "or rather, the nation I belong to, has been fed on a diet of lies for years. It can't tell the difference between caviare and fish-paste. And what makes things even more frightful is that this applies not only to the masses but to a substantial proportion of the people who ought to act as their conscience."

"Generals, for instance?"

"They call themselves generals!" Grau exclaimed. "They pretend to be the high priests of Prussian-German tradition, but a lot of them are just miserable hypocrites who let millions of soldiers think they see Hitler as an embodiment of that tradition. They've turned into stooges and bootlickers."

"But what's a general, when all's said and done? There must be thousands of them. You can't expect them all to be geniuses and heroes."

"No, but I don't expect them to behave like a flock of sheep, scattering to the four winds just because a dog barks at them. Whenever one of them breaks out—Beck, say, or Hoeppner—dozens of others rush forward to take his place. It seems as though generals are more expendable than anyone else in Germany these days. They stand to attention in front of that sewer-rat, let him chew their balls off and say 'Yes, sir, thank you, sir!' It makes me sick to think of it."

Prévert busied himself with the cheese-board. He appeared to be concentrating on a ewe's-milk cheese from south of Pau, noted for its peculiarly sharp and bitter flavour. "Tell me," he said deliberately, "aren't you impressed by the fact that one or two generals seem prepared to risk their necks?"

"It's too late." Grau leant back in his chair wearily. "Killing Hitler now would be like assassinating a corpse. He's on his last legs, anyway. If the army had made a stand at the outbreak of war, or three or even two years ago, it would have been a historic decision. Now, it's just self-preservation."

"But you'll help them, won't you?" Without waiting for a reply, Prévert continued: "Whatever you do, remember one thing. There's precious little worth dying for in this world, but there's a hell of a lot worth living for."

Lance-Corporal Hartmann put a call through to Lieutenant-Colonel Sandauer at the appointed time, hoping that General Tanz's G.S.O.1 would be either unavailable or disinclined to take a telephone call from a humble N.C.O. His hopes were dashed. It seemed that Sandauer had nothing better to do than sit around waiting for Hartmann to ring.

"Hartmann," he said without any preamble, "the General is satisfied with you. You can regard that as a special commendation."

Sandauer's words did not fail to have their intended effect on Hartmann. He felt a glow of pride at his achievement, though he overlooked one minor point. The appreciative remarks emanated not from Tanz but from Sandauer, and Sandauer was a military technician who knew exactly where and when a machine needed a drop of oil.

"In addition to your duties as driver and—if I may so describe it—guide," Sandauer went on, as though reading from a prepared statement, "General Tanz wishes you to take over the duties of his No. 1 orderly. This must mean he has confidence in you. I hope you will justify that confidence. Your unit has been notified and General Kahlenberge has given his personal consent."

Hartmann did not hear the crackle of the bad line. He was unconscious of his surroundings and aware only of the tinny, impersonal voice in his ear. He registered orders and instructions as they came over the wire but had no time to reflect on them. It was as though he were shooting rapids on a raft or clinging to a life-belt in a boiling sea—he didn't know which.

"To enable you to be available to the General at all times you will be quartered in the Hotel Excelsior. A room has already been reserved for you, so ask the porter for the key. You will move in immediately. Between eight o'clock and ten-thirty this evening General Tanz will be dining with General von Seydlitz-Gabler. During that time you will be off duty. From ten o'clock onwards you will remain in your room. There's always a chance that your services will be needed. Is that clear so far?"

Hartmann humbly repeated his instructions. The crackle on the line became worse, forcing the speakers to continue their dialogue at a shout. There was a pause, and in spite of the interference Hartmann thought he heard Sandauer draw a deep breath before asking: "Is everything all right in other respects, Hartmann, or have you anything special to report?"

Hartmann pondered on whether and how to answer this question, but the four or five seconds he spent deliberating proved to be four or five seconds too long. Before he could reach a decision the G.S.O.1's disembodied voice broke in again, monotonous as ever but unmistakably tinged with relief.

"All's well, then, I take it. That's all I wanted to know. Carry on—and all the best."

Hartmann didn't know whether to be pleased, astonished or annoyed. Eventually, he shrugged his shoulders and gave up the struggle.

Reporting to the Hotel Excelsior with his belongings, he found that he had been given a room on the fifth floor. His window gave on to a narrow air-shaft pervaded by a sweetish odour reminiscent of dustbins, lavatories and kitchens. If he leant right out he could just glimpse a patch of sky through a narrow aperture between the roofs.

He took out his message pad and wrote a note.

Am staying here in the hotel. How about that! My room number is 548. Will be in the usual place until 10.20 this evening. Looking forward to seeing you again.

Yours, R.H.

Tearing off the sheet he folded it up telegram-fashion and took it down to the foyer. "For Fräulein von Seydlitz-Gabler," he told the porter. "For her personally, though. Please don't give it to her unless she's alone."

"Understood," said the porter, taking the banknote which Hartmann pushed discreetly across the desk as though he were wiping a speck of dust off its polished surface.

Somehow, this incident gave Hartmann a pleasant sense of

anticipation. He had a sudden feeling that the world—and Paris in particular—was his oyster. And whatever life in Paris cost in the next few days it would all go down to expenses under the heading of General Tanz's special leave.

Hartmann slid behind the wheel of the Bentley and the engine purred into life, its hundred horse-power making no more noise than a brace of contented cats. He depressed the throttle, piloted the car rather dashingly round the few corners that separated the hotel from the Mocambo Bar and drew up outside the dimly-lit blue frosted-glass door.

Hartmann entered the establishment, which he now regarded as his "local," with something of General Tanz's possessive air as he strode down the great steps at Versailles that afternoon. Unfortunately, he marred his entrance by tripping over the last step, which was crumbling and uneven.

The first person he saw was Raymonde, who raised both arms in greeting, bottle in one hand and glass in the other. The second thing he registered was a man in sergeant's uniform dancing with two girls at the same time, rapturously but with the ungainliness of a bear. He was leading them through a sort of square-dance and his face was puce with exertion.

The wildly gyrating figure looked familiar, but it was a moment or two before Hartmann realized to his unbounded astonishment that it was Kopatzki—Sergeant Paul Kopatzki, until that morning General Tanz's No. 1 orderly and now a mere mortal once more.

Deserting his two partners, Kopatzki lurched over to Hartmann and flung his arms lovingly round his neck, exuding a smell like a wine cellar. His hands beat a clumsy but welcoming tattoo on Hartmann's shoulders. Kopatzki was evidently in the grip of strong emotions.

"What are you going to have?" he croaked. "The drinks are on me. I'm celebrating my return to the land of the living, and I owe it all to you. What about some champagne? You can have a bucketful if you like."

Kopatzki embraced Hartmann in another access of remorseless bonhomie. He seemed to have as many arms as an octopus as he dragged the reluctant Hartmann over to his table. Sergeant Stoss sat there, grinning cheerfully.

Stoss said: "So you're still alive, young 'un!"

"He's survived so far," said Kopatzki, "but he may be at

the top of the black list tomorrow. Whatever happens, we owe him a lot. Don't you agree, Stoss?"

Stoss nodded portentously and made room for Hartmann on the bench. Hartmann sat down and Kopatzki squeezed in beside him so that he was hemmed in by sergeants on both sides.

"I'm glad I ran into you," Hartmann told Kopatzki. "If I'm going to take over your job you'd better tell me what to watch out for."

"What to watch out for!" Kopatzki laughed until he was on the verge of asphyxia. "Just watch out you don't get your teeth kicked in, that's all."

"Bump the bugger off, that's the only way you'll get any peace," Sergeant Stoss recommended succinctly. "I can't say fairer than that."

"They say miracles happen," said Kopatzki, draining every glass within reach, "but do you know the biggest miracle I can think of? That no one's ever put a bayonet through his belly or hit him over the head with the butt-end of a rifle. Maybe you're the right man for the job."

"You're tight!" exclaimed Hartmann.

"Yes, thank God!" said Kopatzki in a sodden voice. "A day without Tanz is a sunny day, and dead drunk is half-way to heaven. And we owe it all to you, my lad. We'll cry all the way to your funeral, believe me."

Hartmann extricated himself and joined Raymonde at the bar. He toyed with one of her hands while she poured him a large cognac with the other. His gaze lingered on the enticing, velvety curve of her breasts, and he pictured the thighs he knew so well, now hidden by the bar counter.

"I wish I could stay with you tonight."

"What's stopping you?" asked Raymonde.

"A general."

"Since when have generals been more important than women?"

"Ever since war broke out."

"Couldn't we try to sleep through the rest of it?"

"Maybe we could start tomorrow, Raymonde."

"Whenever you like."

He drank his cognac and then glanced at his watch. Ulrike obviously wasn't coming. He held Raymonde's hand and thought of Tanz, Ulrike, the hotel and the Bentley. He hoped it wouldn't rain. He dreaded to think of the work it would make.

"You know where I live," said Raymonde, deftly uncorking a bottle of white wine. "You know where the key is and you know where your pyjamas are. I won't say any more."

Hartmann looked at his watch again. He pulled Raymonde towards him and kissed her affectionately. He felt the softness of her supple tongue, inhaled the fragrance of her skin and was tempted by thoughts of her bed—but he wrenched himself away. Climbing into the Bentley, he drove back to the Hotel Excelsior and went up to his room. There he flung himself on the bed and reached for a book, but found he couldn't concentrate on it. He waited, without exactly knowing what for. Eventually the telephone rang. He answered it promptly, hoping to hear Ulrike's voice, but it was the General.

"Get the car out," said Tanz—nothing more.

Hartmann got the car out and the General climbed in. The sky above Paris was a deep luminous blue, as though the now languid and compliant city had wrapped itself in a diaphanous negligée.

"A night-club," said Tanz.

Hartmann was prepared for this request. He drove to Montmartre and pulled up outside an establishment in the Rue Fromentin called the Don Juan. Advertisements in the press spoke of antique furniture, Spanish décor, rare paintings and "atmospheric" music.

The General, still in his pearl-grey suit, got out of the car and entered the club, leaving Hartmann at the wheel. He was not gone for long. After half an hour he re-emerged and climbed in again. "I meant a night-club, not a women's institute. Understand?" His tone was contemptuous.

Hartmann thought he did. He drove on for a couple of blocks, this time to a night-club calling itself the Eve Discrète. The General alighted and swept through the doors like a tank. Hartmann saw his broad shoulders disappear into the murky interior.

This time he waited for three hours.

Tanz emerged from the Eve Discrète like a granite monolith mounted on oiled wheels, his face the brittle grey colour of weather-beaten stone. Without a word he slumped into the back seat of the car, slipping sideways when Hartmann spun the wheel but sliding back into an upright position at the next convenient corner. Hartmann might have been chauffeuring a statue.

Yet when Hartmann drew up in front of the hotel the block of granite began to move. It rose from the cushions, stood erect and glided towards the hotel entrance. Then it vanished, leaving the interior of the car filled with a throat-catching reek of alcohol.

Hartmann went up to his room. His bed-clothes were rumpled, and curled up beneath them lay Ulrike von Seydlitz-Gabler.

INTERIM REPORT

DOCUMENTS FROM VARIOUS SOURCES, ALL RELATING TO THE EVENTS OF A SINGLE DAY: 18TH JULY 1944

Extract from the diary of Frau Wilhelmine von Seydlitz-Gabler:

"Am more and more inclined to the view that Paris is not a place of any particular merit. The Parisians regard pomp as greatness, confuse a disorderly past with historic immortality, and pass off light-mindedness as *joie de vivre.* This city has a detrimental effect on people with frivolous tendencies. Herbert, too, suffers from this realization. At lunch he said to me: 'Paris sorts the sheep from the goats.'

"How true, Herbert, how true! I have never found the worthy Tanz so profoundly Prussian as in these surroundings. He is also suffering, though he naturally doesn't show it. No one notices it. Only I, with a woman's intuition, sense it.

"As a mother, I feel a secret current of happiness in Ulrike. The way her hand brushed Tanz's when she passed him the salt during our animated little supper party this evening. . . . Such an intimate, affectionate gesture! I looked at Herbert and Herbert looked at me—then we heard the glass fall. Could his hand really have been shaking? There was no doubt about it—Ulrike had actually put our battle-seasoned hero to flight.

"Am still agreeably excited as I write this. Although it is approaching midnight I feel an irresistible urge to see my little Ulrike. I shall go to her room. Am sure she is longing for a confidential chat—woman to woman."

Taken from correspondence with Lieutenant-Colonel Sandauer, retd., formerly G.S.O.1 of the Nibelungen Division:

"You inquire if I ever noticed anything exceptional about

General Tanz, in one instance mentioning the word 'peculiarities.' You also request information about details such as trembling hands, tics, headaches, consumption of tobacco and alcohol, etcetera.

"Before I reply—reluctantly, may I add—I would draw your attention to the following points:

i While in action at Leningrad during November-December 1941, General Tanz and a small group of men were cut off and surrounded for three days and nights. He did not once close his eyes throughout that time. Only four men out of thirty escaped.

ii During operations against the Resistance in Warsaw a mine exploded under the General's car, hurling him into the air. He was unconscious for a considerable time and did not regain his hearing for twenty-four hours.

iii During the Don crossing a temporary bridge collapsed and the General was carried downstream for some kilometres, several times colliding with rocks in the process. Once again he sustained no serious injury, but was almost insensible when rescued.

"It is possible that these experiences may have resulted in certain very occasional nervous disorders, but I can only repeat that the General possessed an exemplary degree of self-control.

"No one could pretend that the General despised alcohol, but he never drank on duty and only in moderation on social occasions. I know that he occasionally indulged in this not unsoldierly pastime out of hours, but to what extent I cannot say. I was never with him at the time.

"You are therefore mistaken when you assert that I sounded worried when discussing the General on the telephone with subordinates. My sole concern was to maintain the requisite contact with those who were responsible for the General's personal welfare. After all, he was in command of the division which at that time claimed my whole care and attention. Those were my only motives. . . ."

Report by a French friend describing his visit to Mme. Raymonde Gautier at Hossegor, a small spa north of Biarritz, during the last week in August 1961:

"The local policeman, obviously a frustrated sergeant-major, herded us together like sheep. I wanted to get across the road junction—there's only one in Hossegor—and tried to brush past his outstretched arms, but he pushed me back and waved on the only car in sight. To teach me a lesson he kept me waiting for another thirty seconds. A woman near me burst out laughing. It was such an attractive laugh that I turned to look, and immediately I saw the woman I felt I had known her for years."

EXPLANATORY NOTE:

Our French friend's report is almost a book in itself. To cut a long story short, the woman reminded him of a picture that had been sent him of Raymonde, the girl from the Mocambo Bar. He asked her if that was her name and received an affirmative reply.

At a subsequent interview he asked her if she still remembered a man called Rainer Hartmann. To revert to the original report:

"'A young man like a spring morning,' she said, and went on to make a lot of equally flattering remarks about Hartmann. She had obviously been in love with him. The fact that he was a German did not worry her, she told me. He was gentle and affectionate and there had been times when he was profoundly happy—not that it could have been much of an effort with a woman like Raymonde!"

FURTHER EXPLANATORY NOTE:

Other details about Raymonde follow, all recorded in an endeavour to convey the interviewer's personal admiration of her charms. In brief: Hartmann must have been a lucky dog. If so, why was her married name Gautier and not Hartmann?

"'In those days,' she told me, 'I often asked myself what could be more important than love, but I didn't know then what I know now. One day, and in my case that day didn't take long to come, it was all over—like a dream. In the end you can't even remember whether a dream was pleasant or not. It gets vaguer and vaguer as time goes by.'"

5

"It's five-thirty, Monsieur!"

The voice seemed to bore a hole in Hartmann's ear-drums, which roared as though he were submerged in a millstream.

The voice came again. "Wake up, Monsieur. It's five-thirty!"

"So what?" It dawned on Hartmann that he was in a hotel room. Slowly, painfully, he began to remember the nightmare drive through Paris, the soul-destroying hours of waiting, the sight of Tanz swaying like a steel mast, the stark naked general's daughter in his bed, the uncorked bottle in the leather case entrusted to him.

The bottle now lay on his bedside table, empty. Undeterred, the porter gave tongue once more:

"It's five-thirty, Monsieur. You have to call the General at seven sharp."

"Damn it all. I can get in at least another hour's sleep before then."

"Monsieur is forgetting the preparations."

"What on earth has that got to do with you?"

"We have our orders, Monsieur."

Arrangements à la Sandauer were functioning perfectly. The night porter had received written instructions from the day porter, who had received them from the manager, who had in turn received them from Sandauer himself.

The main points from "Special Directive regarding Suite No. 12 for the duration of its use by General Tanz (hereinafter referred to as 'The Guest')" were as follows:

"No hotel employee is to enter the suite while it is occupied by The Guest except when expressly and directly requested to do so by The Guest or his personal orderly.

"The Guest's personal orderly (at present Lance-Corporal

Hartmann) is to be woken at 5.30 a.m. and served with breakfast immediately.

"Between 6 and 7 a.m. The Guest's personal orderly will be allocated a manservant and chambermaid. They will take their orders directly from the orderly, who is the only person permitted to enter The Guest's suite."

Hartmann was acquainted with these and other details when he joined the porter in the hall. The latter regarded him with grave concern.

"I admire your composure, Monsieur."

"I feel absolutely ghastly," Hartmann groaned.

"Never mind, Monsieur, your coffee's ready."

Hartmann was the only guest in the hotel to be up at this hour, so he breakfasted in solitary state. He filled himself with scalding coffee, plastered his croissant with butter and jam and devoured it, meanwhile studying the special instructions issued by Sandauer's department. It didn't need much imagination to grasp what lay ahead.

Accompanied by a silent but curious valet and chambermaid, Hartmann betook himself to Suite No. 12. Here he gathered up the General's scattered clothes and issued his orders.

"Kindly brush and iron the suit and remove any stains. The shoes must be cleaned and highly polished—but make sure you take the laces out first. You, Mademoiselle, will carry out general cleaning duties."

Hartmann spent the next half hour cleaning and polishing an attaché case and two briefcases belonging to the General. He used two woollen cloths and half a tin of Glissando, a special high-grade leather polish which he found in a box marked "C". A list headed "Cleaning Materials and Accessories" was pasted to the inside of the lid.

On the stroke of seven Hartmann presented himself at the door of Tanz's bedroom, having set his watch not by any old church clock but by the Grossdeutscher Rundfunk's time signal. He knocked discreetly and heard the General's low but penetrating voice bid him enter.

Tanz was standing at the bedroom window, his sinewy frame swathed in a brown dressing-gown of some strong, coarse material. In one hand he held a lighted cigarette, in the other a pocket-watch. He nodded approvingly.

"Seven o'clock, sir."

"Seven o'clock and thirty-seven seconds, Hartmann. Always try to be as accurate as possible in your statements."

Tanz looked as though he had enjoyed a long and refreshing night's sleep. His short white-blond hair was carefully combed and his eyes sparkled with the cold fire of cut diamonds.

"My bath, Hartmann. Thirty-one degrees."

Hartmann disappeared into the bathroom, noting as he went that the General's bed had been stripped and tidied. The pillow bore traces of saliva but looked smooth and virtually unused. Warm summer air streamed in through the wide open windows. It was as though the preceding day and night had never been.

Hartmann ran a mixture of hot and cold water, gauging the temperature by means of a thermometer which he found lying on the edge of the bath. He put out a new piece of soap, checked the hand-towels and bath-towel, straightened the bath-mat and satisfied himself that the mirror above the basin was free from splash-marks. As he did so he saw the reflection of General Tanz standing motionless in the doorway, watching him.

"Have you anything to tell me, Hartmann?" There was a hint of urgency in the General's tone.

"No, sir."

"All's well, then?"

"Yes, sir."

Tanz detached himself from the door-frame and took two paces towards Hartmann. He halted in the middle of the bathroom. The noise of running water robbed his voice of none of its incisive clarity.

"I insist on absolute frankness, Hartmann."

"Yes, sir."

"Well?"

"You're a man, sir. All men have certain things in common."

"Go on."

"Well, in the General's place I shouldn't have hesitated to visit places of entertainment either. After all, we're in Paris, and the General is on leave."

"That has nothing to do with you, Hartmann."

"No, sir."

"Your job is to carry out orders. Nothing else matters. Watch the bath."

Hartmann brought the bath water to a temperature of thirty-three degrees—two degrees above the required level—calculating that it would have dropped by the time Tanz had disrobed and climbed in. Tanz registered his every move like a time-and-motion expert.

"In the meantime, see to my breakfast," he commanded. "Black coffee without sugar, five raw eggs in a glass with salt and pepper, two slices of ham, one cooked, one raw, and a treble measure of cognac—my favourite brand."

While Hartmann waited next door the General bathed and dressed. Then, with Hartmann stationed against the wall by the door, immobile as a piece of furniture, he began his breakfast. He did not speak again until he had drained his first cup of coffee.

"We shall be leaving at nine, Hartmann. In the meanwhile you can check the condition of the car—and don't forget to replenish the contents of my briefcase."

Hartmann produced a stereotyped "Yes, sir," judging it inexpedient to say more. He would have welcomed any opportunity to leave the room, but Tanz made no final gesture of dismissal.

"Hartmann," he said, stirring his glass of raw egg, "I'm not wholly dissatisfied with your performance so far. You possess certain qualifications, and I only hope that you continue to live up to them. How does your programme for today look?"

Thanks to Sandauer, Hartmann had worked out his schedule with due attention to detail. "My suggestions are as follows, sir. This morning, the Greek and Egyptian Collections in the Louvre. This afternoon, the Military Museum, the Palais Chaillot and possibly the Balzac and Rodin Museums as well, depending on the amount of time available."

"That doesn't sound bad." Tanz rose to his feet, slender-hipped as a dancer, and leaving his eggs and coffee vanished into the bedroom. He returned carrying a bunch of postcards, which he tossed on to the table. They spread out like a fan.

"What do you think of those, Hartmann?"

Hartmann didn't know what to think of them. They were the cards which Tanz himself had selected during his visit to the collection of Impressionists in the Jeu de Paume the day before. They were all reproductions of paintings which he had personally examined with a certain degree of interest.

Hartmann remarked diffidently: "Of course, sir, they're nothing compared with the originals."

General Tanz gave a nod of assent, as though his deepest suspicions had been confirmed. "I don't know how they turned up in my bedroom," he mused. "Presumably the hall porter obtained them for me. He must have been told to draw my attention to items of particular interest."

Hartmann stared at Tanz as if the man had suddenly grown two heads. He was utterly bewildered.

"These," Tanz went on, gesturing vigorously at the post-cards, "might interest me. I'd like to see them. Arrange it, Hartmann."

Hartmann withdrew as soon as he could and ran down-stairs to the porter's desk, where he put through a call to the number Sandauer had given him. He asked to speak to the G.S.O.1 on a matter of extreme urgency, but was informal that Lieutenant-Colonel Sandauer was not available.

It was July 19th 1944. Place: the Hotel Excelsior, Paris. Time: thirteen minutes to nine.

Lance-Corporal Hartmann decided that he must have been labouring under a temporary delusion. The exertions of the previous night had been too much for him. It was the only possible explanation.

Hurrying round the corner to get the Bentley, Hartmann told himself that he must have misheard Tanz. Either that, or the man wanted to test his reactions. Who could tell what went on inside a mind like that?

With an arduous and sleepless night behind her, Frau Wilhelmine von Seydlitz-Gabler prepared to face what promised to be an equally arduous day. Too much was at stake for her to have abandoned herself to sleep.

The stations of her nocturnal Calvary had been as follows:

11.42 *p.m.* Frau Wilhelmine completes the daily entry in her journal flushed with hope for the future. She sees her husband Herbert going from strength to strength in his professional career, her daughter Ulrike married to General Tanz, and herself firmly established as the wife of a military leader and the mother-in-law of a national hero. Fired with enthusiasm at this burgeoning prospect, she feels prompted by maternal solicitude to pay her daughter a visit with a view to probing and reinforcing her moral fibre.

11.47 *p.m.* Frau Wilhelmine enters her daughter's room on the second floor. It is empty, but Frau Wilhelmine ascertains that her daughter's absence can only be temporary. All Ulrike's clothes seem to be there, including the sensible underclothes which she has personally selected for her. The only missing items: a pink nightie, a blue dressing-gown and Ulrike herself.

Logical inference: Ulrike cannot be far away.

Likeliest explanation: a call of nature.

11.51 *p.m.*–12.07 *a.m.* Frau Wilhelmine makes her way to the second-floor ladies' lavatory. This too is empty. What now? Frau Wilhelmine concludes that it must have been occupied by someone else at the critical moment. If so, two other alternatives present themselves: the ladies' lavatory on the first floor and its counterpart on the third floor. These are also vacant. Frau Wilhelmine is filled with foreboding.

12.07–4.12 *a.m.* Frau Wilhelmine waits for Ulrike in her room, at first sitting in a chair, then perched on the bed and eventually—for comfort's sake and because she feels in urgent need of sleep—lying at full length. Hours of feverish anxiety ensue. Distressing pictures conjured up by a usually inhibited imagination show Ulrike wandering through the night, trustful as a child, falling victim to some brutal assault or overpowered by some shadowy, lust-maddened figure. The only common denominator of all these pictures: Ulrike with a man. Beside him, beneath him, on top of him, entwined around him like a rope. Oh, fearful thought!

4.13 *a.m.* Frau Wilhelmine emerges from an uneasy doze with a start and sits bolt upright. Ulrike has returned. As expected, she is wearing a pink nightie and a blue dressing-gown. Both garments are crumpled and her hair is in disarray. Frau Wilhelmine's opening question: "Where have you been?" elicits the reply: "That's my business."

4.14–4.28 *a.m.* Frau Wilhelmine bombards her daughter with questions. Ulrike remains silent. Frau Wilhelmine appeals to her family loyalty, her sense of responsibility, her sense of decency, her better nature, understanding, goodwill—even her common sense. In vain. Frau Wilhelmine switches to massive threats of parental intervention, paternal power and influence. Ulrike yawns wearily and says: "If you only knew how tired I am, Mother. I've hardly had a wink of sleep." Frau Wilhelmine snaps: "Neither have I!" To which Ulrike: "For entirely different reasons, I trust."

4.30–8.47 *a.m.* Back in her room once more, Frau Wilhelmine throws herself on to her bed and stares heavenwards, seeking inspiration but conscious only of the ceiling above her with its scattering of plaster ornamentation—roses issuing from four cornucopias, one at each corner of the room—now greyish-white in the light of early dawn. After four hours Frau Wilhelmine closes her eyes.

8.48 *a.m.* One minute later Frau Wilhelmine's slumbers are cut short by a knock at the door. It is the day porter, a man with wide experience in the ways of the world. After listening politely to Frau Wilhelmine's opening remarks he diverts the storm which is threatening to break over his head on to the night porter. Only the latter, he assures her, would have any information on the subject under discussion.

The night porter, who is on the point of signing off, finds himself summoned to Frau Wilhelmine's suite. He stands there respectfully, also a man with long experience of awkward guests and equally confident of his ability to handle any situation.

"A porter sits at his desk, Madame," he says patiently. "He sees and notes everyone who comes in or goes out, but he has no idea what goes on upstairs. It's not his job."

"Whose is it, then?"

"No one's, Madame. From midnight onwards there are no floor waiters or chambermaids on duty."

"And whatever happens on the upper floors—no one worries about it?"

"Why should they, Madame?"

"But that means anyone can walk into any room in the hotel!"

"Always providing he has a key to it or the room in question is unlocked—which usually means in practice that it's been left open on purpose."

Frau Wilhelmine dismisses the porter, who retires thankfully. She puts a call through to the Moulin Noir and asks to speak to her husband. "Please come at once, Herbert! I have something to discuss with you—urgently. No, don't try to dodge the issue. There's a scandal in the offing."

"A Monsieur Prévert to see you," Otto announced.

General Kahlenberge leafed through some routine reports submitted by lower echelons, noting as he did so that Lieutenant-Colonel Sandauer's requests for replacements on behalf of the Nibelungen Division would, if granted, drain the Corps of all its effective reserves.

"What does he want?" Kahlenberge was glad of any distraction these days. He was so impatient for the crucial moment to arrive that routine work was beginning to get on his nerves.

"He wants a chat with you," Otto said. "At least, that's what he says."

"All right, I'll see him." Otto opened the door and ushered Prévert in. Kahlenberge offered his visitor a chair.

Prévert introduced himself without preamble, his tone that of a tramp regally dismissing the suspicion that he may be after the price of a drink.

"I'm by way of being a link between the German and French authorities in Paris. I'm also a police officer, and I have reason to believe that you may be interested in my activities."

He was right. Kahlenberge scented at once that Prévert was one of those people who were simply "there," who couldn't be by-passed and were a factor to be reckoned with.

Prévert concealed the sly glint of anticipation which shone in his eyes by gazing at his lap as though lost in thought. Then he said:

"Sometimes I think of my department as a refuse dump, General. You wouldn't believe how much garbage it accumulates."

Kahlenberge did not reply immediately. He had lowered the shiny dome of his head and was contemplating the endless columns of figures on the desk before him, repelled by the thought that they were his staple form of intellectual diet. He looked up abruptly.

"And what have I got to do with your refuse collection?"

"Most of the material I collect consists of so-called confidential reports, each of them associated with a particular name. Your own name has turned up on more than one occasion, General."

Kahlenberge leant back in his chair. "What do you want, Monsieur Prévert?"

"Just to see you. I wanted to see what you looked like."

"Why?"

"I'm the inquisitive type. I wanted to see a man I had sold without getting to know him too well."

"Sold?"

"In a manner of speaking." Prévert might have been discussing the merits of this year's vintage. "You're a form of purchase price, General, a price paid for the freedom of another man with political ambitions—one of the leading members of the Marseilles Resistance, to be precise."

Kahlenberge's face retained its masklike immobility. Only a slight movement of his hand expressed regret at his failure to understand what his visitor was driving at. He took care not to utter a word, fully aware that in such a situation the smallest slip could have disastrous consequences.

Prévert stroked his almost non-existent chin.

"It's quite simple. Firstly, although words are intended for certain ears they sometimes reach ears for which they are not intended. Secondly, microphones are easily concealed. Thirdly, some people have an overwhelming urge to confide in others. Fourthly, even conspirators gossip occasionally. Need I say more?"

Kahlenberge shook his head, his face the colour of ashes.

"No doubt you'll want to know who I've sold you to, General—sold you without knowing you. I must confess that I did so without too much heart-searching. The only reason why I made the deal was that it seemed a particularly advantageous one, not only for me and my cause, but also for the object of the transaction—that's to say, you."

A change came over Kahlenberge's strained expression. It did not exactly relax, but it betrayed a glimmer of surprise. As gingerly as if he were disarming a time-bomb, he said: "May I inquire what you mean by advantageous?"

"Just that, my dear sir. I look on this operation as a form of insurance policy. Allow me to explain. Every system based on brute force has its determined opponents as well as its fanatical adherents. History—French history too, of course—is crammed with examples of such opposition. But you Germans seem to have evolved a completely new species of rebel—a sort of avenger of slighted honour. This individual doesn't hate the Nazis, he merely despises them because fundamentally his attitude is conditioned by historical criteria. He feels that if the Nazis' stooges are stupid or criminal enough to get themselves involved in mass murder they're welcome to do so until they end up as cold meat themselves. What he can't condone at any price is the craven 'wait-and-see' approach and apathetic readiness to compromise of people whose intelligence and education should have imbued them with at least a modicum of dignity and courage. In short, what may be excusable in a horse-butcher cannot be sanctioned in a general."

"You know Colonel Grau fairly well, don't you? I imagine he's one of your sources of information."

Prévert nodded approvingly, gratified that he was not wasting his time on someone who was unworthy of his attention. Kahlenberge evidently had a swift and sure grasp not only of circumstances but of their underlying implications.

"That also has a bearing on the insurance policy I mentioned earlier. Grau could send you and a number of your associates to the gallows tomorrow if he wanted to, but that isn't his intention. He's waiting, and do you know what for? He's waiting for what may be the German officer corps' last chance to make a clean break with an unsavoury past. But if the German officer corps shirks its last chance or botches the job, God help it! You must excuse me if I sound dramatic, General. My sole object is to give you an idea of how Grau's mind works."

"Thank you for being so frank."

Prévert hazarded a smile. "Naturally, you will have gathered that my motive for telling you all this is not just a desire to impress you with the extent of my candour. I'm much more interested in doing business with you." His smile deepened as though he were sniffing a glass of full-blooded burgundy.

Kahlenberge gave a brief but incisive nod of assent. "State your terms. I presume I shan't be able to avoid paying a high price."

Prévert fumbled in his breast-pocket and withdrew a small sheet of paper about the size of a visiting card. It bore three telephone numbers. "I can always be reached at one of these three numbers. Would you be good enough to note them down and keep them handy—or, better still, commit them to memory. Incidentally, do you know Alexandre Dumaine of Saulieu? He's one of the best chefs in France and a friend of mine. It's almost time I paid him another visit. His *coq au vin* is incomparable."

"I understand," said Kahlenberge. He noted the telephone numbers in his diary. "You wish to be informed when the time comes. According to my information, things could happen almost hourly." He shrugged. "All right, it's a deal. You shall be the first to be told."

"Thank you," said Prévert. He cocked his head on one side and smilingly pinched his nose. "A *coq au vin* certainly has its attractions, but it would be tempting to witness one of the most memorable moments in history. I really don't know which I shall decide on, but it will be something at least if you give me a chance to make up my mind in good time."

"You'll hear from me, Monsieur Prévert—in good time."

"And not for the last time, I trust."

General Tanz's second sight-seeing tour began as punctually as the first. At nine o'clock precisely he emerged from the Hotel Excelsior dressed in his pearl-grey suit. Hartmann pulled open the near-side rear door of the Bentley. The morning sun glittered on the car's spotless carriage-work.

General Tanz halted. Not a muscle of his face moved, but his eyes travelled over every inch of the Bentley, taking in the headlamps, the bonnet and wings, the windscreen and windows, the paintwork on the doors, the tyres, rear mudguards, wheels and hub-caps. His expression was completely inscrutable.

"Open the bonnet, Hartmann."

The General took two paces forward—then, after a short pause, a third. He bent over the engine and examined it closely. Pulling a snow-white handkerchief from his breast-pocket he rubbed it round a sparking-plug and held it up to the light, apparently without discovering any dirt. Then he bent down again and rubbed his still virgin handkerchief against the engine block, concentrating on the distributor-head.

Hartmann stood there in his brown reach-me-down and possessed his soul in patience, knees braced, chin in, chest out and fingers aligned with his trouser seams in the regulation manner, thinking what all other ranks think on such occasions—an unprintable phrase meaning roughly: "I couldn't care less!" For all that, his palms were moist with sweat.

Tanz again scrutinized his still spotless handkerchief, his face as expressionless as before. Then, with a brisk sweep of his arm, he poked it back into his breast-pocket and climbed into the Bentley. Hartmann closed the bonnet.

"A tour of the city," commanded Tanz.

Hartmann experienced a transient sense of relief. He closed the near-side rear door without excessive noise, slipped into his seat and drove off, grasping the wheel in his smartly begloved hands. This time he drove without any preconceived plan. Tanz didn't seem to care what he saw or which direction the car took. He issued no orders and made no suggestions, registered neither approval nor dissent. He just sat there drinking in silence.

Hartmann criss-crossed Paris at random, chauffeuring the Bentley along the Left Bank, crossing the Seine by one of the many bridges, driving along the Right Bank for a spell and then repeating the process. Above the scarcely audible hum of the car's superb engine Hartmann became aware of a noise which he could not immediately identify. It sounded like the monotonous patter of falling rain, yet the streets were dry and the sun shone as brilliantly as ever on the gleaming expanse of windscreen in front of him.

The monotonous drumming sound persisted. Very cautiously, Hartmann leant sideways until he could see the General in his driving-mirror. He saw Tanz's stern woodcarving of a face, then his left hand holding a half-filled glass, then his right hand. His fingers were drumming on the leather arm-rest with the rhythmic regularity of a metronome. They continued to do so for minutes on end, like the moving parts of some intricate machine.

"Stop," said the General suddenly. The car rolled to a halt. "What's that building?"

"The Invalides, sir." Almost before the words were out of his mouth, Hartmann remembered Sandauer's express warning on the subject. The Invalides was one of the places to be avoided.

"Let's have some details," said Tanz.

Hartmann reached for the guide book which lay ready on the seat beside him. He opened it and read the appropriate section aloud, carefully omitting any passages which might offend the General's alleged susceptibilities. The Invalides—a classical edifice dating from the reign of the Roi Soleil—the Jesuit cathedral annexed to it, begun in 1679, consecrated in 1706—a military museum from 1905 onwards.

"I'd like to see it," Tanz announced. "Wait here."

He got out and advanced on the Invalides with his habitual air of ownership. Hartmann gazed after him resignedly, aware that he had been guilty of suppressing an important fact, namely that the Invalides contained the tomb of Napoleon and sundry other captains of war. But surely Tanz must realize that? It was a piece of information which even a German general should know.

Hartmann shrugged his shoulders and systematically began to clean the Bentley with dusters, wash-leathers, dust-pan and brush. He had ample opportunity to indulge in this diverting pastime.

After two hours the General reappeared, looking white and sick. He strode up to Hartmann and fixed him with a piercing stare. "Was that your idea of a joke?"

Hartmann thought it wiser not to reply, guessing that any attempt at an apology would be dangerous. He took refuge in the role of chauffeur and silently opened the near-side rear door.

"Tombs!" The General spat out the word contemptuously. "I didn't come to Paris to look at graves. I've seen enough to last me a lifetime." His voice grew menacing. "People don't take liberties with me, Hartmann. Another blunder like that and you'll find yourself carting dung, not driving a general."

Tanz climbed in. He fished about in one of his briefcases and produced a notebook—Hartmann could not make out its colour—in which he made a lengthy entry. Hartmann scarcely dared look in the driving-mirror, but when he plucked up courage to do so he saw that Tanz's forehead was heavily beaded with sweat as though he found writing an immense physical effort.

"Fresh air," he said eventually.

Hartmann drove westwards in the direction of the Bois de Boulogne. He kept close to the Seine at first, warned by recent experience to avoid the Place de L'Etoile and the Tomb of the Unknown Soldier. Passing the Palais de Chaillot—

innocuous because it only contained pictures—he made for La Inférieur.

Hartmann's sense of relief at having reached the Bois without incident was marred by a sudden fear that its long tree-lined avenues might remind his passenger of a military cemetery. This seemed unlikely, but Tanz's reactions were unpredictable.

However, once Tanz had lunched at a local inn, a certain measure of harmony returned to the atmosphere. Trout with almonds followed by half a chicken from the spit, white wine with the former, red wine with the latter, a pernod before the meal, a cognac after it, a cigar with coffee and cigarettes between courses—all seemed to have had a mellowing effect.

"This whole business disgusts me," Tanz confided when he was once more installed in the car, "but even I have to relax once in a while. It's like voiding one's bowels—revolting but inevitable."

"Do you have any particular plans for the afternoon, sir?"

"The paintings in those postcards of mine, Hartmann—I'd like to see them."

"The Impressionists, sir?" Hartmann could not hide his incredulity.

Tanz gestured impatiently. The right side of his face twitched twice, and when he spoke his voice was as sharp as a razor.

"Don't stare at me in that stupid way! I refuse to be gawped at, do you understand?"

"Yes, sir."

"Well, what are you waiting for? Move off!"

Hartmann cowered over the wheel as if a cold and steely hand might grip him by the nape of the neck at any moment, though he knew that all he could feel was the General's cold and steely gaze. There was no escaping the sensation, so the best thing was to accept it as calmly as possible. This must be just another of the bewildering eccentricities for which Tanz was noted.

Hartmann traversed the Place de la Concorde and parked the car beside the Jardin des Tuileries on the corner of the Rue de Rivoli—exactly where it had stood the day before. Tanz climbed out and stood there surveying his surroundings like a man who was seeing them for the very first time.

"You go on ahead and buy the tickets," he told Hartmann. "Then get hold of a catalogue and follow me round the exhibition. I want details, but only constructive ones. Don't try and blind me with science."

What followed was an exact repetition of the previous day's performance. The General stalked past the paintings as though he were inspecting a guard of honour. Methodical as ever, he examined No. 1 in the catalogue first, then No. 2, then No. 3 and so on, allotting each picture precisely the same number of seconds.

Hartmann followed Tanz as he had done twenty-four hours earlier, reading out the same details in the same discreet undertone.

"Edouard Manet, *Vase of Peonies,* painted 1864-65, signed, oils 91 x 69 centimetres. . . ."

General Tanz's tour of inspection was such that he never entirely came to rest. It was impossible to tell whether or not his pale eyes registered what swam into their field of vision. From time to time he clasped his hands together behind him, kneading his fingers until the knuckles cracked under the strain. His pursed lips resembled the coin slot in a telephone booth. For a full hour, not a word emerged from them.

Hartmann felt dazed and apathetic. The exertions of the previous twenty-four hours had sapped his powers of resistance and left him as weary as a dog after a long day's hunting. He began to tell himself, in so far as the interminable catalogue notes left him time, that there was a reason—some reason—for everything. A man like Tanz always knew what he was doing. Any other explanation was unthinkable. The man was a general.

At last, the end of Hartmann's ordeal came in sight. They had already reached the upper floor and only a third of the pictures, at most, remained to be seen. When they passed Monet's three remarkable versions of Rouen Cathedral—in the light of dawn, early morning and high noon—General Tanz seemed to be on the point of shaking his head. He evidently failed to grasp why anyone should have bothered to paint the same scene three times, but that did not prevent him from appreciating the artist's seemingly futile perseverance.

Then, as though drawn to them by a loadstone, Tanz strode up to the central group of van Gogh's paintings. At first it seemed as if he found them no more than agglomerations of paint, wall-coverings, catalogue numbers. He reacted negatively to the Arles section as to the Auvers. Neither Dr. Gachet nor the church nor the inn were capable of holding his gaze or halting his progress.

Suddenly he stopped as if brought up short by a wall. Before him hung the van Gogh *Self-Portrait*, "Vincent in the Flames," a glowing, glassy-green inferno of icy, all-devouring flames, a human being at the seething heart of the Universe, a man's last glimpse of himself before night falls on his soul for ever.

Tanz stood rooted to the spot. Minutes passed. Then Hartmann saw his granite shoulders begin to sag as though weighed down by a massive but invisible load. His head drooped, but his eyes remained fixed on van Gogh's merciless expression of man's ultimate torment.

At length, and with a visible effort, the General mustered his reserves of energy. He straightened up, turned, and walked to the staircase, body erect but feet trailing. His right hand groped for the banister as he made his way downstairs. Emerging into the open, he stumbled across the gravel forecourt, past the weather-worn garden benches, to the balustrade.

Here he stood supporting himself, breathing heavily like a marathon-runner breasting the tape. His back slowly straightened and his gaze travelled across the Place de la Concorde, where the guillotine had once stood, to the Champs-Elysées and the Arc de Triomphe at its further end, in the shadow of which, probably unknown to him, lay the Tomb of the Unknown Soldier.

Hartmann posted himself behind the General at what he considered to be an appropriate distance, not understanding what had happened, merely waiting without knowing what for.

He waited for thirty-five minutes.

Frau Wilhelmine von Seydlitz-Gabler thought she knew the world—her world—pretty well. She was aware of her husband's weaknesses and of his commendable efforts to conceal them, efforts which succeeded admirably with everyone but her.

"Your daughter's honour and future happiness are at stake, Herbert."

"Perhaps so," said General von Seydlitz-Gabler, hedging, "but I have a nasty feeling that our daughter's idea of her honour and future happiness differs considerably from yours."

"These are the facts, Herbert. Ulrike was out of her room almost all night, but she didn't leave the hotel. That much is certain. The only question is: whom could she have been visiting in the hotel?"

"Whom indeed!"

"Why not Tanz?"

Frau Wilhelmine produced this trump card from her sleeve with studied composure. She measured the world by her own standards. Why, she asked herself, shouldn't Ulrike have taken the gamble she herself had taken almost a quarter of a century ago? In her own case, not that Herbert seemed to remember, it had virtually been a question of confirming a *fait accompli*, but Ulrike might easily be capable of doing the same thing under less favourable circumstances.

"Impossible!" Von Seydlitz-Gabler's voice rang with conviction. "Not Tanz!"

"We obviously can't remain indifferent to Ulrike's goings-on, but I admit that we may be biased. What we need is to discuss it with—someone who can be regarded as neutral and reliable. You know who I'm thinking of?"

Von Seydlitz-Gabler was in no doubt whatsoever. The only name which presented itself was that of Kahlenberge—Kahlenberge the reliable, the experienced, the crafty. He was just the man for a ticklish problem of this sort.

Kahlenberge appeared wearing an air of cheerful deference.

Frau Wilhelmine had no intention of rushing things. She proceeded diplomatically, first fulfilling her social obligations by ordering the floor waiter to serve coffee and brandy. Then, after a monologue on the subject of maternal solicitude, she produced her punch line:

"Could it have been General Tanz whom my daughter visited last night?"

"Quite possible," Kahlenberge replied laconically, "but scarcely probable. After all, he's not the only man who was staying here last night."

"General Kahlenberge," Frau Wilhelmine said urgently, "I can see that you know something about this affair."

"Your ladyship is very acute."

"I insist on the truth, Kahlenberge," von Seydlitz-Gabler demanded.

"Of course, sir, though I'm a little reluctant to give a frank answer in this particular case. It may lead to misunderstandings."

"Not with me," Frau Wilhelmine assured him. "Please go on."

"When a young girl stays away from her room all night," Kahlenberge said smoothly, "why should the man in question be a general? Why shouldn't it be someone of her own age—a young lance-corporal, for instance?"

"A lance-corporal!" Frau Wilhelmine's spontaneous yelp of outrage could not have been more heartfelt if she had caught a butler adulterating vintage burgundy with common tap-water. "May I inquire what prompts you to make such a suggestion?"

"I occasionally have a chat with Otto, my chief clerk," said Kahlenberge. "He can be very interesting at times."

"And do you make a practice of discussing private matters with this man?"

"Only private matters. It isn't my habit to discuss official business with my subordinates."

"Quite right," put in von Seydlitz-Gabler, who evidently felt it necessary to advertise his presence from time to time. "When we're on duty we issue orders and give instructions."

"I'm not unaware of that, Herbert." Frau Wilhelmine's eyes remained fixed on Kahlenberge. "The only thing I am unaware of is the precise nature of General Kahlenberge's conversations with his clerk."

"Otto is rather like an old and trusted retainer. He's a gossip of the first order—knocks any woman into a cocked hat, saving your presence. He makes a habit of telling me all he knows, hears or suspects on any subject."

"My daughter included?"

"Your daughter included. You see, Otto has a friend, a lance-corporal named Hartmann."

"Hartmann?" said Frau Wilhelmine.

"You may remember him. You were kind enough to take him under your wing in Warsaw."

"It can't be true!" von Seydlitz-Gabler exclaimed in outraged tones.

A gentle flush mantled Frau Wilhelmine's neck and rose to her cheeks. It was an alarm signal. "My constant concern for the welfare of your men is entirely disinterested and has never overstepped the bounds of propriety, Herbert. Surely you wouldn't reproach me for it!"

"Forgive me, my love!" von Seydlitz-Gabler said hastily. "Of course I'm not blaming you. It's this young swine—what's he called again?—Hartmann, that's right, I'll remember the name. How dare a person like that intrude into our private affairs? I just can't believe it."

"Go on, General Kahlenberge," Frau Wilhelmine urged dramatically. "Don't spare my feelings."

Her request was totally superfluous. Kahlenberge hadn't the least intention of sparing anyone's feelings.

"Your daughter got to know Hartmann in Warsaw, though how well I cannot say. They exchanged letters, and since they reached Paris they've been seeing each other again."

"Seeing each other again!" interjected Frau Wilhelmine, clutching at a straw. "That needn't necessarily mean anything. It may be quite harmless. Besides, lance-corporals don't stay at the Hotel Excelsior."

General Kahlenberge cleared his throat significantly and glanced at von Seydlitz-Gabler as though he were a placard bearing an important announcement. Frau Wilhelmine followed his gaze.

"Have you something to tell me, Herbert?"

"Absolutely nothing, my dear, except for one small detail. Lance-Corporal Hartmann is staying in this hotel on Kahlenberge's orders and with my approval."

"And what's he supposed to be doing here?"

"Lance-Corporal Hartmann's job," Kahlenberge announced cheerfully, "is to make General Tanz's leave as pleasant as humanly possible."

"Incredible," said Frau Wilhelmine tonelessly. "Well, Herbert?"

"The situation will be rectified," promised the G.O.C.—"through the proper channels, of course. I refuse to tolerate such an infamous breach of trust. Take the necessary steps, Kahlenberge."

INTERIM REPORT

EXTRACTS FROM FURTHER DOCUMENTS, RECORDS AND STATEMENTS

Information volunteered by Hector Meurisse of Paris, hall porter, still employed by the Hotel Excelsior when interviewed in 1960

"Our hotel, which you tactfully call the Hotel Excelsior—and I'm sure the management will be most grateful to you for being so discreet, monsieur—was one of the most reputable in Paris, and still is. We weren't directly controlled by the German authorities during the Occupation. We were merely instructed to give priority to special guests, and the guests they allotted us were all V.I.P.s—though not by international standards, of course.

"May I take another look at your list? Ah, yes, Frau Wilhelmine von Seydlitz-Gabler. . . . Do I remember her? As if I could forget her! An extremely civil lady, but her wishes were law. She liked things to be just so, though her taste in food and wine wasn't entirely above reproach.

"Fräulein Ulrike von Seydlitz-Gabler. . . . She was the lady's daughter, wasn't she? Let me think. . . . Ah, yes, that's right. Didn't take after her mother, as far as I remember. A charming young lady, though she didn't look too happy. There were some unpleasantnesses. The police made inquiries about her, I recall. I never knew any details.

"Lance-Corporal Hartmann? No, I don't remember the name. General Tanz's orderly, you say? It's quite possible, but I don't think he could have been with us for more than a night or so. I've no idea when he arrived or left or what became of him.

"General Tanz? I'll never forget him. Every inch a general even in civilian clothes. I imagine he was spending his leave at the hotel. We had to charge him for several broken glasses and a mirror—they said he'd had an accident. Still, he carried himself like royalty."

From an interview with a former member of the S.D. in Paris, now a textile salesman in Frankfurt-am-Main. He was visited in the hope that he could fill in some background details:

"You're welcome to give my name and full address if you want: Horst Torgauer, Frankfurt-am-Main, Zeil 17. Why should I object? I've got nothing to hide. Sure, I served with the S.D. in Paris, but in a subordinate position. There's nothing to be ashamed of in that, is there?

"Things are growing clearer these days, now that all these books of memoirs are putting the facts into their proper perspective. An oath's an oath, after all—not that it stops one being humane. I helped a lot of Jews in my time. Would you like details? I had some copies run off. Always treated our Resistance prisoners well, too. But then I've always been soft-hearted. A dyed-in-the-wool democrat, that's me.

"Lieutenant-Colonel Grau of the Abwehr? Yes, well . . . you just can't work with some people, can you? Once in a while he used to ask us for something, but whenever we wanted anything from him he made a hell of a fuss. A difficult man altogether, Grau. Pity we didn't get on. Of course, I never knew exactly what they had on him, but I remember Dr. Knochen—that was our boss—saying, the first time he met him: 'That man won't last long.' "

Unedited shorthand notes of a procedure which might loosely be termed instruction or training. They were made by a Lance-corporal who was selected, with several other O.R.s, for training as potential successors to General Tanz's two permanent orderlies. He later held the post for three weeks. Originally delivered by a Lieutenant Klaus-Dieter Zirsch, A.D.C. to General Tanz in spring 1944, these remarks were read aloud in 1961 to a circle of cronies known as "The Friends of Conviviality" who gather every Monday evening in a public house on the outskirts of Cologne. According to a statement made by ex-Sergeant Otto, to whom we owe our ccess to this document, the reading was a great success and vas greeted with roars of laughter.

Lieutenant Zirsch, spring 1944:

". . . stop gawping at me like a row of cabbages and keep a tight arsehole or your brains'll drop out you've all got pencils and paper so keep your mouths shut and your ears open the first thing you've got to remember is that you're poor little sods without minds of your own imbeciles are getting rarer thanks to euthanasia so watch it if you want to stay alive the main thing is keep your fingers glued to your trouser seams and say yes sir the General's keen on hygiene so don't forget to shit shave shoe-shine and shampoo and woe betide the filthy bugger who wipes his arse with his fingers when you finish a tin of polish replace it immediately the motto is full tins and hearts that beat for Greater Germany but don't forget that as far as you're concerned the General is Greater Germany have you got that down you idle shower the floor must be clean enough to eat off lick it clean if necessary there may be a shortage of mops and pails but you've always got tongues which brings me to the joys of civilization the General's very particular about his handkerchiefs he's the only one who's allowed to blow his nose on them the rest of you snotty-nosed bastards can use your bare hands for all I care but woe betide anyone who wipes his paws on his trousers or on the car which reminds me the car's got to shine like a whore's eyes on pay-day even if it's raining or snowing or the sky falls in or you shit your pants and I wouldn't put it past some of you but woe betide anyone who pongs sweat may be the result of honest toil but you're not required to prove it underclothes and hands must be clean at all times also teeth anyone with dirt under his nails can kiss his sweetheart good-bye now remember not a word about sickness or death the General doesn't like it the main thing is to obey orders and keep your leather polished watch the rims of cups and glasses also don't forget to clean his nail-files with a brush after use and as I said before keep a tight arsehole have you got that written down you idle bunch of nignogs. . . ."

6

That evening, the evening of 19th July 1944, General Tanz dined at Versailles. Having partaken of a sole washed down with white wine and a spring chicken washed down with red wine, a whole bottle of each, he felt inclined to complete the meal with a large brandy.

He stared through the restaurant window at the Château, which stood outlined against the rich blue of the night sky like a mighty treasure-chest brimming with history. His mind dwelt pleasurably on the unique and massive grandeur of the great steps. It had been an unadulterated delight to cross their broad expanse, even for the third and fourth time.

Tanz ordered a large brandy. The waiter served him with the deferential respect which his capacity for and single-minded devotion to food and drink merited. Tanz raised his glass, sniffed it and set it down again. Then he beckoned to Hartmann, who was standing in the doorway of the restaurant.

"Would you care to drink a cognac with me, Hartmann?"

There was only one correct reply to this, and Hartmann made it without a moment's hesitation, satisfied that he had already adapted himself to Tanz's devious ways.

"I'm on duty, sir."

The General nodded without any noticeable sign of approval. It was a mechanical movement reminiscent of a shop-window dummy. "Sit down all the same."

Ordering his guide and chauffeur a bottle of Vichy water, Tanz put his hand in his breast pocket and drew out the bundle of postcards which he had acquired the day before. He spread them carefully on the table before him and produced a propelling-pencil.

"I'm extremely pleased with you, Hartmann. I was particularly interested in the pictures. Since you obviously know something about painting, define the term Impressionism."

While Hartmann strove to comply, Tanz jotted down notes on the backs of the postcards in front of him. The observant waiter appeared and discreetly pushed the candlestick closer. Hartmann discoursed at length above the distant clatter of crockery from the kitchen.

"Now try to give me some positive differences between Manet and Monet," the General demanded. "A layman might find them easy to confuse, mightn't he?"

Hartmann felt he was seeing a new and entirely unexpected side of General Tanz. The man seemed to absorb unfamiliar facts like a sponge. Tanz was capable of anything, Hartmann told himself. He wondered uneasily whether there was some ulterior motive underlying this sudden interest in things aesthetic, but Tanz left him no time to dwell on the thought.

"Have you spoken to Colonel Sandauer about me on the telephone?" he asked suddenly.

"No, sir."

"Why not, Hartmann? Didn't you have orders to give him a running report on our activities?"

"No, sir—no direct orders." Hartmann omitted to say that he had tried to reach Sandauer several times but failed to get through. Perhaps Sandauer hadn't wished to hear from him at all. It was as though he and Tanz were alone in a little world of their own.

"Are you worried about me, Hartmann?" Tanz asked almost gently. "Don't be. Any conclusions you may have drawn from my behaviour are false—and dangerous. Or is there anything you'd like explained?"

Hartmann preserved a bewildered silence, paralysed by the General's glassy, snakelike stare. His face betrayed utter helplessness.

"I have a question for you," said Tanz, examining a postcard reproduction of Gauguin's *The Gold of their Bodies.* "Who, in your opinion, is more important—you or I?"

Hartmann had no difficulty in answering. His verdict—that a general is infinitely more important than a lance-corporal—carried conviction.

"Good," said the General with a thin smile. "I shall remember your answer. I may even remind you of it some time."

The corners of his mouth twitched in a grimace that might have been interpreted as a mocking smile. Picking up his brandy glass in both hands, he conveyed it to his lips and drank thirstily, closing his eyes as he did so. It was some moments before he spoke again.

"I presume that you checked the car and its equipment while I was eating, also that you found time to eat something yourself. You can relax for the next half hour. Drink your Vichy water in peace and smoke a cigarette. I'm going for a short stroll to settle my dinner. All clear?"

"Yes, sir."

General Tanz glanced at his watch. "It is now seven minutes past nine. Do you agree? Good. At nine forty-five you will be waiting outside the entrance of this restaurant with the car. Any questions?"

"No, sir."

Tanz rose to his feet, straight and slender as a willow wand. Two bottles of wine and a large cognac had produced no visible effect on his athletic frame, which wavered not a fraction of a millimetre. He handed Hartmann a wallet stuffed with bank-notes.

"Settle the bill and leave an adequate tip. Then take care of my wallet for me."

"Yes, sir."

Just as Tanz was leaving he turned back. "I may feel like studying a few more details of Parisian night-life later on, so you'd better be prepared. Think up something special—something different. The place you recommended last night was more like a temperance hotel. Know what I mean?"

Hartmann thought he did. He watched the General's erect figure disappear through the door, then ordered himself a large cognac and a hip-flask of Calvados, putting them on the bill. Tipping the waiter liberally, he tucked Tanz's wallet into his pocket and strolled outside.

The vast, empty gardens of the Château lay before him, at once monotonous and sublime, their magnificent wrought-iron railings silhouetted elaborately against the night sky. It was a study in soft shades of dusky blue and luminous, almost tangible black.

The outline of the main gate was broken by an attenuated, misshapen-looking shadow. A man was standing there, a man who could only be Tanz. He was urinating copiously into the perfection of the summer night.

General von Seydlitz-Gabler drove through the darkened streets of Paris. He had successfully survived a *dîner à deux* with his wife, submitting to her barrage of reproaches and exhortations with his usual exemplary self-control. Now he was returning to headquarters.

His driver, whose name he didn't know, chauffeured him across the almost empty Place de la Concorde. Of the few vehicles still about at this hour nearly all belonged to the German authorities. Some were on patrol duty, others were transporting dead and wounded, and still others were carrying personnel to places of work or entertainment.

The narrow fingers of light which escaped from the grilles masking the headlamps swept across tarmac and cobbles, fitfully illuminating the house fronts. They looked bare and jagged in the deepening gloom of incipient night, like rock formations seen by starlight.

The war was getting depressingly close. Even though it was still raging more than a hundred kilometres away in Normandy, where it was hoped to stem the tide of invasion, the city seemed to sense impending disaster. There was unease in the air.

Von Seydlitz-Gabler was far from overjoyed at the prospect of crawling into his camp-bed. He was equally unattracted by the thought of Melanie Neumaier's avid attentions. Besides, Kahlenberge was bound to look in on him. He shook his head ruefully. One thing was certain: whatever the reason, he found it impossible to sleep these days.

"Actually, I had no wish to go on leave at all," Tanz told Hartmann, who sat in front of him at the wheel of the Bentley. His voice sounded almost affable.

Hartmann preserved an attentive silence.

"I had more important things to do. However, I was told that I deserved a rest—that I needed one. They were worried about me. What do you say to that, Hartmann?"

"I can understand it, sir."

"That they were worried about me?"

"That they thought you deserved some leave, sir."

Tanz sniffed audibly and relapsed into silence. The Bentley's engine purred gently. A soft clink of glass indicated that the General was pouring himself a cognac.

Hartmann was pained by the repetitious sound and forced himself to ignore it. He stared ahead at the dark, almost deserted street as it swam into view in the dim light of the masked headlamps. As the Bentley turned into the Boulevard Montmartre the General began to speak again.

Tanz evidently had his communicative moments, few and far between though they might be. He even leant forward a little as he spoke, wafting a reek of spirits over Hartmann's shoulder.

"This is my first leave for years, Hartmann. I was ordered to take it—ordered! What do you think of that?"

"A very agreeable order, sir."

"Not altogether, Hartmann, but an order, and orders have to be obeyed. That goes for generals as well as lance-corporals. Can you understand that?"

"Yes, sir."

There were few people about, even though midnight was still an hour away. Paris seemed to be a deserted city.

"When a man's on leave," Hartmann heard Tanz saying, "he must make the most of it. No half measures. Either you do a thing properly or not at all. That's why entertainment is just as much a part of leave as cultural education. I only hope you've found somewhere really lively for me tonight."

Hartmann had done his best. His choice had fallen on a newly opened *boîte* in a cellar in the Rue Drouot. It bore the promising name of L'Ecurie de Madeleine. Although he didn't know the "stable" from personal experience, he had heard unanimous reports that Madeleine's fillies were in a class by themselves and equal to the most exacting demands.

"Stop a hundred yards from the place," Tanz ordered. "Park where you can keep an eye on the entrance."

Hartmann parked the Bentley accordingly and raced round to open the door. Tanz got out, glancing keenly about him like a hound taking scent. Then he said: "Give me a few of the large notes from my wallet."

Hartmann opened the wallet and extended it to him. Tanz pulled out several notes at random—five or six thousand francs in all—and marched off down the street at parade-ground pace. Just before reaching the door of the establishment he ducked as though preparing to inspect a fox-hole. Then he disappeared from view.

Resigning himself to a long night's wait, Hartmann climbed back into the Bentley and switched on the dashboard light. He got out a packet of cigarettes and the hip-flask of Calvados and removed a copy of *Père Goriot* from the glove compartment.

Hartmann smoked, drank and began to read. When he looked at his watch a short while later it was still three-quarters of an hour before midnight.

Hartmann was jolted out of his Balzac by a screech of brakes as a jeep-style Mercedes 220 ground to a halt beside the Bentley. A portly figure tumbled out and bounced over to him like a rubber ball.

"So you're still alive, old cock!" roared Otto with boisterous delight.

Hartmann proffered the packet of cigarettes and the still half-full flask of Calvados. The fat sergeant helped himself without hesitation.

"What are you doing here?"

"Just touring the area," Otto replied casually, putting the flask to his lips like a trumpeter. He seemed to enjoy the tune. "Things couldn't be better. All the generals are away for the night so I'm making the most of it."

"Don't let me keep you," Hartmann said ungraciously.

Otto grinned. "You look as if butter wouldn't melt in your mouth, don't you, laddie, but you're not above shitting on your own doorstep. I'm talking about Mam'selle Ulrike—if you'll pardon the comparison. You've really gone and done it there, you know."

"Give me the bottle back," said Hartmann. "You've obviously had more than you can take."

"The drunker I get," Otto announced loudly to the darkened street, "the sharper I get. When I'm really pissed I'm as sharp as a razor. You're either a cool customer or you're dead stupid—one of the two. Don't you realize what you're in for? People don't just lay generals' daughters and get away with it. Why in God's name did you let them cotton on?"

"I don't know what you're talking about."

"You don't?" Otto shook with laughter. "You're about the only one who doesn't. Her mother knows and her father knows, and since her father's General von Seydlitz-Gabler his C.O.S. knows—i.e., Kahlenberge—and so I know. And if I know it might just as well be posted up on Part One Orders."

Hartmann went cold as he began to visualize the implications of this. Absently, he relinquished the bottle again. The surrounding gloom seemed to take on a sinister aspect and the moon disappeared behind a cloud, turning it into a sheet of frosted glass and blurring the outlines of the neighbouring houses. Only the dim blue lamp above the entrance of L'Ecurie de Madeleine seemed to glow brighter than before.

"That's bad," Hartmann said bleakly.

"There's worse to come. You've been relieved of your duties and your marching orders are signed and sealed. But that's only the half of it. Your girl-friend Ulrike isn't just a general's daughter—she's likely to become a general's wife soon, by all accounts. You would have to pick on Tanz's girl-friend, wouldn't you! If he gets his teeth into you even Kahlenberge won't be able to do much. It won't be just a question of a posting to the front and a hero's death. You'll probably wind up in front of a court martial."

"Don't swig the lot," said Hartmann dully, reaching for the bottle.

"If I were you I'd beat it."

"But you're not me, Otto."

"No, thank God. I'll burn a couple of candles in Notre Dame the next chance I get. But what I wanted to say was —if you do a bunk, with or without a pass, you can rely on me to look after Raymonde properly for you."

"Get lost," said Hartmann.

"With pleasure. But just in case you put your foot in it again, forget you ever saw me. I haven't said a word, understand?"

"All right, as far as I'm concerned you don't exist."

"Fine," said Otto. "You're a real pal. And talking about pals, could you slip me a franc or two?"

Hartmann produced General Tanz's wallet and took out two notes. Otto gave an appreciative whistle, clapped Hartmann on the shoulder and stuffed the money into his pocket.

"One more question, old cock—man to man: did you really lay her?"

"Push off!" Hartmann shouted furiously. "Or I'll tell them everything you've said."

"I'm going," said Otto, clambering into his Mercedes. "All the best, old cock. You're going to need all the luck you can get!"

"Abnormal situations," Inspector Prévert declared suavely, as though he were offering someone a glass of vintage Meursault, "call for abnormal measures."

Having bearded Lieutenant-Colonel Grau in his office, Prévert now gazed about him with undisguised interest. He surveyed the naked and unassuming expanse of wood and cement, the almost monastic simplicity of the furniture, the charts and plans, standing orders and troop dispositions covering the walls—and, in the midst of it all, Grau, illumined by the harsh glare of an overhead light.

"A room like this in the heart of Paris!" mused Prévert. "I'd scarcely have believed it. Even our suburban police stations look luxurious by comparison."

"I'm a symbol," Grau said, "and this office is my shop-window. Believe me, creating this atmosphere of shabby insignificance was quite a work of art—but then I'm a stage designer *manqué*. However, knowing you as I do, monsieur, I realize that you didn't come here to discuss office décor. What can I do for you?"

"I've been busy since we last met. I couldn't resist taking a closer look at General Kahlenberge."

Grau nodded without the least sign of surprise. He picked up a file lying on his desk, extracted a sheet of paper and passed it to Prévert. Headed "Visit of Prévert to Kahlenberge", it gave the exact date, time, place and duration of the interview.

"So you're having me watched." Prévert smiled wryly.

"I'm only playing the new party game. It's all the rage these days."

"Am I on your black list?"

"But of course, Monsieur Prévert—though I have a number of black lists, as you can imagine. You don't figure on all of them."

"Excellent," said Prévert. "It all confirms my theory about

you. If the conspiracy comes off you'll support it indirectly, probably remaining under cover for the time being until the new line-up becomes clearer. However things turn out, all you'll have to do is select the appropriate list and emerge on the right side. Am I right?"

Grau gave a faint smile. "That's your theory, is it? I expect you think I'm playing a pretty shabby game."

"I don't pass moral judgments, Colonel. All I want to do is avoid burning my fingers on your belated display of patriotism. I'm a Frenchman and a policeman. I've no wish to die for the greater glory of the German Reich. I want to insure myself."

"Against all contingencies, if I understand you rightly."

"Perhaps you'll understand me better if I put forward a concrete proposal. For instance, I assume that it's impracticable for you to establish direct personal contact with the conspirators. I've already done that. Why not use me as a go-between? You'll benefit whatever the outcome—and so will I, of course. If the conspirators succeed as we both earnestly hope, even if for different reasons, you'll be on the right side. If they fail, nobody will be able to prove that you ever communicated with them."

"You're wrong, Prévert. There's one man who will."

"You mean me?" Prévert sadly shook his gourd-shaped head. "You're overlooking the vital point. If any questions are asked you'll be able to say that I was supplying you with information about the conspiracy and that in this sense we've always been working together."

Grau nodded. It was an arrangement after his own heart, the sort of game which only a past master in police technique could play. It enabled one to score off the mighty, combat criminality and protect the rights of the individual without entirely sacrificing one's own personality.

Seen from that aspect, Grau and Prévert were cast in the same mould—or at least their methods were similar. First they insured themselves. Then, phase by phase, they worked out their alternative plans. Version One, directed against the conspirators, envisaged the compilation of duplicate files containing material, ideas, suggestions and views, one copy to be held by each party. The material would be clear in its implications but so phrased that it would neither facilitate nor impede any subsequent action against the conspirators.

Version Two, in favour of the conspirators, was discussed in similar detail. It entailed keeping in touch with developments but preserving enough independence to guarantee that if things went awry nothing would be lost.

"Splendid," said Prévert at the close. "I feel distinctly happier now."

"I only hope Kahlenberge's people are equally painstaking."

"If everyone were like Kahlenberge our problems would be halved."

"What about the other three or four thousand generals?" Grau asked quietly.

"Aren't you sure of them?"

"Shall we say—I'm distrustful. I know my fellow-countrymen. But I can tell you one thing: if they fall down on the job again it will be for the last time. They'll have proved, contrary to intention, that the German soldier has forfeited every last scrap of self-respect. That's something no one will ever forgive them for, and I'll be one of the first to say so aloud when the day comes—and act accordingly. I'll spit in their faces, the cowardly, dim-witted swine."

"What a performance," Prévert murmured to himself. "I'm not sure I want to be in at the kill."

"This is nothing to do with you!" Grau snapped. "It's our business. But if you knew what some of these generals are capable of you'd lose your palate for burgundy."

Lance-Corporal Hartmann read on, fully resigned to hours of waiting. The Rue Drouot was almost deserted. On the opposite side of the street a man shuffled along in the shadow of the houses. A woman was leaning against the newspaper kiosk on the corner, haggling with her male companion in a low voice. Two cats spat at each other in the gutter, and there was a rumbling sound in the distance as of heavy freight trains on the move. All at once, whether spontaneously or in response to some external stimulus, Hartmann looked up from his book. Standing beneath the dim blue lamp outside L'Ecurie de Madeleine he saw a shadow, thin, elongated and sharply defined.

The figure raised its hand as though signalling and moved towards the Bentley. Hartmann hurriedly switched off the light and the radio and put his Balzac away. Then he pocketed his packet of cigarettes, corked the almost empty flask of Calvados and started the car. The exhaust puttered softly.

Tanz approached, silent as a shark circling a swimmer. He climbed in and slumped back on the cushions, breathing stertorously. Then he began to speak, enunciating his words with extreme care. "Move off, but keep your speed down." His voice sounded as if it had been steeped in glycerine.

Hartmann let in the clutch and the Bentley crept forward. Then he saw what he might have expected—a woman of uncertain age and medium height with blonde hair and a protuberant bust. She was standing in the entrance, watching the Bentley's approach with an air of appraisal. Her eyes glittered hungrily.

"Drive up to her, Hartmann."

Hartmann crawled the remaining thirty yards and then stopped. The Bentley stood there purring quietly. The General pushed open the off-side rear door and said: "Get in."

The woman's ample mouth emitted a shrill giggle of pleasure. Agreeably surprised and flattered, she slid on to the seat beside Tanz and began to wriggle her bottom luxuriously. The venerable Bentley creaked indignantly, and waves of strong scent assailed Hartmann's nostrils.

"Where do you live?" asked Tanz, his voice suddenly hoarse.

"Rue de Londres, just next to the Gare St. Lazare."

"I know it," said Hartmann, and trod on the accelerator.

He tried to ignore what was going on behind him, but the woman's voice, strident with artificial gaiety, kept breaking through. She was going through the usual routine. Tanz could call her "*tu*" if he liked. He needn't be shy with her—she was the broadminded type. Live and let live was her motto. Eat, drink and be merry—tomorrow might be too late. Would he like to know her name? Should she try and guess his? Or was he one of the strong, silent sort? Well, still waters run deep, etc., etc.

"Later," said Tanz. He sounded as if he were engaged in some form of violent physical exercise.

Hartmann glanced in the driving-mirror. Tanz was sitting stiffly in the extreme right-hand corner of the car while the woman sprawled snugly and expectantly across the seat. She had a mottled, coarse-looking face with lips like slabs of moist red rubber and small porcine eyes. Even she seemed reluctant to force her attentions on Tanz unbidden.

"You're different," she told him confidentially. "It's a long time since I met someone with a chauffeur."

"Watch the road," said Tanz. He might have been talking either to her or to Hartmann.

The woman leant forward, and Hartmann smelt a thick animal stench of perfume, sweat and alcohol. He put his foot hard down in an instinctive attempt to leave it behind. The Bentley raced through the darkened streets of Paris, far exceeding the regulation speed limit.

"Slower," the woman said in his ear. He felt her fingers caressing the nape of his neck and bent forward to avoid them. "We're nearly there. That's it—the grey house on the corner."

Hartmann pulled into the kerb, jumped out and hurried round to open the door. The woman got out first, followed by Tanz. "Where, exactly?" he asked.

"On the third floor. It's really cosy. You'll like it, no one'll disturb us."

"Go on ahead," he told her. He looked round him as though checking military dispositions. House fronts with blacked out windows like blind eyes, an unobstructed stretch of street and in the background a towering pile of steel, glass and concrete thickly coated with a layer of soot—the Gare St. Lazare—all veiled in the numbing inactivity of the night.

"Wait here, Hartmann," said Tanz. His eyes glowed phosphorescently and his face had become the same chiselled mask which he seemed to wear every hour of the day. "I may need you. Watch the windows on the third floor."

"Yes, sir."

Hartmann heard the woman's shrill laugh ring out once more before she disappeared into the house. Tanz followed her with the purposeful tread of an infantryman advancing to the attack. Then the front door closed behind him with a dull thud.

Hartmann lit a cigarette. He saw a narrow chink of light appear at a third-floor window, then another in the window next to it. From this he deduced that they had reached her flat and gone into an inner room—presumably the bedroom.

Strolling back to the car, he drank what was left of the Calvados and lit a second cigarette. Then he began to pace up and down, automatically, as though he was on guard duty and the Bentley was his sentry-box.

Although he felt tempted to brood on Ulrike's relationship with him and his relationship with Raymonde, he forced himself to banish distracting, titalating thoughts of that kind. Instead, he concentrated on Tanz. He tried to picture what was happening behind the darkened window on the third floor, but found it impossible. Grotesque images flitted erratically through his head.

He gazed up at the third-floor windows as though they might provide the answer to a riddle. Then he saw the strip of light widen as a curtain was pushed to one side. A familiar silhouette appeared, a stark black shape not unlike the dummy figures painted on pistol or machine-gun targets.

"Are you there?" Tanz inquired in a low but penetrating undertone.

"Yes, sir."

"Come up here."

Hartmann wasted no time. Taking a torch from the car, he walked over to the house, opened the door and started up the stairs. The beam of the torch shone on walls which looked as though they had been soiled by generations of grubby, sweaty hands.

Then he saw the silhouette again, outlined against a rectangle of light. Tanz was waiting for him in the doorway of the woman's flat.

"Come in," he said.

Tanz appeared to be smiling. His face looked drained of tension, as it might have done at the successful conclusion of a hard-fought engagement. His eyes were filled with the self-absorbed, almost blissful languor of someone who has weathered a storm, and his gesture of invitation had the relaxed grace of a dancer who has just performed his *pièce de rêsistance* before an appreciative audience.

"Take a look next door."

Hartmann obediently crossed the living-room, noting the old and shabby furniture with its thick powdering of dust and the flowered wallpaper hanging in shreds from the walls. The curtains were threadbare and the carpet so worn that only remnants of its original pattern survived.

"Next door," Tanz insisted.

Hartmann had to fight his way through a wall of thick, viscous air. He was met by the same foetid aroma of cheap perfume and stale sweat which he had smelt in the car, only infinitely stronger. His eyes focussed on a large dishevelled bed lit by the rosy glow of a standard lamp. On the bed, like meat displayed on a butcher's slab, lay a tumbled mound of flesh.

It was as white as the belly of a fish but interspersed with thick streaks of crimson. Starting at the throat, the deep gashes progressed across the breasts and belly and merged into an oozing crimson mess between the thighs.

"Have a good look," said Tanz, "but don't stand there too long. I've got to talk to you."

Hartmann backed away from the corpse and out of the bedroom with dragging feet, pursued by the stench of blood. Queasily, he tripped over a mat and staggered sideways, colliding with the door-post like a sack of flour. Feeling a dull throb of pain he clutched his head, and his hand came away covered in warm, sticky moisture. He had struck his temple and broken the skin. It was only a superficial cut, but the pain was enough to clear his head and jolt him out of an attack of anguished retching.

"Sit down," said Tanz. "You look like a drowned rat. But then you're a sensitive lad. It doesn't take much to turn your stomach."

General Tanz sat in the middle of the living-room, picked out with painful clarity by the centre light. He sat there as erect as ever, but there was something almost nonchalant about his contented smile. Nestling elegantly in his right hand was an automatic—a 7.65 mm. Walther.

"You really ought to sit down," he repeated, and this time it was an order. He indicated a chair with the hand that held the pistol, then pointed to a bottle and two glasses lying on the table between them. "Have a drink, Hartmann. I can see you need a pick-me-up."

Hartmann groped for the bottle with a trembling hand. He filled one of the glasses and drained it. His stomach heaved, but he poured himself a second glass and swallowed its contents at a single gulp. Looking at Tanz, he saw that the General was noting his every movement with an attentive smile. A wave of indignation surged through him.

"So now you know what's happened, Hartmann. It's obviously made a deep impression on you. Why, may I ask? Is your experience of death really so limited? I've seen a man staggering across a field of stubble with his entrails hanging out, trying desperately to escape from enemy rifle fire. He fell over, wriggled like a worm and tried to get up, over and over again, but he became entangled in his own guts. So he tore them out with his bare hands, screaming like a wounded horse. He was the only person I ever really loved. When I reached him he was past recognizing me. He died babbling a woman's name—the name of a woman I regarded as a whore."

"What has that got to do with what happened here?"

"It happened."

"But why, why?"

"Must you have an explanation, Hartmann? It happened, that's all. There were a number of reasons, I've no doubt, but it was war which activated them. That's probably part of the price we have to pay for war. A lot of people have to pay one way or another, often with their lives. Human beings have no control over natural phenomena."

Tanz delivered this statement as though he were reading out an operational order. His voice preserved its cool, matter-of-fact timbre, but the frozen fixity of his smile had become tinged with melancholy.

"That may be one explanation," he said, delicately caressing the pistol in his right hand with the fingers of his left. "There must be others, but why should I bore myself and you with them? Let's stick to facts and not waste time on unnecessary speculation. It has happened, and not for the first time. Months or years hence it may happen again, but there's no point in thinking about that now. Pour yourself another glass, Hartmann. You may smoke too, if you like —it won't disturb me. Nothing disturbs me any longer. I feel fresh as a daisy. Take a look at my hands." He held them out. "Steady as a rock, aren't they? You may also have noticed that I'm not drinking or smoking. I don't need to any more, nor shall I for a long time to come, I hope."

Hartmann stared at the General as though he were seeing him for the first time. Tanz's renowned sang-froid was complete and his manner was a combination of rocklike inflexibility and elemental calm. Under other circumstances

Hartmann might have found it impressive, but nothing could banish his memory of the corpse in the next room.

"A dead body like that one," Tanz said coolly, "will probably attract a certain amount of attention even at a time like the present—quite unjustifiably, in my view. Who was the woman, after all? Just a worthless, slatternly, degenerate whore, a piece of human flotsam. During the last moments of her life she served a certain purpose, but our age has witnessed a million deaths more deplorable than hers. Can't you see that?"

"No," said Hartmann.

"You will," Tanz assured him. "There are bound to be inquiries. That could be embarrassing, though not necessarily dangerous. However, there's always a chance that unwelcome witnesses will come forward. The very fact that the Bentley may have been seen could cause complications. That's why—and I've weighed my decision very carefully—we're going to leave some clear and comparatively straightforward clues. Can you guess what their implication will be?"

"It's a clear-cut case."

"To us, Hartmann, yes. Not to anyone else."

Tanz raised the pistol and peered at it, but the muzzle pointed at Hartmann. "Do you recall a question I put to you earlier today? I asked you which was more important—to the army, the Führer, Germany, anyone—a general or a lance-corporal."

"And I said: a general." Hartmann's gorge rose. He felt on the point of choking and had to fight hard to overcome the sensation. "But now, after this, I can only say: the general was—*was!*—more important. Or rather, I thought so at the time."

"You're mistaken," Tanz said amiably, "and it won't be long before you see your mistake. When that time comes you'll do precisely what I expect of you and accept responsibility for this business."

"Never!" cried Hartmann, shaking with impotent rage. "Never! It was a bestial, abominable murder, and you're the one who'll pay for it."

General Tanz leant back slightly, looking as if he might burst out laughing at any moment. He was apparently incapable of any such outward expression of emotion, but it was evident that he was being racked by a spasm of violent, almost painful amusement. His blue eyes sparkled like a sunlit northern sea.

"How little you know me!" he said. "And how greatly you overestimate the strength of your own position. I like you, Hartmann, I find you congenial and I appreciate your pleasant disposition. We have spent two interesting and enjoyable days together. Our visit to the Impressionists in the Jeu de Paume was an event in itself. You have looked after me with tact and discretion, hence my forbearance. I should hate to have to put a bullet through your handsome but stupid head."

Hartmann shrank back in his chair. The graze on his forehead stung violently as rivulets of perspiration trickled down his scalp. His palms were sweating freely and he breathed through his mouth.

"Try to collect your scattered wits, Hartmann," Tanz told him kindly. "As I said, the surest method of avoiding prolonged and embarrassing inquiries is to provide some unambiguous clues. I have already made certain arrangements and shall shortly complete them. My original plan was simply to shoot you out of hand. It would have been only too easy to explain that you had deserted, taking my car and briefcase with you, that I followed you here, caught you red-handed and shot you in self-defence."

"And you think people would have believed you, just like that?"

"Naturally. I'm a general. Who or what are you?"

Hartmann shivered as though smitten with an ague. "You won't get away with it, not this way."

"You overrate the importance of a lance-corporal, Hartmann."

"I'll deny the whole thing."

"Dead men can't deny anything."

"But they'll make inquiries. They'll find out that this woman was at Madeleine's before she was murdered and that you spoke to her. A place like that is always packed with people. Someone's bound to have seen you together."

Tanz raised the hand that held the pistol. His smile grew more sombre and a look of indulgent contempt flitted across his features. "Do you take me for a fool, Hartmann? I must confess that I find it a displeasing idea. You surely know the form in such establishments. There's no need for any lengthy discussion. You just raise your thumb, that's all. I didn't exchange a single word with the creature. She was sitting three tables away from me. No one noticed me make any sort of rendezvous with her."

Hartmann reached for the bottle. In the middle of the movement, he stiffened, remembering with dismay that it bore his finger-prints. So did the glass and probably other objects in the room as well. What was more, there would be blood on the door-frame where he had hit his head.

"I told you they would find clues, Hartmann." The General spoke with quiet triumph. His usually masklike features had become endowed with expression, his eyes sparkled with life and his voice conveyed emotion. He seemed to have emerged from a deep and lasting state of lethargy. "But that's not all. Earlier on, while you were alone in the restaurant at Versailles, I removed your papers from the glove compartment of the car. Your pass is hidden somewhere next door, somewhere where the police will find it. That's just one of many clues, all of which will be supported and corroborated by my own testimony."

A cloying stench of blood came from the next room, so penetrating that Hartmann half expected to see a sticky red stream oozing across the floor towards him. Numb with horror and fatigue, he closed his eyes.

"It's up to you," said the General. He sat there like a panther crouching for the kill, the muzzle of his pistol levelled at Hartmann's head. "Either I shoot you or you make a run for it."

Hartmann heard himself say: "I'll try."

"Good." Tanz nodded contentedly. "That's much the best solution—and far pleasanter for me personally. As I told you before, I've grown to like you. You weren't perfect, of course. You even had the audacity to intrude into my private life. Don't imagine that anything escapes me. I know all about your affair with Ulrike von Seydlitz-Gabler, though it's a matter of complete indifference to me."

Hartmann stared at the pistol without answering.

"Get away from here, Hartmann—as far away as possible. Go to ground somewhere. You can have the money in my wallet. You can even have the Bentley. You're already wearing civilian clothes and you've got nearly a whole night ahead of you. Make the most of it."

"What about you?"

"I shall take a little stroll and then go to bed. I shan't notice your absence officially until tomorrow morning. I'll say that I dismissed you on our return from Versailles this evening and that you haven't reported for duty. There will naturally be inquiries, though I can't say what their immediate result will be. It probably depends how soon this—" he indicated the bedroom—"is discovered and how quickly the police get to work. But now get going, Hartmann. You're wasting valuable time."

Hartmann walked to the door, then paused and looked back into the room. "You really think you'll get away with it?"

"I've already done so. You're the one whose life is in jeopardy."

INTERIM REPORT

DEPOSITIONS, COMMENTS, REPORTS, CONJECTURES AND ASSERTIONS CONCERNING THE EVENTS OF THE NIGHT 19TH-20TH JULY 1944

Alexandre Petit, at the time in question a waiter at the Boule d'Or in Versailles; now—sixteen years later—head waiter at Chez Pierre (Mediterranean specialities) in the Avenue Victor Hugo, Paris:

"Even in those days I used to divide people into three categories: those who enjoyed eating, those who ate a lot, and those who enjoyed eating a lot. I regarded anyone who didn't fall into one of those three classes as ill-bred.

"The guest in the pearl-grey suit, whom I still remember to this day, probably belonged to the third category. He ate with what might be described as fervour. I heard the man with him address him respectfully as '*Herr General*'.

"My recollection of the other individual is far less favourable. He drank Vichy water and guzzled a quantity of kitchen waste, commonly known as sandwiches. I was forced to conclude that he was a highly uncultured and inferior form of life. The General, on the other hand . . ."

Communication received from Frau Wilhelmine von Seydlitz-Gabler:

"I consider it an impertinence of you to pry into our past. Naturally we have nothing to hide, but we find it repugnant to assist notorious subversives and pathological muck-rakers in their unsavoury work.

"I will tell you this much: if any degraded literary hack dares to libel us we shall institute proceedings against him. In particular, we shall contest the insidious and malicious allegation that a personal or intimate relationship existed between ourselves and General Tanz—or was even contemplated.

"My daughter, who is now a married woman with two fine children and lives abroad in an allied country, is immune to any such denigrating and slanderous insinuations. But I give you fair warning—my husband is on intimate terms with the Minister of Justice and is fully able to defend our daughter's honour—and our own."

Madeleine V., formerly the proprietress of L'Ecurie de Madeleine in the Rue Drouot and now manageress of an international art agency with an office in the Champs-Elysées:

"A *boîte* is a *boîte*, not a Sunday school. Anyone who comes in, orders something to drink and pays for it, is a customer. Some customers are male, others female. What men and women do to each other doesn't concern the proprietor—so long as they don't actually do it on the dance floor.

"That's just what I told the police at the time. The Stable was always packed. It was a popular place. My wine merchant, who was under a personal obligation to me, made sure that the drink never ran out. There were always barrels of Bordeaux. Did I ever have anything to do with a general—on the premises, you mean? It's possible. Ministers came sometimes, not to mention prominent painters and authors.

"Yvonne—the girl from the Rue de Londres? Yes, she was a regular customer of mine. Not what you'd call a pin-up, but a willing girl and extremely good value for money. She disappeared suddenly that evening, but for the life of me I couldn't tell you when and who with. Excuse me, won't you? I'm rather busy."

Otto the Fat, clerk and confidant of General Kahlenberge:

"Don't you believe it, old cock! Of course we painted the town red occasionally—we were in Paris, after all. But always within limits, mind, so have a care! Don't go saying anything you can't prove.

"Why should I waste my time talking about Hartmann? What's the point? I'm not a historian or a fortune-teller. We got pissed together sometimes. Anything the matter with that? There you are, then. That's all there was to it.

"I'm ready to stand up and swear I never told Hartmann

he was for the high jump. Everything was correct and above board between us. There wasn't any question of threats and so on. Hartmann just hopped it. Why, God only knows."

M. Paul Victor Magron, formerly a detective-inspector in the homicide division of the Paris police, now a chief inspector in the South of France:

"War is to crime what the coming of spring is to a garden, if you'll pardon the poetic simile.

"Please don't expect me to remember every detail, monsieur. Prostitution paid enormous dividends at the time and the mortality rate among *filles de joie* was correspondingly high.

"As usual, prostitutes got themselves murdered far oftener than housewives or office girls. The commonest motives were greed or revenge, though there were also abnormal crimes which could not be classified as sexual murders proper. All such cases were routine, so to speak. However, the murder in the Rue de Londres had certain unusual features. All crimes of violence are inhuman, monsieur, but this one was nothing short of bestial. What was more, suspicion fell on a member of the former German Wehrmacht.

"Thanks to that, the case was taken out of my hands. I was only too glad to obey instructions. I passed on the particulars to the official responsible for maintaining contact between the French and German authorities.

"Did I hear you mention the name Prévert? Well, monsieur, it was you who did so, not me."

Colonel Martin Volges, Army Medical Corps, retd., formerly attached to the Nibelungen Division and now chief medical officer at a Hamburg clinic:

"I'm a specialist in organic diseases. I also have a knowledge of surgery, but I have never devoted any time to the study of psychiatry, psychoanalysis or related subjects. I think it only fair to stress this.

"I cannot claim that General Tanz was ever one of my patients. As far as I am aware, he flatly refused all medical treatment. General Tanz consulted me on only a few occasions —five at most—and at no time did I subject him to an exhaustive physical examination. He merely told me that he had been suffering from severe headaches and recurrent sleeplessness, so I confined myself to prescribing the appropriate medicaments. Since I was never in a position to conduct a full examination I must decline to make any further comment. Subject to that proviso, however, I can state that General Tanz enjoyed what might have been described, under prevailing circumstances, as normal health. I further state that I had neither occasion nor cause to believe that General Tanz showed symptoms of any unusual ailment."

Captain Kahlert on the subject of Lance-Corporal Hartmann:

". . . I had abundant and repeated opportunities to observe and assess Lance-Corporal Hartmann, who was directly under my command. As his immediate superior, it was one of my duties to submit official reports on him. Their gist was roughly as follows:

"Hartmann, Rainer, is an extremely intelligent and adaptable soldier. He is versatile, possesses a pleasant appearance and may be described as well-read, even cultured. He is hardworking, but careless and not endowed with any great sense of duty. He might even be described as unstable.

"His character is not easy to define, nor does it seem noticeably well-formed. He lacks toughness and drive and would be incapable of shouldering any major responsibilities. His soldierly qualities are far from developed.

"It would not, therefore, be advisable to entrust him with special duties of an exacting nature. It is also conceivable that his unbridled imagination could lead him to make statements which, while they might be unconscious exaggerations, might equally be lies.

"On the basis of this assessment, H. must be regarded as an unreliable individual and an awkward subordinate. Consequently, caution is indicated."

Extract from a letter written by ex-Lieutenant-Colonel Sandauer:

". . . I must confess not without a profound sense of shock, that your allegations have shaken me to the core. I shall resist the temptation to ask you how you have the effrontery to make them. Instead, I shall take into consideration your evident conviction that you are acting in good faith, and try, with all the tolerance at my command, to answer your questions as objectively as possible.

"First, kindly note the following: I should never have taken it upon myself to ignore, let alone hush up, any suspicious or pathological behaviour. It necessarily follows that I was never aware of anything which might point to behaviour of that sort. If I had been, my conscience would have compelled me to intervene regardless of the consequences.

"The only possible inference is that spiteful and malicious tongues have been at work—or rather, that one man's pathological condition has prompted him to impute the same condition to another. I have no idea where your information originates, but I am convinced that this is a case where 'Stop thief!' is being shouted by the perpetrator of the theft.

"I implore you to think again before you proceed to cast aspersions on the honour of a veteran military commander. There is such a thing as a duty to history. Woe betide the man who tries to evade that duty, especially if he lives in Germany and means to go on living there."

Extracts from two letters taken at random from several dozen replies received by the author. The first was written by ex-grenadier Matthuber of the Nibelungen Division, the second by a fellow-grenadier of the same division named Biermann:

". . . I only hope you realize the truth. That man was war personified. He had eyes like a snake. We used to tremble when he looked at us. Sometimes we were absolutely petrified with fear. . . ."

". . . I can only warn you! Don't trample on our sacred beliefs. He was a hero, the sort of man whom only the Third Reich could have produced. We went through hell for him and we'd be ready to do so again. . . ."

7

Diary of a day in Paris; 20th July 1944

Circa 1.15 a.m.

Murder in the Rue de Londres, estimated on the basis of subsequent medical findings to have occurred between midnight and 3 a.m.

General Kahlenberge was making renewed efforts to enlist his G.O.C.'s support for the conspiracy against Hitler and his henchmen. Von Seydlitz-Gabler was being as evasive as ever.

Frau Wilhelmine was sitting up waiting for Ulrike to return.

Inspector Prévert and Lieutenant-Colonel Grau had ironed out their differences so successfully that they were now indulging in an exchange of views on red wine, horses and women.

Lieutenant-Colonel Sandauer, G.S.O.1 of the Nibelungen Division, was poring over his reorganization plans.

Otto the Fat was drunkenly—and fruitlessly—endeavouring to seduce Fräulein Melanie Neumaier, the G.O.C.'s lady-in-waiting.

Sergeant Stoss, General Tanz's driver, had been laying siege to Raymonde in the Mocambo Bar, but had now given up and was applying himself to a bottle of *crème de menthe.*

The Allies had penetrated the Normandy front at several new points. In a month's time Paris would no longer be in German hands.

In the East, Russian armies were moving inexorably towards the frontiers of the Third Reich.

A briefcase containing a time-bomb was standing in a certain Colonel Stauffenberg's room in Berlin.

Hitler was trying to sleep.

Hour by hour, thousands of soldiers and civilians were vanishing into the insatiable maw of total war. Thousands more were begetting new life.

Sergeant Engel of the Abwehr, who had just completed one of his nocturnal interrogations, was in a philosophical mood. "Why do human beings cling to life?" he mused. "Probably because they haven't a clue what it's all about."

2.21 *a.m.*

Lance-Corporal Hartmann emerged from the house in the Rue de Londres. He stood forlornly in the darkness for a minute or two, then got into the Bentley and drove off in the direction of the Champs-Elysées.

Abandoning the car there, he made his way on foot to the street in which the Mocambo Bar stood. He stationed himself in a doorway opposite the establishment and waited. A glance at his watch told him that if all went well he would not have to wait much longer. He lit a cigarette, shielding it in the hollow of his hand. The chill night air made him shiver.

He began to count the trees in the street, then the houses, then the windows. He noted numbers and forgot them immediately. Then he started counting again, determined not to think about what had happened.

Shortly after three o'clock the last customers left the Mocambo Bar, gently prodded by the bouncer. Some slipped away like shadows, others loitered to discuss weighty matters in loud, drunken voices and one man began to sing, but they all eventually vanished into the darkness.

Except for one hulking figure standing alone in the middle of the street, swaying slightly but solid as a baulk of timber. Like Hartmann, Sergeant Stoss was waiting for Raymonde.

A quarter of an hour later Raymonde appeared, having made up her books for the night. Stoss bore down on her, cooing like a loftful of pigeons. When his blandishments had no effect he started making massive bids: a hundred marks—three hundred marks—five tins of canned food and a hundred marks—three tins and two hundred marks—seven tins and . . .

Raymonde shoved him in the chest. He staggered backwards and sat down hard on the cobbles. Still sitting there, he began to curse vehemently, pouring out a stream of unflattering epithets of which "dirty French tart" was one of the mildest.

Raymonde hurried off and Hartmann ran after her on tiptoe, hugging the walls. After three hundred yards he caught up with her. She flung her arms round his neck.

"Can I come with you?" he asked.

"Of course."

"Can I stay with you?"

"The whole night?" she asked hopefully.

"Maybe even longer."

"What are we waiting for?" said Raymonde happily, tugging at his arm.

3.00 *a.m.*–7.00 *a.m.*

Death may be the great leveller, but sleep is not. If there is a sleep of the just it is only logical that there should be a sleep of the unjust. There are numerous other categories as well.

Frau Wilhelmine slept the sleep of the watchdog. Ulrike dozed uneasily, either because her conscience pricked her or because the thick *duvet* on her bed was too hot for her. General von Seydlitz-Gabler sweated profusely and dribbled into his pillow. Kahlenberg tossed and turned, dreaming of labyrinthine intrigues. Grau lay curled up like a worm. Prévert stared wearily into the darkness. General Tanz lay supine, deathly still and smiling faintly like a marble effigy on some medieval tomb. Hartmann clung to Raymonde with a desperation which Raymonde was only too glad to construe as passionate abandon. When they finally slept it was as though they were one body.

The summer night was warm and the sky clear as glass. It promised to be a hot and sultry day.

7.03 *a.m.*

General Tanz woke up as though roused by a mental alarm clock. He sprang out of bed with his brain refreshed, skin clear and movements supple and relaxed. He performed some callisthenics, surveying the radiance of the morning from his window as he did so. Then he telephoned the porter.

Question: where was Hartmann, his orderly?

Answer: the porter had gone to wake him at the normal time but found his room empty. There was no indication as to where else he could be. His bed had not been slept in.

Question: was the car—a Bentley—in the courtyard? Outside the hotel? In the garage? Parked in the Place Vendôme? In a side street?

Answer, half an hour later: the said Bentley was not in any of the places mentioned nor anywhere else in the vicinity of the hotel.

There followed a lengthy telephone conversation with Lieutenant-Colonel Sandauer. Tanz reported that Hartmann and the Bentley were nowhere to be found. Sandauer was thunderstruck. No one had yet uttered the word "deserter," but Sandauer jotted it down on the pad lying in front of him.

Tanz told Sandauer that whatever lay at the bottom of it all he relied on him to make the necessary inquiries. He was feeling full of beans, he announced, and intended to cut short his leave at once. He asked for Stoss to be sent over with his staff car, adding that he greatly looked forward to getting down to work with his men again.

8.19 *a.m.*

A man named Jean Marceau entered the house in the Rue de Londres. Marceau acted as pimp to the woman on the third floor and had come to collect his cut, which usually amounted to fifty per cent. His women were selected for their efficiency and high return on capital, hence his appearance of solid prosperity. His official profession: commodity broker.

Marceau was aghast at the slaughter in the bedroom and would have beaten a hasty retreat, but since the concierge had seen him come in there was nothing for it but to do the right thing and call the police.

In less than half an hour Detective-Inspector Paul Magron of the Sûreté arrived with a small band of assistants. He recognized Marceau's function without difficulty, examined the body and soon discovered a piece of paper under the commode by the bed.

This document, obviously a form of military permit, was written in German.

Magron pocketed it, happy in the knowledge that once routine inquiries were complete he would be able to hand the case over to Inspector Prévert, the connecting link between the French and German authorities. No one was better qualified to handle it.

9.02 *a.m.*

Kahlenberge called on von Seydlitz-Gabler.

"Something's come up which could make things extremely awkward," he reported. "Hartmann seems to have vanished into thin air. He didn't turn up for duty this morning, and Tanz apparently sees this as a heaven-sent opportunity to cut short his leave. He's planning to return to his division."

"I knew it!" exclaimed von Seydlitz-Gabler. "My wife warned us that something like this would happen, if you'll remember. I thoroughly distrusted Hartmann myself. Well, Kahlenberge, your little plan has landed us in a nice mess, I must say."

"But the arrangement was made with your approval, sir."

"Only because I saw no reason to doubt your usually excellent judgment. I take it for granted that you weigh your advice carefully before giving it. In this instance I appear to have been wrong."

Kahlenberge was visibly annoyed. "I suggest we institute an official search for Hartmann."

"Do as you think fit," snapped von Seydlitz-Gabler. "But don't forget: it'll be your fault if General Tanz starts treading on our toes. My plan was a good one. With Tanz out of the way, reorganization could proceed according to plan. Now the ball's in the air again. He'll go on battering away at us until he's squeezed us dry of reserves—and all because you, Kahlenberge, made a palpably ill-advised choice. God knows where it'll lead to."

9.59 *a.m.*

The battalion commanders of the Nibelungen Division had turned out in full force to hear General Tanz deliver his first situation report since returning from leave.

They stood there like statues as General Tanz entered his temporary office, a studiously spartan room with whitewashed walls and bare wooden furniture, unrelieved by any splash of colour except the red and blue markings on the maps displayed for inspection.

General Tanz was a picture of masterful energy. He radiated enthusiasm. His eyes had a glint of newly whetted knife-points in a ray of sunlight and his voice filled the room like the middle register of an electronic organ.

"Headquarters gave us three weeks to patch up the Division. My G.S.O.1 estimated that it would take two weeks. I put the time at ten days. Well, we're going to beat that. During the course of this afternoon I shall start inspecting units for combat readiness. Stand by for my arrival."

10.10 *a.m.*

A telephone rang on a desk in an office building in the Rue de Surène. The desk belonged to Colonel Finckh, Chief of Staff to the Quartermaster-General, Western Command.

Picking up the receiver, Finckh heard the exchange announce a call from Zossen, near Berlin, headquarters of General Wagner, Quartermaster-General of the Army. Then an unfamiliar voice said: "Exercise."

Nothing more.

The Colonel was hearing the word for the third time in a fortnight. He had already heard it on the 6th and 11th of July, and he knew what it meant.

As an initiate into the inner circle of the conspiracy, Finckh realized that his one-eyed, one-armed friend Colonel Stauffenberg was already on his way by air to Wolfschanze, the so-called Leader's "lair" in East Prussia.

Hitler's end seemed imminent.

11.15 *a.m.*

Inspector Prévert began his regular daily conference at the Sûreté. Persons present: an inspector of the secret police, a municipal police officer, a detective-inspector from the criminal branch and two officers on special duties. Purpose of the meeting: a review of the general situation with special reference to any points which might have a bearing on Franco-German co-operation.

It was extremely rare for surprising or unusual matters to be raised at such meetings, and no one expected to hear anything very startling or sensational. The men round the table were familiar with every form of brutality, intrigue, vileness, perversion, violence and homicide.

"There's been a murder in the Rue de Londres," reported the detective-inspector on duty. "Inquiries are being pursued by Inspector Magron. The victim was a woman of about thirty—probably a prostitute. Preliminary findings indicate that the murderer was a sexual maniac. A number of prints have been found."

"Anything special about it?" Prévert asked mechanically.

"A sort of identity card in German, giving the number of a car and the name of its driver. It's stamped by the issuing authority, but I can't identify the signature."

Prévert said: "Let's see it."

The detective-inspector passed it across to him. Only one unusual feature caught Prévert's eye, and that was the signature. It read: "Kahlenberge, Lieutenant-General, Chief of Staff."

11.47 *a.m.*

Lance-Corporal Rainer Hartmann gazed at the sloping ceiling above his head. It was decorated with pictures cut from magazines. There were no illustrations of people or buildings, only woods and fields, flowers and animals.

He felt the warm body lying next to his. He knew every detail of it and he seldom tired of telling himself how enticingly lovely it was, but his blood was cold now, even though the sultry summer heat beat on the shuttered windows of the little room.

"What's the matter?" Raymonde asked softly. "There's something different about you—I can feel it."

"Did I disappoint you?"

"No, no, it's never been so good with us before." She bent over him, nuzzling his ear with her lips, and whispered tenderly: "I could have died with happiness."

Hartmann closed his eyes. "What has dying got to do with happiness?" he asked bitterly.

Raymonde sat up and looked at him. "There is something the matter. What is it?"

"I'm what they call a deserter."

"What do I care?"

"You're not worried?"

"Don't be silly!" Raymonde said firmly. "You're here with me—that's all I care about."

"Can I stay?"

"As long as you like—for the rest of your life, as far as I'm concerned."

Hartmann's expression did not alter, but his eyes flinched

rom her look of tender concern. "They'll come looking for ne."

"They won't find you."

"What about the others in the house?"

"It doesn't matter to them who I live with. They won't noop on us. When a man and a woman are together all the ime it's as good as being married—or it's a start, anyway. They'll all understand."

"I've got to hide, Raymonde."

"That's all right with me," she told him, smiling. "I'm not o keen to show you off in front of people, you know. More han half the world's population are women! I'll keep you all o myself for as long as possible."

12.30 *p.m.*

In answer to an urgent summons, General von Seydlitz-Gabler went to see his wife at the Hotel Excelsior. He found her in the drawing-room of her suite with Ulrike. Both women ooked resentful.

"I'm very disappointed, Herbert!" remonstrated Frau Wilhelmine. "General Tanz has left the hotel without saying good-bye to us. Has he been given a new command? If so, why didn't you let me know in good time? It's not that I want o pry into official matters, but I should have been glad of a chance to clear up a few things with General Tanz in private before he left. Now the ideal moment seems to have passed."

"A combination of unfortunate circumstances," said von Seydlitz-Gabler.

"Created by you, Herbert?"

Herbert repudiated the suggestion indignantly. "It's that frightful fellow Hartmann. He's simply vanished—deserted, without a doubt. Tanz has obviously cut short his leave because Hartmann's left him in the lurch."

"Hartmann a deserter?" Frau Wilhelmine regarded her daughter's waxen face with unabashed triumph. "You see! That's the sort of man you've been consorting with! A thoroughly untrustworthy specimen—a deserter!"

1.25 *p.m.*

Prévert and Grau had left their respective offices and gone to meet each other—half way, so to speak—at the Relais Bisson, a restaurant on the Quai. Their pretext for this meeting, a plausible one, was a consignment of fresh lobsters and a bottle of Chablis. Grau had recently exploited every available opportunity to profit from Prévert's extensive knowledge of cuisine, cellar and criminal procedure.

They set to with a will, and while they were doing so Prévert asked casually: "Are you interested in murders, too, Colonel?"

"Only unusual ones."

"In our daily report, which you don't normally receive until late afternoon, as you know, you'll find a reference to a rather unusual murder. I would ask you to take special note of the case. In fact, it might even be advisable for you to take it over before the S.D. or the Gestapo get their hands on it. You see, judging by the evidence before me, I'd say that one of our mutual friends may find himself facing some awkward questions. I refer to Kahlenberge."

Grau looked up from his lobster with an expression of amazement. "General Kahlenberge?"

"A military permit was found near the body. It was made out to a Lance-Corporal Hartmann and signed by Lieutenant General Kahlenberge. Murder complete with visiting card —rather curious, don't you agree?"

Grau sat up, his eyes alert. "It wasn't a sex murder, was it?"

It was now Prévert's turn to interrupt his intense preoccupation with his lobster. He looked genuinely surprised. "It was, but how did you know?"

"The victim was a woman," Grau said excitedly. "She was murdered and then riddled with knife-wounds like a sieve— from throat to thigh."

"That's what it says in the report. How did you get hold of it?"

Grau's voice had gone harsh. "I haven't seen the report but I know what the body looks like."

"How on earth . . ."

"I'll tell you later, Prévert." Grau pushed the remains of his lobster to one side and got up. "For the moment, take it from me that this is a most important case. The man who did it slipped through my hands once, but he won't get away a second time. It's lucky I've got you to help me, Prévert."

"It's a pleasure," said Prévert with a mixture of indulgence and curiosity. "I'll put some of my best men on to it, if you like."

"The best man!" Grau insisted with the stubborn determination of someone who will stop at nothing to gain his objective. "The best possible man—and that's you, Monsieur Prévert, you personally, backed by all the resources at our joint command. If you solve this case and bring me the man responsible you can name your own price."

"Anything?"

"Absolutely anything. A whole wagonload of French patriots, if you like."

1.50—2.07 *p.m.*

A telephone conversation between Inspector Prévert and General Kahlenberge, conducted from the porter's lodge of the hotel attached to the Relais Bisson. The house exchange was cut off and Lieutenant-Colonel Grau listened in. After a few preliminary courtesies, the following dialogue took place:

Prévert: "Do you have a Lance-Corporal Hartmann under your command—Rainer Hartmann?"

Kahlenberge: "I do."

Prévert: "Where is he now?"

Kahlenberge: "Not a clue. It's possible that he's deserted. He was given the job of escorting General Tanz, on the G.O.C.'s orders. Hartmann and Tanz were both staying at the Hotel Excelsior, but Hartmann disappeared some time last night."

Prévert: "Am I right in thinking that you issued him with a permit?"

Kahlenberge: "That's right—a permit for a requisitioned car, a Bentley. Why do you ask? Have you run him to earth somewhere?"

Prévert: "Has the car been found?"

Kahlenberge: "Not yet."

Prévert: "Where is General Tanz now?"

Kahlenberge: "With his division. But what's this all about, Prévert?"

Prévert: "I'll gladly tell you as soon as I know more details myself. May I ask whether plans for the forthcoming operation are complete yet?"

Kahlenberge: "They appear to be. It may already be under way."

Prévert: "Good. All the best, then. I'll keep in touch."

2.04 *p.m.*

Once again the Quartermaster-General's office at Zossen came on the line asking for Colonel Finckh, and once again Finckh heard the quiet, unemotional unfamiliar voice. This time it said: "Gone off." Then the 'phone went dead.

This meant that Colonel Stauffenberg's bomb had exploded, that the sands had run out at last, that the Führer was no more.

Why wait any longer?

2.08 *p.m.*

Inspector Prévert outlined his plan of action to Lieutenant-Colonel Grau:

"I'll look through the reports so far submitted and have a word with Detective-Inspector Magron, who has been handling the case. Then we'll inspect the scene of the crime. In the meantime we ought to look for the missing Bentley—and Hartmann too, of course."

"I'll contact the Provost Marshal and get him to authorize special patrols."

"I shall need information from Wehrmacht personnel, Hartmann's friends in particular. It's important to know who he was friendly with, what his habits were, whether he had any favourite haunts, what women he was seeing—routine questions of that nature."

"I'll put Engel on to it. He's good at that sort of thing."

"Excellent," Prévert declared. "One of my men can handle inquiries at the Hotel Excelsior, but who's going to collect statements from Tanz and the other generals?"

"I'll deal with them," Grau replied, adding grimly: "It'll be a pleasure."

"If you take my advice, Colonel, you'll wait until we've completed our preliminary investigations and have the basic facts at our finger-tips."

"Of course. But then I'll make a thorough job of it."

2.52 *p.m.*

General von Seydlitz-Gabler was resting. He had doffed his uniform jacket, pulled off his glossy shoes and opened his waist-band. He lay motionless on the bed, his slightly parted lips emitting an occasional rattling sound.

A series of loud knocks roused him from his well-earned afternoon nap. He woke up with a snort, frowning.

"I don't wish to be disturbed!" he called.

It was a vain hope. The door opened to reveal Melanie Neumaier, looking distraught. Then she was pushed almost brutally to one side and General Kahlenberge appeared. He closed the door behind him and walked swiftly to the G.O.C.'s bedside.

"The time has come," he said.

Von Seydlitz-Gabler propped himself on one elbow. He looked as exhausted as if he had just returned from a route march, but his eyes were cold and censorious.

"The time for what?"

"I've just had a personal call from Berlin, from an old and trusted friend of mine in the Bendlerstrasse. He promised to 'phone me if anything unusual occurred. According to his information, a bomb went off in the Führer's headquarters during the morning conference. They say Hitler is dead."

"Is it official?" von Seydlitz-Gabler asked.

"We're expecting code-word 'Valkyrie' at any moment."

"But you haven't received it yet, so it's not official. What do you expect me to do, Kahlenberge? Why must you insist on pestering me with vague assumptions? I badly need my afternoon sleep. Kindly bear that in mind."

3.45 *p.m.*

A preliminary conference in Inspector Prévert's office at the Sûreté. Those present: Lieutenant-Colonel Grau and Inspector Prévert. Matters under discussion:

i Aforesaid Bentley found abandoned in the Place de la Concorde by a military police patrol and taken into custody.

ii Inquiries at the Hotel Excelsior virtually useless. Impossible to check on the movements either of General Tanz or Lance-Corporal Hartmann. The porter, though willing enough, had apparently been asleep for a large proportion of the night.

iii Existing findings confirmed by further investigation at the scene of the crime. Motive for murder almost certainly sexual. Copy of particulars submitted to Abwehr, i.e., Grau.

Those corresponded in every respect to the unsolved murder in Warsaw.

iv Inquiries made by Sergeant Engel had elicited a few clues and a lot of gossip, particularly about Hartmann's so-called love-life. Two names emerged: those of Ulrike von Seydlitz-Gabler and a girl called Raymonde, the latter employed at the Mocambo Bar.

Inspector Prévert walked over to the gigantic street map of Paris which covered one entire wall of his office. He tapped two points with his fingers: the Place de la Concorde, where the Bentley had been discovered, and the Mocambo Bar, where Raymonde worked.

"Here's where we'll start," he said. "You know, Colonel, elementary reasoning turns up trumps again and again, mainly because people tend to be elementary themselves. They think and act accordingly, especially when they're in a hurry. Leave this part of it to me and concentrate on your generals."

4.06 *p.m.*

The Headquarters of the G.O.C.-in-C., France, were located in the Hotel Majestic. The conspirators waiting there included the G.O.C.-in-C. himself—General von Stülpnagel—and several members of his staff, among them Lieutenant-Colonel Cäsar von Hofacker, hub of the conspiracy in Paris.

The officers waited with pale, strained faces. No definite news had come through yet. Plans were complete, but the code-word which was to set them in motion had still not arrived.

At last Lieutenant-Colonel Hofacker was called to the telephone. Berlin was on the line. Hofacker listened with bated breath as von Stauffenberg himself gave him the news. Then he replaced the receiver and turned to the others.

"The *coup d'état* is under way. Government offices are being occupied at this moment."

4.26 *p.m.*

After a brief but vigorous interrogation of the proprietor of the Mocambo Bar, Inspector Prévert was directed to an address in the Rue de l'Université, near the Pont des Invalides. Here he climbed to the third floor, which comprised two studios and a number of attic rooms.

Leaving a police escort on the landing, Prévert entered

the room alone. As expected, he found two people inside. They were scantily dressed and looked thoroughly alarmed, though not for reasons of modesty.

"No need to get excited," Prévert told them soothingly, "I'm not from the vice squad. All the same, I'd put something on if I were you. You can catch cold even in the middle of July."

"You're in the way!" Raymonde said belligerently.

"I'm quite certain I am," agreed Prévert, "but I have a job to do, and in this particular case my activities take precedence over yours."

"I can live with whoever I please," said Raymonde, undeterred.

"But of course." Prévert smiled. "There's nothing so inalienable as the right to make a mistake."

He turned to Hartmann with an expression of endearing benevolence on his pudgy face. The young man intrigued him. "I don't suppose you want to identify yourself as Lance-Corporal Hartmann of the Wehrmacht, do you? If you did I should have to hand you over to the German authorities—and I hardly imagine you'd want me to do that."

"What do you want?" Hartmann asked.

"To begin with, I'd just like to have a chat with you—but not here. May I ask you to accompany me?"

"Over my dead body!" Raymonde cried dramatically.

Prévert's smile broadened. "If my information has any basis in fact, it might well have come to that!'"

"What if I refuse to come with you?" asked Hartmann.

"Don't worry," Prévert said encouragingly. "I have a feeling that you're over the worst. You may be luckier than you know, if anyone can be described as lucky in times like these."

5.52 *p.m.*

General von Stülpnagel, G.O.C.-in-C., France, summoned the G.O.C. of the Greater Paris area.

He said: "There's been a Gestapo *Putsch* in Berlin. The Führer has been assassinated."

The G.O.C. clicked his heels.

Any questions? No questions.

The G.O.C.-in-C. said: "You're to take the Paris S.D. into

custody. All senior officers of the S.S. must also be detained. Fire-arms are to be used in the event of resistance."

The G.O.C. took the proffered map showing the location of all S.S. and S.D. barracks, clicked his heels again, and withdrew.

5.58 *p.m.*

General Kahlenberge received more news from Berlin, again via his old and trusted friend in the Bendlerstrasse. Apparently, all was going according to plan.

Kahlenberge urgently demanded to know whom he could consult in Paris, stressing that he needed definite orders, not for himself but for his commanding officer. His friend apologized for not being sufficiently well-informed but mentioned the name Hofacker.

Kahlenberge cursed vigorously as they were cut off. He and his friends did not belong to the inner circle of the conspiracy and lacked the necessary contacts. The situation called for decisive measures, but what measures?

Faithful to his undertaking, he put through a call to Prévert and gave him the news.

Prévert promptly called Grau. "The die is cast—or whatever one usually says on such occasions. We must act accordingly. How would a trip to the provinces appeal to you? I recommend the Lyons route. They have the best chefs in France down there."

"Later!" Grau said impatiently. "At the moment wild horses wouldn't drag me away from here—let alone a *cordon bleu.*"

"Think it over carefully, Colonel, and don't take too long about it. Why stay here? The conspiracy seems to have got off to a promising start. You'd only be in the way. Why endanger yourself unnecessarily? Your best plan is to get out of the firing line. I'm going to."

"No!" exclaimed Grau, stubborn as a Provençal donkey. "I'm staying put—for the moment, anyway—and I beg you to remain here too, at least until the Rue de Londres affair has been cleared up."

"But my dear friend, don't you realize that things could become dangerous for people like us? There may be a massacre. At least let's go to ground in Paris for the next twenty-four hours. I just can't understand why you're ready to risk your neck for the sake of a comparatively straightforward murder case."

"It's anything but a straightforward murder case to me, my friend. To me it's a job that's got to be done. When I saw the first body two years ago it meant more to me than a human being who had been bestially murdered. I saw it as a symbol of degradation, a symbol of the criminal brutality which was infiltrating the nation I loved. Forgive me for sounding pompous. I just want you to know how much this means to me."

Prévert sighed. "In that case," he said laconically, "I don't suppose there's anything more I can say."

"You'll stay?"

"Perhaps, but I suggest we keep on the move. It would be foolhardy to sit around in our offices waiting to be picked up. You know at least three places where I can be reached. I've got a couple of your telephone numbers. Let's try our luck. One more thing: Lance-Corporal Hartmann is locked up in a cell at the Sûireté. He's not ready to talk yet, but it can only be a matter of minutes. I'll keep you posted."

6.08 *p.m.*

The code-word "Valkyrie" reached von Seydlitz-Gabler's headquarters. As soon as the signal came through, Kahlenberge hurried in to see the G.O.C.

"Now it's official!" he said.

"Are you sure there's no mistake?" von Seydlitz-Gabler asked apprehensively.

"It's here in black and white."

Von Seydlitz-Gabler squared his shoulders. "Well, an order's an order. There are no two ways about it. But I insist on being informed immediately if the order is rescinded."

Kahlenberge at once alerted all units within the Corps, including the Nibelungen Division. In doing so, he alerted General Tanz. Lieutenant-Colonel Sandauer, imperturbable as ever, asked for more details.

Once Kahlenberge had told him what he knew, all Sandauer had to do was to consult the carefully compiled list of Divisional emergency procedures. Under it, General Tanz's division had to occupy several strategic points, among them power-stations and waterworks in the southern outskirts of the city, the communication centre at Fontainebleau and a number of ammunition and supply dumps. In addition, the maximum possible number of up-to-strength combat units had to be mustered ready to move off.

Sandauer silently took notes. He read back his orders word for word and then went to see General Tanz.

Tanz received the instructions from Corps Headquarters impassively. "Well, let's get moving!" was his sole comment.

"I advise against it," Sandauer said drily.

"Why?" Tanz inquired.

"I don't like it, sir. There's something funny about the whole business. I can't believe our S.S. units would back a *coup d'état* against the Führer—the idea's absurd. In my opinion, any mistake we make in a situation like this could be fatal."

"What do you suggest, then?"

"A personal call to Supreme Headquarters, sir."

"Why not?" said Tanz. "After all, the Führer has told me more than once to consult him personally if I have any problems."

"I consider it vital to clarify the situation, sir."

"Right, get through at once."

Sandauer's efforts to reach Supreme Headquarters were not immediately successful. Even the code-word "Lightning" failed to secure the necessary priority. Undeterred, Sandauer asked for the Propaganda Ministry in Berlin.

The Ministry switchboard answered promptly, and thirty seconds later Sandauer was told that Dr. Goebbels would speak to General Tanz. Shortly afterwards, the ear-piece vibrated with the nasal tones, once heard never forgotten, of Hitler's right-hand man.

"A clique of unprincipled and reactionary officers is trying to seize power. These individuals allege that the Führer is dead, but this is not the case. This very day, Adolf Hitler will broadcast to the German people. In a situation like this, the Führer counts on the support of his loyal followers."

General Tanz listened intently. He knew where his loyalties lay. Fidelity was no empty delusion, especially when it could prove profitable.

"Heil Hitler!"

He turned to Sandauer. "Alert all units under my command. And make it clear, in case anyone needs reminding of the fact, that in my division only my orders count. No one else has any jurisdiction over it."

6.18 *p.m.*

Inspector Prévert looked at his watch. Hours had passed, and that at a time when every minute was precious. Prévert had taken off his coat, loosened his tie and opened his collar. He was chain-smoking.

Rainer Hartmann stood in front of him, pale and silent. His head drooped like a wilting flower.

"Haven't you any faith in me?" Prévert asked hoarsely.

"No," said Hartmann, "no faith in you or anyone else."

Prévert looked up. There was a trace of perplexity in his expression, but his eyes showed that he was not in the least tired. Although he was on the verge of losing his temper, professional experience told him that this would be the worst possible thing to do.

"Hartmann," he said, concentrating afresh, "you have refused to make a statement, and I regard that as a point in your favour. Criminals normally try to exonerate themselves, whatever they've done. They try to explain away their conduct or lay the blame on others. You've made no attempt to do that. Why not?"

"If I told you the truth you wouldn't believe me."

"Perhaps you underestimate my powers of imagination."

"Maybe." Hartmann contemplated his clasped hands.

Prévert began again from the beginning. He ran through all the findings which had so far been evaluated: the permit found beside the bed, the finger-prints on the cognac bottle and glass, the blood on the doorpost—belonging to Hartmann's blood group—and the graze on Hartmann's forehead, the Bentley, which had been seen parked outside the house in the Rue de Londres, and finally Hartmann's flight, which could be construed as indirect evidence of guilt.

"For all that, Hartmann, I refuse to believe that you could have committed this crime. Everything I know about you, both from Raymonde and your personal dossier, speaks in your favour. I'm genuinely convinced that you didn't commit this frightful crime—in which case, who did?"

"I distrust everyone!" Hartmann shouted. "Why should I confide in you? I don't know who you are or who you're working for. I've seen everything now. As far as I'm concerned, anything's possible, and the viler it is the more likely it is. You can string me up for all I care. It's only what I'd expect."

6.49 *p.m.*

Lieutenant-General Tanz, escorted by a motorized unit, drove to Corps Headquarters. As his staff car screeched to a halt, Tanz pumped the sub-machine-gun in his right hand up and down three times. Men swarmed from the trucks and raced to take up their prearranged positions, blocking every exit and entrance and occupying the surrounding area.

Tanz advanced on the G.O.C.'s office flanked by two chosen officers in battle-dress and steel helmets. He was accompanied by four N.C.O.s and twelve men with hand-grenades in their belts.

General von Seydlitz-Gabler received Lieutenant-General Tanz standing. He omitted to extend his hand.

"What brings you here?" he asked.

"The Führer is alive," Tanz said ominously.

"I should be overjoyed if that were so," von Seydlitz-Gabler answered promptly, "but I am otherwise informed."

"Your information is incorrect," declared Tanz. He proceeded to quote verbatim from his telephone conversation with Dr. Goebbels. "A clique of unprincipled and reactionary officers is attempting to seize power."

"That information may be equally incorrect."

"No," Tanz said stolidly. "I have spoken to Berlin on the 'phone. The Führer will be addressing the German people later today."

"If that is so," said von Seydlitz-Gabler after a brief pause, "I have been labouring under a temporary misapprehension. General Kahlenberge certainly regards the 'Valkyrie' order as genuine. He has taken all the appropriate steps."

"With your approval, sir?"

"I firmly believed that I was helping to implement a genuine order, and General Kahlenberge encouraged me in that belief. I naturally assumed that my Chief of Staff would have double-checked. I can only hope I was not mistaken in that assumption. If I was, I shall call General Kahlenberge to account immediately. Surely no one can doubt my loyalty to Führer and Reich?"

Tanz demanded to know General Kahlenberge's whereabouts, but it appeared that the Chief of Staff was *en route*, inspecting the implementation of emergency procedures. When Tanz roundly condemned these measures as high treason von Seydlitz-Gabler did not contradict him.

"You may rest assured that I know where my duty lies, General. If I have been deliberately misled I shan't hesitate to deal severely with those responsible."

Tanz slapped the butt of his sub-machine-gun, with that one gesture assuming effective command of von Seydlitz-Gabler's Corps. "There's only one way to deal with them," he said.

Von Seydlitz-Gabler hastened to assure Tanz of his unqualified support. "This is an emergency. No one shall say that I failed my country in its hour of need."

7.04 p.m.

Telephone conversation between Inspector Prévert and Lieutenant-Colonel Grau:

Prévert: "I'm getting virtually nowhere with my inquiries, but I'm convinced that we must rule Hartmann out. The murder's entirely out of keeping with his character."

Grau: "Who was it then?"

Prévert: "Someone—but not Hartmann."

Grau: "Have you checked the generals' alibis?"

Prévert: "Yes, as far as it was possible to, with the hullabaloo that's going on at the moment. As far as I can make out, von Seydlitz-Gabler and Kahlenberge were in conclave at Corps Headquarters during the time in question. General Tanz may have been at his hotel, but there's no positive proof of that."

Grau: "Well, at least we've got something to go on."

Prévert: "My dear friend, I implore you to let the matter drop, for the time being, anyway."

Grau: "I'll get the swine if it's the last thing I do."

7.19 p.m.

General Kahlenberge walked into the Hotel Majestic, headquarters of the Commander-in-Chief, France, and made his way to General von Stülpnagel's office. The place was buzzing like a beehive, and Kahlenberge's heart beat higher at the sight of so much bustling activity. He asked to speak to the G.O.C.-in-C.

"I'm extremely sorry, General von Stülpnagel isn't here."

"Where is he?"

"He's with Field-Marshal von Kluge."

"Who's deputizing for him?"

"G.O.C. Paris—officially, at least. But he's not available, either. He's out somewhere on a special assignment."

"And Lieutenant-Colonel von Hofacker?"

"Accompanying the Commander-in-Chief."

Kahlenberge swore roundly. He urgently wanted to get into touch with the main group. It would be folly to operate independently in a situation which called for concerted action, but there was no one he could turn to. The officers at the Majestic were a first-rate bunch, but without their generals they carried no weight.

"Goddammit!" Kahlenberge said helplessly.

7.52 p.m.

Going in search of General Tanz, Lieutenant-Colonel Grau found him at Corps Headquarters. Tanz was sitting at the G.O.C.'s desk in full battle order except for his steel helmet. General von Seydlitz-Gabler, virtually demoted for the time being, was obligingly signing or confirming all orders issued in his name.

It was clear that plan "Valkyrie" had been superseded, at least within this command. Von Seydlitz-Gabler had declared a state of emergency, relieved General Kahlenberge of his duties and ordered his arrest—as soon as he could be found. Like Mary's little lamb, von Seydlitz-Gabler followed the flag wherever it went.

Grau was admitted into Tanz's presence at once, though his greeting could hardly have been called cordial.

"Haven't you anything better to do than get under my feet? Why aren't you at your post?"

"I'm looking for a murderer."

Tanz shook his head reprovingly. "This is absurd. The Reich is in danger and you waste your time on trivialities. I don't understand your attitude."

"Last night," said Grau, "a woman was brutally murdered in the Rue de Londres."

"Colonel Grau," snapped Tanz, "earlier today someone tried to murder the Führer. A clique of unprincipled and reactionary officers was at the bottom of it. That should be your sole concern at the moment. Do your duty accordingly."

"I intend to do my duty," replied Grau. "However, what concerns me is not an attempted murder but a murder which has actually taken place."

"Why bother me with it?" Tanz asked impatiently.

"Somebody must have committed this murder. This circle of potential suspects is small, and my investigations have narrowed it down still further."

"So what?" said Tanz. "At a time when the Fatherland calls us you seem to be more interested in the fate of a French tart. Kindly don't smirk at me, I forbid it! Get out of here!"

"Certainly, as soon as you've answered a few questions."

"How dare you interrupt my work with your ridiculous flights of fancy? Who do you think you are, anyway?"

"Where were you last night between midnight and 3 a.m.?"

"That's nothing to do with you. I don't have to answer your questions."

"A refusal to make a statement usually means only one thing."

Tanz drew himself up, his eyes glacial.

"Colonel Grau," he said majestically, "at this moment I am the embodiment of the Führer's will. An attack on me is an attack on Greater Germany, and anyone who tries to hinder my work automatically stands revealed as an enemy of the Third Reich. I would go further: anyone who tries to destroy me must necessarily be trying to destroy the sacred ideals which inspire our great nation."

"Ridiculous," said Grau in a choked voice.

"No, true! That is why I have no alternative but to arrest you, Grau. You will leave this room a prisoner. You have shown yourself to be an enemy of the people. In a state of national emergency, there can be only one penalty for that."

8.20 p.m.

At the operational headquarters of Army Group West in La Roche-Guyon, Field-Marshal von Kluge turned to General von Stülpnagel and his companions. "Well, gentlemen," he said tersely, "they've bungled it." With that, the Field-Marshal had said all he had to say. His mind was made up. General von Stülpnagel turned deathly pale.

A short while before, von Kluge had exclaimed to Hofacker: "If only the swine were dead!" A short while later, the following congratulatory letter was on its way to Hitler:

"The dastardly and murderous attempt on your life, my Führer, has failed, thanks to a gracious dispensation of Providence. . . .

. . . I congratulate you and assure you, my Führer, of our unswerving loyalty, whatever may come."

signed: Field-Marshal von Kluge

8.57 p.m.

General Kahlenberge went to look for Inspector Prévert. He found him not in his office but in a bistro near the Sûreté, whither Prévert's secretary had directed him after a brief glance at her notebook. "Ask the landlord for Henri" were her exact words.

The landlord jerked his thumb in the direction of the door leading into his back room. Here Kahlenberge found Prévert leafing through a wad of papers and drinking *crème de cassis* diluted with white wine.

"I put a call through to Corps," Kahlenberge reported, "but I couldn't reach the G.O.C. Tanz seems to be in charge there now."

"Are you surprised?"

"Von Seydlitz-Gabler is obviously burying his head in the sand."

"He's not the only one."

"What's the form now—in your opinion?"

Prévert shrugged. "Your resistance movement seems to have been a flop."

Kahlenberge thumped the table with both hands. "It's easy for you to make snap judgments. What do you know about Germany?"

"Nothing," Prévert conceded readily. "I don't even pretend to know much about France."

"We're blown about like drift sand from one dune to the next."

"Sounds almost poetic," said Prévert. "What sort of excuse is that?"

"It's an explanation, not an excuse. Even so, there were men among us who were prepared to push Hitler off his pedestal. That's something, anyway. But what I can't get over is the way this whole fiasco has proved me right—*me*, Prévert!"

"You sound almost like our mutual friend Grau."

Kahlenberge raised his hands in protest. "What do I care about the theories of that sleuth-hound? All I know is, the masses are just as hair-raisingly stupid or criminally indifferent as I always thought they were—and generals are one degree worse."

"You're a general too."

"I'm a soldier," Kahlenberge said bitterly, "but I suppose it took me too long to realize that soldiers forfeit the right to exist as soon as generals start jockeying for position."

"It's an old, old game, General."

"Yes, but we've turned it into a sort of national sport for the ruling classes. All you have to do is anesthetize the masses by telling them they're an élite, that they've got a mission, that they're making history, that they're fulfilling their destiny and fighting for a better world—and they swallow it like lambs—even when a guttersnipe says it."

The proprietor of the bistro opened the door a crack and poked his head in.

" 'Phone for you, Henri."

Prévert nodded and disappeared. When he returned three minutes later he said:

"I've left orders that I'm only to be informed of major developments from now on. My men know what that means. The latest major development is that two single cells have been reserved at Sous-Bois, one of them for Lieutenant-Colonel Grau. He's been arrested by General Tanz, and General von Seydlitz-Gabler countersigned the order."

"Who's the second cell meant for?"

"For you, I imagine, my dear General."

9.20 p.m.

Inspector Prévert's influence had so far remained unimpaired. The police departments under his supervision still obeyed his orders and his network of contacts appeared to be functioning as well as ever.

However, certain changes had taken place during the evening, and this was nowhere more apparent than at a local prison which had the merit, or disadvantage, of being close to the headquarters of a Corps—to be precise, the Corps commanded by General von Seydlitz-Gabler but temporarily controlled by General Tanz.

Even under prevailing circumstances, Tanz tried to maintain a façade of extreme rectitude. He saw to it that his orders were signed by the G.O.C. and made sure that every action he took was confirmed, though generally after the event. One of his first steps was to ensure the safe keeping of Lieutenant-Colonel Grau and possible accomplices by requisitioning a number of cells in the neighbouring prison at Sous-Bois and detailing a subaltern and twelve men to guard them. When Prévert reached the prison he found that the usual division of labour prevailed: the German soldiers detailed for the job were striding around barking orders while the experienced French prison staff did the actual work. It didn't take him long to realize that the subaltern in charge was a typical product of the Nibelungen Division—hard as nails, unimaginative and unswervingly obedient.

Prévert circumvented the subaltern with some finesse by getting the governor of the prison to engage him in conversation on an appropriately official matter.

"Don't get any wrong ideas," Prévert told Grau when he had gained admittance to his cell. "It's not in my power to get you out of here." He grinned. "The most I can do is smuggle your ideas out for the benefit of posterity."

Grau stood with his back to the wall, smiling. "Well, Prévert, you're looking at a traitor. How do you like that?"

"You find the role amusing?"

"The German Army has become a tragic joke. This is just one more proof."

"My dear Grau, when you talk like that you remind me of Kahlenberge. You were brothers under the skin, not that either of you ever realized it. It's a crying shame. Together, you might have achieved a great deal. Still, this isn't the time for edifying speculation. It wasn't easy to get in here. There are two battalion commanders and a staff officer locked up next door and the cell opposite is probably reserved for Kahlenberge, but you, *cher ami*, appear to be a sort of public enemy number one."

"I'm the one who knows who the murderer is. Since the murderer knows I know, he means to murder me, too."

"Plausible enough," Prévert conceded. "That's why you

must get out of here. But how? I can't take you with me. Your personnel have presumably been black-listed, Engel included, so they'll be under surveillance—that is, if they haven't already been locked up. We need at least twenty stout lads to crack this little nut."

"There's always my 'flying squad'," said Grau. "It's a special branch of our organization which I recently formed against just this sort of emergency. They're all reliable chaps and armed to the teeth. No one but me knows about them. Give me a pencil and paper."

Prévert tore a sheet out of his notebook and unscrewed his fountain-pen. He handed them to Grau, who wrote:

I am being forcibly detained. The bearer will give you more details. Mobilize the whole squad at once. My guards are almost certain to resist.

Grau, Lt-Col., 20.vii.44, 21.30 hrs.

"I'll arrange their visit personally," promised Prévert, making for the door.

"One more thing, Prévert. If I don't get out of here alive, do your best to get Hartmann away. I'm certain he knows all about the murder, and his evidence could be vital."

"From his behaviour I'm inclined to agree with you." Prévert gave a mock bow. "Your wish shall be granted. Let's hope it's not your last!"

9.35 p.m.

An "order of the day" issued by the Commander-in-Chief of the German Navy reached Paris. It opened with the words:

"The treacherous attempt on the Führer's life fills each and every one of us with righteous indignation against our criminal enemies and their hirelings. Divine providence has saved the German people and the Armed Forces from this indescribable misfortune. In the miraculous preservation of our Führer we see fresh confirmation of. . . ."

This order of the day was signed: *Doenitz, Grand Admiral.*

10.30 p.m.

The military commander of the Greater Paris area, Lieutenant-General Boineburg-Lengsfield, directed operations against the S.D. and S.S. in person, escorted by members of his staff. He was bold enough to wait until this juncture because Retreat was at 10 p.m. and he wanted to bottle up as many men as possible simultaneously.

Surprise was complete. The S.D. and S.S. allowed themselves to be disarmed and taken prisoner without offering the slightest resistance. Barely an hour later, twelve hundred men were under lock and key, some in the military prison at Fresnes and others in the casemates of the Forts de l'Est at St. Denis. Senior officers of the S.S. were detained in custody at the Hotel Continentale in the Rue Castiglione.

All this happened just as the Bendlerstrasse end of the conspiracy had degenerated into a bloody shambles. Hitler, Goering and Goebbels were composing their speeches to the German people, and General von Stülpnagel, Commander-in-Chief, France, had been relieved of his command by Field-Marshal von Kluge.

10.38 p.m.

Grau's flying squad drew up outside the prison. His picked men overran the sentries and stormed into the cellars, where they came up against the battle-seasoned detachment from the Nibelungen Division. The two parties flew at each other's throats like beasts of prey—or, in more prosaic language: fierce hand-to-hand fighting took place.

Tanz's shock-troops retreated step by step, blazing away savagely in all directions. It was like a battle in the Warsaw sewers, and although the Nibelungen Division had been well-grounded in Warsaw techniques, Tanz's men were picked off one by one.

Having served his apprenticeship under General Tanz, the young lieutenant acted precisely as he had been ordered to act under such circumstances. He called for covering fire, crawled into Grau's cell, and shot him.

Grau collapsed without a word. His eyes were wide open as he fell.

11.23 p.m.

Side by side, Generals von Seydlitz-Gabler and Tanz listened intently to their Führer's words. It was a soul-stirring moment. Von Seydlitz-Gabler, in particular, registered deep but manly emotion.

The Führer yelled: "A small clique of ambitious, unscrupulous and criminally stupid officers. . . ."

"Quite right!" said General Tanz.

"A small gang of criminal elements, who are now being ruthlessly exterminated. . . ."

"Serve 'em right," put in General von Seydlitz-Gabler.

An A.D.C. poured champagne into two waiting glasses. After Hitler came Goering and, after Goering, Doenitz. As the last impassioned phrases died away, von Seydlitz-Gabler declared solemnly: "To our Führer, guided and guarded by Providence."

General Tanz drained his glass.

General von Seydlitz-Gabler drafted a telegram conveying his humble respects to the Führer and Supreme Commander of the Armed Forces. He expressed his full and unqualified appreciation of Lieutenant-General Tanz's services and composed a report to that effect. Furthermore, he proclaimed General Kahlenberge a traitor and deserter and issued a warrant for his arrest.

"Well," declared von Seydlitz-Gabler with an unclouded brow, "I think we can congratulate ourselves on coming through a trying time with flying colours."

"Casualties were unavoidable," said Tanz. "The attempt to rescue Grau had to be foiled at all costs, especially as he was in close touch with traitors like Kahlenberge. He also appears to have been in contact with the French Resistance. We had no choice in the matter. Don't you agree, sir?"

"Certainly," said von Seydlitz-Gabler after a moment's hesitation.

"May I count on your full support if the point is raised?"

"That goes without saying, my dear chap. You can count on me in every respect. Haven't the last few hours proved that? Well, then, what about a modest victory celebration? I'm sure the ladies will be delighted to join us."

11.50 p.m.

Three men made their way southwards in the direction of Marseilles: Inspector Prévert, General Kahlenberge and Lance-Corporal Hartmann.

"Well," Kahlenberge said grimly, "the war's as good as over for us. The night of the long knives is here again—or should I say the night of the generals? We'll have to become civilians if we want to survive. We've no option."

"The war will never be over for me," said Hartmann. "I'll never be able to forget what's happened."

Inspector Prévert's harsh absinthe-coated voice broke in. "We must accept war for what it is—murder, pure and simple. Anyone who's gutless or indifferent enough not to make a stand against it is abetting murder. He's just an accomplice. Is that what you want to be, Hartmann?"

There was no reply

INTERIM REPORT

EXTRACTS FROM THREE ARTICLES DEALING WITH THE PROBLEMS RAISED BY 20TH JULY 1944

The following articles were written and published one month, ten years and sixteen years after the event respectively. Their most noteworthy feature is that all three were written by the same man, the self-styled historian Karl Kahlert, formerly a captain on von Seydlitz-Gabler's staff.

From the periodical "Officer and Reich," August 1944, an article entitled "The Mark of Shame" and signed K.K.:

". . . it fills us front-line soldiers with profound indignation to see defensive victories which have been won with the blood of our comrades placed in jeopardy. An ambitious and unprincipled clique of un-German, treacherous and reactionary elements. . . ."

From the periodical "Officer and People," August 1954, an article entitled "The Hour of Trial" and signed K.:

". . . deserves our deepest respect. It was an act which enabled us to raise the flag of honour once more. We stand, profoundly moved, before the great dead of that day, men answerable only to conscience and the dictates of the heart. . . ."

From the periodical "Officer and State," August 1961, an article entitled "A Day of Conspiracy" and signed Kahlert:

". . . there are moments in history whose distinguishing feature is their very uniqueness. They are, by definition, unrepeatable. . . .

"Even though their ranks included some whose motives were, to say the least, not entirely unequivocal. . . .

". . . forced to conclude that while the men of 20th July merit respect, they should not be heedlessly, and thus irresponsibly, held up as an example. The young officer of today should be deeply conscious of this. All that need concern him is what we in this country have always felt to be the essence of military tradition and the inviolable duty of the soldier: unquestioning obedience. . . ."

PART THREE

The Reunion

BERLIN, 1956

1

Herr Kahlenberge's 'plane was nearing Berlin. Not a cloud obscured his view of the city, and general visibility was good. As the Air France machine came in to land the sun shone forth in all its glory as though the heavens had decided to put on a show of welcome.

Kahlenberge hugged his soft leather briefcase almost tenderly. It contained the draft of a lecture which he was to give before what would undoubtedly be a select and well-informed audience drawn from Berlin's upper crust.

The ponderous machine lumbered across Templehof aerodrome and rolled gently to a halt. The passengers extricated themselves from their seats and streamed up the aisle to the exit. As he passed the smiling air hostesses, Kahlenberge smiled back and bade them good-bye in impeccable French. His knowledge of languages had improved considerably in the past few years. The air hostesses were patently charmed, and Kahlenberge was not too old to feel gratified.

Cheerfully, he walked across the tarmac to the main building. He was fond of Berlin and its inhabitants. To him, the city was the only vantage-point from which Europe could be viewed as a whole, and he was flattered by the thought of being asked to lecture there. He had prepared his address with due attention to detail. It was entitled "The Conquest of the Past"—a conquest which Kahlenberge felt that he himself had successfully achieved.

BRIEF NOTE: *Kahlenberge in the intervening years*

At the end of July 1944, escapes to Southern France with Inspector Prévert and Lance-Corporal Hartmann. Resident in Marseilles until 1945. Thanks to some wire-pulling by Prévert, employed in an administrative capacity by the French Army of Occupation in Koblenz between 1945 and 1947. From 1948 until 1952, senior executive in a commercial vehicle and agricultural machinery firm based in Essen. Since 1953, director in charge of planned production in the same firm. Contributor to newspapers and periodicals. Occasional lectures. Author of memoranda commissioned by the ministry responsible for industrial planning.

"Thank you, Herr Generaldirektor," said the man at the barrier, handing back Kahlenberge's passport.

Kahlenberge smiled indulgently. In his firm he had been known as "General" long before he officially earned his civilian appellation. He had recently forbidden his staff to use the new title, but since they seemed to enjoy doing so he had resigned himself to it.

Kahlenberge scanned the arrival hall. He owed his invitation to Professor Kahlert, once a captain on his staff and now a historian of some repute. It seemed improbable that the usually punctilious Kahlert had forgotten to send at least a couple of his minions along to meet him, but Kahlenberge could see nothing that even faintly resembled a welcoming committee. He was a little disappointed until it struck him that this would give him a chance to look round his beloved Berlin at leisure.

Kahlenberge was about to lift his suitcase off the baggage counter when a pudgy hand closed over his and a husky voice said quietly: "May I help you?"

There was no mistaking the voice. With a start of surprise, Kahlenberge spun round to face the little man who was standing beside him.

"Prévert, my old friend, what a coincidence."

Prévert grasped Kahlenberge's outstretched hand and shook it warmly. They smiled at each other like men who have just received an unexpected present.

The Frenchman seemed to have grown even shorter. His flat, round, inexpressive face was covered with a network of fine wrinkles, but his eyes sparkled with the crystalline brilliance of emeralds. Looking into them, Kahlenberge felt almost dazzled. With a touch of misgiving, he asked: "It was a coincidence, I suppose?"

"Don't bank on it!" Prévert told him drily.

BRIEF NOTE: *Prévert in the intervening years*

Late July 1944, decamps from Paris accompanied by Kahlenberge and Hartmann. Finds lodgings for Kahlenberge in Marseilles and Hartmann in Antibes. 1944-45, works with the Maquis. 1945, returns to Paris. 1945-49, heads the Crimes of Violence Department at the Sûreté. 1950-51, helps to reorganize the national police services. 1954 onwards, co-ordinating director of the French police departments associated with the International Police Organization—Interpol.

"I wouldn't put anything past you," said Kahlenberge.

"Very wise of you!" Prévert replied, motioning him to follow.

A man in a smart grey suit silently took charge of Kahlenberge's luggage and led the way through the swing doors. They emerged on to the pavement, where a large dark saloon stood waiting by the kerb—a Renault with a Berlin numberplate.

They got in, Prévert raised his hand and the car drove off towards the centre of the city.

"Don't worry," Prévert remarked. "You won't miss your lecture. Have you got it taped yet?"

"Not quite."

"Never mind," Prévert said equably. "I may spare you enough time to correct a point here and there."

"So it wasn't a coincidence," Kahlenberge did his best to look amused. "You obviously suffer from the same old vice—moving people around like pawns on a board."

"Just take a look at this city," said Prévert. "Don't you feel it bubbling away just beneath the surface? Berlin always reminds me of a gigantic barrel full of fermenting wine—if you'll pardon the analogy. I'm still fond of my drink."

They drew up outside the Dollhagen, the celebrated delicatessen shop in the Kurfürstendamm. The driver opened the door, still without a word, and Prévert and Kahlenberge got out. People streamed by without giving them a second look. Kahlenberge revelled in the sense of anonymity. He enjoyed being just another face in the Berlin crowd because it made him feel he belonged.

"Let's fortify ourselves a little first," Prévert suggested.

"I'm sure you could do with a bite and it won't do me any harm either."

They climbed the stairs to the first-floor restaurant, where a table had been reserved for them beside a window in the far corner. The head waiter bowed and smiled. All Prévert had to do was to raise his hand like a president unleashing the waters of a dam, and two plates of baked oysters appeared, bedded in red cabbage and accompanied by a bottle of Chablis '53.

"Almost like being in France," said Kahlenberge.

Prévert nodded. While they ate he expatiated smilingly on an acquaintanceship with culinary refinements. If ever a nation took it into its head to make war on France for that reason—but only for that reason—he, Prévert, might be able to sympathize with its motives.

"Well, I feel twice the man," Kahlenberge sighed, when nothing remained but a litter of shells and two squeezed lemons. "You can come to the point now."

"With pleasure," said Prévert, dividing the rest of the Chablis equally between their two glasses. "What I have to tell you can be summed up in a few words. We haven't seen each other too often in recent years, as you know, but we've been admirable correspondents. You know that last letter of yours—the one I got a few days ago? There was one sentence in it which made me sit up."

"There wasn't anything special about it, as far as I can remember."

"The sentence I'm referring to," said Prévert, "ran something like this: 'Even General Tanz seems to recognize the signs of the times. They say he'd like nothing better than to make contact with the West.' "

Kahlenberge wagged his hairless, glistening head, which looked more like a billiard ball than ever. "I don't see anything unusual in the fact that one man has lost his taste for life in East Germany. Millions share his opinion. Nothing could be more natural."

"On the contrary," said Prévert firmly. "I can't imagine anything more unnatural—in Tanz's case."

BRIEF NOTE: *Tanz in the intervening years*

Promoted to Corps Commander at the end of July 1944, after the successful quelling of the revolt in the Paris area. Transferred to the Eastern Front in this capacity and fights first in Silesia, then in Brandenburg. Taken prisoner by the Red Army. 1945-49, prominent inmate of a camp for generals near Moscow. 1949-51, confidential adviser to the Russian Army of Occupation in the Saxony-Thuringia area. From 1952 onwards involved in the creation of the so-called National People's Army of the so-called German Democratic Republic. Since 1955, frequently tipped as a potential Deputy Minister of Defence in the same political set-up.

"What's so worrying about it?" asked Kahlenberge, smiling at Prévert with a hint of curiosity. "What do you deduce from it?"

"Certain things," Prévert said. "I've got my fair share of imagination, you know. It can be awkward sometimes, for other people as well as myself."

They emptied their glasses, ordered another bottle and waited in silence until the wine waiter had finished serving them. While he did so they stared out at the Kurfürstendamm with apparent interest, each man covertly eyeing the other's reflection in the polished glass of the window. They smiled as their eyes met.

"If I understand you correctly," said Kahlenberge, leaning forward, "I owe my invitation to Berlin to you."

"Shall we say—I arranged it."

"May I ask what your motives were?"

"I had several, *mon cher*. In the first place, it seemed a good opportunity to see you again after all this time, and, in the second place, I felt I might be able to offer you an entertaining experience. In fact, I may be able to lay on a performance which you would not have missed for worlds. But that's not all. I may well need your assistance."

Kahlenberge smiled wryly as the last words sank in. "I expected something of the sort," he commented. "You plan to use me as a sort of bait—for Tanz, of all people. I suppose I oughtn't to be surprised."

"The idea annoys you?"

"Put your cards on the table, Prévert. What do you want with Tanz?"

"Can't you guess?"

"I imagine you want to win him over. For some reason, you

want to lure the revered General Tanz into the Western camp—with my help. On the other hand, you may be doing a little wild-game hunting and you need me to help beat the covers."

"You could be right."

"I'm shocked at you," said Kahlenberge, "shocked at what you've turned into. You treat yesterday's enemies like old friends. Next, you'll be telling me there were no Nazis, only Germans. Go ahead, then—scrub out three wars and call history a whore. Let's all indulge in an orgy of spurious bonhomie."

"I could argue that it's the trend of the times."

"And I could tell you to take your trend of the times and go to the devil!"

"Thank you for those few kind words," said Prévert with unabashed amusement.

He raised his glass to Kahlenberge, small eyes sparkling like greenish water lit by a ray of sunshine. Then he put his glass down and rubbed his hands together as though he had concluded a particularly advantageous business deal.

"Do you remember the strange yarn Hartmann told us on the way south from Paris?"

"Morbid nonsense!" declared Kahlenberge. "The product of an over-heated imagination. You thought so, too, didn't you?"

"What he told us certainly sounded morbid, but I'm beginning to wonder if it was such nonsense."

"Really, Prévert! You were sceptical enough about his story yourself—to put it mildly."

"Yes, I was," Prévert conceded, "then."

"But not now?" Kahlenberge shook his head wonderingly. "My dear chap, it's absurd—absolutely crazy!"

"A lot of things are absurd and crazy, war most of all. The more I think about it, the more convinced I become of one thing: there's nothing a human being isn't capable of, especially when war has destroyed all his inhibitions. The question of rank doesn't enter into it."

"It's all very well theorizing, but don't forget that the boy was in a state of nerves at the time. He was at the end of his tether."

"But he wasn't a murderer, I'm absolutely positive of it. Hartmann wasn't a sex maniac."

"I didn't say that, Prévert. Don't misunderstand me—I've no doubt he'd been through a lot of things which would have unbalanced stronger personalities than his. Think what he must have gone through in Russia, for instance. But all that blood-curdling poppycock about Tanz . . . Just the product of an over-heated imagination, I tell you."

"I thought so too, at the time," admitted Prévert. "That's why I dropped the case like a hot potato. Besides, I had more important things to do. There was a war to be won, if you remember, and after that we had our hands full paying for the privilege of having won it."

"Have you heard anything of Hartmann since?"

"I've been hoarding him like buried treasure," Prévert said. "However, it wasn't until yesterday that I knew with any certainty what a treasure I was hoarding."

BRIEF NOTE: *Hartmann in the intervening years*

End of July 1944, escapes to the South of France. Goes to ground first in Marseilles and later in Antibes, where he lodges with a fisherman from August 1944 onwards and works on boats and nets. From March 1945 onwards, employed by a master mason who specializes in the rebuilding of harbour installations. From summer 1947 onwards, works as a casual labourer, mending roads, building walls, repairing fences and erecting houses at Antibes and Cap d'Antibes. Now living there in a room near the Castell, quietly tolerated and protected by former members of the Resistance, once all-powerful but still influential. Passes for a Frenchman locally.

"It's characteristic of the man," said Kahlenberge. "He's buried himself—cut himself off from the world. Obviously, he prefers to live like a hermit. But that often happens when someone finds life more than he can cope with. I'm not surprised by his reaction in the least."

"People like Hartmann are commoner than you think, *mon vieux*. It's just that they don't all behave as logically. He refuses to compromise and insists on living as he thinks he was destined to live. But it's precisely because Hartmann is what he is, and nothing else, that he's given me so much food for thought. I've asked myself again and again if he mightn't have been telling the truth—and, if so, what to do about it."

Kahlenberge drained his glass. The wine was dry, fruity and full-bodied, but he got no pleasure from it. His head had grown suddenly heavy.

"How much do you really know, Prévert?"

"Tanz wrote to von Seydlitz-Gabler, hinting that he wouldn't be averse to changing sides. Von Seydlitz-Gabler informed you and you wrote to me. My first reaction was: why?"

"Why? You know what I think of Tanz, but in this case his motives may be entirely above reproach."

"They may be, yes, but not necessarily so—particularly with a man like Tanz."

"Perhaps you underestimate von Seydlitz-Gabler's influence. He's still got a lot of pull, you know."

"I've taken his influence into consideration from the start. I realize that generals like von Seydlitz-Gabler are an institution in Germany. Just because they lose battles or campaigns or even wars, it doesn't mean they forfeit their influence."

BRIEF NOTE: *Von Seydlitz-Gabler in the intervening years*

End of July 1944, promoted to Army Commander. Invested with the oak leaves to his Knight's Cross for exemplary conduct during the 20th July crisis and honoured with a personal citation from the Führer and Supreme Commander. Exemplary conduct maintained until the last day of the war. Preferential treatment while a prisoner of war at Schloss Beil near Stuttgart, where he writes essays on the reasons for Germany's defeat, larding them with veiled allusions to Hitler's incompetent generalship. 1946-49, a peaceful interlude at the Villa Friedhold near Berchtesgaden. 1950, elected one of the three honorary presidents of the Combat Veterans' Association. 1951 onwards, essays, articles and lectures. Their general theme: the integrity of the German soldier, in particular his sense of honour. A noted spokesman for the revival of military self-reliance, currently known as defensive preparedness. Now preparing a comprehensive book of memoirs to be entitled "Every Inch a Soldier."

"You're right," said Kahlenberge. "Von Seydlitz-Gabler may be an overgrown schoolboy, but his contacts are legion. If Tanz wanted to break with the East he couldn't turn to a better man."

"But to resume, *mon cher*. It is my habit to glance through international police reports occasionally—out of sheer boredom, if you like. Well, whether you call it coincidence or fate, on the very day when I received your letter telling me that Tanz was contemplating a change of scenery I happened to see a confidential report from East Germany. It referred to a crime of violence."

Kahlenberge was breathing heavily now, like a man toiling up a mountain-side. "A crime similar to the one described by Hartmann?"

Prévert nodded. "Not only similar, but identical in almost every detail with what he told us. One more thing: the crime was committed in Dresden, and General Tanz is quartered in the Dresden area at the present time."

"I can promise you one thing, you won't be bored." Prévert snapped his fingers for the bill. "But that's all I can guarantee."

Kahlenberge regarded his companion with a quizzical smile. "And what part do you envisage for me?"

"Principally that of a friend," Prévert said cordially. "I am operating in a somewhat unfamiliar field, you know. My experience of generals has been rather limited hitherto, and I lack the special knowledge which you, my dear friend, so abundantly possess. Your main function will be to draw my attention to any features of my plan of action which you consider faulty. I rely on you to be frank."

"What else do you want me to do?"

Prévert slipped a large note under the bill which had been presented to him and gently drew Kahlenberge towards the exit. "You, *mon cher*, are here to give a lecture. That's the official version, as it were. However, your lecture won't claim all your time, so you may get a chance for a chat with one or other of your old friends—about your unforgettable times together in Warsaw and Paris, for example."

"Not with von Seydlitz-Gabler, surely? How are you going to entice him here?"

Prévert raised his hands like a salesman defending the

quality of his goods. "General von Seydlitz-Gabler," he sai blandly, "has been invited here by a publisher to discus his memoirs. It wasn't too difficult to find a potential buye incidentally. To cut a long story short, our former hero ha already arrived—complete with lady wife, needless to say All expenses to be paid by the publisher."

"That only leaves his daughter."

"Ulrike von Seydlitz-Gabler has been living in Berlin fo some years. At the moment she is working as secretary to a industrial consultant."

BRIEF NOTE: *Ulrike von Seydlitz-Gabler in the intervenin years*

Immediately after 20th July 1944, quarrels with her parent whose efforts to make her see "reason" are entirely un availing, and breaks away from the family fold. 1945-8, durable affair with an American colonel, already married Stays on in Berlin after his departure and tries her hand a modelling (dress-house and photographic) and acting—al with only moderate success. 1952, learns shorthand and typing Has since been employed by various industrial concerns

"Exactly what do you hope to achieve by this family reunion?"

"To be honest, Kahlenberge, I'm not quite sure—excep that it's one way of getting Tanz to Berlin. To begin with von Seydlitz-Gabler—and you as well, to a certain extent provided you're willing to make a show of burying the hatche —will act as a draw. Later you may be able to render me valuable assistance as witnesses or advisers."

"That's all very well, Prévert, but how do you hope to conduct your case without your star witness? Surely you can't hope to get Hartmann here?"

"I'm in the process of making the necessary arrangements."

They stood in the Kurfürstendamm and looked across at the Gedächtniskirche. The sombre, smoke-blackened spire dominated the long street far more effectively than any of the new buildings with their glass and chromium façades. Its tortured, shattered silhouette seemed to claw the sky in a desperate effort to retain its equilibrium. No memorial could have been more melancholy or more mutely eloquent.

"Your hotel's just across the street," said Prévert. "I've reserved you a room with bath. You'll find your bags already installed there, if I'm not mistaken."

"First-rate planning," remarked Kahlenberge. "I congratulate you."

Arranging to meet in the hotel foyer at seven that evening, they shook hands grinning like a couple of old cronies indulging in a piece of youthful folly. Then Kahlenberge crossed the Kurfürstendamm to the hotel and Prévert got into his waiting car.

"Friedrichstrasse," said Prévert. Friedrichstrasse lay in the Eastern sector of the city, but Prévert's driver betrayed not the slightest surprise.

The car passed through the two check points at the Brandenburg Gate without incident, glided down the Unter den Linden and turned left into Friedrichstrasse. There, a few blocks beyond the Admiralspalast, it drew up in front of a bleak façade of grey stone broken by dim windowpanes set in narrow, elongated embrasures and interspersed with unadorned but massive pillars—a piece of severely uniform architecture which had once been the lair of Prussian officialdom.

Once inside, Prévert turned into what he was, a senior administrator of the prestigious Sûreté and an Interpol co-ordinator. In this capacity, he was admitted into the presence of Commissioner Karpfen of the East German Ministry of the Interior. These days, policemen were the only civil servants in the world with any real community of purpose, and then only where capital crimes were concerned.

A lengthy discussion on professional matters developed between the two international police experts. They swapped information on the rapid comparison of finger-print records, moved on to possible methods of tightening up communication procedures and ended by discoursing—semi-officially, now—on narcotics and the use of lie-detectors.

Prévert skilfully fostered an atmosphere of insidious familiarity because he was aware of Commissioner Karpfen's weaknesses and was clever enough to interpret them as an indirect source of strength. Herr Karpfen, round as a rubber ball but endowed with the wrinkled physiognomy of a sad-faced clown, warmed to his visitor, flattered that his almost legendary colleague from Paris was treating him like an intimate friend.

"I don't have anything to do with politics," Karpfen declared with spirit. Then, alarmed at his own temerity, he back-pedalled vigorously and nipped this perilous line of thought in the bud by adding: "Though I'm fundamentally a political animal, of course, and as such I'm a staunch upholder of democratic ideals."

"But you're a policeman first and foremost."

"True," Karpfen conceded.

"And if we lend each other a helping hand it's purely for reasons of professional solidarity?"

"What else are colleagues for?"

"Then tell me," said Prévert, folding his hands like a man in prayer. "You had a particularly gruesome sex murder in Dresden the other day, didn't you?"

Karpfen looked surprised. "Where did you hear that?"

"Come now, Commissioner, we hardly need explain the nature of our information services to each other, need we?"

The Commissioner made a gesture of resignation. There were certain things which had to be accepted. "It's a fundamental principle of ours not to suppress information, but we are equally careful not to divulge it prematurely. After all, it might endanger the success of our investigations."

The case quoted by Prévert—the Dresden murder—had actually caused quite a stir in the East German C.I.D. Public success in the fight against non-political crime was the breath of life to the East German C.I.D. if it was not to degenerate into a poor relation of the political police. Consequently, headquarters in Berlin had dispatched one of its ablest investigators to Dresden at the local C.I.D.'s request, so far without tangible results.

"I may be able to help you, Commissioner," said Prévert.

Karpfen snapped eagerly at the bait. "We're more than grateful for any assistance from our foreign colleagues, but what form is your help likely to take?"

"As far as I can judge, we seem to have a similar case on our files. It happened some time ago, in Paris."

"Most interesting!" said Karpfen. "Could you place the necessary particulars at my disposal?"

"Of course." Prévert's display of disinterested co-operation was convincing in the extreme. "Though it would eliminate any undesirable misunderstandings if I were given an opportunity to study your findings so far."

Karpfen shied like a nervous horse. "Is that essential?"

"Absolutely. I don't want to make any blunders. The results might be embarrassing, and I can't afford mistakes in my position."

"Quite, quite." Commissioner Karpfen nodded gravely, conducting a lightning review of the situation as he did so. The Dresden murder was clearly a criminal case which had nothing whatsoever to do with politics or related matters. His brow cleared.

"My dear and esteemed colleague," he said, "it will be a pleasure and a privilege to work with you. I shall make arrangements for you to see the full particulars—and the officer in charge of inquiries. Shall we say here in my office early tomorrow afternoon?"

"Many thanks," said Prévert with exaggerated cordiality. "That's agreed, then. I have yet another favour to ask you. It's a private matter, but I should be most grateful if it could be arranged. In fact, I shall look forward to expressing my personal thanks to you in Paris."

"Paris!" breathed Karpfen with scarcely suppressed enthusiasm. "Who knows when I shall have a chance to visit your delightful city again."

"Next month at the latest," Prévert said firmly. "The routine matters we discussed earlier need working on as soon as possible. I intend to arrange a conference in Paris when I get back there next week."

"Splendid," said the Commissioner with a sigh of satisfaction. "Now what's this personal request of yours?"

Prévert did not hesitate for a moment. "Please make a note of this name: Frau Constanze Hartmann, No. 14 Giebichensteinstrasse, Halle. She's an elderly lady, the widow of a former government employee. I should be grateful if she could make a trip to Berlin, preferably at public expense. I leave the details to you."

"The grounds for such a visit could be either social—a medical examination, for instance—or cultural—a visit to the State Opera, say, or the Schiffbauerdamm Theatre, or the State Museums."

"Any excuse will do, *cher collègue*. The main thing is that the old lady gets to Berlin as soon as possible. I'm asking this as a favour to a young friend of mine—her son, to be precise. He's been living in the South of France ever since the end of the war, and it would mean so much to him to see his old mother again."

"A touching story," Karpfen said, not without irony. "It also sounds comparatively innocuous. I shall be delighted to grant your request—as a personal favour."

"You won't regret it," Prévert assured him. "As long as we policemen stick together there's still hope for mankind."

INTERIM REPORT

An extract from the draft of General von Seydlitz-Gabler's memoirs:

"The events of July 20th moved us deeply. However, they did not accord with Prussian tradition, and any would-be comparison with the Convention of Tauroggen is absurd. There, the King sanctioned an overt proceeding by virtue of his divine right. In Hitler's case, circumstances were quite different. However one regards him, it cannot be denied that he was elected by a majority of the people. He owed his position to what was, in essence, a democratic process, and we soldiers had no real choice but to obey the voice of the Fatherland.

"For all that, I find myself profoundly and repeatedly moved whenever I reflect on the events of July 20th. My soldier's heart belonged to the rebels but my soldier's conscience owed allegiance to the Reich alone, for ever since the beginning of recorded history the axiom has always been: good is what serves the State, evil what harms it.

"I do not mean by this that I stood aloof, but I was extraordinarily conscious of the deep conflict, the vast gulf that divided otherwise like-minded brother officers. At this period I used to pace up and down for hours on end, seeking a solution which would be acceptable to all. I confess now that I never found it. One thing, however, I could do. I refrained from victimizing anyone. On the contrary, I protected those who were venturing the impossible for maintaining an attitude of chivalrous forbearance. Not a few of them owe me their lives, but gratitude is not what the true soldier expects. He merely does his duty.

"That, and that alone, is what I and many of my best friends did. Only this makes it possible for us to look history in the eye today."

Telephone conversation between Commissioner Karpfen in Berlin and Detective-Inspector Liebig in Dresden, conducted on 21st September, 1956 and recorded in writing by a member of the East German State Security Service. This man, whose name is unimportant, abandoned the German Democratic Republic in May, 1959, bringing a number of official papers with him, among them the following shorthand transcripts:

Karpfen: "How far have you got with your inquiries?"

Liebig: "On-the-spot investigations are complete."

Karpfen: "Any clue as to who did it?"

Liebig: "No. All the leads we have are vague and obviously misleading. However, I've put every available man on to the case, so far without definite results."

Karpfen: "Is there any indication that the crime could have —hm, political connotations?"

Liebig: "Absolutely none. It's a straightforward murder. Revolting, though, the way the body was mutilated."

Karpfen: "To make myself even plainer, Liebig—is there anything to suggest that the crime was committed by someone—how shall I put it?—of a certain standing—someone who might need handling with a certain measure of discretion?"

Liebig: "Not the slightest indication, sir."

Karpfen: "Monsieur Prévert, whom you probably know by name, thinks he knows of a parallel case. What's your reaction to that?"

Liebig: "If a parallel case did exist it would help us considerably."

Karpfen: "I'm glad you think so, Liebig. Kindly report to me here tomorrow and bring all the particulars with you. We'll see where we go from there."

From a letter written to Rainer Hartmann by Ulrike von Seydlitz-Gabler. There are at least eighty such letters in existence, though none of them ever reached its destination. Ulrike von Seydlitz-Gabler wrote them over a period of twelve years but never sent them because she had no idea of the addressee's whereabouts, or even if he were still alive:

"If I go on writing to you over and over again it's because I can't think of any more soothing and absorbing occupation. Why are women such fundamentally helpless creatures? I believe that of all the millions of men in the world there's only one who's right for a particular woman. Since the odds are against her ever meeting him, she has to adapt herself to another man—which she usually does with loyalty and devotion. But if you have the luck or misfortune, whichever way you look at it, to find a man—one man among millions—who stirs you to the bottom of your soul, what do you do then? There's nothing to do but wait, even if it means waiting for a lifetime.

"It's hopeless—I know it is—but I refuse to think about it logically. I go on waiting and hoping. Did you know I had a photograph of you? During the day it stands on my desk and at night it lives beside my bed. It's just an ordinary snap-shot, blurred and fingered and faded after all these years, but it shows you and me together in Warsaw, where it all began. God only knows how it will end, and when."

Two telegrams, both sent from Berlin on 21st September, 1956. Telegram to R. Hartmann, 13 Rue Victor Hugo, Antibes:

"Visiting Berlin. Ideal opportunity to see you. Staying Niederschönhausen with Aunt Grete. Longing to see you. Please fly at once to your old Mother."

Telegram to Edouard Manessier, borough councillor and building contractor, Place de la République, Antibes.

"Need Hartmann urgently. Have sent wire on mother's behalf. Please eliminate difficulties advance money arrange passport personally. Will reimburse all expenses. Treat as important confidential urgent. Regards Prévert."

2

Kahlenberge appeared in the lobby of the Hotel am Kurfürstendamm punctually at the appointed hour, but Prévert was not installed in any of the handsome armchairs which were scattered around for the convenience of guests. Strolling over to the reception desk, he asked for an evening paper and seated himself near the entrance, from which point of vantage he studied the hotel's luxurious décor with a pensive eye.

A page approached discreetly. "Herr Kahlenberge?" he murmured. "There's a call for you, sir—Herr Prévert on the line."

Kahlenberge followed the boy to the phone booth and picked up the receiver.

"I've been detained, *mon vieux,*" Prévert said. "So I must ask you to wait for me. I hope you won't be bored—in fact, I'm quite certain you won't."

"No?" drawled Kahlenberge.

"It's quite possible you may run into an old friend of yours."

"Good God, Prévert, you haven't billeted von Seydlitz-Gabler here, too, have you?"

"But, of course. Why should we disperse our forces? Besides, my dear fellow, you might bear in mind that an invitation to Tanz will carry more weight if it comes from von Seydlitz-Gabler."

Returning to the lobby, Kahlenberge sat down again and resumed his vigil, this time concentrating his attention on the stairs leading to the first floor. Before many minutes had passed he saw a figure descending with stately tread, an elderly gentleman with silver-streaked hair, patrician features and the erect carriage of a regimental sergeant-major. He moved with a regal dignity that would have put a Shakespearean actor to shame.

Von Seydlitz-Gabler gave a momentary start when he caught sight of Kahlenberge, and for a brief few seconds his sublime composure deserted him. Then he stretched out both hands and summoned up a smile.

"Kahlenberge! What an unexpected surprise! The age of miracles isn't past, after all. What brings you here, my dear chap?"

"I'm supposed to be giving a lecture here."

"And I'm bringing out my memoirs," von Seydlitz-Gabler explained with a hint of pride. "It seems to have got around. I've had publishers literally battering at my door. They scent the truth, I expect, and truth's a saleable commodity these days. We're thinking in terms of three volumes and an illustrated prospectus. There's a possibility of selling the film rights to Hollywood. I've already had a number of offers from abroad."

"Splendid! And how's your lady wife?"

"In great form, all things considered."

At length, Frau Wilhelmine appeared—like her husband, the acme of timeless self-assurance. She thrust her bony hand confidently into Kahlenberge's and shook it with apparent warmth.

The next half hour belonged to her ladyship. Kahlenberge listened with good grace, answering questions and receiving a detailed account of the von Seydlitz-Gabler saga in return. He waited patiently for a chance to implement Prévert's plan. Eventually Frau Wilhelmine paused for breath and Kahlenberge leapt into the breach.

"How pleasant to have this opportunity for a quiet chat with old friends. It makes one want to resurrect the past. Do you know what would complete our little gathering? General Tanz."

"General Tanz?" Frau Wilhelmine exclaimed spontaneously, as though overwhelmed by a sudden flood of memories. "What a man!"

"A first-rate general, too," von Seydlitz-Gabler declared firmly. "At least, during his time with me."

"And now he's in the service of the East." Kahlenberge's tone was cool. "He virtually draws his pay from the Russians."

"You never were a friend of his," said Frau Wilhelmine.

"If I had given him half a chance," von Seydlitz-Gabler said quietly, "our celebrated friend Tanz would have signed my death warrant because of the 20th of July."

Frau Wilhelmine laughed harshly. "I imagine he felt he was only doing his duty, Herbert."

"It was a tragic business, there's no denying it," mused von Seydlitz-Gabler. "Still, one ingredient of tragedy is greatness."

Kahlenberge returned to his earlier theme. "What a pity Tanz isn't here, though. I'd be so interested to see him again. Don't you think we ought to try and invite him here? An opportunity like this doesn't come twice."

"A splendid idea," announced Frau Wilhelmine. "Don't you agree, Herbert?"

Von Seydlitz-Gabler nodded. "The bonds of comradeship which exist between brother officers," he said, as though reading from his memoirs, "have nothing whatsoever to do with the flags or frontiers of the moment. With us, even opponents are treated chivalrously. When I found myself compelled to sign the armistice documents on behalf of my army—on orders from above, I may say—even a Russian general saluted me."

"Then why not drop our old friend a line?" Kahlenberge suggested. "Invite him to pay us a visit."

"Gladly." Von Seydlitz-Gabler agreed with alacrity, prompted by the glances of approval which Frau Wilhelmine was flashing him like signals in Morse. "But if I do ask Tanz to join us, what guarantee is there that my invitation will ever reach him?"

"As a business man," said Kahlenberge, "I have to operate on as wide an international basis as possible. Don't worry, I'll see that the letter reaches its destination safely."

Von Seydlitz-Gabler fished a correspondence card and matching envelope from his breast pocket, both of them die-stamped "von Seydlitz-Gabler" in Gothic script. Then he took out a pen and wrote:

My dear and esteemed friend,

We—Kahlenberge and yours truly—would be more than delighted to see you again after all this time. We look forward to swapping experiences with you and discussing future plans, though it goes without saying that we fully appreciate your special position. We shall be here for some days, so please look us up at the above address.

Your old friend,

von Seydlitz-Gabler

Within an hour the note was in Prévert's hands. Kahlenberge described its contents and the circumstances under which it had been written. The two men smiled at each other gleefully.

"I hope you're pleased with my performance so far," Kahlenberge said with a hint of irony.

They drove to a *Weinstube* near the Schiller Theatre run by a character called Mother Neuhaus. It was a long narrow cellar like a stretch of underground railway, lit discreetly and furnished with a large number of separate tables, heavy affairs of polished oak. The chairs were comfortable and the clientele quiet. The sound of their voices never drowned the agreeable clink of bottle against glass.

Mother Neuhaus waddled up in person as soon as she caught sight of Prévert. She greeted him with blunt good humour, treating him like a Berliner born and bred. Although she had only seen him a handful of times in the past ten years, it had not taken her long to realize that the little man with the pudgy face and sharp eyes was an excellent judge of wine.

"I'll get the letter forwarded to General Tanz tonight," Prévert said, when a bottle and two glasses had been set before them. "It may be in his hands tomorrow, so with a bit of luck he'll be here the next day. I'm certain he'll come."

"I hope you're not overestimating his readiness to accept the invitation."

"He'll be overjoyed to get it, believe me. Unless I'm much mistaken, he'll snatch at it like a drowning man."

"It's always been one of Frau Wilhelmine's pet ambitions to see her daughter married to a general—Tanz, for choice. I'm sure the idea's still lurking at the back of her mind. Lucky the girl never married, isn't it?"

"We'll have to protect her from her mother's ambitions."

"Of course, though from what I remember of her she'll be quite capable of protecting herself." Kahlenberge smiled. "You enjoy playing around with people's lives, don't you?"

Prévert gave a shrug of distaste. "You know, *mon cher*, sometimes I get the depressing feeling that we policemen hunt down the sick and abnormal and let the real criminals of this world get away—the people who play with death and destruction like a child playing marbles."

"Don't lose too much sleep over it," said Kahlenberge, and his sarcasm was as mild as the gentle rain from heaven.

Prévert spent the next morning sitting by the telephone in his room in the Hotel am Steinplatz, poring over a thick bundle of Sûreté files. They dated from 1944 and contained all available information about the murder which occurred in the Rue de Londres during the night of 19th-20th July.

While he was engaged in this absorbing pastime, news reached him from Antibes. His local representative there confirmed that Edouard Manessier had contacted Rainer Hartmann as requested and that Hartmann had reacted favourably on receipt of the spurious telegram from his mother. He had booked a seat on a flight from Nice to Berlin via Geneva and Munich and would be arriving at Templehof at 7.47 p.m.

After that, Prévert put a call through to Ulrike von Seydlitz-Gabler. A series of veiled hints captured her interest so effectively that, after a brief hesitation, she agreed to meet him when she finished work that evening. They made an appointment for 6 p.m. in the Restaurant Kopenhagen.

Shortly before midday, Prévert received the call which he had been awaiting so impatiently. Commissioner Karpfen announced that Detective-Inspector Liebig had arrived from Dresden with the requisite particulars and would be at Prévert's service from 2 p.m. onwards.

Prévert arrived at Friedrichstrasse punctually and was greeted by Karpfen, who introduced him to Liebig and then left the two men alone together. For some minutes they conversed in general terms and exchanged a few compliments on the efficiency of their respective police forces, skilfully avoiding any excursions into politics. Then they got down to business.

Detective-Inspector Liebig of Dresden was a stolid, heavily built man resembling a football with arms and legs. He looked as though he would survive a kick in any portion of his anatomy with complete impunity, and his smile was as deceptively mild as the moon on a Romanticist's canvas.

"If my information is correct," he began, "you believe you

know of a case similar to the one I've been working on in Dresden."

"It's not entirely out of the question," Prévert said cautiously.

Detective-Inspector Liebig opened his briefcase, which was as capacious as a small trunk, to reveal a mass of documents. "Perhaps the simplest thing would be to exchange files."

Prévert warmed to Liebig's straightforward approach. He seemed to be a typical representative of his profession. A crime was a crime, and the only pertinent question was: who committed it? Tracking down the criminal was all that mattered; any other considerations were unimportant.

They swapped files, each aware that the other's documents were not entirely complete. Certain facts and certain aspects of police procedure had to be kept secret, but both took this for granted, especially as they had no choice in the matter.

So Prévert and Liebig sat opposite each other in two hard and unyielding chairs which had once belonged to the Prussian civil service. They had probably been used by generations of public servants—officers of the Imperial police, security officials of the Weimar Republic and members of the Gestapo and S.S. Their latter-day equivalents leafed through each other's files in silence. Years of practice had taught them to take in essentials at a single glance. Detective-Inspector Liebig was the first to speak.

"Well, it really does seem to be a parallel case." He sounded genuinely impressed.

"I'm inclined to think so, too," said Prévert.

"A lot of it could be coincidence, of course."

"Let's try to establish the exact points of similarity," Prévert said placidly. "I suggest we simply jot down which factors are common to both cases."

"Comparative analysis would undoubtedly be the most appropriate method," replied Liebig. "However, I suggest that we postpone further examination for the time being. It may be premature."

"Why?" Prévert leant forward attentively.

"Just before I left Dresden this morning I received a wire from the homicide branch of the Warsaw police. It was signed by a man called Liesowski. Do you know what it said? According to Liesowski, a parallel case occurred in Warsaw some years back."

"When?" Prévert asked, his expression tense.

"In nineteen forty-two."

"Then we must get Liesowski here at once. Can you arrange it?"

"I can," said Liebig, "and I will."

Prévert took up his station in the Restaurant Kopenhagen a quarter of an hour early. He had never seen Ulrike von Seydlitz-Gabler before, but he recognized her immediately from her photographs.

The young woman who entered the restaurant on the stroke of six o'clock fitted his mental picture of her almost exactly. She had an athletic and wiry figure, but there was something lithe and graceful about the way she moved. Her blonde hair was short and wavy, and her expression would have seemed almost defiantly casual if it had not been for her eyes, which were coolly alert.

Prévert felt satisfied that he knew exactly how to proceed. There would be no suspect compliments, no devious manoeuvres, no paternal condescension. From the look of her, Ulrike von Seydlitz-Gabler would respond to candour alone.

"To begin with," said Prévert, after preliminary introductions were over, "I should make it clear that I know you, or parts of your life, better than you probably imagine."

"When you spoke to me on the 'phone you mentioned the name Hartmann. That's why I came. What do you know about him?"

"A great deal. My friendship with Herr Hartmann dates from July nineteen forty-four."

"That was when my friendship with him ended," said Ulrike. "Or, rather, that was when we lost touch with each other."

"I'm a police official from Paris. Perhaps that will make things a little clearer."

"And yet you talk of Rainer Hartmann like a close friend. I'm surprised."

"Why?"

Ulrike looked disconcerted. An expression of pain and helplessness crossed her face, but she quickly recovered her composure. "What do you expect me to say to that?"

"Nothing," Prévert answered simply. "At least, nothing you don't want to say."

"Are you really on good terms with Rainer?"

"I'm more than that—I'm his friend. He may not realize it, but it might be a good thing if you did."

"I believe you—I don't know why."

Ulrike took a sip of the Danish lager which a waiter had brought her. She studied Prévert's face attentively as she did so, and the longer she looked at him the greater her confidence in him became. She began to tell him all she knew. It was not much, but it was informative.

"In Paris, back in July nineteen forty-four, they said Rainer had deserted—that he was involved in some frightful crime or other."

"But you never believed he was capable of such a thing?"

"I regarded the charges as utterly ridiculous."

"I'm glad to hear you say that. It may make things easier."

"What things?" asked Ulrike, her eyes again filled with sudden alarm. "Have you got something unpleasant to tell me?"

"You can relax. What I've got to tell you isn't unpleasant, but what I propose to ask you to do may well be anything but pleasant."

"Tell me one thing first: how is he?"

"Quite well, all things considered."

"When did you see him last?"

"Last summer. I regularly spend my leave at the place where he's living now. We have supper together at least once a week—we share the same taste in rosé."

"Please go on."

"If you're interested in details," Prévert said politely, "I can tell you that he's still unmarried. I don't know if he's ever contemplated marriage, but I know one thing: it would have been virtually impossible for him to marry. He couldn't have got hold of the necessary papers without endangering his existence. Perhaps I should explain that in nineteen forty-four I left Hartmann with some reliable friends of mine in the South of France, and he's been there ever since. My friends had a certain amount of influence, so they managed to get him a French identity card, but he's only had a French passport since yesterday."

"Why did you help him? If you still look on him as a friend, it must mean that you're convinced of his innocence."

"Shall we say—I had no good and sufficient proof of his guilt. Quite apart from that, I was indebted to him for telling me the strangest story I had heard in the course of a not uneventful career, a story, incidentally, which still lacks an ending—and if there's one thing which worries me, mademoiselle, it's a story without an ending."

The restaurant was slowly beginning to fill up, and the rush-hour traffic flowing past the windows outside in the Kurfürstendamm was growing denser. The cramped city hummed with life. Prévert glanced at his wrist-watch.

"Am I keeping you?" Ulrike asked quickly.

"Forgive me," Prévert said. "It was I who should have asked you that. I gather your parents are in Berlin at the moment."

"Don't worry, I had dinner with them yesterday evening and I'm due to see them again tomorrow for lunch—but how did you know they were here?"

"An old friend of mine called Kahlenberge is staying in the same hotel. But, of course, you know him. Herr Kahlenberge is due to give a lecture here, and I'm hoping to be able to supply him with a little worth-while material."

"Please tell me something more about Rainer Hartmann."

"Well, he's hardly changed at all, outwardly. He's still got that gentle, melancholy angel-face of his, but inwardly it's a different story. The business in Paris seems to have left him with what our psychologist friends would call a trauma. A little while ago his chances of recovery seemed slender, but things could always change."

"Hasn't he ever been back to Germany in the meantime?"

"He couldn't do so without risking arrest. To begin with, he was officially posted as a deserter. The end of the war disposed of that charge, but he's still under suspicion of murder, even now. A man called Grau, a member of German counter-espionage in Paris, was probably the only person who knew the whole truth, but he was killed. That's how the Hartmann case got into the hands of your police.

'here's no statute of limitations governing murder, so his ame is still on their files. Hartmann knows that these recrds exist and that they contain enough circumstantial evience to put him away for life."

"It must be a terrible weight on his mind," Ulrike said oftly. "He was a sensitive person."

"He tried to get over it by resolving never to speak or hink about it again, but it was hopeless, of course. He's one f those rare people who would genuinely like to begin a ew life."

"What sort of life?"

"Ah, that's the vital question. Perhaps you'd like to ask im about it yourself?"

Ulrike had turned very pale. "You mean it would be ossible for me to speak to Rainer in person—here in Berlin?"

"That's precisely what I mean," said Prévert. "When I ooked at my watch earlier I was only making sure we vouldn't miss the arrival of a certain aeroplane. Will you ome with me?"

"Yes," she said, then added: "But I shan't know how to ehave."

"Behave naturally," Prévert advised her. "I'll give you a ew hints on the way to Templehof. The rest I leave to our instinct."

"I feel absolutely at sea."

"You're wrong," Prévert smiled encouragingly. "I'm the only one who's entitled to feel that. I feel as though I had just handed over the keys of a safe. I may be the only person who knows the combination, but without the key I'm powerless to open it—and the key is in your hand, mademoiselle."

INTERIM REPORT

FURTHER DOCUMENTS, NOTES AND RECORDS RELATING TO EVENTS IN BERLIN

Extracts from notes made by Lieutenant Felix Steinbeisser, formerly a serving officer in the so-called National People's Army. Steinbeisser graduated from the ranks of the Free German Youth and, after a spell of regimental duty, joined the East German Ministry of Defence as a political staff officer. In 1957 he left the German Democratic Republic because of a "crisis of conscience" and transferred his allegiance to West Germany, where he set up as a military expert on Eastern affairs. The following notes, which he described as an expert opinion, were supplied in return for a fee:

"Although he kept himself in the background, General Tanz was a prominent figure in the National People's Army. If he lacked popularity, it was because he seemed either unable or unwilling to come to terms with the political questions of the day. He was strictly a soldier.

"After his capture in Silesia he spent several crucial years in the Soviet Union, and although his name was never explicitly mentioned in connection with the 'National Committee for Free Germany,' I regard it as conceivable that he maintained some degree of contact with that body.

"General Tanz probably played a major role in the creation of the National People's Army and is said to have been responsible for much of its high-level planning. From March 1955 onwards he was transferred to active duty in the Dresden area, where he commanded an armoured corps.

"In 1956 General Tanz withdrew from the public gaze, and I have never (officially) heard of him since. My innate respect for historical accuracy forbids me to discuss current speculation on the subject."

Extracts from instructions given to Kahlenberge by Professor Kahlert, formerly a captain on General von Seydlitz-Gabler's staff. They have been reconstructed from notes made available by Herr Kahlenberge.

"First I must extend our sincere thanks to you for offering to give this lecture. When I say 'our' I am referring to a group of people with similar ideals. Our political club, whose full title is the Society for the Revival and Protection of Traditional Responsibilities—'The Traditionalist Club' for short—draws its membership from distinguished ex-officers, patriotic students, reliable graduates from other associations of various kinds, responsible scientists and enlightened artists. In short, you will have an audience to whom you can speak bluntly and with the candour of an old army man.

"I hardly need tell you that we believe in complete freedom of thought. This does not, of course, mean that we fail to uphold the inalienable validity of certain fundamental national rights. I say this solely for your information and in the implicit belief that in your case, my dear sir, such explanations are totally superfluous. If I give them nevertheless, it is purely a matter of routine.

"Bear in mind, first, that the reunification to which we all aspire so earnestly has always been imperilled by the other side, never by us; secondly, that ours is the only Germany with a claim to sovereignty; thirdly, that Bonn is not Pankow; and, fourthly, that if Germans ever start shooting each other we should be quite clear from the outset which side the good German is on. Ours is the only just cause.

"But why am I telling you all this? You must be fully alive to the true state of affairs in Germany today. You were a general. If we cannot rely on men like you, on whom can we rely?"

Telephone conversation between the Ministry of the Interior, East Berlin, and Central Police Headquarters, Warsaw. The speakers: Detective-Inspector Liebig of Dresden and Detective-Inspector Roman Liesowski of Warsaw. This conversation was noted down by the East German renegade whose shorthand records have been quoted in an earlier interim report. It was conducted in German.

Liebig: "I got your wire about the possible connection between Warsaw 1942 and Dresden 1956."

Liesowski: "It's only a possibility. Not having seen your files I can't give a firm opinion."

Liebig: "I had a long conversation with Monsieur Prévert of the Sûreté today. Do you know him?"

Liesowski: "Only by reputation."

Liebig: "Prévert has particulars of a third case which occurred in Paris in 1944. I've looked through them. The details bear an astonishing resemblance to those of the Dresden case."

Liesowski: "It can't be pure coincidence."

Liebig: "No, but what if Prévert's got something up his sleeve?"

Liesowski: "Look, you're dealing with a sex crime, that's all. What are you scared of?"

Liebig: "Nothing I can put my finger on. I just feel uneasy about working with the man. He's a tricky customer. That's why I'd like you to come to Berlin."

Liesowski: "I'll take the first 'plane—be with you by midday tomorrow. We'll see what happens then."

Instructions given to Ulrike von Seydlitz-Gabler by Prévert during the drive from the Restaurant Kopenhagen to Templehof Airport. Their gist was as follows:

"Try to give the impression that your meeting was accidental. Don't go rushing at him. On the contrary, give him a chance to recognize you. He'll need a moment or two to get used to the idea.

"The more you get him to talk about himself, preferably in general terms, the less likelihood there will be of his asking you awkward questions—though in my experience people remember the questions they've asked far better than the answers they get.

"I'm most anxious to create a pleasant atmosphere for

Hartmann. I want him to feel at home—and therefore secure.

"Try to put over the following points: it's never advisable to travel into the Eastern sector in the evening or at night, so it would be better if he spent the night on this side of the border. Advise him to stay at the Pension Phoenix in the Nürnberger Strasse. Here's the address. I've made sure there's a room available for him.

"The main thing is: don't mention my name if there's any way of avoiding it. As soon as he hears it he'll know what's going on. I promise you I'll tell him in due course, but if he found out prematurely it could be dangerous. For whom? I don't want to worry you unnecessarily."

3

Early the following morning a young man appeared at the Hotel am Kurfürstendamm. He wore a tight-fitting grey worsted suit and was carrying two capacious, almost new briefcases, one in either hand.

When the page-boy on duty tried to take one of the briefcases the young man gave him a curt "No thank you" and marched up to the reception desk.

The chief receptionist studied the approaching figure attentively. He found himself unable to classify it with his accustomed precision, which stimulated his curiosity. Perhaps the young man had wandered into the hotel by mistake, but judging by his air of solid self-assurance this seemed unlikely.

"General von Seydlitz-Gabler," said the young man.

The chief receptionist pretended not to know what was expected of him. "I beg your pardon?"

The young man looked as though he were incapable of being disconcerted or over-awed. His eyes, which had an appraising glint, were slightly narrowed like those of a man squinting along the sights of a rifle. He continued to grasp the briefcases firmly in both hands.

"I'd like to speak to General von Seydlitz-Gabler."

"In what connection?"

"That's none of your business," said the young man with compelling simplicity.

The chief receptionist bridled almost imperceptibly. The youth was right. It wasn't any of his business, but there was no need to be grossly offensive about it. People just didn't talk to chief receptionists like that—thought the chief receptionist. The young man evidently had no such inhibitions.

"I can't stand around here all day."

"What name shall I give?" The chief receptionist was breathing heavily now, like someone who was being forced to run up a mountainside at pistol-point. With barely concealed animosity, he added: "Your name, please."

"My name is unimportant."

"Really, sir!" expostulated the chief receptionist, on the verge of losing his self-control. "What do you mean? I can't just tell General von Seydlitz-Gabler . . ."

"Yes, you can," said the young man with undiminished composure. "All you need say is that I'm here on the orders of General Tanz."

The chief receptionist picked up the 'phone and asked to be put through to General von Seydlitz-Gabler's suite, eyeing the young man with mounting repugnance as he did so.

The object of his resentment stood there surveying his surroundings like a yokel on a village green. The luxuriously appointed foyer appeared to leave him completely unmoved. On the contrary, the chief receptionist thought he detected a look of unalloyed disdain in his eyes. He was tempted to wag his head reprovingly, but his telephone conversation temporarily precluded any such display of emotion.

"The General is expecting you," he said reluctantly. "I'll have you taken up to his suite." He snapped his fingers for a page-boy.

The young man followed the boy to the lift, still carrying his two briefcases and striding across the Persian carpets as if they were a stretch of asphalt.

Upstairs, von Seydlitz-Gabler was already awaiting his visitor. He stood in the centre of the sitting-room of his suite clad in a blue silk dressing-gown, a grey silk scarf at his throat and his feet thrust into a pair of stylish travelling-slippers. He looked benevolently paternal.

"Well, my boy," he inquired sonorously, "what have you got for me?"

"A letter from General Tanz, sir." The young man put down one of his briefcases, felt in his pocket and produced an envelope.

Von Seydlitz-Gabler's practised eye immediately spotted what the chief receptionist had failed to comprehend. The young man confronting him was a soldier in civilian clothes. From his manner he could only have one function—that of personal orderly.

"Name?" von Seydlitz-Gabler asked benignly.

"Wyzolla, Alfred, sir," came the prompt reply.

"Rank?"

"Sergeant, sir."

"Which arm?"

"Infantry, sir."

"Excellent," declared von Seydlitz-Gabler in tones of approval, and devoted himself to the contents of the letter which he had been handed. It was written on unheaded paper in a large, imposing hand, and ran as follows:

My dear General,

Many thanks for your extremely cordial letter. I have never forgotten the momentous hours which I was privileged to spend in your company. I gratefully accept your kind invitation and look forward to seeing you again. Please convey my warmest regards to your lady wife.

Yours very sincerely,

Wilhelm Tanz

Von Seydlitz-Gabler scanned the strong, angular characters intently for a moment. They marched across the paper like columns of well-disciplined soldiers, visible testimony of General Tanz's fighting spirit. Then he went into the bedroom next door.

Frau Wilhelmine was just putting the finishing touches to her toilette. Seeing her husband's reflection, agreeably reduced in size, in the mirror before her, she turned to him with an indulgent smile. Von Seydlitz-Gabler held out the letter.

"He's coming," he announced with scarcely suppressed triumph. "You see—a few lines from me did the trick, even after all this time." He bent forward confidentially. "Do you know, it's suddenly like old times again—I can feel it. Tanz has sent an orderly along in advance, just as he always did. A fine youngster—first-rate material. It's deplorable to think of a lad like that serving under the Communists!"

Frau Wilhelmine steered her husband back to the point

with her usual objectivity. "You ought to invite General Tanz to lunch."

"An excellent idea."

"Especially as Ulrike will be eating with us. I call that a fortunate coincidence. We must make the most of it."

Von Seydlitz-Gabler nodded and returned to the sitting-room, where he found Wyzolla, Alfred, standing exactly where he had left him. The boy was evidently waiting for instructions, directions or orders, and von Seydlitz-Gabler was only too happy to supply them.

"Right!" he exclaimed with youthful zest. "What's the form?"

The position, as summed up by Wyzolla, was as follows: Tanz had sent him on ahead with instructions to hand over the letter and then make sure that suitable accommodation, i.e., a hotel room, was available. If so, he was to make immediate preparations for the General's arrival; if not, he was to inform the General without delay. The General had travelled up to East Berlin for a conference. Unless otherwise notified, he would automatically arrive at the Hotel am Kurfürstendamm in three hours' time, at 1 p.m.

"First-class organization," von Seydlitz-Gabler commented admiringly, "but only what I should have expected. We've made some arrangements too."

They had—on Kahlenberge's advice. A suite had already been reserved for Tanz, and it proved easy enough to obtain a comparatively modest single room for Wyzolla.

Wyzolla picked up his briefcases, froze smartly to attention in a way that gladdened von Seydlitz-Gabler's heart, and betook himself to the suite which had been earmarked for General Tanz.

Once there, Wyzolla alerted chamber-maids, floor waiters and valets and issued them with precise instructions on how to cater for General Tanz's needs. He then instituted and supervised the spring-cleaning of the entire suite. When this had been carried out to his satisfaction—not that he voiced it—he dismissed the staff and carefully unpacked the contents of his briefcases.

Meanwhile, von Seydlitz-Gabler rang Kahlenberge and informed him, with an unmistakable note of self-congratulation in his voice, of General Tanz's forthcoming visit. "He wasted no time in accepting my invitation. I should welcome it if you could turn up at my suite for coffee, any time after two."

Kahlenberge thanked him and promptly rang Prévert. "Tanz is arriving about midday," he told him.

Prévert asked for details and Kahlenberge repeated his conversation with von Seydlitz-Gabler word for word. "That's all I know at the moment, but it's good enough for the time being. I'll be seeing Tanz shortly after two, then. Is there any special way you want me to behave?"

"Just help to create as pleasant an atmosphere as possible."

"I'm afraid I won't find it easy."

"Try to all the same, *mon cher*. I want Tanz to feel at home."

"Like a donkey on thin ice, you mean?"

Prévert chuckled. He was familiar with most of the German proverbs and admired their applicability to any given situation. "I should be greatly obliged if you could arrange a small party this evening—a rather select affair, you understand."

"I'm crazy about parties," Kahlenberge said caustically.

Rainer Hartmann, domiciled in Antibes and, according to his passport, a French national, had returned to Berlin at last. He was walking on air and everyone seemed to be in step with him. Even the buildings smiled down on him kindly, and the sky was bright. Hartmann felt happy.

Virtually the first person he had met in Berlin was Ulrike, who had apparently been seeing someone off at the airport. "It's almost too good to be true!" he exclaimed joyfully, and Ulrike felt like a traitress for not disillusioning him there and then. The years melted away as they talked, until what had once been seemed to have happened only yesterday. Ulrike and he suddenly became the focal point of the universe, wreathed in a golden haze of memories.

Hartmann spent the night at the Pension Phoenix, a night filled with roseate dreams of the future. He awoke to find that the weather matched his mood. Ulrike joined him for breakfast, during which they drank champagne and held hands under the table, chattering away happily like carefree children playing truant from school. It was a glorious day outside, with a sky that looked like a lavish flower arrangement in pastel shades.

After breakfast, Hartmann and Ulrike walked arm in arm to the nearest underground station. They got out in the vicinity of the Iderfenngraben, where Hartmann deposited Ulrike in a neighbouring bar and ordered her—at ten-thirty in the morning—a beer and a schnapps. Then he hurried round the corner and ran excitedly up the four flights of stairs that led to his aunt's flat.

Aunt Grete was the pride and joy of the family. She had been lucky enough to find a husband who adored her unstintingly. They had ten or twelve children at a rough count, and the family was a living example of the old saying that children are a form of wealth. Since three or four of them were already earning, the weekly income of the household which Aunt Grete administered so indefatigably was considerable.

Hartmann's old mother was waiting for him. He held her at arm's length for a moment, studying her face as though he had never seen it before. She was thin and grey, and her cheeks were seamed with a multitude of fine wrinkles, but her eyes were still as blue and serene as a mountain lake on a day in midsummer.

They hugged each other without speaking, surrounded by the younger members of Aunt Grete's family. A baby crawled under their feet, a small boy gazed at them with rapt attention, and a girl of about school-leaving age looked as though she intended to smother Hartmann with cousinly caresses. He was hard put to it to keep his feet under such a violent onslaught of affection. Oblivious to what was being said, he held his mother's hand and revelled in the cosy warmth enclosing him as the children clustered round. At least two of them perched on his knees, and the adolescent girl hung over the back of his chair with her arms round his neck.

"You must be hungry," said his mother. "Children are always hungry."

"Yes, always!" clamoured half a dozen voices.

Aunt Grete had baked a monster cake in his honour and laid out an array of cold meat, sausage and jellied eel. Encircled by dishes, Hartmann began to tuck in, urged on by the children, who knew that the left-overs would belong to them. Today was a red-letter day!

"Thank you for your telegram," said Hartmann. He stroked his mother's arm, dividing his attention between her and the jellied eel. "What a wonderful spread! I haven't been so spoilt since I was a boy. My God, I feel good! But you know what would be real heaven? How about frying me a couple of potato pancakes?"

"As many as you like," Aunt Grete replied promptly.

A few of the children looked disappointed. They had potato pancakes at least once a week.

"What telegram do you mean, Rainer?" asked his mother.

Hartmann looked perplexed. "You sent me one, didn't you?" A tempting aroma came from the heaped dishes before him, but for the moment all he wanted was an answer to his question.

"No."

A brooding expression came over Hartmann's face. He tasted everything that was set before him, stuffing himself with food he didn't really want and temporarily yielding to the notion that he could eat his way back into the halcyon days of his boyhood, dish by dish.

"Never mind," he sighed between mouthfuls. "I'm happy to be here with you, that's all that matters."

At length he took his leave, promising to come back very soon—if not that evening, certainly at lunch-time next day. He held his mother close, pressing his cheek against hers, while a dozen childish hands plucked at his sleeve. Aunt Grete looked on with a contented smile, satisfied that she had warded off starvation for a few hours.

Hartmann hurried back to the bar, where Ulrike had ordered herself another beer and was still waiting patiently. She looked tired but happy. "Well, aren't you glad you came?" she asked.

"Of course," Hartmann replied automatically. His face had darkened as though a thin veil had been drawn across it. "But there's something queer going on. You know that telegram I got from my mother? She says she never sent one. I don't know what to think."

"Maybe she misunderstood you." Ulrike sensed that this was the moment Prévert had warned her about. "Perhaps she didn't understand what you meant—or you misunderstood her."

"The fact remains that she says she didn't send me a telegram."

"Did you discuss it with her?"

"Of course not. I didn't want to upset her. She was so happy to see me."

"Perhaps that's the answer," Ulrike said persuasively. "You didn't question her thoroughly enough. The telegram needn't necessarily have been sent by your mother—it could have been your uncle or aunt, or one of the neighbours. There are any number of explanations. I don't see the slightest reason for you to worry."

"All the same, maybe I ought to leave Berlin straight away." Hartmann sounded morose. "There's something going on. I can feel it in my bones."

"Cheer up, darling!" Ulrike smiled at him fondly. "Look outside—it's a glorious day, you're back in Berlin, and I'm here with you. What more do you want?"

The meeting scheduled for noon in Commissioner Karpfen's office opened harmoniously enough. It broke up barely an hour later in an atmosphere of strident discord. Those present, apart from Karpfen, were Prévert of Paris, Liesowski of Warsaw and Liebig of Dresden.

Karpfen was determined not to miss this exchange of views, which promised to provide a welcome break from his otherwise arid routine.

"No formalities, please, gentlemen," he said with heavy bonhomie. "Permit me to bid you a cordial welcome, and thank you for the prompt way in which you accepted my invitation. May our common efforts prove fruitful!"

Commissioner Karpfen raised his glass and the other three followed suit, smiling politely. Liesowski had brought a bottle of smoky Bison Vodka with him from Warsaw. He preferred Polish vodka to Russian.

"Right, let's get down to business," said Karpfen.

The three investigators started to remove documents from their briefcases, eyeing one another covertly as they did so. Each realized that the other two were weighing him up, and this led to a certain amount of restrained amusement.

"If we're looking for common features," Liesowski said, "the case to concentrate on is the one that's still warm, so to speak. I think we should start from there."

"Precisely," agreed Prévert. He regarded the detective-inspector from Warsaw with the interest which he would have lavished on a century-old brandy. "That's it in a nutshell."

At a nod from Karpfen, Liebig obediently spread out his files on the table.

"The only thing I can give you any firm details about," he began, "is the crime itself. The motive seems clear enough and the victim has been identified, but so far we have no clues as to the murderer's identity. There have been a number of tips and false leads, but nothing which could be called conclusive."

"Perhaps we shall be able to offer some suggestions on that point," said Prévert. "But not, of course, until we've heard the results of your investigations."

Liebig launched into a summary of his findings, and the further he got the more attentive Liesowski and Prévert became. They glanced at each other fleetingly from time to time, their initial reserve giving way to something resembling tacit understanding.

Commissioner Karpfen, who thought he was already in possession of the full facts, brooded absently in his chair. He failed to detect anything in the case which could be called particularly interesting or sensational. In his opinion the crime was the work of a complete lunatic, and such individuals existed in the best-regulated countries.

Detective-Inspector Liebig's report, reduced to its basic essentials, was as follows:

During the night of 12th-13th August 1956, screams were heard issuing from No. 7 Sterngasse, Dresden. They came from a flat occupied by a certain Erika Mangler, of no fixed occupation. The local police were notified at once. On reaching the premises, they found the mutilated body of a woman, presumed to be Erika Mangler herself. Homicide was called in and immediately identified the crime as the work of a sexual maniac. Inquiries, which were instituted without delay, had elicited conflicting and, in some cases, implausible statements from a number of witnesses. Erika Mangler's name appeared in the current list of known prostitutes.

According to the pathologist's report, Mangler had been stabbed thirty-three times with a sharp, pointed instrument, e.g., a stiletto-type knife, in the region of the throat, breasts and genitals. Most of the wounds were in the latter area. It could be assumed with certainty that death had intervened after the first few blows had been struck.

"Most interesting," declared Liesowski, when Liebig had finished. He spoke quietly and without apparent emotion. "I worked on a very similar case in Warsaw in 1942. Place, victim and method were much the same, and the pathologist's findings were almost identical."

"The same goes for me," said Prévert. "Rue de Londres, Paris 1944."

"Really?" Karpfen was slowly emerging from his lethargy. "But how can that be? I ask you—the same type of crime in three entirely different places?"

"There's quite a simple explanation," Prévert said. "The murderer is a man who has moved around a lot. The last war was an indirect cause of mass migration, and historic events of that sort often have strange side-effects. In our particular case, all we've got to do is find someone who was in all three places at the times in question."

The Commissioner smiled indulgently. "How do you propose to do that? Europe was upside down in 1942 and 1944."

Liesowski said: "In the course of my inquiries I came across a peculiar point—so peculiar that the German authorities took the case out of my hands at once."

"The officer in charge was called Grau, wasn't he?"

Liesowski stared at Prévert in amazement. "You're right! The salient feature of my inquiries, as far as they went, was that a witness stated that he'd seen a man in Wehrmacht uniform."

"A soldier near the scene of the crime?" Liebig pricked up his ears. He hurriedly thumbed through his papers until he found what he wanted. "I have a similar statement here. Someone saw a soldier sitting in a parked car just round the corner. He was there for some time. My men interviewed him, but they didn't find anything suspicious. He was an N.C.O.

named Wyzolla, an army driver. But he was a young man. That rules him out—he must have been a child at the time of the Warsaw and Paris murders."

"I think we've reached the end of the road," said Prévert. He looked across at Liesowski. "Do you agree?"

The policeman from Warsaw nodded. "This is the decisive factor, there's no doubt about it."

"Wait!" cried Karpfen. He was wide awake now, and puffing like a grampus. "Take it easy, gentlemen, please! I feel we're skating on thin ice."

"Why?" inquired Prévert. "We're after a murderer. What's so ticklish about that? Besides, I already know the murderer's name, and have done for twelve years. These parallel cases were all I needed to complete my chain of evidence. Now, I'm absolutely sure of my ground."

"I thought I knew who the murderer was, too," said Liesowski. "I managed to find a witness who was prepared to make a detailed statement. Major Grau, the German officer we mentioned earlier, appeared to share my suspicions, but he never succeeded in clearing the case up. It was hardly surprising, considering the unusual nature of the evidence before us. For a long time even I felt disinclined to believe it."

"I was in exactly the same position." Prévert nodded understandingly at his Polish colleague. "I also felt chary of accepting it."

"Please be more specific!" Liebig demanded impatiently. He was all detective now, nothing else. He seemed to be blind to his superior's warning glances and deaf to his snorts of protest. "Theories are no good to me on their own. I need positive proof."

Prévert made a gesture of invitation to Liesowski. He might have been lowering a poised dagger in deference to someone who had a better claim to strike the first blow.

Liesowski said: "The man in question is a general named Tanz."

Commissioner Karpfen leapt to his feet, purple in the face. He appeared to be on the verge of apoplexy.

"I declare this meeting adjourned," he said peremptorily, "and I regard the last remark as stricken from the record. Please act accordingly, Herr Liebig. I request you to close your files and release no more information until further inructed. I regret having to make this decision, but I have no :her choice."

"Why?" asked Prévert. "Do you want to obstruct the ɔurse of justice? I can't think of any other way of describing ɔur attitude."

Karpfen subsided into his chair. He sat back with legs ɔlayed, fished out a handkerchief and began to mop his row.

"Gentlemen," he said wearily, "you are police officers nd experienced members of your profession, but I am rst and foremost a civil servant. As such, I have special esponsibilities. Apart from that, I serve a country which having difficulty in gaining the recognition it deserves— or reasons which we need not go into here. But you, Herr révert, and you, Herr Liesowski, belong to nations which an never be expected to entertain any particular sympathy or us."

"What about opening a bottle of that Crimean cham- agne?" asked Prévert.

"I'm all in favour," said Liesowski. "After all, we have omething to celebrate."

Liebig seemed to welcome the distraction. He rose with lacrity and busied himself with the bottle, presenting his road back and equally imposing posterior to Karpfen in the rocess.

The Commissioner pressed on doggedly. "I would ask 'ou to remember that we—my comrades and the State we erve—have been compelled to rearm, even though our sole bject has been to help defend the cause of peace. It has ot escaped us that our action has aroused a certain sneak- ng distrust here and there. Moreover, gentlemen, there has lways been a considerable degree of fellow-feeling between 'oland and France."

"I second that last remark," said Prévert, unabashed.

"And I drink to it," Liesowski chimed in.

"We cannot permit you," Karpfen said heatedly, "to jeop- rdize the results of all our hard work and self-denial. I ay this in all seriousness, gentlemen: we shall further the nds of justice, but not at the expense of a scandal. Our enerals are not clay pigeons—as far as we're concerned, hey're a necessity of life. I implore you to show some ympathy for our position."

"I have remarkably little sympathy for murderers," said Prévert, draining his glass, "but my appreciation of good food and drink is almost unlimited. All I can think of at the moment is that caviar over there."

General Tanz entered the Hotel am Kurfürstendamm on the stroke of one o'clock. His slim, powerful frame was clad in a suit the colour of autumn leaves. His face might have been cast in bronze and his eyes seemed to be focussed on invisible armies deployed in the far distance.

He was met in the hotel foyer, predictably, by Wyzolla. The young man looked as though he was about to salute but controlled himself and came forward to make his report in a subdued voice. A suite had been duly reserved for Tanz and General von Seydlitz-Gabler was expecting him for lunch.

Tanz gave a suggestion of a nod. He did not seem to have changed much in the intervening years. The tanned skin covering bone and sinew, the sharply defined, pugnacious set of the jaw, the sea-blue sailor's eyes, the mouth like a knife-wound—all looked the same. The grooves running from his nostrils, past the corners of his mouth, to his chin were deeper, but that was all.

Ignoring the chief receptionist, who bowed repeatedly, doubling up like a jack-knife, Tanz mounted the stairs leading to the first floor, accompanied by Wyzolla. He motioned to his escort to station himself outside the door and then entered von Seydlitz-Gabler's suite.

The ensuing ceremony of welcome was positively affecting in its cordiality. The two men gazed into each other's eyes, extended their arms and shook hands warmly and at great length.

"At last, at last!" breathed Frau Wilhelmine with well-rehearsed if slightly theatrical fervour.

"Just like old times, eh?" said von Seydlitz-Gabler as they sat down to table.

"The only one missing is our Ulrike." Frau Wilhelmine never lost her grip of essentials. "The dear child will be along later. She's a working girl, you know—extremely efficient, too, I'm told."

"Well, my dear chap, how have things been with you since we last met?"

Tanz had been expecting this question and was ready for it. He regarded von Seydlitz-Gabler calmly, like a doctor meeting the gaze of an anxious patient.

"I did my duty."

"It must have been very difficult for you sometimes," hazarded Frau Wilhelmine.

"I ask you," von Seydlitz-Gabler said jovially, "when was it ever easy to do one's duty? Certainly not in times like these, I know that."

While the floor waiter was serving lunch they chatted amicably about things in general, but Frau Wilhelmine soon steered the conversation back to Ulrike.

"All young girls try to kick over the traces occasionally, but she has never forgotten her duty towards us and the traditions of our family."

"I have often thought of you, General," Tanz said. "You and your family have always meant a great deal to me."

Von Seydlitz-Gabler was touched and Frau Wilhelmine seemed equally moved. A mouth-watering aroma rose from the saddle of venison and red cabbage in front of them.

"It has always been part of a soldier's job to make the best of any given situation," Tanz went on, when the floor waiter had left the room. "Fate decreed that I should end up on the other side, but I was still in Germany."

"Everyone appreciates that," von Seydlitz-Gabler assured him, inserting a forkful of red cabbage into his mouth and following it up with a substantial helping of cranberries. "When you come down to it, my dear fellow, you've probably been going through the same sort of things we went through when the Bohemian corporal was in charge. They were difficult times but not inglorious ones. We stuck to our posts through thick and thin. Let's face it—it was our legal duty to do so, if only to prevent something worse happening. If we'd been irresponsible enough to default, a pack of bloodthirsty and unscrupulous career-hounds would have stepped into our shoes."

"I've been in much the same position myself during the past few years," said Tanz. "My intentions have always been of the best. Whatever I've done, Germany has always been uppermost in my thoughts. After all, the people I've been dealing with over there are Germans too."

"Absolutely," agreed von Seydlitz-Gabler. "Magnificent

material—you've only got to look at Sergeant Wyzolla to see that. Stout lad, Wyzolla. I gave him a careful once-over."

"He's only one of many. It was chaps like that who made me realize that I couldn't evade my responsibilities. For all that, it's become clear to me that if there are two Germanies one of them must be more——" he paused as if searching for the right word "—more worth-while than the other."

"Bravo!" exclaimed von Seydlitz-Gabler, deeply moved. "A very creditable sentiment."

Frau Wilhelmine said: "You can't imagine how delighted we are to have you with us again. We've missed you."

"You're very kind," Tanz replied. He grasped her hand and kissed it with a convincing display of chivalry. "If there were more people like you, dear lady, it would make everything very much easier. As things are, I fear there will be awkward misunderstandings."

Von Seydlitz-Gabler leant back, savouring the blissful sensation of having lunched excellently in congenial company.

"You must realize, my dear friend," he began importantly, "that the Federal Republic has gradually regained its respect for real values and its readiness to listen to men of long experience. The days of namby-pamby self-recrimination and mental confusion, the days when it was fashionable to foul one's own doorstep—well, they're gone for good. Just after the war they taught children to look askance at us. Young people were talked into pouring scorn on us. Even some of our old friends started to waver. But that's all over now."

"You can't imagine how much we suffered," put in Frau Wilhelmine, "though we kept a stiff upper lip, of course."

"It was absolutely humiliating in the early days." Von Seydlitz-Gabler bowed his grizzled head. "I'm ashamed when I think of the drivel published by German newspapers, of the muck written by German authors, of the filth spewed out by the German radio—buckets of it, I tell you! Still, let's forget it. A lot of misguided individuals have realized their mistakes and mended their ways. Open our newspapers today—they've regained their character. Read a good book—authors are no longer ashamed of referring to our glorious past. Listen to our radio broadcasts—you won't hear a word uttered against the forces of reconstruction and tradition."

"That," Tanz declared approvingly, "is what I call true national awareness—something really worth fighting for."

"I don't wish to exaggerate my own importance." Von Seydlitz-Gabler spoke with unaffected simplicity. "We've been through some hard times, but what are hard times for, if not to teach us the art of survival? Conscientious objectors and pacifists are as good as dead today. They can say and write what they please, but they're not socially acceptable."

"It's much the same over there—where I come from," said Tanz, looking thoughtful.

Von Seydlitz-Gabler's voice took on a note of justifiable pride. "You'll see how far the country has travelled back along the road to sanity when I tell you that people not only listen to old soldiers like us but actually seek our advice. For instance, they've snapped up these memoirs of mine. Negotiations for an English edition are complete and a big American magazine is bidding for the pre-publication rights."

"Splendid news," Tanz said appreciatively. "That's the sort of air a man can breathe in. I congratulate you. No one deserves success more than you."

"Of course, I'm not telling you this just to blow my own trumpet. I merely quote it as an illustration of how things are with us. There's only one sphere of operations for men with ideas, and I hope you'll have decided by now which side of the border it's on. Tell me in all honesty, my dear fellow, wouldn't you like to join us?"

Tanz, who had been sitting there stiff as a poker but with his body slightly inclined, now drew himself up to his full height. His granite features seemed to be illumined by a gentle ray of sunlight. "My sense of duty comes first," he said, punching out the words like a machine, "but it must be a spontaneous sense of duty. To me, service is not an end in itself. It must have a higher purpose."

"Does that mean you've already decided to make the break?" von Seydlitz-Gabler asked expectantly.

"I'm not averse to the idea—given some guarantee of fair treatment."

"How wonderful!" Frau Wilhelmine laid her hand affectionately over Tanz's. "I know you'll feel at home with us. We have a wide circle of friends and our social functions are regaining their old cachet. Even cabinet ministers feel honoured to be invited."

"And so they should!" cried von Seydlitz-Gabler in high good humour. "But you will be especially welcome, my dear Tanz. There are any number of possibilities open to you. You can relax in private, or do a bit of writing for the papers, or go into industry with our friend Kahlenberge's assistance, or write memoranda for government departments, or become a military consultant, or even return to the active list again—the choice is unlimited."

Tanz nodded curtly. "My motto has always been deeds rather than words, as you know. The last thing I want is to draw attention to myself."

"Your wishes shall be respected, rely on me. This evening, subject to your approval, we plan to give a small private reception. Only eight or ten people—a dozen at the most—including men with influence in the right quarters, friend Kahlenberge among them. You'll be able to explore the ground—entirely without obligation, of course. What do you say?"

"I shall be glad to come," said Tanz. He sounded almost moved. The glass which he was holding shattered between his clenched fingers and blood started to drip from his palm, but he appeared not to notice. With formal courtesy, he added: "I'm greatly indebted to you."

INTERIM REPORT

FURTHER DOCUMENTS, INCLUDING EXTRACTS FROM MANUSCRIPTS, TELEPHONE CONVERSATIONS AND LETTERS

The following are excerpts from the draft of the lecture which Kahlenberge planned to give before an invited audience in Berlin:

". . . it is my intention, so far from putting the concept of soldiership on a par with that of war, to make a deliberate distinction between the two. If you train a man for war alone you are automatically training him for murder; but if you claim, in all sincerity, that you are training him to preserve peace you must train him to be a human being. You have no other choice.

"To train a man in blind obedience is tantamount to fostering stupidity. It may be the most convenient form of man-management, but it has nothing whatsoever to do with leadership. An attempt to inculcate culture and knowledge, on the other hand, presupposes culture and knowledge on the part of the teacher. Building up an army must be a mental process, not a piece of routine planning. An army should not be in the hands of adroit power politicians but in those of equally shrewd but responsible men.

"If the course of history conforms to any so-called historical rules, then we have reached the end of the road. If it means learning and experience, then we must finally acknowledge the necessity—the vital necessity—or making a radical break with the past. As long as the soldier is only a fighter, a warrior, a recipient of orders, a gunman and a potential murderer, he will always be at the mercy of bloodthirsty and unscrupulous war-mongers. . . ."

These remarks had been heavily deleted in red pencil. The same pencil had written in the margin: "Too late!"

but the exclamation mark after the words had been replaced by a mark of interrogation.

Extracts from a letter written by Frau Wilhelmine von Seydlitz-Gabler to her sister-in-law, whose husband, Frau Wilhelmine's brother, was head of a government department:

". . . I'm sure you still remember General Tanz. I told you so much about him. You know I never enthuse about people, but I've always had a soft spot for General Tanz. He's a man of action—perhaps the last of his kind. If only he would take Ulrike off my hands. I'm so worried about her.

". . . Fate sent General Tanz to the East. He made every effort to do his duty even there, and he succeeded. What a price he paid, though! You can see it in his face.

". . . He has boundless faith in Herbert—and in me as well. If ever a man followed the dictates of his conscience, it is he. Do tell Adalbert about him. Something definite must be done. It's none of my affair, but when I think what those Russians have done. . . ."

Verbatim notes of a telephone conversation between Detective-Sergeant Hornträger of Dresden:

Liebig: "I've come across an interesting memo in my files—something of yours. I gather you found some witnesses who saw a saloon car parked in a side street near the scene of the crime."

Hornträger: "That's right, sir. It was there for some time."

Liebig: "Well, did you follow the information up?"

Hornträger: "Of course—as far as it seemed necessary. The driver was a chap called Wyzolla—a sergeant in the National People's Army."

Liebig: "Go on."

Hornträger: "Well, nothing came of it—at least, nothing that seemed to have any bearing on the case. I naturally made the usual routine inquiries, discreetly, of course. His superiors had nothing but good to say about him. They gave him an excellent report. He turned out to be the G.O.C.'s personal driver."

Liebig: "Damnation! What's the G.O.C.'s name?"
Hornträger: "Tanz."
Liebig: "That settles it. I want you to interrogate Wyzolla at once—no holds barred, mind you. Squeeze him like a lemon and don't worry about the consequences. Keep a mobile squad on call and 'phone me as soon as you've got something to report. I'll wait for your call here."

From the memoirs of General von Seydlitz-Gabler. The following passage is taken from a chapter entitled "The Path of Duty":

"There were certain problems which I, personally, never evaded. I say this not out of vanity but as a matter of plain fact. I always strove to be a father to my men and never contemplated surrendering to Corporal Hitler. In that way, I not only helped my men to lead a comparatively worthy existence but also managed to protect many of them from the more unpleasant aspects of our situation. By refusing to desert my post I was serving the future of Germany.

"Similar, though not identical in every respect, was the position in which one of my highly esteemed and often-decorated brother officers, General Tanz, found himself after the Second World War. Whatever he did, his thoughts were centred upon Germany, upon Germany as a whole, upon the German as a soldier and an individual, upon the need to safeguard the achievements of the Western world. . . ."

Verbatim report of a further telephone conversation between Detective-Sergeant Hornträger of Dresden and Detective-Inspector Liebig, temporarily in East Berlin:

Hornträger: "I tried to get hold of Wyzolla, as you requested, but it proved to be impossible. Sergeant Wyzolla is away on an official trip at the moment. He's escorting General Tanz to Berlin. Tanz's chief staff officer told me that he's attending a conference at the Ministry of Defence, but that's all I could get out of him. He left at about two o'clock yesterday afternoon and they don't know when he'll be back."
Liebig: "Damn and blast!"

4

Rainer Hartmann opened his eyes, blinking sleepily. His bedroom curtains were drawn, but the subdued afternoon light hurt his eyes. He was lying fully clothed on his bed in the Pension Phoenix. It might have been minutes or hours since he dozed off—he didn't know. Something seemed to be groping for him, oppressing him, enveloping him. He couldn't identify it, but it was there. Shaking off his lethargy with an effort, he sat up abruptly.

A squat, dimly defined figure was standing at the foot of his bed. It looked familiar, even in the half-light.

"So it's you!" Hartmann grunted.

Prévert pulled up a chair and sat down. "My dear Hartmann, don't pretend you're surprised to see me."

Hartmann leant back against the bed-head, almost as if he were flinching away. "Considering what's happened to me in the past few days, I should have guessed that you were behind it all. I just couldn't bring myself to believe you were capable of such a dirty trick."

"It's part of my job," said Prévert. "How do you imagine I could deal with unscrupulous individuals effectively if I were a mass of scruples myself?"

"What do you want?"

"Why ask a question you know the answer to—subconsciously, anyway. All right, if I must be explicit: it's time."

"I suppose you're waiting for me to say 'Time for what?' Well, I won't. I just don't care. The only thing that matters to me is that you've seen fit to take advantage of a number of decent people, including our mutual friends in Antibes, my mother and Ulrike."

Prévert settled himself comfortably on the hard wooden

chair. "My dear Hartmann, that's what friends are for. I'll give you some good advice: don't underestimate a mother's unselfishness—and as far as Ulrike is concerned, I can only congratulate you. That girl has the sort of courage most men only dream of."

"Do you mean Ulrike's in on this, too? Do you mean she's playing your game—letting herself be used for the sake of something she doesn't understand?"

"My dear boy," Prévert said patiently, "that remarkable young lady of yours immediately grasped what it has taken me weeks and you years to realize: the past cannot be dismissed; it has to be overcome. A man can't always do that on his own. He needs people to help him—in your case, Ulrike and—please believe me—myself."

Hartmann hitched up his socks, straightened his trousers and buttoned his shirt—all mechanical acts designed to gain time.

"You're welcome to go on living as you have been doing—if that's what you really want. There's a 'plane leaving for Nice via Munich and Geneva in just over an hour's time. You can catch it comfortably." Prévert spoke like a ticket-clerk giving information. "My car's waiting outside. You only have to say the word and you'll never see me again, or Berlin—or Ulrike, probably."

"Or General Tanz either, I suppose?"

Prévert chuckled gleefully. "He's in the bag," he said. "I only have to pull the string, but I can't do it unless you help me."

"And what's likely to happen if I do?"

"A lot of things," Prévert conceded. "Loaded pistols sometimes go off and typewriters can be just as dangerous in their own way. Wherever there's power there are men who abuse it. Human beings are the most unreliable creatures in the world. For all that, there are such things as friends."

"And are you one, Prévert?"

"Where my friendship for you is concerned, all I can say is—try me."

Hartmann drew a deep breath. "All right. Maybe I've nothing more to lose. If I'm wrong, at least I'll know how much I did have."

"How I envy you," Prévert said softly, "and how well I understand you. Life has dealt you one slap in the face after another, but you still cling to your faith in human nature. You've lost nearly everything that makes a normal person's life bearable—and yet, when I claim to be your friend, you don't hesitate to return the favour. Ah, my dear boy, what have I done to deserve this moral incubus? Fundamentally, even I believe in the existence of goodness. How do you account for that?"

Frau Wilhelmine was making the necessary preparations for the reception in honour of General Tanz, aided by Wyzolla, who had been made available to her for the purpose by Tanz himself. Wyzolla had proved an able assistant, instantly carrying out anything that sounded remotely like an order. Frau Wilhelmine watched him with a tinge of nostalgia. The dear dead days were not so dead after all.

"You've been extremely helpful," she told him.

"Thank you, ma'am," Wyzolla replied with ingenuous self-assurance. "I try to be."

The hotel management had reserved the so-called "Green Salon"—also known as the "Hunting Room"—for the von Seydlitz-Gablers' reception. Frau Wilhelmine checked the arrangements in person and then telephoned Kahlenberge. He seemed delighted, and promised to come, adding: "I'd very much like to bring a friend of mine—a Frenchman."

"Is he an influential person?"

"Definitely," Kahlenberge assured her brightly. "You might describe my friend Prévert as a power behind the throne. He can make careers and break them. Given the right combination of circumstances, even the President of France would find it hard to evade his clutches."

"In that case, bring him by all means." Frau Wilhelmine sounded impressed.

Her next victim was a junior minister who happened to be visiting Berlin. Being a man who accepted all invitations on principle, he proved easy meat, as did a visiting diplomat from the Benelux countries. The latter was reputed to be a very minor force in the Council of Europe, but Frau Wilhelmine threw him into the pot for good measure. His function would be mainly decorative.

The next name on her list was the managing director of a famous electrical engineering firm. After putting up a brief but fruitless struggle, he weakened when Kahlenberge's name was mentioned, reflecting that Kahlenberge's firm manufactured special vehicles for transporting turbines and marine cable.

Frau Wilhelmine then proceeded to rope in a member of the Berlin Senate, who was noted for his vast network of contacts. He was also noted for his slightly wry sense of humour, which he took care to display when accepting her invitation. "I shall be delighted to come, dear lady, and so will my latest wife."

The last remark drew Frau Wilhelmine's attention to a problem of secondary but undeniable importance: the so-called gentler sex. Since no great reliance could be placed on Ulrike and the Senator's "latest wife" was an unknown quantity, she would have to hunt up two or three females, preferably attractive.

The appropriate source of supply in this case could be defined by the collective term "show business" in its widest sense, i.e., television, radio and films. Within a few minutes Frau Wilhelmine had secured acceptances from a much-misunderstood film actress of Scandinavian origin, an uncommonly attractive "pop." singer and a junior woman announcer from the local television station.

While Frau Wilhelmine was thus engaged, Wyzolla had been polishing glasses with the concentration which he would have devoted to cleaning rifle ammunition. It was one of Tanz's axioms that nothing should ever surprise a soldier, and Wyzolla's attitude conformed to it perfectly. Hence, he remained utterly unimpressed when a page appeared in the Green Salon and sidled up to him.

"There are two gentlemen downstairs."

"Well?" Wyzolla shrugged and resumed his glass-polishing. "There may be three or four, for all I care."

"They want a word with you," the page persisted in a whisper.

"Maybe," said Wyzolla, "but I don't want a word with them. Can't you see I'm busy?"

He ignored the page, who retreated in some confusion. Frau Wilhelmine crossed out some entries on her notepad and made some more. The page reappeared.

"The two gentlemen are still waiting in the hall. They say it's important."

"Not to me it isn't," Wyzolla said laconically.

"They say they only want some information."

"Can't give them any," said Wyzolla. "Not competent to. Don't bother me. Got things to do."

Prévert, Hartmann and Ulrike were sitting in a café in the Nürnberger Strasse.

"Don't worry, Rainer," said Ulrike, "I know Monsieur Prévert won't let us down." She smiled at Prévert. "General Tanz has turned up already—with an escort, as usual."

"An escort?" asked Prévert, without betraying undue interest.

"A sort of body-guard, I suppose. A tough young man who doesn't say much—I saw him earlier on when I visited my mother. She's making arrangements for the party and he's helping her. Tanz generously lent him to her for the occasion."

"What's the youngster's name?" asked Prévert.

"Wyzolla."

Prévert leant back in his chair contentedly. "Excellent," he said. "Tell me more."

Ulrike ran through the list of invitations. "Mother had put a note beside Kahlenberge's name: 'plus French guest.' Is that you, Monsieur Prévert?"

"Yes, I'm a guest of a guest, and if Kahlenberge can invite someone I don't see why you shouldn't."

"In that case, my guest's name is Rainer Hartmann."

"Clever girl—that's what I hoped you were going to say."

"I can't ask Ulrike to do that," Hartmann said promptly.

"My dear boy," said Prévert, "what do you mean? The fur's going to fly tonight anyway. We needn't worry about a little subterfuge like that."

"I've remembered something else," Ulrike said. "While I was with Mother she invented an errand for Wyzolla to get him out of the room. While he was gone she 'phoned reception and asked for more details about the two men who had asked to speak to him."

"Well? Did she get what she wanted?"

"Apparently not. She looked rather at a loss when she put the 'phone down, and it's unlike my mother to be flummoxed by anything."

Prévert had suddenly assumed an air of urgency. He got

up, issued a few final instructions and took his leave. "I'll leave you to yourselves now. You could put it down to my sense of delicacy if you like, but you'd be wrong."

"I wouldn't disturb you unless it was absolutely necessary," said Prévert as he entered Kahlenberge's room. "I see you're doing some more work on your lecture."

"I'm making a genuine attempt to finish it," Kahlenberge said, pointing to his manuscript, "but I don't feel I ever will."

"Very perceptive of you," Prévert commented cheerfully.

Kahlenberge shuffled his papers together. "I can't remember a time when you didn't have some special request to make. Well, what is it now?"

Prévert lowered his bulk on to the sofa, carefully arranging the cushions first.

"Of course I want something," he said. "My primary concern is to entertain you as pleasantly as possible—while at the same time interesting you in the next phase of my plans. I should also like to make a couple of telephone calls at your expense. I think they'll intrigue you."

Prévert's first call was to the West Berlin Senator. "Just mention my name," he told officials who tried to be obstructive.

Within a few minutes the Senator was on the line. He sounded pleased to hear from Prévert again, and since both men were seasoned veterans of a thousand telephone battles and neither had any marked predilection for complex formalities they reached agreement in a surprisingly short space of time. Prévert merely expressed a wish for some co-operation from an experienced Berlin police officer, and the Senator said: "Leave it to me." That was all.

Shortly afterwards, Chief-Inspector Müller-Meidrich telephoned. Müller-Meidrich had learned his trade under Chief Superintendent Tantau, formerly head of the Berlin homicide department and highly thought of in professional circles. He received the following information: at about 3 p.m. two men had turned up at the reception desk in the Hotel am Kurfürstendamm and asked to speak to someone called Wyzolla. Who were these men and why had they come?

"We'll soon find out," said Müller-Meidrich. "I'll call you back."

"Who's Wyzolla?" Kahlenberge asked Prévert when he had rung off.

"A young man who was sitting in a car in Dresden the other night—to be precise, in a street just round the corner from the Sterngasse."

Kahlenberge shook his bald dome of a head in exasperation. "And what's that supposed to mean?"

"A murder was committed in the said Sterngasse—and I may say that murder is a pale description of what took place there."

Kahlenberge raised both hands as though he were about to protest, then let them sink again impotently. "And I always thought," he said with an effort, "that you revelled in the bizarre and mysterious. I thought that was the reason why you didn't dismiss Hartmann's story as a piece of grotesque nonsense, but I'm beginning to see now—you're in dead earnest."

"I've never been capable of dismissing violent death as a sort of diabolical joke."

Kahlenberge rose to his feet abruptly, knocking the draft of his lecture off the table as he did so. It fluttered to the floor and lay there like so much waste paper. Neither man looked at it.

"If your assumptions are correct," he said in a dull voice, "if what you suspect turns out to be based on fact, where do we go from there?"

Prévert smiled grimly. "Call a general a general, by all means, but never hesitate to call a criminal a criminal."

The telephone rang shrilly. Prévert picked up the receiver and gave his name. Müller-Meidrich was on the line again.

"We're extremely grateful for your tip, Herr Prévert. I got in touch with the hotel receptionist at once. He's pretty certain that the two men who wanted to speak to Wyzolla were detectives or agents of some kind. I immediately consulted all our departments, but none of them had detailed any men for such an assignment."

"They needn't necessarily have been members of the Berlin C.I.D.," Prévert said. "There are American, British and French agencies here in Berlin, don't forget."

"I know," replied Müller-Meidrich. "There's a wide choice. However, even hotel receptionists have flashes of inspiration occasionally, and this seems to have been a case in point. Apparently, he sent one of the hotel staff after them, not a uniformed page but a man from the accounts department. He saw them get into a car parked near the Gedächtniskirche. It had an East German number-plate."

"Even that doesn't prove anything."

"True, even that," Müller-Meidrich conceded blandly. "But Berlin is a city of boundless possibilities. That's why it's not surprising that the two men have turned up again. We arrested them a quarter of an hour ago. They're keeping mum for the moment, but something tells me that they belong east of the border. What shall we do with them?"

"Put them on ice temporarily," Prévert suggested. "We'll thaw them out when the time comes."

"And until then?"

"Let them cool their heels."

"Any other suggestions?"

"Yes, my dear Herr Müller-Meidrich. Play the innocent—telephone the Hotel am Kurfürstendamm and ask one of the guests, a man named Tanz, if he would like police protection. Tell him that two men, assumed to be from the Eastern Zone, have been trying to get at him."

"Nothing else?"

"Nothing else. That will do for the time being."

Frau Wilhelmine's meticulously planned reception in the Green Salon of the Hotel am Kurfürstendamm promised to be a *succès fou.* The guests were greeted with American-style martinis—high-proof gin with a dash of vermouth—which coursed down their throats like liquid fire and created an agreeably relaxed atmosphere. The ever-increasing hubbub of conversation seemed to indicate that a spirit of gregarious cordiality reigned.

The von Seydlitz-Gablers' select little gathering had acquired rather larger proportions than they had originally intended. Almost everyone present knew everyone else. Innumerable encounters at similar functions, ostensibly held for political, cultural or professional reasons, had bred long-standing mutual familiarity. Names figured on certain lists, and their owners turned up because they wanted to keep them there. The only variable factor was the current celebrity: the circle round him remained almost unchanged.

Whether he was a cabinet minister, a film star, an international playboy, a sportsman or an American hotel magnate, the same figures always rotated round him.

This time the focal point of the gathering was a composite of General Tanz and General von Seydlitz-Gabler—the battle-scarred hero and the great strategist respectively. To those present, who regarded them as men who had helped to make history, they seemed to radiate an aura of spine-chilling grandeur.

Tanz stood there like a crag protruding from a blasted heath. His monolithic appearance evoked universal admiration and his steadfast silence was readily construed as profundity.

"He looks like an eagle soaring above the prairie," twittered the junior television announcer, spell-bound. "A man like a bottle of champagne," breathed the recording star, melodiously, her bosom heaving like a stormy sea.

"Is it true what they say about him?" asked the wife or girl-friend of a senior liaison officer in the Federal Government. "Did he really build a wall out of frozen bodies during the Russian campaign?" She addressed the question to her hostess with a thrill of expectant horror.

"I couldn't tell you," replied Frau Wilhelmine. Her tone was noticeably cool.

The senior liaison officer hastily nudged his over-impulsive wife or girl-friend, aware that she had just broken an important taboo. For a considerable time now, it had been bad form to dwell on the horrors of war in case it weakened the spirit of self-defence. In a loud and convincing voice, he said: "My view has always been that we need the best men on our side. No stone should be left unturned in the case of General Tanz."

Frau Wilhelmine rewarded the senior liaison officer with a grateful smile. His wife or girl-friend shot him an oblique glance, but he ignored her and raised his glass in the direction of their host.

Von Seydlitz-Gabler was busy playing Pythia to Tanz's oracle. He was never at a loss for an answer and, what was more, his answers had the spurious validity of the printed word. His publisher beamed happily. The General certainly knew how to sell himself. In his mind's eye he pictured serried rows of dust-jackets in bookshop windows and a high rating on the best-seller list.

"You ought to write your memoirs, too," he told Tanz enthusiastically.

"Some men can write," replied Tanz in measured tones, "others are destined to act. I belong to the latter category."

"Talking about action," said the managing director of the electrical engineering firm, "how would you like to join us, other things being equal?"

"I regret that I am not an expert in your field," Tanz said majestically.

The managing director, who specialized in communications systems, smiled understandingly. He was familiar with the modesty of senior army men and appreciated its material value. The priceless importance of such people consisted in their automatic knowledge of the right contacts and their unerring sense of good form.

"A man can serve his country in a variety of ways," said the managing director.

"Quite right! The main thing is to serve it," boomed von Seydlitz-Gabler, who never neglected an opportunity to air what he considered to be one of his maxims.

"How are you feeling?" he asked Tanz.

"First-rate." Tanz produced the word like a slot-machine ejecting a packet of cigarettes. The skin of his face looked taut and shiny.

"A really nice crowd, eh?"

"A nice crowd—really."

At that moment the recording star gave a sudden screech. Someone had poured champagne down her cleavage. The offender was trying to apologize, but the recording star hooted like a siren and smote her bare wet bosom dramatically. Frau Wilhelmine bore down on the group like a life-boat.

"Every cake has to have a little icing," said von Seydlitz-Gabler with laborious gaiety.

Tanz had gone deathly pale. His hands were clenched and his cheek-muscles rigid. He looked as if he were grinding his teeth in agony.

"Disgusting," he said in a choked and almost inaudible voice. Then he pulled himself together with an effort. His lips twitched in a semblance of a smile. Kahlenberge was standing in front of him, and Kahlenberge was saying, indicating his companion:

"May I introduce Herr Prévert?"

In the narrow ante-room leading into the Green Salon sat Wyzolla, who had installed himself, legs apart, in a chair near the door and was waiting. What he was waiting for, he didn't know. He was merely carrying out his General's orders and acting as a body-guard.

With him in the narrow ante-room was Hartmann, also waiting. He stood leaning motionless against the wall for some time, observing Wyzolla with interest. Prévert had drawn his attention to Tanz's orderly and offered a few suggestions on how to handle him. The longer Hartmann watched Wyzolla, the more he succumbed to the strange sensation that he was looking at himself as he had been twelve years before.

"Does he still insist on having his shoes polished with three brushes and two dusters?"

Wyzolla sat up alertly. "Who?"

"Has he got used to glass ash-trays, or do they still have to be china?"

"What's that got to do with you?" Wyzolla asked suspiciously.

"In my day he always wore night-shirts. They had to be white, not coloured. He couldn't stand anything fancy. All the creases had to be ironed out beforehand, and there had to be a clean linen handkerchief in the right-hand breast-pocket —a small white one."

"Man alive!" said Wyzolla, impressed. "How do you know all that?"

"I had your job once," Hartmann told him. "It doesn't seem so long ago, really, when I come to think of it."

Wyzolla asked for information and Hartmann supplied it, soothing the alert young N.C.O's. misgivings with an abundance of detail. Wyzolla began to thaw, and before long a highly animated conversation was in progress.

"He used to sit in the back seat and lower a whole bottle of brandy inside two hours," Hartmann said. "But he didn't show it. He just held himself straighter and spoke clearer. He could drink like a fish."

"He still can," Wyzolla declared with a touch of pride.

"Except that he hardly ever drinks brandy these days. Brandy's in short supply with us, you know, but there's plenty of vodka. The General keeps cases of the stuff in his quarters."

Hartmann took secret pleasure in the fact that Wyzolla was already addressing him with the familiar "*du.*" It showed that he had gained his confidence, which was exactly what Prévert had instructed him to do.

"You're on a cushy number," he told Wyzolla. "Your cars are shoddy old tin cans—you can't be expected to put much of a shine on them. Back in Paris I was driving a Bentley. Every grain of dust showed up. I had a whole collection of stuff in the boot—linen cloths, woollen cloths, leathers, sponges, brushes and so on."

"So have I!" Wyzolla assured him vehemently. He seemed to regard Hartmann's aspersions on his range of cleaning materials as an affront to his honour. "Three sets—one in use and two in reserve."

"What about women?" asked Hartmann.

"Women?" Wyzolla shook his head in disapproval. "The General doesn't go for anything like that."

"That's what I always thought," Hartmann said confidentially. "He never seemed to notice them—and there were some real smashers in Paris, I can tell you."

"We don't do too badly in Dresden," said Wyzolla.

"He did pick one up once, though, in Paris."

"Well, he's only a man—out of the ordinary, but a man like anyone else. I've been driving him for two years now, and as far as I know he's only been on the job once in all that time."

"When was that?"

"A couple of days ago. I drove him to some bar or other and he picked up a tart there. I took both of them back to her flat."

"Did you wait?"

"Yes, but I didn't have to wait long. About half an hour later he came rushing back. Just flopped down on the back seat and told me to take him home. It was funny, he sounded quite mild for a change. Hasn't touched a drop or smoked a cigarette ever since."

Hartmann nodded thoughtfully and Wyzolla looked gratified at his reaction, but they had no opportunity to continue their edifying conversation. At that moment, Ulrike appeared in the doorway leading to the Green Salon.

"It's time," she said. "Prévert has given the signal."

"We've never met in person before," Prévert said to Tanz, "but you're not unknown to me."

"I, too," said Tanz, endeavouring to be sociable, "have a feeling that I've heard your name before, but I can't place it."

"I work for the Sûreté," said Prévert, "in Paris."

"My knowledge of Paris is limited to the war. I was there in nineteen forty-four."

"In those days," said Prévert, "my task was to provide a link between the French and German authorities—eliminate friction between them, and so on."

"An interesting job, I'm sure," Tanz said, polite as ever.

Feeling instinctively that this line of conversation might be less innocuous than it seemed on the surface, von Seydlitz-Gabler made an attempt to cut it short. He was skilfully distracted by Kahlenberge, who started talking about a foreword for something he was writing and his need to find someone with sufficient reputation and expert knowledge to supply it—for a suitable fee, of course. He had immediately thought of von Seydlitz-Gabler, and would appreciate his comments on the subject. Flattered by this display of confidence, von Seydlitz-Gabler allowed himself to be drawn into a corner.

Meanwhile, Prévert and Tanz eyed each other steadily, each man attempting to smile but neither succeeding to any marked degree. Tanz saw two frog-like eyes and a fish-like mouth set in a wrinkled expanse of flesh. Prévert saw an ideal model for a sculptor who wanted to portray the essence of unflinching, adamantine heroism. Everything about Tanz seemed big, impressive and imbued with classical beauty, though his face bore a few deep lines which looked as if they had been carved into it with a razor-edged knife.

"In those days," Prévert said cautiously, "I worked with a certain Lieutenant-Colonel Grau. Perhaps the name rings a bell?"

"It does," said Tanz. He stepped back slighly, as though to get a better view of Prévert.

"A remarkable man, Grau." Prévert leant forward as

though anxious not to increase the distance between himself and Tanz. "He was obsessed with a strange craving for absolute justice. His arguments and methods were quite out of the ordinary."

"I'm unable to share your enthusiasm," said Tanz. His eyes glinted frostily like slivers of ice. He raised his right hand, only to let it fall again in an attempt to disguise the fact that it was trembling violently. "And now—if you'll excuse me."

"One moment, please!" Prévert moved fractionally so that his corpulent body blocked Tanz's route of escape. "Perhaps you'll find our little chat considerably more interesting when I tell you that in July nineteen forty-four I was responsible for investigating a murder in the Rue de Londres."

Tanz froze. His eyes had gone as blank as the windows of a deserted house.

"I'm not interested," he said eventually.

"Even if I can prove that the crime in the Rue de Londres exists in triplicate?"

"You're insane."

"I might reciprocate that," said Prévert.

"What do you want?" asked Tanz with scarcely suppressed fury. "You're becoming a nuisance. I won't tolerate it."

"Warsaw nineteen forty-two, Paris nineteen forty-four, Dresden nineteen fifty-six. Need I say more?"

Tanz looked as though he were on the point of collapse. His body lost its unwavering poise. He tottered backwards into the wall behind him and leant against it, a ruined marble column.

Even then, his square jaw jutted pugnaciously and his parted lips seemed to suck energy from the surrounding air. When he spoke again, his voice had regained its crystalline clarity.

"Kindly spare me your theories. You can't prove anything. It's all guesswork."

Prévert glanced across at Ulrike and raised his hand. This was the signal for Hartmann's appearance. Ulrike nodded and disappeared.

"You've spent the past twelve years in the East," he said, turning back to Tanz, "and now you want to change sides. A lot of people look on this as a triumph of conscience—an action worthy of respect. They're even ready to fête you for it."

"'And you dislike this?"

"I dislike it very much indeed, Herr Tanz. You see, I can't regard it as mere coincidence that the murder committed in Dresden the other day was an exact replica of the murders in Paris and Warsaw."

"Pure speculation!" Tanz exploded.

"I don't agree with you." Prévert's manner was irritatingly serene. "There are a number of facts which add up to something more than coincidence. For example, two detectives from the Eastern Zone tried to get into conversation with your orderly this afternoon. They were arrested by the West Berlin police, who are now taking an interest in you. You won't be particularly impressed by all this, but perhaps it may interest you to know that this afternoon a conference took place between Detective-Inspector Liesowski of Warsaw, Detective-Inspector Liebig of Dresden and myself. We reached a unanimous decision."

"Suppositions aren't evidence." Tanz's voice sounded muffled, as though he were speaking through a piece of baize.

"I agree with you there," said Prévert imperturbably. "Nothing I've said so far is capable of proof. The Warsaw case is still open, the Dresden case is unsolved, and in the Paris case the vital witness doesn't appear to be forthcoming."

"Precisely!" said Tanz.

"That's where you're wrong, General. As you well know, we're speaking of someone called Hartmann—the only surviving witness of one of your crimes."

"Who is Hartmann?" asked Tanz. Pin-points of cold fire danced in his eyes. "Or, rather, where is Hartmann?"

"Over there," replied Prévert, pointing to the figure in the doorway.

Slowly, Tanz propelled himself forward. His limbs functioned stiffly and mechanically like those of a marionette operated by a novice. His body seemed to be hinged at the joints.

Prévert followed at his heels. The General moved with great deliberation, still determined to give an impression of dignified composure. This enabled Prévert to overhaul him without undue effort and made it look as though he were clearing a path for him. As he went, Prévert issued brief instructions:

"Hartmann, look after Ulrike."

"Frau von Seydlitz-Gabler, your husband will be in urgent need of your support."

"Kahlenberge, come with me."

Prévert opened the door leading to the ante-room and Tanz passed through, followed by Kahlenberge. Wyzolla jumped up from his chair and snapped to attention. For several seconds Tanz stood motionless as a mountain pine, seemingly unshakable despite the axe-strokes thudding against its base. Then he appeared to sway, but it was an illusion: he merely inclined his body a few millimetres towards Wyzolla.

"Give me your pistol," he said.

Wyzolla obeyed the order exactly as he would have done if Tanz had asked him to produce a handkerchief. He reached into his trousers pocket and brought out an 8 mm. automatic.

"Loaded, sir. Safety-catch on."

"Thank you," said Tanz, taking it.

Wyzolla stepped back smartly. Where his General was, there was his parade-ground. Kahlenberge stared fascinatedly at the weapon in Tanz's hand, then tore his eyes away and glanced at Prévert. Prévert shook his head very slightly.

Tanz lowered the pistol until it nestled in his hand with its muzzle pointing at the floor. Once more, he began to move. Wyzolla automatically started to follow, but Prévert said: "Wait here!" The words sounded like an order, and since they were uttered in the General's presence they carried almost as much force as if the General had uttered them himself. Obediently, Wyzolla stayed where he was.

Tanz walked on down the corridor to the door of his room, where he halted. From behind, Prévert and Kahlenberge could see him brace his shoulders and raise his head, slowly, as though jacking it up. Then he turned to face them. In a choked voice, he said:

"I have no explanation to offer."

"Why should you have?" Prévert replied in an icy tone his friends would not have recognized. "There's nothing to explain—Tanz!"

Tanz winced as though he had been stuck with a needle. The contempt with which his name had been uttered—just his name, no rank, not even the rudiments of civility, plain "Tanz" and nothing else—seemed to hurt him more than anything anyone had dared to do to him so far. His right eyelid twitched violently. He spun on his heel, flung open the door of his room and, stumbling inside, slammed it shut behind him.

"That's it, I think," Prévert remarked flatly. "Have you got a cigarette for me, Kahlenberge?"

Kahlenberge's hand was unsteady as he proffered the packet. Prévert helped himself and struck a match. They both lit up, audibly exhaling the first gulp of smoke, their eyes fixed on the door which now hid Tanz from view.

They waited, each aware that further conversation was superfluous. Both men were breathing fast but neither was conscious of the fact. They smoked their cigarettes down to the butt and ground them out on the imitation Persian carpet, then lit fresh ones immediately.

Kahlenberge could hardly control his restlessness. "You're really counting on him to behave like an officer and a gentleman?" he asked in an undertone.

"If you like to call it that—though officers and gentlemen aren't the only people who know how to do the right thing."

"Sometimes I wonder what category I belong to myself."

"I'll tell you what you are—an incurable idealist, though you probably wouldn't admit it."

They went on waiting, studying their feet and the carpet beneath, tracing its pattern until their gaze returned to Tanz's door. Even when they turned and looked out of the corridor window their eyes met the reflection of the door, clearly mirrored in the glass.

At last the brooding silence was broken by a muffled report like the bursting of an out-size toy balloon. It was the sound they had been expecting for almost half an hour.

Kahlenberge started forward, but Prévert held him back. "Don't rush it," he said.

Prévert's lips moved almost imperceptibly. He might have been praying, but it was more likely that he was counting. Being a practical man, he was giving Tanz time to fire again in case the first shot had proved ineffective. After about sixty seconds, he said: "Now!"

They threw open the door leading into Tanz's suite. On the table was a tumbler and an empty vodka bottle, which had fallen over. Sticky wet traces of half-digested food, evidently the result of vomiting, led from the table to the carpet.

Tanz lay there in a puddle of blood with his skull gaping.

"*C'est ça,*" Prévert said tersely.

A SPEECH WHICH HAS BEEN OFTEN PONDERED BUT NEVER DELIVERED

From a soldier to his general:

"A general commands thousands of men, thousands of whom he may never have seen, exchanged a word with, or learnt the names of.

"To generals, most of these thousands are no more than components of a battalion or brigade, faceless creatures who go to make up daily strength reports, items to be disposed of by a word, a signature or a command. One word from a general and thousands of soldiers stand to, move off, attack, withdraw, or march to their deaths.

"There is no other form of absolute power so great and all-embracing as that wielded by generals at a time when martial law and a state of emergency prevails. But, for the soldier, even the intervening periods are dominated by the figure of his general, regardless of whether he knows who his general is, where he comes from, where he is going, whether he is an unemotional pedant or a genial father-figure, a strict martinet or an equable personality, a daredevil or a temporizer.

"Generals are like shadows from which no soldier can escape. They define the boundaries within which their subordinates can operate. They also specify the objectives to be attained by divisions, corps and armies composed of finite numbers of men, finite numbers of weapons and finite quantities of ammunition—columns of figures headed simply "credit" and "debit," the deductions being accounted for by dead, wounded, missing, sick, postings and transfers—only numbers, never names.

"This is so, was so and will always be so. It may be deplorable, but it is unavoidable. Wherever human beings conglomerate they lose their face, name and individual existence, whether in factory bays, football stadiums or barracks, the waiting-rooms of war.

"Generals, on the other hand, do have a name. Soldiers learn it by heart as soon as they come under a particular general's command. They meet it again and again on written orders or when decorations and promotion are being conferred. It appears in military dispatches, is mentioned in newspaper articles or on the radio, and occasionally finds its way into books and, thus, into history.

"Generals also have a face. It occasionally glides past soldiers bound for the front or returning from it. It turns to look, for a fraction of a second, at rows of motionless figures standing to attention. It stares from publications or is captured in photographs destined to adorn the walls of billets or canteens.

"Generals also have an individual existence. They stand apart from the surrounding masses much as the manager of a factory or the star coach of a famous football team does. Like them, generals have power, influence and importance. Like them, they have to shoulder responsibility. But it is responsibility of a very special kind, and it is that alone which makes their position so incompatibly different.

"A general's responsibility is immeasurably greater than, say, that of a factory manager, who is only worried about production and turn-over, nor can it be equated with that of the manager or trainer of a football team. It does not consist merely in knowing how to deploy troops skilfullly or employ them methodically. Intelligent planning, the art of strategy and an outstanding capacity for coherent thought all pale into insignificance beside a fact which is inseparable from victory or defeat: generals operate with human lives.

"Generals' decisions, therefore, are life-or-death decisions. They do not affect the odd individual alone, as in the case of judges and doctors, but thousands of human beings simultaneously. Indeed, the total losses incurred in wars conducted by generals can run into millions.

"Teachers can either spoil their pupils or show them the true nature of beauty, dignity and worth; politicians can either stupefy nations and pander to their basest instincts or rouse them to a genuine sense of freedom and justice; but generals make decisions which directly affect human lives, and continue to do so, again and again, for as long as they remain generals.

"A general knows that in war-time he must be prepared to take this hardest of all decisions unflinchingly. That being so, he has no choice but to approach his task with profound humility. He must be fully aware of his special relationship to the highest price a human being can pay—unless, of course, he is inspired by a ruthless quest for power, fatal stupidity or a penchant, conscious or unconscious, for bloodshed, all of which lead, in the last analysis, to murder.

"It is a cheap excuse, nothing more, to mouth platitudes like "sacrifices are inevitable" or "the innocent always suffer with the guilty" or "human beings are the manure of history because their death prepares the ground for national greatness." In the view of certain historians, the road that leads to a better world has always been paved with corpses—not that they themselves are, or would wish to be, among those corpses.

"Yet how can anyone who remembers his mother, who has known and loved a fellow-being, who knows what children are, even look on human life as a form of war material to be employed with mechanical indifference?

"Such generals do exist, but there are other kinds.

"Some generals are 'soldier's generals' who do their best to live like the humblest private soldier under their command. They try to think like him and they often die like him. General Modersohn (principal character in the novel *Officer Factory*, by the same author) was one such, and he is far from unique.

"There are other generals who not only serve their country selflessly and responsibly but whose thoughts range far beyond their immediate horizon, who ponder on the meaning of life, the merits of their nation and their personal responsibility not only toward the individual but toward history as a whole. The men of July 20th, junior officers as well as generals, belonged to this category, as does General Kahlenberge. Many of them proved their worth during their country's lowest ebb and darkest hour.

"Still other generals do no more than act as willing lackeys of the strong-man of the moment. But what may have been understandable in Kaiser Wilhelm's day becomes unscrupulous, if not criminally irresponsible, under a man like Hitler.

Utterly foolish as it may seem to us today, some generals genuinely believed in Hitler, not that this was necessarily a mark of dishonour. Others, again, half-believed in him but maintained certain reservations, while still others inured themselves to the idea that it was their patriotic duty to believe in him. General von Seydlitz-Gabler may be classified as one of the latter.

"There were, however, a considerable number who were well aware that Hitler and his clique constituted a danger. In private, they called their Supreme Commander "the sewer-rat" or simply "that swine." They reviled him, abused him or poked fun at him, probably with justification in each case. Yet it is an undeniable and incomprehensible fact that the same generals did not hesitate to send thousands upon thousands of poor, brave, unwitting soldiers to their deaths for the sake of the man they called a sewer-rat and a swine.

"Still other generals were, and are, merely artisans of war—regimental sergeant-majors on a grand scale. They drill their men for a hero's death in the simple belief that they are doing the right thing and are immune to criticism. They have equally simple explanations for their activity and presumably cherish an implicit faith in them. They enjoy talking about love of country, defence of home and hearth, preservation of freedom, call of duty. They spoke of Hitler and Germany in the same breath, never faltered, never erred, and far-sightedly defended the West against Communism. Men like these fight and die, armed with water-tight explanations for doing both.

"It is frightening that men of this type should become generals. In almost every other sphere of life, people are prepared to take such individuals for granted. We are familiar, for instance, with business men who will gladly ruin their competitors for the sake of profit, with industrial tycoons and financiers who try to squeeze out rival concerns with every means at their command and even enlist government support in their endeavours, with public idols who turn out to be monumental fools or ravening sexual hyenas, with corrupt and power-hungry politicians who finally lose their ability to exploit the benign gullibility of the masses.

"In the realm of generalship, however, we cannot afford any imperfections, ambiguities or inadequacies. The price of failure has to be paid in blood, and errors which might be termed 'human' in any other sphere of life are fatal here. In the final analysis, generals are entrusted with the fate of nations, and it is they who make the ultimate decisions.

"Generals are unable to look into their soldiers' eyes while making such decisions, yet if they do not think of them while doing so they have failed both God and their fellow-men. Countries and nations—even generals—depend for their existence on the individual soldier. Anyone who sees fit to burn human beings like coal is not a human being himself.

"Even when generals are ready to die for their men, it does not follow that they know how to live for them. To do this successfully entails at least an attempt to convince the soldier that he is not just another entry in a casualty list.

"Some generals, perhaps a substantial number, try to cultivate this state of mind. Others have abandoned the struggle, and still others regard the questions as one of supreme indifference. The dead of their divisions and armies are merely laurel-leaves in the victor's crowns which are their constant preoccupation. Their path is paved with corpses.

"From such an assortment of men, all of whom bear the common title of general—unjustifiably, since one is unlike the next, all are dissimilar, and insignia of rank are no indication of merit—from such an assortment of men, constantly exposed to the gravest and most extreme demands, there sometimes emerges a human enigma.

"Ever since the beginning of time, humanity has occasionally thrown up creatures of appalling and monstrous perversity. Some of them have been called kings, others statesmen; at least one was a Pope and others have been soi-disant scientists or outwardly respectable citizens. Some, needless to say, have been soldiers.

"Tanz was the personification of war—of a war which was nothing more nor less than a cruel, pointless, uncontrolled blood-bath. A man who devotes himself to war in the same way as others fall prey to an irresistible vice is exactly like someone infected with the plague, syphilis or any other virulent disease.

"Thus the face of the general named Tanz—christened General Totentanz ('Dance of Death') by one of his men—was merely the mask of war, an iron mask concealing blood-lust, destruction—perhaps, even, Hell itself."

FINAL REPORT

ADDITIONAL PARTICULARS RELATING TO THE "TANZ CASE"

Statement by Wyzolla, made a few days after the foregoing events and taken in West Berlin at a so-called emergency recording session:

"It was like this: I only did my duty in the East, that's all. Of course, I had a good think about things—saw a lot of mistakes, too. Wyzolla, I said, that's not right, you can't do things like that. What mistakes? Well, for instance, take all this fuss about war-mongers. Take Adenauer, for instance. He's one—yes, that's what they tried to make out. Well, I thought it over and I said to myself: Wyzolla, I said to myself, that can't be true. How can a man who's never seen service be a war-monger? And they said to me: There you are —that's just it."

"And so it went on. I got pretty puzzled sometimes, I can tell you. For instance, they told me Krupp was a war criminal. Well, I found that easier to believe—all those guns and so on. But then I read something about the Leipzig Fair—and what do you think it said? Krupp was exhibiting there. Yes, sir, in the German Democratic Republic. Well, I reckoned that if Krupp was a war criminal and in the G.D.R. as well he couldn't be in West Germany. So which side are the war criminals on? You see how they pull the wool over your eyes?

"You want to know how I joined the army? I was drafted. No nonsense about volunteering. The most you can say is, I joined up to avoid being sent to a forced labour camp or a uranium mine as an enemy of peace. What's that, press-ganged? Yes, that's right. Not that I've got anything against military service as such. Someone's got to do it, but not on the wrong side. Anyway, now I'm—what do you call it?—following the dictates of my conscience.

"I don't know a thing about Tanz. Orders are orders and duty is duty. I was his driver, that's all."

Letter from Prévert's secretary to a newspaper editor who had requested answers to specific questions:

". . . M. Prévert greatly regrets that he is unable to accede to your request. His visit to Berlin in July 1956 was of a purely official nature. M. Prévert considers that it would be improper to disclose any details, especially as no written notes were kept and he was not engaged in any specific inquiries.

"M. Prévert also regrets to inform you that the files appertaining to the murder in the Rue de Londres in July 1944 are not available for inspection. He is only at liberty to tell you that, as far as the Sûreté is concerned, the matter is closed and is no longer being treated as an unsolved case.

"Furthermore, M. Prévert wishes to draw your attention to the fact that the name Hartmann, which figures repeatedly in your questions, does not appear in our records. No one by that name had anything to do with the above-mentioned case or any other case within our jurisdiction. Assertions to the contrary may render you liable to severe penalties. M. Prévert hopes that you will profit by his advice. . . ."

Closing remarks from Kahlenberge's lecture:

". . . I venture to submit, therefore, that it is impossible to dismiss all that has happened in the past few decades as a tragic and deplorable, but unique and exceptional phenomenon. What confronts us is the dissolution of a social stratum which has been inexorably bypassed—perhaps I should say, trampled upon—by the march of history. Within the brief span of half a century, the German officer has had to come to terms with Prussia, Kaiser and Reich, with the Weimar Republic, with Hitler, with democracy and, finally, with ideologies and power blocs which span whole continents.

"It is stupidity, self-delusion or conscious deception to go on talking of the good old values—e.g., of a tradition which people not only cherish but propose to borrow from substantially in future. What could be more ridiculous than to put yesterday's bankrupt in charge of tomorrow's business?

"Only fundamental changes in structure can produce new and hardy growth. We do not want a further instalment from a torn, dog-eared, obsolete history book. We must have the courage to make a fresh start, deliberately and unflinchingly. The alternative is self-destruction."

(This lecture was never delivered.)

Excerpt from Frau Wilhelmine von Seydlitz-Gabler's diary:

"I have seen many things in my time, but the Tanz affair shook me to the core. He was such a magnificent person. I was one of the last people he spoke to. 'Dear lady,' he said, 'how wonderful it is to be among friends again.' He was chivalrous to the very last.

"Herbert considerately spared me a last sight of the man we had valued so highly. 'Remember him as he was', he said. Herbert is like that.

"Kahlenberge—my friend no longer—thought fit to tell us a story like something out of a penny dreadful. It was so indelicate and disrespectful to the dead that I was speechless with anger. Herbert merely nodded and said: 'Who knows the real truth about anything?' "

From a letter to the Author by Herr Kahlert, the historian, dated 18th December 1961:

". . . I can assure you that I followed the events in question very closely, if only for academic reasons. Exhaustive inquiries have led me to conclude that the suppositions still entertained by a few individuals today—entirely without justification, I hasten to add—spring from a series of fortuitous coincidences and questionable deductions.

"To sum up the result of my investigations: General Tanz was not murdered by either side. Furthermore, there is no question of suicide. I can adduce a whole mass of convincing evidence, all of it psychologically sound, to support my contention. I will not go into details here. Suffice it is to say that, judging by his natural disposition (on which there is ample corroborative evidence), Tanz was not the sort of man to raise a hand against himself.

"The only valid inference is that it must have been an accident, probably caused while cleaning a pistol.

"As for the absolutely fantastic allegations made by Hartmann, I believe I have already made it clear that I had ample opportunity to study that unfortunate individual at close quarters. He has undoubtedly had a hard time, but my sympathy for him cannot be allowed to obscure the plain and unvarnished truth: the man is a pathological liar."

Remarks made by the popular recording star Britta B. during the later stages of a party held in honour of an internationally famous film actor on the occasion of the première of an American film dealing with the rehabilitation of Germany:

"He was crazy about me—General Tanz, I mean. Not that he showed it, of course, but a woman can tell these things, deep down inside.

"The press breathed down my neck for days afterwards. Well, it was only to be expected with a sensation like that, wasn't it? It didn't last long, though. The story only made the front page for one day. They ran it on the inside pages for the next three days, and two or three weeks later the subject was dead as a door-nail. All the same, my disc—you know, *Kiss me when the sun shines, kiss me in the rain*—stayed in the Top Twenty for nearly four months. Just shows you, doesn't it?

"Get to the point? What do you think I'm doing, sweetie? Well, someone rushes into the room and yells: 'He's dead—shot!' It gave us all an awful shock. I was standing next to von Seydlitz-Gabler—he's a field-marshal or something like that, all kinds of decorations—lots more than Mende—anyway, a hero—and do you know what he said? Go on, have three guesses.

" 'A pretty kettle of fish!' That's what he said—I promise you."

From von Seydlitz-Gabler's memoirs, concluding section:

"The repercussions arising from the death of one of our finest soldiers can only be construed as a deplorable misunderstanding. Once again, and perhaps for the last time, the news-hounds scented a stag at bay. They leapt at him, avid and remorseless, eager to vent their pathological hatred and besmirch his memory.

"I vividly recall the moment when I was told of his death. It was at a select gathering. We had, I believe, just been discussing the reconstruction of the true Germany and the new orientation of Europe, a subject close to all our hearts. Then the tragic news reached us. I was profoundly shaken, and could only murmur: 'How frightful!' adding, a little later: 'But we must not be deterred, even by this.'"

Further statement by Wyzolla, this time made in East Berlin several weeks after the foregoing events. The occasion: a press conference arranged by the East German Ministry of the Interior and presided over by Commissioner Karpfen, who was promoted shortly afterwards:

"It was like this: I only did my duty, that's all. Of course I had a good think about things—and how! I'm no fool. I've always known where the real war criminals are. Over there, that's where. That's my belief, anyway. Anyone care to disagree?

"I was General Tanz's driver. A fine man, no two ways about that. Promoted me to sergeant. Yes, I'm a sergeant-major now. I escorted the General to West Berlin. Just a private visit—man to man. Everything went like clockwork to begin with. The General said: 'Makes a bit of a change, doesn't it?' 'Yes,' I said. It did, too. Everything was different over there—not like here, you understand.

"Then two blokes turned up. Right there in the hotel. Wanted a word with me. 'Wyzolla,' I said, 'watch out! Get shot of these two lads.' Told the General. He was sarcastic. 'Cloak-and-dagger merchants,' he said.

"A bit later another man came up—a Westerner. Name of Hartwich or Hartmut or Hartmann—something like that. Reeked of perfume and spoke French into the bargain. I heard him chattering to a Frenchman. Talkative type, he was. Tried to chum up with me. Gabbed about the General the whole time—interested in his personal habits, etc. Wanted to pick my brains, but I wasn't playing. I led him up the garden path all right, take it from me!

"Then the gendarmes arrived. Stuck a pistol in my ribs and said: 'Come with us or else!' Well, I'm not stupid. I made the best of a bad job—steady as a rock, though. Never said a word against the National People's Army. Not on your life!"

Letter from Rainer Hartmann, Antibes, to Chief Inspector Prévert, Paris, dated May 1961:

". . . the weather is gorgeous. Our greenhouses are packed with flowers and the roses are just coming into bloom. The palms in the Botanical Gardens are looking lush and green, and there are a hundred candles burning in the chapel beside the light-house. I lit them becuase my wife has just given birth to a son. With your permission, we intend to name him after you.

"This means that you will have to come down here. We're planning a celebration in the auberge, and next day Félix will be concocting the best bouillabaisse of his life, down at the harbour.

"Ulrike is firmly convinced that you'll want to see our son. . . ."

Telegram from M. Prévert to M. et Mme. Hartmann:

"Already on my way. Get the Hotel Juana to put a bottle of Rosé Provence '53 on ice."

From a speech delivered before delgates of veterans' associations and similar bodies on the occasion of Heroes' Memorial Day, 1961. Official speaker: General von Seydlitz-Gabler.

". . . Thus, men like General Tanz have become a symbol

to us. He was one of those officers whose men would have gone through Hell for him. To him and his like, there was only one thing which existed—and triumphed—above all others. That was, is, and remains: Germany!"

Interjection: "Which Germany?"

ABOUT THE AUTHOR

HANS HELLMUT KIRST was born in 1914 in East Prussia and grew up in the countryside which is now part of Poland. Before becoming a soldier in the Second World War, he had worked as road builder, gardener, surveyor, dramatist and critic. His war experiences in Poland, France and Russia led him to write a series of novels which have made him Germany's best-selling author. Among them are the Gunner Asch tetralogy (*The Revolt of Gunner Asch; Forward, Gunner Asch; The Return of Gunner Asch;* and *What Became of Gunner Asch*), *The Officer Factory, Soldiers' Revolt* and *Brothers in Arms.*

See next page for coupon.